MW00460019

Andrew O'Hare grew up in Northern Ireland. He trained as a nurse, and spent several years in the Merchant Navy, before specialising as a butler to celebrity clients. *Green Eyes* is his first novel, and he is currently working on a science fiction project.

GREEN EYES

Andrew O'Hare

GAY MEN'S PRESS

First published 2001 by Millivres Ltd,
part of the Millivres Prowler Group,
Worldwide House, 116-134 Bayham St, London NW1 0BA

World Copyright © 2001 Andrew O'Hare

Andrew O'Hare has asserted his right to be identified as the author of this work
in accordance with the Copyright, Designs and Patents Act 1988

A CIP catalogue record for this book is available
from the British Library

ISBN 1 902852 24 9

Distributed in Europe by Central Books,
99 Wallis Rd, London E9 5LN

Distributed in North America by Consortium,
1045 Westgate Drive, St.Paul, MN 55114-1065

Distributed in Australia by Bulldog Books,
P O Box 300, Beaconsfield, NSW 2014

Printed and bound in the EU by WS Bookwell, Juva, Finland

To Bobby, Colin and Peter, in recognition
of your unwavering belief and support.
With love, guys.

Thanks are due to Morris Fraser
and David Fernbach. Without
their help, advice and hard work,
Green Eyes would have been stillborn.

For Mike and Roger, work colleagues,
in appreciation of your encouragement.

For Sam. With love.

Part One: Accidents and Meetings

1

"Mmm... Such amazing green eyes."

He'd been horribly embarrassed. More so by my tone of voice than by what I'd said.

Then the haziness and pain had swooped. My hands were burning, throat all wet, something was stabbing my chin and I felt so giddy, so very sick. The smell of shit, cowshit this time, was alarmingly strong. Though I could feel the damp solidity of the ground under me, I had the sensation of teetering on the edge of a vast drop.

A woman's voice, indecipherable.

Blankness descended.

Later? Those eyes again. Peripheral vision had everything in white. Still teetering on the edge. Hands now apparently stuffed into hot, tight, wet gloves. Chin sending electric shocks.

What a fantastic shade of green, and, a sunburnt snub of a nose. The blue-black hair falling over the white forehead, long sensitive face and naturally laughing mouth just did not register at all.

"Eyes! Hi, don't go..."

Blankness conquered the light again.

Jolted back to the light and back on the bike. Down the hill. The T-junction. Mouth suddenly bone dry. Too FAST. I was going too FAST. Sickness like a punch in the stomach as I froze. The fear. The foreknowledge of what was to come. Unable to turn. Unable to brake. SHIT! SHIT! SHIT! Straight across the junction. Car horn's sudden blare at my left knee. Vision filling with the white-thorn hedge coming to swat me. Whirling blue sky...Amazing green eyes.

Another jolt. It was over. I knew I was in hospital. Was I very badly injured? Fucking motorbikes.

* * *

"Easy son, easy," as my eyes opened and the tears of fright which had been building were released.

"Sorry Dad, Mum." The feeling of imminent sickness again.

"It's sorry you are is it?" Little brown eyes bulging, as always, seemingly on the point of popping out of their sockets. Smug expression unalloyed by worry or concern.

One of the first lessons in life that I'd learned was not to run to Mum with skinned knees or a sore stomach. The first would earn me a clout on the ear 'for running round like an eedjit' and the second would likely result in a sore arse 'for gorbing yoursel' on all them sweeties', followed as like as not by a dose of Syrup of Figs, which seemed to be her panacea for all ills.

Dad on the other hand, though his words might carry the same message, could always be relied on to provide the hugs and hankie when needed. His salt-water hardened hands were ever gentle in the washing of scrapes, or holding my forehead whilst I retched over a bowl after a surfeit of 'all them sweeties', and, a genuine childhood illness would earn me long periods curled up on his lap. Warm, secure and comfortable. Protected and reassured in his embrace.

Had I not felt so disorientated, so fuzzy, I would probably have been cringing, wondering what Mum was due to mete out. If you got a sore ear after a tumble, what would you get after crashing a motorbike?

"Sorry won't wash with me my man. I telt you, I telt you and I telt you till I was blue in the face, but would you bloody listen? No! Well, I always said you'd come to no good. Look at you now! Crippled no doubt. Lucky you weren't kilt. Well, you listen to me my man, as the Blessed Virgin is my witness, NO MORE MO-TORBIKES!!!" The spittle was fairly flying by now. Dad squeezed my arm. "And another thing, if you for one minute think that I'm giving up my wee job to look after the likes of you... you can stay here till you mend or the other thing happens. A lifetime I've spent scrimping and saving on what little your father bothered to give me, and as the Blessed Virgin is my judge I'm not going back to cleaning your shitty hole." She ran out of breath panting triumphantly and Dad cut in.

(Why did I keep having flashes of green eyes? Dad's were brown, like Mum's. Well, not angry like hers. More soft, concerned and full of love.)

"Don't worry son. You've just had a wee bit of a bang." Squeezing my arm again and drying my tears with his hanky. "Stitches in the chin and your hands are a bit cut up, but nothing serious. The doc says you'll be as right as rain by tomorrow." Another squeeze and a half smile. "You're going to be alright son. You're just a bit shook up. Can you remember what happened?"

Vision of thorned hedge reaching for me broken by Mum.

"What happened? WHAT HAPPENED? That blackhearted wee get of an Orangeman run him off the road. THAT's what happened. Just like the rest of the breed. Them wi' their fancy cars and swanky ways. Think they own the road along wi' everything else round here. May the Blessed Virgin forgive me, but I hope the Divil toasts their shrivelled wee souls for all eternity."

"Shut up Winnie." Turning back to me: "They'll keep you overnight, just to make sure they haven't missed anything." Squeezing again. "X-ray results and all that. I'll bring clean clothes up tonight."

"Sorry Dad."

"Hush now son. It's just the shock, the reaction, you know. Really Shaun you'll be alright."

"Alright? ALRIGHT? He might have been half right if you'd taken your belt to him when he was wee. As it is it'll be, like father like son. Good for nothing the pair of you and a bad end just waiting. The Blessed Virgin be my judge in that."

"Jesus Christ Winnie WILL you shut up! Everybody can hear you."

"And what should I care about the scum of Newry? They should be saying their prayers not minding other people's business. And what do you care anyway? Off on your wee boat again tomorrow. It's me'll have to do the running roun' after him. Feeding him, dressing him, no doubt cleaning his arse for him."

"Please keep the noise down or you'll have to leave." Starched nurse. "There are sick people here."

"SICK? Sick you say." She stood up, all five foot two of her. "More like the divil's got his hooks in half of them. Claiming his own." Crossing her arms and hugging herself. "And who might you be, to be telling abody what to do? HOORS the lot of ye, in or out of uniform."

The nurse's face set like stone as she advanced.

"I wouldn't stay here a minute longer. Not if the Blessed Virgin and all the saints got down on their knees." Snatching her handbag off the chair, digging Dad in the shoulder. "You! Take me back to work this minute. I'm losing no more money because your eedjit son can't do anything right." Sneering over her shoulder as she left: "Oh, he's your son alright." The double doors swung twice as she barged through them.

Momentary silence in the ward, then a clearing of throats and the murmur of renewed conversation. I felt too woozy to be embarrassed and, like Dad, I was so used to it by now I doubt I would have been anyway.

"I'll have to go son. You know the scene she'll make if I don't." Releasing my arm. "I'll come back this evening." Rueful smile as he stood. "Young Hannah will want to see you. I'll send him in."

I started to tremble as he left and couldn't stop.

What young Hannah?

Tears started again and wouldn't stop.

And there they were. Green and misty, looking very concerned. Or was that my imagination?

"Nurse says you're going to be okay." They were definitely wet, and the face was very white.

Blankness swooped again and I still hadn't said a sensible thing.

* * *

Harry told me later that the woman I had heard was Mrs Collins. She had been cautioning him not to move me and saying that she had called the ambulance. He'd blushed when I asked if I'd said anything.

"Something about green eyes." Apparently Mrs Collins had been on my other side at the time and he had found himself at a loss for words. The ambulance had arrived shortly afterwards and off I went to Daisy Hill Hospital, still wearing the helmet and smelling slightly of cowflops.

Harry had followed in his black Mini, though at the time he wasn't sure why. He'd been about to turn into the Scrogg Road when I'd whizzed across inches in front of his bonnet. The bike had buried itself in the hedge and he had a vivid memory of my trainers disappearing through the branches. Pulling onto the verge he'd run back to the gate into the field. I was lying about twenty feet from the hedge.

"Your face and neck were covered in blood. I thought your throat was cut." Smiling as he ran his fingers lightly over the ridge of scar tissue under my chin. "Your right hand looked as if it had been minced." (I must have thrust it before me for protection as I came off the bike.)

Mrs Collins had seen it all from where she'd been working in her garden and, after calling the ambulance she'd joined him to render first aid. Right about then I'd come round momentarily 'Mmm.

Such amazing green eyes.'

She had found my driving licence, so they knew I was Shaun McKenna of 4 St. Joseph's Cottages, Scrogg Road. After the ambulance had left, with Harry following, she had gone down to the harbour and found Dad working on 'The Maid o'Mourne'. He had borrowed Hugh Green's car, picked Mum up from the fish factory and arrived at the hospital a little more than an hour after I had. Which was why the first time I came round there were green eyes and the second, two sets of brown.

* * *

When next I woke there were no eyes to see. In fact there was very little to see and it took a few minutes to realise that it must be late night or early morning. That I *was* in hospital and that no, I was not going blind, it was just that very few lights were on.

Various aches and pains rapidly made themselves known and, as I became genuinely aware, for practically the first time that day (was it still the same day?), my head felt clear and more or less normal. I must have made some sound as a man seemed to materialise at the side of the bed. I was looking to my left, so his voice coming quietly from the right made me start.

"Hi, I'm Dennis the night nurse."

As I turned my head I received several sharp jabs from my chin and kindled a dull ache in my left shoulder.

"Can I get you anything?" Placing a hand on my forehead "A drink?"

"I need to pee." Suddenly aware of the pressure.

"Just a sec." Pulling screens round the bed.

I could not manage the bottle myself with both hands bandaged. So whilst I raised my arms he rolled back the bedclothes and placed it between my legs. My face was burning as he fished my limp dick out of the front of the hospital-issue pyjamas and fed it into the neck of the bottle. I prayed that he would go away and I wouldn't get a hard-on. Although I was almost bursting I could not perform with him watching.

He gave me a moment's consideration, then: 'I'll get that drink, back in a minute," and he slipped out through the screens. God! The utter relief as I relaxed and the flow began. Oops! What if I overfilled the bottle? But I couldn't have stopped if I'd tried. No disaster ensued and just as I finished Dennis returned with a beaker of orange juice and a feeding cup.

"All done?" Raised eyebrows.

I nodded. Chin cried out. "Oh shit!"

"Try not to move too much," he advised after setting the beaker down, as he proceeded to milk the last few drops of urine from my (thankfully) limp and passive dick. Was it my imagination or was the squeezing, milking motion of his clammy fingers somewhat prolonged? Removing the bottle, tucking me back into the pyjamas he straightened the bedclothes before offering me a drink.

"Orange juice." Proffering the spout to my lips.

"Slowly now," as I gulped feverishly. Not realising until just then how dry my mouth and throat had been. Three times he filled it before my thirst was slaked. "Good." Setting the empty cup down and making an entry on a chart.

"What day is it?"

"Tuesday night, early Wednesday morning. It's three-fifteen." Still the same day.

"I'll come back in a little while. See if you are still awake." Pushing back the screens. "Give you another drink. Do you need a bedpan?"

I looked blankly at him.

"You know. Do you need a crap?"

My face burned "No. Thanks."

"Well, okay." Sounding somewhat disappointed. (My imagination again?) "Try to go back to sleep. Best thing." As he prepared to leave: "You'll be up and about later today. So don't be worrying. Doc only kept you in to make sure that you hadn't damaged your head."

"Nurse." Quietly from a few beds away.

"Okay then, see you later." Walking away, half-full bottle in one hand, empty cup in the other.

I tried to get comfortable. The pyjamas were unfamiliar and constricting. 'Did I need a crap?' I blushed in the semi-darkness. Following on from the morning's performance I was of the opinion that I wouldn't need another for at least a week.

* * *

I'd woken about ten to the feel of something warm and wet on my belly, now cooling rapidly as it ran down my side. Throwing the duvet back I'd jerked upright in the bed only to be severely jabbed in the stomach. Cock was staring straight up at me, his one eye beaded with moisture. SHIT! I'd almost pissed the bed. Something I couldn't ever remember doing. I needed to piss RIGHT NOW. Another spurt hit me on the throat before I could control it. NOW. DAMN IT. NOW!

Fucking cock so hard it wouldn't bend in any direction, but stuck out the waistband of my briefs, nestled against my belly. The bathroom was right on the other side of the house. Palpitations followed by relief as I remembered it was Tuesday. Mum, Dad and elder sister at work. Little sister at school. Sensation of relief almost leading to disaster as I raced across the living room. Through the kitchen and into the bathroom. My legs were trembling. Slam and bolt the door, almost falling into the shower. Too hard to have any chance of pointing it into the bowl. No time to remove the briefs. Only let go. Initial spurt cut off like a light as a new pressure, an overwhelming urge to shit took over. (I'd had my first pint of Guinness the previous night. Decided later that was the culprit.)

"For fuck's sake!" I couldn't sit down because as soon as I'd shit I'd pee and it would go everywhere, I was TOO hard. Tears of mortification slid down my face, I couldn't stop it. My arse gave way. As the soft warmth pushed me open my cock started bouncing and jerking. The sensation was too good to ignore. I felt light in the head, half triumphant, half disgusted as the soft heat forced its way under and between my legs up to my balls, I just HAD to beat off.

How to describe it? And then, the panic when reflex shut my arse just as I felt the onset of the most incredible orgasm. Couldn't stop NOW. Also couldn't believe what I was doing, but the urge was not to be denied and I forced myself to continue what felt like a truly monumental crap. The briefs couldn't hold it all and the sensation of warm stickiness sliding down the back of my legs and inner thighs was bringing me to a peak I'd never before experienced. I could not stop myself yelling out as the cum shot out, hitting the underside of my left arm with which I was braced against the back wall of the shower. God, what a buzz, what an incredible high! (JESUS, what an incredible pong). Seconds after cumming, dizziness and gasps were cut short as the original culprit (the bladder) took over. My open mouth and hanging head took the full force of the initial blast. Salty yet slightly sweet and warm, I almost choked, spluttering like a stranded fish.

As the flow eventually diminished I stood erect. I was tingling all over. Although the smell was overpowering, the continued trickle which by now had reached my knees was just too, too much. I would quite often wank two, three or four times in succession, on one famous day five times in less than an hour, but I'd split my foreskin and paid for it by not being able to have a proper wank for over a week. I'd had to resort to very gentle strokes and a lot of ball pulling and fondling to achieve even a half-hearted release. My arse had shut when I'd cum, but I knew by the heaviness there that more was on the way. Pressing lightly only served to confirm what I already knew and also brought cock (who was just beginning to wilt) back to ramrod stiff attention.

How COULD I bring myself to do this! I did it anyway. My right hand between the thighs getting smothered in soft warm shit. Using it as lubrication and pressing at the same time, the sensations just experienced seemed to repeat themselves in slow motion. As I reached for the second orgasm I pressed so hard that my head felt as though it might burst. Bright little sparks floated before my eyes. Briefs, soaked and overburdened, began slowly sliding down my legs, managing to heighten feelings I'd never known existed. I kept on pressing as I reached the point of no return and almost blacked out. Empty now of both cum and shit I leant against the shower wall, feeling not just drained but slightly sick as well.

It must have taken poor old heart a minute or two to come out of overdrive. GOD! – the *mess*! My briefs were round my ankles. There was shit and cum slithering down the walls and door of the shower and one brilliant brown handprint on the back wall about head height.

Even though everything was at least semi liquid it still took twenty minutes to clean me and the shower using the detachable jet. I must have put a whole bottle of Dettol down the drain as I washed the evidence away. Then almost a full container of airspray throughout the house .Yesterday's T-shirt, jeans, briefs and socks into the washing machine. Eventually I was back on my bed for half an hour to cool off. Then into the girls' room to pinch some of Kathleen's talc for my bum, balls, and still semi-turgid prick. I hadn't the energy to oblige him with another round and tucked him away with the solemn promise of attention later.

Finally, dressed in jeans, blue T-shirt, black leather jacket and Nike trainers (no socks, but plenty of talc) I studied myself in the hall mirror before leaving. Not bad! Five foot five, real strawberry blond hair flopping every which way, seven and a half stone (soaking wet), pointed pixie face, stone grey eyes (which I thought terribly menacing) and little ears hidden under the thatch. On with the helmet and out the door. It was the second day of my two-week holiday from the aircraft factory (we didn't actually make planes, only the seats). I'd started the previous year three weeks after leaving school and worked in the stores section.

By now it had gone midday and I decided to head down to the harbour to see if Dad needed a hand with painting the boat. I wrestled the bike off its stand and promptly had to fight with it when it wanted to fall over. I'd had it four days and, although I refused to admit it (even to myself) it terrified me. And so, off to meet my Waterloo.

2

'Young Hannah' turned up at the hospital shortly after lunch the next day. By then my dressings had been changed on the hands (I already had partial use of the left), the new dressing being really only a pad on the palm. The right was a different story, it had cuts to the fingers as well as the palm and lower inside arm. I had not enjoyed the process one little bit. However I'd managed to perk up a little and my chin had stopped screaming every time I moved my head. Cock was complaining bitterly at the lack of attention, having been ignored for over twenty-four hours and it wasn't helping any that I kept running the previous morning's shower sequence through my head. He was threatening to fire off unassisted when 'those amazing green eyes' approached the bed. Hannah was actually blushing slightly and looking a little on the nervous side.

A good three inches taller than me, I reckoned. I noted the blue-black hair this time and the eyebrows like a straight black bar across the top of the snub nose, full red lips, thin face and high cheekbones.

"Hi." He came to a stop at the bedside. "I hope you don't mind?"

"Hi, Eyes. Sit down." Indicating a chair. I also noted the tight white T-shirt and the rather looser chinos. Loose or not they seemed to be reasonably well filled. I can't help it, but the crotch is usually where I look first. Really cockeyed, that's me. I didn't know quite why at the time, but I've learned since.

"Why or, what should I mind?" Trying to ignore cock who was twitching (quite visibly, I felt certain). He didn't seem to notice as he brought the chair over.

"Coming to see you, I mean."

"Why should I mind?" Raising my left knee a little to obscure what I was sure must be an enormous bulge in the bedclothes. "I'm glad you came, Eyes. I was getting bored."

Now he was really blushing. "Why 'Eyes'?" and he grinned.

Oh Golly! I could have swooned (if I'd known what a swoon was).

"But why Eyes?" he repeated and started to giggle.

I realised that his gaze was no longer directed at my face but was focused on what appeared to be a very small tent in the middle of the bed. My leg had gone flat. Just a touch on cock would have triggered him off. Oh God! I wanted him to slide a hand under the clothes and touch me.

"I don't know your name," as I started to laugh and blush at the same time. That brought chin to full screaming mode, which in turn produced, "Oh shit. Don't make me laugh. Please," and a collapse, at least partial, of the tent.

"I'm sorry Shaun." Leaning closer. (Oh closer yet. Please, closer).

"Actually, I really don't know your name or why you're here?" I tried a very small grin. "And you do have the most startling eyes I've ever seen."

"Harold John Hannah at your service." Half standing to give a mock bow. "And I'm curious as to why you don't take corners?"

"Shaun Peter McKenna," I replied. "I froze up. I only got the bike and I just froze." I could see the hedge coming for me and remember my inability and the fear.

A warm dry hand clasped my wrist. "Hey! Hey! Don't go getting all upset," he urged. "It could have been much worse. Come on. Please?"

"I feel like such an idiot. I'll never ride it again. Never."

"Please Shaun, don't worry. I'm just glad you are alright." He told me about the feet disappearing through the hedge and the 'amazing green eyes' bit in the presence of Mrs Collins. She had looked up from wrapping my hands and agreed that they were indeed quite remarkable.

"Well after that introduction, I just had to meet you and talk. You know?" and he squeezed my wrist but didn't let go. "You weren't really with it yesterday and with your parents here I reckoned it wasn't the best time." Blushing again he looked away from my face. "To tell the truth I think I had a bit of delayed shock myself – the smell of the hospital, you looking so ill and your mother shouting. I felt quite faint. Thought I'd pass out." Shrugging he finally relinquished my wrist. "Your dad made me sit down and put my head between my knees." Looking back at me: "If you don't want me to stay?" and he started to rise.

"No. Please." Reaching out to catch his hand. "Please stay Harry."

He gripped my hand. Hard. Made me yelp.

"Sorry Shaun. Jesus I'm sorry." Panicking a little and stroking my arm.

"It's okay. Really, I'm okay." When I'd managed to get my breath back: "Can I call you Harry, or is it Harold?"

"Harry it is, but maybe I should go anyway." Making no movement. "Your mum and dad are bound to come soon."

I held onto his hand, no way was I going to let go.

"No. Dad's sailing tonight. He works on Green's boat and Mum doesn't drive." I looked away "Anyway she works, and she doesn't like me much."

"Oh come on, she's your mother."

"I know. I know, but we never get on over anything." I closed my eyes and gave his hand a light squeeze. Looked at him again "But what about you?" I protested. "You must have things to do. Don't you work?"

"Holidays," he said.

Two hours later, after the ward orderly had given us both a cup of tea, Harry left. Arrangements hade been made for him to collect me the next afternoon and bring me home. Sex had not been mentioned, though we hadn't realised that we had spent the most of the time holding hands until the tea arrived. By then I couldn't have cared less. I was, for the first time in my life, head over heels in love. When he did eventually leave, I had to go to the toilet and cry. I didn't want him to go.

Jean, Harry's mother, told me later that she knew when he came in that evening that he was in love. It took Harry a few days to realise it for himself.

"I was glad for him." She sighed and stroked my hand. "Even when he told us what had happened and I realised that it was another boy he was in love with."

* * *

Harry turned up at the hospital around eleven the next morning, only to have to wait around until I was eventually discharged just after one o'clock.

Dad had returned to the hospital on Tuesday evening but I'd been asleep. He'd left clean clothes for me and – surprise surprise –

a new razor and shaving foam. I wasn't shaving then, so I took it as a kind of reverse compliment: 'Old enough to have accidents. Old enough to shave.'

It really is very difficult to get dressed when you only have the use of one hand and not even full use of that. The briefs I managed and the jeans part way, but my hand was hurting. I peeked out of the screens surrounding the bed hoping to see Harry, but caught the gaze of a senior nurse. She bustled in, saw the problem and brusquely took over. In what felt like thirty seconds, and gave me some idea of what a piece of meat feels like in a butcher's hands, I was zipped up, shod and (blush-making) hair *wet*-combed. Hustled out to the nurses' station I received a long list of instructions regarding visits to outpatients for dressings (every day for ten days), visits to my own doctor, plenty of rest, no alcohol etc. Then, having an envelope for the 'Mourne District Hospital' thrust at me along with a bag containing my things, I was forgotten. Harry had been hovering in the background and he sprang forward to rescue the envelope and bag.

"How do you feel?" Solicitously taking hold of my left arm. "This way," nodding towards the right.

"A wee bit giddy, Harry," and in all honesty I did a little; but I think it was more from the clasp of his warm dry hand on my arm than from any physical reaction to being discharged.

"Will you be alright?" Hand tightening fractionally, "It's a little way to the car." He looked into my eyes causing me to stumble slightly, at which he grew alarmed. "Are you sure they should be letting you out. Do you think you need to sit down? You look awfully pale." His eyes were saucer-large and the voice nervous, a little panicky.

"No, I'm alright. Really, I'll be okay once we get into the fresh air." I tried a small smile. Small so as not to upset my chin. Small so as not to give my thumping heart away. Every second with him my heart's commitment grew. I could have sung, except that I can't. I could have danced, but didn't want to give him a reason to let me go. I could have cried with joy, but didn't want to worry him. How was I to know how he felt? I didn't want to scare him off. I promised myself not to rush things. How to stop him losing interest? (Found out later that I need not have worried too much.)

"I'm always pale," as we descended the stairs towards the exit to the car park. "Dad says too much... alcohol in the blood stream." I had been going to say too much of something else, but in keeping with the just made resolution changed it at the last second.

"Do you drink a lot then?" Looking into my face again, he almost missed a step and we both nearly took a tumble.

"Shit." Simultaneously.

He giggled and I laughed, waking chin into full screaming mode.

"Oh shit. That hurts." My eyes were watering.

"Sorry Shaun." His grip on my arm so tight that it hurt too, but no way was I about to complain over that. "But do you?" releasing my arm to hold the swing doors open.

"Do what?" Crossing both arms over my chest, frightened of being struck by the doors.

"Drink a lot, I mean?"

"No! One pint of Guinness and I'm anybody's." Breaking my 'no rush' resolution straight away. Actually I'd wanted to try that line for ages but the chance never came up. I held my breath as I followed him threading his way through the cars.

"Oh, that's alright then." Relief in the voice.

What was alright? That I didn't drink a lot or, that I was anybody's?

"Here we are." Cheerfully, stopping beside a shiny black Mini.

"Golly! It's new isn't it?"

"Yes. Birthday present from Mum and Dad." and he sort of stroked the roof. "Well, Dad really." Unlocking the door, slinging my things on the back seat. Coming round to open the passenger door, holding it for me.

"Mind your hands," as I swung in. "And your head," anxiously. He closed the door and bounced round to the driver's side, giving me a good eyeful of fascinating crotch. Brown Levi's today.

"Put your seat belt... " He giggled: "Oh, I forgot. Here, let me," and he leant across me, his cheek only a fraction from my lips, his shoulder pressing into mine. The aroma of shampoo from recently washed hair. How I managed not to cross that small gap and kiss his cheek, ear, hair, anywhere! I think it was due more to the unexpectedness of his sudden proximity, rather than self-restraint on my part.

"Mind your hands." The touch of the back of his hand on my chest even through the T-shirt as he brought the belt across, made me gasp.

"Shit! Did I hurt you?" Stopping with his hand still lightly touching me.

"No, no. It's just that I must have bruised my shoulder when I was learning how not to fly."

Clicking the seat belt in. Hands moving to the steering wheel. "Did they look at that?" as he started the engine; resting his left hand partially on the seat back and partly on my shoulder, he twisted round to reverse out of the space.

"Ooh yes. X-rays, the lot. Just bruising, honestly." Failing miserably at trying not to look between his legs. Hurrah for tight jeans. Wondered as we came to a halt whether he wore briefs or boxers. Made a bet with myself on boxers. I was right. But the intervening days until I had the proof were amongst the most frustrating I've ever endured.

"Straight home Shaun?" as we moved off.

"Yes. I think I'm supposed to get plenty of rest for the next few days." Leaning my head back slowly so as not to stretch the skin under my chin too abruptly. Silence from the driver. Turning my head a little I caught a slightly disappointed set to the face as he used the mirror and indicated left. I could have kicked myself. That had sounded like a put-off even to me. "That doesn't mean I'm going to be in bed twenty-four hours a day, or that I'm refused visitors. I'm not THAT ill," I protested. "I just feel a bit shaky. You know?"

The expression lightened immediately like a lamp being switched on."How will you get to the Outpatients' at the Mourne?" snatching a quick glance at me. "What time do you have to be there?" God. His face, it was SO open, SO readable.

"Eleven o'clock. I'll walk." Held my breath, and right on cue.

"You can't do that." Indignation evident "I'll take you."

"Oh come on Harry. That would spoil your holiday and what will your parents say?"

"They won't mind." He grinned as we swung round the roundabout at the top of the Rostrevor road. "It's a good excuse to take the car out."

"Do you need one?" I wondered out loud.

"Well no," he admitted. "You know what I mean, and it'll be fun."

I held up my right arm encased in bandages from fingertips to halfway to the elbow.

"Well, maybe not so much fun for you." His face was distressed again. "But it will give us the chance to get to know each other."

"Are you really sure that's a good idea Harry?" It just had to be said, and of course he took it the wrong way.

"I thought we could be friends." Sounding both hurt and surprised at the same time. "But if you don't want to."

"Come on. You know it's not that at all... HEY, hey keep your eyes on the road," as we drifted across into the next lane.

"Oops. Sorry Shaun, sorry." Straightening up. "But what is the problem then?"

"You know, I don't think you and I would have a problem. But, this *is* Northern Ireland!"

"So?" His eyebrows inverted over his nose and my heart gave a little skip and a jump.

"But Harry, you are Protestant and I'm Catholic."

"*So?*"

"Aren't you worried about the reaction from your family and friends if you start going round with me?"

"Why should I be worried, are you?" Looking at me, eyebrows still inverted.

I thought for a few seconds and realised: no, I wasn't concerned at all, my only concern was to get as close as possible to him, and I suspected that was a good deal closer than he had yet taken time to envision.

"Nope. No worries. I really would like to get to know you, and I think we are going to be the very best of friends."

His grin threatened to swallow his ears as reaching over he squeezed my right leg just above the knee.

"Good. That's alright then."

God! The shock of his touch raced straight to cock's tip. One way or another I needed to have a wank very soon. I'd go crazy else.

We swapped stories the rest of the way home. I told him about the factory and of course he knew a lot of the people there. I found out that he was thirteen months older than me. Doing part-time studies in computers at Newcastle Tech. Didn't much want to go to university. (My heart sank at the thought of his going anywhere.) I already knew in a general way that his family were well off, with a couple of trawlers (he'd had a week on one the previous year. Been sick the whole time and was never ever going to set foot on one ever again), a brickyard and building business, hardware store at the top of the Harbour Road with the family house on the opposite corner, and of course 'The Arrandale Hotel' in Newcastle. He worked there doing whatever was necessary.

"If you get fed up with the factory you could always come and work with me at the hotel." Swinging the car into the Scrogg road. "Which one is it?"

"There, with the yellow roses round the gate."

Pulling up, he unclipped the seatbelt for me, ensuring it didn't snap back against my shoulder. Carrying the bag with the helmet and clothes plus the envelope he followed me round to the back door.

"Who's home?" he whispered as I opened the door into the kitchen.

"Nobody."

"Don't you lock your door?"

"Nah. I don't think anyone round here bothers."

"Where do you want your things?"

"Can you bring them through?" Leading the way to my bedroom. "Just sling them on the bed." Mum had obviously taken the opportunity to spring-clean in my absence. There were no clothes on the chair. The bed had been changed, all my books were standing to attention and there wasn't a shoe in sight.

"Ooh, lots of science fiction."

"Yes. Do you like Anne McCaffrey, or how about Marion Zimmer Bradley?" Taking *Darkover Landfall* and *Dragonquest* off the shelves.

"Are they any good?" Reading the back covers.

"Brilliant. Look, sit down a minute Harry, I'm bursting."

"Where is it?"

"Come on. I'll show you," as we trooped back into the kitchen. "It was only added four years ago" – as I opened the door – "Now, you first, me first, or both together?"

"Nah. You first." Blushing and stepping back.

"But I don't think I can manage by myself." Waving bandaged hands in front of his face and trying to keep my own straight. His eyes widened. (Actually I was pretty sure I could manage to pee unaided.) "Your face!" I had to grin, chin or no chin "Why don't you put the kettle on," closing the door, "We'll have a coffee."

It was more awkward than difficult to wrestle the zip down and hook cock into the air. Much more difficult to get him back out of sight, particularly as he didn't want to go. Later, later I promised silently, honestly, soon soon! Pressing the flush I realised that in no way could I get the zip back up again.

The kettle was beginning to hiss as I came out. "Sorry Harry," adopting what I hoped was a suitably sheepish tone, "but I really can't manage the zip." Stopping beside him at the sink. "Would you?" His hand trembled as he grasped the tag and pulled it up over the bulge. "Thanks. Sorry."

He bolted into the bathroom. Now, how many zillion times

had I pulled that zip up and down? I had no memory of it feeling like that except when I was really horny and couldn't wait to get hold of cock! Anyway, he'd got his nerve back in the short while he was in there and he seemed quite relaxed as I showed him where the coffee things were. Back in the bedroom with him on the chair and me perched on the bed we drank coffee and talked books for over an hour before, looking at his watch, he announced that he would have to go home. He'd told his mother that he would be back in time to help her with the dinner.

"I'm learning to cook," proudly. "Mum promised to show me how to make a bannock." Standing up, "I'll bring you some tomorrow if it turns out alright."

I didn't want him to go and yet at the same time I desperately needed to lie down. At the back door I laid my semi-good left hand on his shoulder. "Harry, Eyes, thanks."

He stood still looking at me.

"I can't shake hands" – small smile – "but I could give you a hug." I was nervous, but couldn't just let him walk away. He didn't say anything, just put his arms round me. I put mine round him and hugged lightly. My head on his shoulder, our hair mingling, for about thirty or forty seconds.

"Thanks again." Releasing him, stepping back. My eyes felt misty and his looked very bright.

"See you at ten-thirty in the morning Shaun," and he was gone round the corner of the house.

I was back in my room in time to see the roof of his car move off on the other side of the hedge. Waved even though I knew he couldn't see me. Feeling suddenly depressed and very tired, I kicked off my shoes and lay down on top of the bed. With Harry's departure the sexual need seemed to have gone as well and, within a matter of minutes I was fast asleep.

3

Eight p.m. had passed when Mum woke me. "There's a good wee dinner on the table so there is," as I slowly swung my feet onto the floor. "Then get yourself into bed properly." Watching me wince as I stood up. "A soak in a hot bath is what you need for them bruises." Picking up my trainers and placing them inside the wardrobe beside my other shoes, all polished and lined up on the rack at the bottom. "But no. NO! We have to have the bath out and a

SHOWER in." Bustling out the door. "No one asks me. But then, what do I bloody know? And, another thing, how are you supposed to wash with all them bandages." Voice trailing away, then loudly. "Come on. Your good wee dinner will be cold." In truth, sleeping in my clothes and being woken up had left me feeling fuzzy. My shoulder ached, my chin had woken up as well and my right hand was pulsing and awfully hot.

Kathleen, my twenty-four year old sister, had been in from work and gone again. Eileen, who was twelve, was sitting at one end of the table sucking on a pen and glaring over her glasses at me. My dinner was at the other end and Mum was crashing around in the kitchen.

"Hiya Frogface," I managed as I sat down. Fish and bloody chips! When your Dad catches it and your Mum packs it, you do tend to get more than your fair share.

"You are in dead trouble." Triumphant ring to her voice, then: "How many fingers did you lose?" edged with delicious dread.

"Little vampire. Only three." Waggling the bandages at her.

"Eeugh. Mum!" she wailed.

"I brought them home." Pretending to search in my left-hand pocket. "I thought we might have a funeral for them tomorrow."

"Mum," lilting wail, "he's being horrible to me."

"That's what brothers are for." Winking at her. "Now give. What sort of trouble this time?" using the fork to break up the fish.

"Oh, just you wait till Kath gets hold of you." Triumph back again.

"Oh shit. What now?"

"Mum, he's swearing."

"If you don't tell me" – putting my hand back to my pocket – "I'll feed these fingers to you one by one and I won't even cook them."

"Oooh YOU!" tossing her head. "I know you didn't lose any fingers really." Smirking. "You used her talc again and you didn't clean up after."

"Oh shit." Suddenly very tired. With Kathleen this was a hanging offence.

"Mum" – warningly – "It's okay really. I saw the mess when I got home from school." Putting out her hand: "That'll be fifty pence. I hoovered it up." Smug little bitch.

"So now you're a blackmailer as well as being a vampire." Pushing the plate to one side. "I'll give it to you tomorrow."

"Now please. You ALWAYS forget and this time I might forget too and let slip about the mess I had to clean up."

"Alright, alright, you goblin. I'll get it."

Mum was looking grimly at the plate when I returned with the money. "Huh! Fine thanks I get. Not good enough for you?"

"No Mum," feeling fuzzier than ever. "I'm just not hungry."

"Oh *aye*." Sarcasm layered thick. "Get to your bloody bed then." Sweeping the plate into the kitchen.

"Here you go, squirt, and thanks."

"Are you really very sore?" Solemn now with the money in her hot little fist.

"Yes. I really am. Goodnight. See you tomorrow."

"Goodnight Shaun. I'll say a wee prayer for you."

"Okay, squirt," closing the hall door then my own. The next few minutes were a mixture of contortions punctuated with the occasional "Shit!" as I unsuccessfully tried to undress without causing any aggravation to my various painful areas. I managed eventually, even got the dressing gown on and through to the bathroom. Trying to brush my teeth resulted in an unmitigated disaster with more paste on my face than round my teeth. I'm no good at that sort of thing with my left hand. I even had to give cock an IOU. I don't remember turning the light out, but do remember seeing *Darkover Landfall* and *Dragonquest* on the chair and thinking I must make sure to give them to him tomorrow.

Every other time I've had a wet dream I've woken up (at least part way) in the final critical moments and, although more often than not I fail to remember the actual dream sequence, at least I've sleepily enjoyed the sensations before being poleaxed by sleep again. So I was pretty miffed to wake up and find my belly and chest crusted with dried cum without the faintest recollection of the event. Cock however was totally unrepentant, staring brazenly at me through partially open foreskin.

"Ready, eh?" Normally I use my left hand just for cupping my balls and pressing the root behind the ball sac, but with my right being out of action I was reduced to a gentle stroke with the thumb and fingertips of the left. Cock didn't seem to mind. I think he was having withdrawal symptoms and any attention being better than none, enjoyed himself hugely. The first blast landed precisely on my left nipple. A truly great way to greet the day. Licked the residue clinging to the thumb and fingers, wondering what Harry's would taste like?

Galvanised by the thought of Harry I shot out of bed. Time! What fucking time was it? Only nine-fortyfive, thank shit. I strolled through to the bathroom in the nude, cooling cum sliding down my belly. I love being in the nude, it feels so sexy.

Doing things left-handed when you are right-handed is awkward, frustrating and downright difficult. I used loo paper to remove the fresh cum and pissed on the paper in the bowl. To get rid of the dried residue from the previous night I was reduced to crumbling it with my fingertips and rubbing with a towel. I needed a shower but didn't have a clue as to how to go about it. By God, I was going to stink if I couldn't wash for ten days! Trying to scrub my teeth was just as disastrous as before, washing the face no more than a lick and a promise but it would have to do. I had a few dicey moments after having a shit. How to clean myself without soiling the bandages? Solved by using a wet sponge and rinsing it thoroughly afterwards. Back in the bedroom I chose my loosest pair of slacks, to ensure that I could do them up. T-shirt and trainers completed the outfit. I'd just boiled the kettle when 'tap, tap' on the door.

"Come on in, boss. You want to make the coffee?" My heart started bumping as he smiled and brushed the hair from his forehead. I don't know why he bothered, it looked just the same afterwards.

"Sure. Morning. Use the loo first?"

"Go ahead. See you in a minute."

He didn't bother to close the door and I watched (back view only). I could see his pee going into the bowl and hear it hit the water. Oh, bliss! He used the sponge to wipe his fingers and my knees almost gave way.

"Hi again. Did you sleep alright?" spooning sugar into the mugs. I wanted to hug him and never let go. "Shaun, are you okay?" looking over his shoulder, kettle poised.

"Yeah sure, just glad to see you." I couldn't not say something.

He grinned. "Same here," adding the milk. "Thought about you a lot last night" – stirring vigorously – "Wondered how you were and all that."

"Bring it through to the table." Seating myself opposite him so that I could look at his face. "Yeah, I'm fine" – shrugging – "Not looking forward to this though," indicating my right hand.

"Is it very bad?" reaching across to take it in a gentle grasp.

"It's just scratches really. But it's a bloody nuisance."

"Well it won't take long to heal then." Finishing his coffee. "We'd better be going. Have you got your letter?" – rising – "Shall I wash these?"

"Please. Don't bother drying them, just pop them on the rack" – going into the bedroom – "Wont be a sec" – returning with the envelope and the two books. "You forgot these yesterday," handing them over.

"Yeah. I could have kicked myself when I got home. I could have used something new to read." Pulling the door behind us. "Are you sure about not locking the door?"

"Don't worry. Nothing worth stealing."

Repeat of the previous day. Holding the car door for me. Fitting the seatbelt, shoulder pressed to shoulder. Surely he must feel SOMETHING. Must KNOW I love him. Almost said it as he leant across me.

"Harry!!!"

"What is it?" switching the engine on.

"Oh, nothing." I felt depressed and yet, somewhere deep inside I was certain that I shouldn't.

"Go on. What is it?"

"Are you sure this isn't an awful drag for you?" I shrugged. "You know you don't have to. I COULD walk."

"Don't be silly." Checking the mirror and pulling away. "I wouldn't be doing it if I didn't want to and besides, I thought we sorted this out yesterday."

"Yes, but that was yesterday. What do you think now?"

He pulled up abruptly at the side of the road. "Do you mind if we talk about this later?" His face! So readable, so very earnest and, the eyebrows were inverted again. "I really like you and I should like it very much if we became friends. Can we take it from there?"

"Harry! I'm sorry." Totally lost in green eyes (with little golden flecks). "Honestly, I do want you for a friend" – and a lot more, cock added, stretching slowly. "It's just that I worry. I don't know why but I do."

He was still glaring under his brows at me. "Is it your side?" Worry there. "Am I going to be trouble for you?" – brows relaxing – "Is that it?"

"No," I assured him. "Mum wont like it, in line with anything I do..." I shrugged. "I've known you three days, Harry. All things being equal, it's unlikely we ever should have met, but now that we have!" – this was getting very heavy very quickly – "Now that we have, I wouldn't want to..." I was struggling to finish, not wanting to go over the top.

"You wouldn't want to change it?" he finished for me.

"Right."

"Nor me."

Nothing more was said during the few minutes it took to reach the 'Mourne' nor did anything seem necessary.

"Should I come with you?" releasing the belt.

"Would you mind, I'm liable to be a bit shaky afterwards."

"Come on then."

Maybe it was only the anticipation, but the whole procedure seemed much more painful than at the hospital. First the chin dressing stuck. "Tut, tut, tut," from the nurse. The left hand not too bad, but the right was sheer hell and I could not hold back the tears as the final layer was soaked and peeled off. I couldn't bring myself to look, I felt faint.

"Tut, tut, tut." Shake of the head. "*Why* will they not use the Melamine squares?" looking up. "What's your name?" – referring to her notes "Shaun. Well Shaun that is the last time you will have to go through that..." applying a bandage over the fresh dressing. "The arm and fingers are coming on nicely, and I've put a Melamine dressing on your chin and hand. Do you know what Melamine does?" – closing the bandage with surgical tape.

I could only shake my head in the negative.

"Well, Melamine prevents sticking" – grimacing – "So, no more soaking and peeling like today."

"Thank you nurse."

"Sure and don't thank me for doing my job properly. Those eedjits in Daisy Hill are going to be hearing from me, I can tell you that."

"Now" – as she disposed of the old dressings – "are you managing to sleep alright, or do you need something to help?"

"No thanks, I'm alright..." – standing shakily – "Nurse?"

"Yes son."

"I need to have a shower" – waving my hands. "How can I?"

"Just you soak in a warm bath. You don't really need soap and all that. Someone at home will surely wash your hair for you."

"Um, we only have a shower." Beginning to blush.

"Well, then you will have to keep your arms up, your dressings covered with plastic bags and have someone do the washing for you. Your Mum?"

I knew I was absolutely crimson as I left the dressing station.

"Same time tomorrow please."

"Yes. Thanks nurse."

I hoped she was right about the Melamine. No way could I go through that every day for ten days.

"Poor you. You look done in. Was it that bad?" He took my arm. "At least I can see your fingertips now" – referring to the right hand.

"I feel sick Harry." I did too. Things were not quite steady. He ushered me to the car.

"Leave the door open a minute." Taking deep breaths of cool disinfectant free air.

"Maybe you should try putting your head between your knees?" squatting in front of me. "It worked for me."

I did as he suggested, and magically everything steadied up. A few more deep breaths. "Thanks Harry, you're a lifesaver, I'll be okay now."

Are you sure?" At my nod he closed the door and got in behind the wheel. "Are you going to go through this every day?"

"No. Or at least she says that the dressing she put on won't stick." I shivered. "I wish I'd never seen a motorbike."

"But then we never would have met." Faint protest as he started the car.

"I know that." Leaning back, recovering rapidly. "But did it really have to be such a dramatic meeting? Where are we going?" as he turned left out of the hospital grounds.

"Well, I did promise you some bannock."

"And?"

"I keep my promises." Left again out of Newry Street and down the hill.

"You wouldn't?" I was appalled and intrigued at the same time.

"Now don't go worrying. Only Mum at home and she is expecting you."

My Mum was very small and plump (very fat really). Her face wore a continually harassed, angry expression. Life for her seemed to be a continual battle which she was frightened of loosing. I had NEVER heard a word of praise from her that I could remember. Everything was criticised. Hair, clothes, attitude, my way of talking or walking. And even though she had more than half of my wages every week, all she said was that I'd have to work a lifetime to begin to repay her for rearing me.

Eileen, now that she was almost a teenager, had recently become subject to the whining and carping that until then had been my sole lot. Kathleen tended to be almost totally ignored, except when she was preparing to go out of an evening. Then there would commence a series of loud sniffs, followed by comments as to how much she (Kath) 'looked like a hoor' and how much better it would be if 'you stayed home with your legs closed'. Adding the warning that she was to 'bring no wee bastards to this house'. Kathleen's only response would be to increase the volume of her Walkman, thereby ensuring an ever more varied and sarcastic tirade from Mum. If Dad was at home he might try to stem the tide with the likes of "Shut up Winnie. Leave the child alone," and once, "She's no different from you at her age."

Looking up from my book I found that VERY hard to believe. Impossible to imagine this angry little fat woman in a short skirt, low cleavage and make-up. However she soon put a stop to that line. "Aye! Och *aye*! And look where it's got me. Should the Blessed Virgin be my judge, I swear, I wish I'd nivir clapped eyes on any of you. I do that." At that Eileen burst into tears, Kathleen slammed her way out the front door and Dad escaped to the back garden. Me? I carried on with my book by the fire. I'd heard it all too many times before. Dad I felt sorry for, but at the same time I could not help but resent what I (then) took for cowardice.

Harry's Mum could not have been more unlike mine if she had set out deliberately to do so. As we pulled into the yard at the rear of the house (huge, three-storey granite), he bipped the horn a couple of times. He raced round the car and practically dragged me into the kitchen, smothering my feeble protests. "Come on. She can't wait to meet the flying motorcyclist from the Scrogg."

"And who's SHE? The cat's mother? You horrid little beast." She folded him in a hug. I thought he might disappear. Everything about her, apart from the warm smiling voice, was huge. Jean must have been over six foot and built to match. You could have slept on her breasts and not worried about falling off when you turned over. Her upper arms were a match for my thighs. Her eyes were his eyes. I'd heard of eyes twinkling, but never seen it until I met Jean. Harry's shone yes, but hers seemed to have little lights flickering on and off at random. Her face was full and round (his snub nose) and perfectly made-up. Only her hair colour, mostly steel grey with streaks of pure white, gave away the fact that she was fifty-eight. The hair was waved and cared for (not like Mum's, scraped back into a bun always).

Jean released Harry and ruffled his hair. "Well? Are you not going to introduce us then? You're not much of a gentleman." Spoiling the reproof with a fond smile.

"Mum, meet Shaun McKenna," and he gave a little bow. "Shaun, meet my mother, Mrs Jean Hannah" – another bow. "What did you do with the bannock Mum?" turning to the cupboards.

"Come away in son," as I continued to stand just inside the door. Coming over she folded me in a gentler version of what Harry had just endured. Holding me away as I reddened. "Well, you can't shake hands now can you?" pushing me lightly towards the table. "Sit down, sit down"– turning – "Harry Hannah, stop wrecking my kitchen this instant and sit down with your friend." Pretending to swat the back of his head. Grinning he ducked and more or less fell into the chair opposite.

"The service in this hovel gets worse" – winking at me.

"Cheeky little monster. Shaun, take no notice."

Sandwiches, bannock, butter, jam, cream, a pot of coffee, cups, plates, knives, spoons and all the rest covered the end of the table where we sat in about a minute. I wasn't sure what to do with the starched cloth on the plate and waited for Harry, copying him as he spread his over his knees. Jean buttered slices of bannock with a speed born of practise. Spooned jam and cream onto my plate. (What on earth was I supposed to do with the cream? I'd thought it was for the coffee.) I was looking to Harry for guidance when she saw my confusion and covered it brilliantly. "Ooh, I forgot your hands. Let me." Smothering the buttered bannock with jam followed by a huge dollop of cream. Then cutting the whole thing into fingers. "There you go. Goodness but you need feeding up." Looking at my arms. "Never mind, you're still growing." Ruffling my hair. "You're just like skinny over there. I do my level best to fill him up and he never puts on an ounce."

"Och Mum!"

He was watching but pretending not to as I picked up the first finger of bannock.

"Well! What do you think?" as I had a sip of coffee.

"Think of what?" All the puzzlement and innocence I could muster.

Jean giggled (his giggle) as his face fell and he looked as though he might burst.

"SHAUN..." drawing it out menacingly – "the bannock of course."

I paused for a moment. "It's great. Really, I love it." Picking up another finger. "You did make sure he washed his hands first?" – stage-whispered to Jean.

"Oh YOU! Just you wait till your hands are better Mr McKenna, I won't forget." The implied threat negated by the grin on his face. That all helped break the ice for me, and less than an hour later I was feeling more at home there than I ever had in my own house.

Jean insisted on 'Aunt Jean' when I wouldn't call her by her first name, "and Mrs Hannah is too formal." She asked a few questions about the accident then, without seeming to, led the conversation round to me personally. On thinking about that first meeting some time later, I realised I had been well and truly grilled without ever once Harry or I catching on. She knew by the time she left to do her shopping that Harry and I were going to be a lot more to each other than just mere acquaintances. As to whether that prospect pleased her or not she never at any time said. She accepted me as her youngest son's friend and made me one of her family. I would later wish that all his family had been so open-minded. She left Harry to put the dishes away, kissing the end of his nose and the top of his head.

"I think Shaun still needs his rest, young man." Warningly. "So, no gallivanting round the countryside until the bandages are off." Poking him in the ribs. "You hear me?" Making him giggle and fumble a plate. "Don't you dare break my china."

"And you!" turning from the door to me. "You're welcome here at any time." Fishing in her bag for car keys. "You listen to me when I tell you, you're not over that accident yet. So, get plenty of rest, and don't be letting my prize idiot son drag you from here to Attical until those bandages are off." Looking stern "You hear me?"

"Yes, Aunt Jean." I almost said "Yes Mum."

"Good." With finality. "I hear you're another bookworm. Well, that will be your best pastime for the next week or so. See you soon again I expect. Now don't either of you go forgetting what I just said." Closing the door.

"Phew! Mothers!"

"I think she's great."

"So do I really." Grinning. "But don't tell her too often or she'll get a big head." Closing the cupboard doors.

"Come on up and look at my books." Leading the way upstairs. "You can borrow whatever you like."

Harry's room was on the top floor, partially in the roof space. It was huge! There were two big beds, not quite doubles but they certainly looked to me as though they might be big enough for two.

"Oh, Graham and I used to share." Putting the key he'd used to open the door in the lock inside. "He got married almost a year ago." That seemed to depress him somewhat.

"Is this REALLY all yours?" I couldn't believe it, I was frankly jealous. Compared to my ten by ten, it was a palace. It appeared to be bigger than our living room at home. There were a couple of big old armchairs, a chess table all set up, a big TV and stereo with a video. Place round the walls were a half-dozen waist-high bookcases crammed mostly with paperbacks, interspersed here and there with large hardbacks and videos.

"AHA! But let me show you something else..." And he opened an odd-shaped door by the front wall to reveal his own bathroom.

"Shit. You are a lucky brute." I shook my head "What else is on this floor?"

"Another room the same as this on the other side of the landing."

"Whose room is that?" Flopping into a chair. "Sorry, don't mean to be nosy."

"No problem." Taking the other chair. "Nobody uses it now, but it was the twins' before they got married."

"Why do you keep your room locked?" Myself, I could think of all sorts of good reasons to lock my bedroom door.

He got embarrassed. "It's Charlie."

"Who's Charlie?" Who was Charlie? Just how many were there?

"One of my brothers." His face was red. "Nosy fucker. Always walking in whenever he pleased." Wriggling in the chair which pulled his slacks tight round his crotch, giving me the first indication that he might more than equal me in that department.

"Borrowing clothes and stuff without asking. Dad put the lock on when Graham got married." He was redder than ever. Springing up from the chair. "You haven't looked at the books. Shall I put some music on? What do you like?"

I received the distinct impression that further questions about Charlie would not be welcome at that time. Nevertheless I determined to find out more at some stage. I felt sure that there was more to it than borrowing things without asking.

"Any 'Take That'?"

We decided that Robbie was our favourite. Me hoping that his reasons were similar to mine. As he squatted by the stereo I became convinced about boxer shorts. No line to betray the wearing of briefs. Suddenly thought, suppose he doesn't wear anything under his trousers! I felt little beads of moisture gather on my upper lip. The mere thought made me twitch.

The clock on the stereo showed 3.15 when I began to feel a bit stretched out and I had the beginnings of a real thumper of a headache. He looked disappointed and anxious when I suggested that I'd better go home.

"Are you alright Shaun?" Locking his door. "Mum will kill me if I get you too tired."

"No, really." Following him down the stairs. All wood panelling and an enormous number of doors. "I expect your mum is right. I'll be more lively in a couple of days." As we got in the car I felt that I had to apologise. "Sorry Harry. I've really enjoyed today, if only I didn't feel so tired."

"Hey, no problem." Accelerating up the hill past the 'Kilmorey'. "It should be easier tomorrow." He glanced at my right hand. "The dressing I mean."

"I do hope so," as we pulled up at the gate.

"Want a coffee?" when he put the books I'd borrowed on the chest in the bedroom.

"Thanks Shaun, but no, I think you should lie down. I'll let myself out." He wrapped his arms round me and hugged hard. Having it returned with interest. It felt so right, I felt so comfortable, I didn't want to let go. At the same time I didn't want to embarrass him. Leaning back a little before releasing him, I looked into his eyes just inches from mine and couldn't help myself. Moving my head swiftly I planted a kiss on the tip of his nose. His arms slackened momentarily and I thought I'd overdone it. But his grip tightened again and his head came to rest against mine, his lips by my ear.

"See you in the morning Shaun. Sleep well." He was gone. I stood by the window to see him come round the house to the gate. He looked up as he closed it, smiling and returning my raised hand before disappearing into the car and away.

I panicked a little. Would he come back? Had I been too forward? The headache in that instant became a crashing, pulsing reality. I swallowed four paracetamol with some water. (It seemed very silly to take two and then wait a couple of hours to take another two). Kicking off my trainers I lay down on the bed. I couldn't concentrate to read, although I really wanted to get stuck into the Robert Heinlein books I'd borrowed. Instead I closed my eyes and thought about the cleft of his arse as he squatted by the stereo and before that, the bulge of his crotch as the material stretched across it. I wasn't altogether sure just what it was I wanted, but knew it had to be more than Padraig and I had ever done together. Really, I supposed I was still a virgin. I wondered if Harry was?

4

I don't know how long I'd been wanking. Probably a year or two, but I do remember the first time I'd spunked. It gave me such a shock and fright, I almost fainted. Then I'd totally freaked. What was it? What had I done to myself?

Often enough when I think back over the years I've had cause to thank Dad, but never more so than on that day. I would have been about thirteen, can't now remember exactly. I do know that Dad wasn't working and it must have been sometime during the summer holidays as we were at Gran's old house at Ballykeel. She had made us dinner and afterwards Dad was cutting the grass with a scythe. I'd been sitting reading on the garden wall when I had to go to the toilet. At that time, every time I had a shit my cock got hard. I didn't know why. No one ever said anything and even now I can't understand why. My shorts must have been sticking out a good couple of inches every time I came out of the loo. Not only then, if I crossed my legs I got an instant hard, sitting on the bus to school and again on the way home. Running made me hard, riding my bike gave me sensations I had no words for. Stroking or squeezing it made me feel as though my feet were six inches off the ground. Mostly it was a nuisance. I didn't know what was happening, or why, and was too ashamed and naïve to ask. Dire warnings from Mum about not touching yourself *'down there'* brought feelings of guilt and reinforced the shame when I ignored her warnings. How could you NOT touch yourself 'down there'? You had to pee, you had to wash, you had to dress and undress. Why could you not pee when it was hard? I was both fascinated and terrified in roughly equal proportions, but never terrified enough to stop pulling or stroking it.

That day, it seemed absolutely imperative that I pull the loose skin on its end back and back. I felt as though I was going to split, but couldn't stop myself forcing it back. The more I did so, the more incredible the feeling. My heart was jumping out of my chest, I was gasping like a stranded fish. Suddenly there was a 'pop', not an actual sound but a feeling of release. Opening my screwed shut eyes I looked down. I was still forcing what had been loose flesh back. It wasn't loose any longer. Stretched to tearing point. (At least it felt that way). There, where there had been white skin! A purple thing. All glistening, and it had a little slit at the point.

A sensation, unique and indescribable was building, threatening to knock me over. I pulled back even harder. I WAS splitting! The flesh parted from the base of the purple thing. By now I was totally petrified, but could no more stop myself than I could stop breathing. I watched as the purple tip bent forward, was it going to fall off? I both cared and didn't care. With another 'pop' (it really is the only way to describe the feeling) the skin released the purple head completely. I was suddenly half an inch longer than before.???

On other occasions when I had been bursting and more than bursting for a pee, the sensation of relief when the piss started flowing was fantastic. Well this was the same, only a hundred times, no, a thousand times more intense. I could feel it coming. Whatever IT was. I was rubbing myself frantically. At that stage I couldn't have cared less if the whole thing had come off in my hand. I must have sounded like a horse in the last stages of exhaustion.

The scything had stopped, although I wasn't aware of that or much else. I'm sure now I must have cried out, screamed, sobbed, groaned. More than likely a combination of the lot. The purple tip seemed to be expanding enormously. I was sure I could hear the skin stretching and not just feel it. Only on very rare occasions since have I been able to reproduce the tingling, shaking-all-over feeling that I had that day as my new purple friend swelled and spat forth a gob of white. It travelled almost the length of the toilet before it hit the floor. Looked for all the world like a very small lump of spit. The whole world spun and for the first time (but not the last) I saw stars.

HAD it come off? I almost couldn't look. But no, it was still there and I noticed at the base of the purple head what looked like a yellowish white collar. Picking at it cautiously with my left hand, I found that it would peel away. Did just that. Got the most incredible jolt of feeling as it came free and a repeat of the sensations just experienced. It was too much. I squeaked. I remember that distinctly. There was no second discharge, though it felt as if there had been.

"Are you alright, son?" Dad's voice outside the door. He almost sounded as though he were laughing. What to *do*? I hadn't a clue. I felt weak. Exultant. Terrified too, but exultant.

"Don't know." Now feeling like crying as the incredible new feelings started to diminish. *Was* crying as he opened the door. (No lock on the outside and only toilet.)

"Aah!" spotting the cum straight away. Me standing, shorts round the ankles, right hand still clutching cock. Still hard, but not quite as hard as it had just been. The formerly loose bit of skin now feeling frighteningly, painfully tight.

"What's that, Dad?" indicating the purple bit which began to shrink quite visibly as we looked at it. "What is that white stuff?" Really sobbing now. "What did I do Dad?... I'm sorry Dad."

He took his hanky from his pocket and dried my face. Took my hand away from cock and looked at it closely. Now it was shrinking rapidly almost as if frightened itself. I suddenly felt embarrassed, standing in front of him nearly naked, and began to blush furiously.

"Give it another minute son," as I went to pull up the shorts.

"Really Shaun, everything is alright." Tilting my head to look into my eyes. "You're not in any trouble son, so don't worry, okay?" I couldn't see it at the time but, he was trying very hard not to laugh out loud. I bless him for that. *Had* he laughed, I think I would have curled up and died right there.

"Try easing the skin back over its head now." I was back to my one inch or so of soft cock. I was almost as surprised by the gradual disappearance of the glans as I had been by its totally unexpected arrival on the scene. It still didn't feel right and it was very painful.

"Pretty sore, eh?" seeing me wince as I pulled my shorts up and caught it on the waistband. "Well, you won't be doing *that* again for a few days." His voice was light. The top of his head threatened to fall off, the smile was so vast. "Come on son, we'll go down to the shore and have a talk." Did that mean that I could do it again? When? How often? Every time it was hard? Would it be as sore every time? I was bursting now with pent-up questions but didn't have the nerve, nor did I know how to ask.

He called out to Gran that we were going for an ice cream and would be back in a while. We had the ice cream and sat on the rocks on the beach while he talked. Had it been anyone else telling me, a lot of it I would not then have believed, but because it was Dad telling me, I had to believe all of it. No matter that a lot of it was offputting , some of it frankly sick-making.

"Are you feeling better now?" as we trudged back up the hill.

"Yeah, but, I'm still sore."

"Well, as I said you'll just have to try and leave it alone for a week, maybe a little longer. If you find that it's still tight or sore afterwards, say over the next couple of months, you promise to tell me?" Nudging my arm and looking into my face. "Promise me Shaun. Because we can easily get it fixed so that it is not sore, okay? Promise?"

"I promise, Dad." Blushing again. "Dad?"

"What, son?" as we walked on.

"Oh, nothing really... I mean..." I hesitated, not wanting to sound soppy, then, "Thanks Dad I love you," all in one breath.

He laughed a little and gave me a dead arm. "You're my son and I love you too."

"Big bully." Rubbing my arm. "I'll get you," and I did. Deadlegged him at the dinner table that night to exasperated cries from Mum.

The subject was only ever raised once again after that day of revelations. Round about Christmas time as the two of us were putting up the tree.

"You alright, Shaun?" apropos of nothing. I looked at him puzzled.

"No problems with your willy I mean?"

I blushed furiously remembering just how naïve I had been. "Oh, sorry Dad. Yes. I mean *no*." Getting hopelessly confused. "I'm fine honestly. No problems." Well, apart from not being able to cum as often as I'd like, but I wasn't going to tell him that, and anyway, he had covered that aspect too at the time.

"Okay, good, but don't forget I was your age once and anything you don't understand you just have to ask." And that was that.

* * *

Padraig and I had just been mutual lust, no emotion involved. We had stumbled into it almost by accident when we were fourteen. Back in school a couple of days after the end of the summer holidays and no one had really settled into the routine as yet. Everyone including the teachers was still getting to know new faces, different classrooms, changed schedules, plus the anticlimax of being locked up again Monday to Friday, nine to four. Renovations to the wood and metalwork department were as yet incomplete, so our class had nowhere to go during the last class period of the day. Luck or bad judgement placed the two or us at the front of the queue outside the door. Mr Swallow grabbed us as he came out of the noise and the dust. "You two! Stay here. The rest of you outside. No woodwork today."

"Please Sir, can we go home then?" from somewhere safely at the rear.

"Those who live locally or come to school on bikes may go now. The rest of you will just have to wait on the usual buses."

"Quietly," in a vain attempt to quell the clatter of feet on the stairs. "You two come with me!"

We followed down the stairs past the Art Room to the Library and the stationery store beside it. When he opened the door and turned on the light we saw stacks of boxes and bare shelves. "Empty all these boxes and put the books neatly on the shelves, make sure you keep all the same sizes and types together" – turning to go – "If you do a good job I'll see that you are this year's stationery and library monitors."

"Thank you, Sir," we chorused as the swing-loaded door closed us in the windowless room.

"I hope we do get the monitors' job," Padraig removing his blazer.

"Yeah, you get to miss some lessons," I agreed.

"If I climb up you can pass them to me," as we set to ripping tops off boxes.

"You'll want to put the smallest ones on the top, Pat?"

"Yeah, let's sort them into piles first."

"Okay."

The room wasn't very big though it was quite high so we tended to bump into each other as we ripped and shoved boxes around. It was also very warm and my blazer soon joined Padraig's on the bottom shelf. All the boxes opened and books sorted Padraig climbed up two shelves and turning awkwardly straddled a corner, feet well apart. His crotch was level with my eyes each time I straightened to pass a pile of books. It wasn't long before my back unused to all the bendings and straightening began to protest.

"God. Sorry but I'll have to stop for a minute," holding my back, eyes glued to his zipper.

"Okay, I need to move some of these along a bit," holding on with one hand and leaning towards me as he rearranged the stacks. I could see the outline of his cock quite clearly. As he abruptly regained his position I noticed that it seemed to be getting bigger. My own was beginning to react and I felt quite breathless. My heart was thudding away and my mouth was unaccountably dry.

"Come on, Shaun, I don't want to be here all fucking day you know." The F word gave me a real twitch. At that time I'd never dared say it out loud.

I couldn't say anything. I know I was beet red. Bending down I passed him a stack of books. Too many all at once. He dropped them. In trying to catch them I inadvertently rubbed my hand up the front or his trousers. It just seemed to stick there. Like a magnet to iron.

My hand on another boy's cock. Padraig didn't say anything, didn't do anything, except continue to grow under my hand. Looking up at his face I slowly pulled his zipper down and slid my hand inside his trousers. Felt the hard hot flesh more freely through his underwear.

"Wait," he breathed and got down. I thought he was going to go as he moved to the door. Looking out he closed the door again, moved some boxes against it. Turned to me with an expectant look on his face. Little beads of sweat on his forehead staining his white blond hair almost black. With trembling fingers I undid the top of his trousers and pushed them down. My eyes momentarily level with the protrusion in the briefs. Upright again, I stretched the elastic of the waistband and released his cock as I pushed the briefs down his hairy thighs. I was surprised by the amount of hair on his legs, but didn't really take it in at the time, eyes fixed on his jutting cock. Curious the differences to mine. It had a definite twist to the left whereas mine was straight. When we got round to comparisons at a later date my suspicion that his was a little longer proved correct. There was a definite and clearly defined brown patch on the side of the shaft.

That day there was no talking. I closed my fist round him as he reached out and set me free. We had to steady ourselves with our free hand on each other's shoulder. I could feel that we were both trembling violently. Every time I pushed his foreskin back too hard he jerked his arse back, letting me know that his was too tight to retract completely. He appeared totally surprised that mine went back so far and kept brushing the back edge of the head with his fingertips. I felt him sag at the knees and concentrated my gaze on his cock which was beginning to twitch in my hand. I could feel his balls rising against my fingers on the down stroke. He was making little moaning sounds in his throat. As for me, I was rapidly approaching something which promised to be very special in the way of cumming. I gripped him more firmly and increased the pace, hoping he would take the hint. I'll give him due credit. He then and every other time was quick to follow my lead. I moved as close as I could without losing sight of our flying fists. I couldn't decide which to concentrate on, his twitching cock in my hand or the pressure of his fist round mine. I came first in a stomach-wrenching spasm that induced the little bright stars again, my cum landing on his shirt. Then he came with a gasp and almost completely collapsed at the knees. I trapped most of it in my hand though it tended to ooze between my fingers. Continued to stroke him using his cum as lubrication (I'd never thought of doing that to myself, but promised cock an experiment that same night). My hand was getting tired, but already he was beginning to twitch again. A quick glance at his face showed eyes screwed tight shut and lower lip clenched between his teeth, breath whistling through his nose. Both his hands were on my shoulders now, holding himself up, and I could see that he was on the point of cumming a second time in as many minutes. It came accompanied by a heartfelt groan. His head falling forward just missing my chin to land on my chest. Thirty seconds later, breathing back to normal, he looked up with a smile, pushing his pelvis forward till our semi-limp sticky cocks touched. That was the first time.

"Shit! You got a hanky?"

"Let's get these books on the fucking shelves."

* * *

After the first time in the storeroom, Padraig and I looked for opportunities to repeat the performance. Not though for a week or so after the first time. I think we were both a bit shy with each other for a few days, but we had obviously done well enough as Mr Swallow did get us the monitor's jobs.

A week or so after the storeroom incident we both got off a music lesson when 'Ould Biddy' discovered that over the summer break our voices had broken and we could no longer sustain a steady note. We were packed off to the library to make a start on indexing the new books and shelving them.

No class in the library. A couple of important visitors in with the deputy Head. Head off sick, so no one monitoring the corridors or loos during class time. As we came to the bottom of the stairs opposite the boys' loos I looked at him and realised that he was having similar thoughts. I nodded towards the loos and he didn't hesitate. Closing the door quietly I bent down and scanned the cubicles for betraying feet. None. Padraig opened the door to the showers, looked in and shook his head. "In there then," I said giving him a push.

"Okay," reaching out to undo my trousers, letting them fall and tugging at my briefs. Me returning the compliment until we were both naked from the waist down. We moved together until our upright cocks were touching. I put my hand down and tried to grip them both at once, Not very successfully but it got us both going. Standing back a little we braced ourselves as we had on the first occasion. He gripped my cock and pushed the foreskin all the way back staring at the bulb revealed, a distinct look of envy on his face. Instead of his cock I took his little balls in my hand and very gently squeezed and pulled them. This was something I'd recently been experimenting with on myself to some quite good effect. He was a bit uneasy at first but soon got into the spirit and began pulling and squeezing me a bit too enthuiastically. "Yeow," I half whispered half yelped. "Here, here, go easy. Go back to this," and relinquishing his balls I gripped his cock. Instead of rubbing or pulling I gripped hard and started a rhythmic clench and release. Fast and then slow as I felt him begin to twitch. He was more interested in the naked head of mine and taking his hand from my shoulder he held the loose flesh right back and traced the contours of my cockhead with his fingers. The tickling scratching sensation brought me off in about ten seconds. Pushing my hand aside he smeared the cum from his fingers onto his bouncing cock.

I found that by holding him quite loosely my fist slid up and down his shaft. I didn't try to push his foreskin back, aware or how much it was likely to hurt. "Harder, Shaun, harder," through clenched teeth.

Leaving him to brace us both with his hands on my shoulders, I took his balls in my other hand and pulled and squeezed trying to keep in time with the stroking of his nearly boiling cock.

"Right. Faster," he was moaning. "Faster. Harder." I gripped more tightly, pushing back very slightly. "Oooh, oooh, oooh, *shit*," I could feel the pulse of it as his balls contracted up to the base of his cock. I pushed my hand between his legs and tickled the shaft behind his balls.

"Oooh, oooh, don't. Please," but not moving or pushing my hand away. As I watched and continued stroking and tickling he shot right into my little patch of pubic hair above my dick.

"Jesus Christ! Oooh, oooh," as he pulsed again landing a small gob on my belly. His head down on my shoulder. He was trembling all over. "Shit, shit, shit. That was great," looking up, breathing beginning to recover. "Can we do it again?" taking hold of my ever willing cock.

"No, not now, Pat."

"Why not? Nobody's coming. I want to."

"So do I," pulling my clothes up. "How about after school?"

"Lunch time," he insisted. And after school."

"Okay then, we'll take a walk up the back of the football field at lunch time."

"But there's nowhere to go up there," rearranging his cock inside his trousers, trying to hide the telltale bulge.

"Yes there is," as he checked the urinals and cubicles. "Oh, come on, Pat, no one is going to see you and we've to get these books done."

When we got into the library he began to laugh. "What's the joke then?"

"You've got spunk on your tie," and he fell about.

"You crazy sod, why didn't you tell me?" scrubbing furiously with an already cum-stiff hanky.

Lunch followed one of my favourite subjects, history. Joining the noisy exodus we threaded our way across the tarmac playing area onto the football pitch. The field containing the pitch was three times the size of the playing area which was marked out at the end nearest the school buildings. On the far side of the pitch there was a long overgrown five to six foot high mound running almost the full length of the playing field. Soil and debris left over from the building of the school which had been left on site. It now provided an ideal vantage point for watching games. Beyond, running to the low stone ditch which marked the extent of the school grounds was sufficient space to insert another full playing field.

Munching on our sandwiches we gradually left the screaming hordes behind. Although the stone ditch was barely eighteen inches high, there was at one corner a drop of about three feet into the next field. When we jumped down only our heads would have been visible to anyone coming from the direction of the school. Looking the other way, there were just small fields, no buildings or roads.

"See!' as we faced towards the school. "You keep watch and I'll do you," sitting on a lump of granite with my back to the wall. Fumbling with his trousers. "Then we'll swop," pushing his trousers and briefs down to his ankles. Running my hands slowly up the inside of his extremely hairy legs. As my hands travelled upwards so his semi-recumbent cock reared its head. I stopped just under his balls and transferred my left hand to his arse, making him jump.

"What are you doing?" buttocks clenching under my hand.

"Just keep your eyes open, Pat," stroking the curve of his arse with my palm and lightly pressing the solid root behind his ball sack. It was fascinating to watch from such close range as his balls contracted and relaxed. Everytime his arse clenched his cock jerked, the just visible slit in the head was beaded with a little clear liquid, sticky, when I touched it with a finger. Made him jump again.

"Jesus, Shaun, DO IT. DO IT," taking a hand from the wall

where he was bracing himself at an angle and grabbing his cock in frustration.

"Leave off," knocking his hand away. Gripping him full fisted and reaching between his legs to hold his bells. Milking him. Stroking, squeezing and relaxing my hold all at the same time. I'd never seen a cock from such a close viewpoint before and was totally involved in watching it to such an extent that I almost didn't move quickly enough when he twitched, groaned and came. Shooting over my shoulder onto the wall. He couldn't take the continued stroking. "Stop, Shaun" – pushing my hands away. "Holy Shit" – collapsing bare-arsed on the ground beside me. Sweat trickling down his face.

"Don't have a heart attack" I advised, standing to keep watch in the direction of school. Plenty of noise, but no one in sight. Cock had gotten trapped down the leg of my trousers whilst I was bringing Padraig off and the relief when he had recovered enough to undo my clothes and release it was almost sufficient in itself to bring me off as the cool air swirled round my balls.

"Wait, Pat, wait," holding his hand away. "Just a second," letting the tension abate slightly. "Okay, now, Pat, but SLOWLY." I deliberately did not look down as I normally do (or watch myself in a mirror), just gave myself over to the sensations. He wasn't doing it quite right, his grip was too high on the shaft and his rhythm was very irregular, but I didn't say anything. I felt divorced from what was happening, yet at the same time it was just about the most intimate moment in my life so far. I couldn't hold off for long. Muttering through clenched teeth, "Cumming, cumming," my knees started to tremble and I felt myself shoot into the open air.

"Phew," sinking down beside him and watching as he rubbed his sticky fingers' through the grass. Trousers still round his ankles.

"Shaun?" he looked at me and down to my wilting cock "Why does your thing go back so far?"

"I just forced it one day," leaning against the wall and rolling the loose flesh back. "And out popped his head."

"Mine's too sore," reclining against the wall looking moody.

"Try it now while it's soft," I suggested sagely.

"It always hurts," he protested, shrivelling up even further.

"No, it won't always," and I leant over taking him in my hand. "Anyway, my Dad says you can get it fixed if it won't go back."

A mixture of shock and fright bugged his eyes and turned his face white. "You TOLD your DAD about..."

"'Do you think I'm fucking thick or something," pulling him down as he made to rise. "I asked him last year and he explained the whole thing."

"Yeah, yeah, yeah. You asked your Dad," disbelief in his voice. "Jesus, my ould fella would beat the shit out of me if I mentioned it," subsiding on the stone again. "What did you say? What did he say?" He glared at me. "You're having me on" – insistent. "Nobody asks their Da things like that!"

"You don't want to believe me. That's okay." I shrugged. "Why should I lie to you? We went for a walk on the beach and he told me. About spunk, babies, wanking and all that." I shrugged again. "And about tight skin on your dick." I pulled my foreskin back slowly. "Mine was just as sore as yours, but the skin stretches as you do it more and more," reaching over to him again.

"You'll stop if I tell you?" through tight lips.

"Surely." He really was tight, and, although he had shrunk almost to the point of non-existence the head was still too large to permit it to come all the way through the hole. It did though, come further than before. It looked a bit odd, even silly, as if it had a belt tied round its middle.

"No more. Stop," seizing my wrist. "Oooo, it's never come that far," looking in surprise at the half-visible bluish tip.

"You're probably better doing it for yourself," easing the sheath back over the bulb. Standing up and turning back towards the school. "Come on, we'd better get back before the bell goes."

"Are we coming back here after school?" – climbing into the playing field.

"They don't like you hanging around afterwards, you know that."

"But we agreed!"

"We can find somewhere else."

He ran and kicked a ball rolling towards us, then returned to me.

"Do you have to go straight home?" He shook his head. "Suppose we walk out the bankhead from the harbour?"

"Okay then," bouncing off towards the scrum. "You playing?"

"Nah, see you later," waving a hand and heading towards the school. I needed a pee.

* * *

Concealed by the long bracken which covered the cliffs on the Newcastle side of the harbour, I encouraged him to show me how he wanked himself off. As he lay back on the ground I opened his shirt, stroked his chest and tummy. "Nuts. Hold my nuts." Propping myself on an elbow I took his balls in my hand and kneading them very gently watched, my eyes flicking from his face to his flying fist. His rhythm varied only in that the speed increased as he came to the point. Just before he came he changed hands, bringing himself off with the left and clutching the back of my neck with his right.

"Oooh fuck. I think I'm going to die." A couple of tears leaked down his cheeks. "Shit, shit, shit" – as the last convulsions of his stomach muscles seemed to pulse in time with the gobs of white landing on his chest and belly. I cleaned him up as he regained his breath and composure.

Suddenly he pushed me flat. "Come on let me see you do it," pulling at my trousers as I raised my arse from the ground. "Can I touch you?" as I lay back.

"Same as I did for you. But don't pull too hard," as he grabbed for my balls. I lay for a few seconds savouring the sensation of my balls being fondled and that of cock coming to full rigidity before wrapping just index finger and thumb round the shaft behind the head and pushing down, releasing the head into the air. My hand contacting his at the bottom of the stroke. I teased myself as usual with half a dozen fast tight strokes followed either by two or three slow loose ones or stopping at the bottom of the stroke and holding the skin taut for a few seconds. The slow strokes and the stops were soon discarded, The thumb and forefinger replaced by a full tight fist.

"Keep going for fuck's sake." His hand had become motionless as he watched.

"Sorry," squeezing hard. That one I didn't mind as it seemed to impel the spunk up the shaft with extra speed. I raised my head, opened my eyes in time to see the head pulse and shoot forth a continuous thick stream of white, which landed on my belly button.

"Oooh," dropping my head back.

"Good one." I got the impression that he was of more than half a mind to try for a repeat, as he released my balls with marked reluctance when I sat up.

"Come on, Pat." My hanky was one sticky ball but would have to do. "Don't know about you but I'm starved."

We parted at the bottom or Newry Street where he lived. "See you tomorrow," and I headed along Newcastle Street towards home.

* * *

That set the pattern of our school life (more or less) for the next two years. There were interruptions of course, sickness on the part of one of us, school holidays, weekends. It became an unwritten rule that we confined our sexploits to school or on the way home. A number of incidents (quite apart from the beginning) remain vivid in my memory. Some weeks after we started I noticed one morning that he looked miserable, uncomfortable, yet excited at the same time. As was not unusual we couldn't find the time before lunch. Yet walking up the playing field he kept lagging behind.

"What's the matter?" as I reached the wall and realised that he'd come to a halt some five or six yards back.

"I can't," face reddening.

"What was that?" not quite catching what he'd said.

"I said, I can't," sounding near to tears.

"What's the matter?" I repeated. "Come on, tell me."

Keeping his head down he came over and carefully climbed down into the field; normally we both jumped. "It's split and it hurts something awful."

"Well, show me then." He was remarkably reluctant.

"For Christ's sake, Pat, I won't touch it."

Grimacing he undid his pants and dropped them. Gingerly he pulled the briefs away from his stomach and lowered them to his knees. Hooked a finger under his limp dick and lifted it up. Hunkering down I looked closely at the swollen blood-streaked flesh. "How did you do that?"

Tears were dripping off his nose. "I've been trying to get it back for weeks," rubbing his sleeve across his face. "Like yours. I had a wank in the bath before I went to bed last night," sniffing furiously. "After, it was really soft so I had another shot at it when I got into bed" – raising his head – "and it just peeled right back" – looking at me. "You didn't say what it would feel like. It got so hard so quick. I couldn't get it back over the head" – really miserable now. "It just split. Jesus I thought it was going to burst," tears again. "Now look at it. I'll have to go to the doctor," he shivered. "My Da will kill me. What am I going to do?"

49

"Don't be so fucking stupid, Pat," standing up. "I told you, the same thing happened to me, and my Dad told me it happens to lots of boys. You just have to keep it clean and leave it alone for a couple of weeks."

"Two weeks," his voice cracking. "Two fucking weeks!"

I had to laugh at the alarm on his face. "You'll find other ways, Pat," undoing my trousers. "If you can't use yours you can always borrow mine."

Sometime after that when he wasn't experiencing so much trouble I brought him off during a class in the Science Lab. We were right at the back perched on those high stools behind the work-bench and I could see that he had a hard on. Whilst he was working with the microscope I slid my right hand into his left-hand pants pocket, knowing that he had ripped the bottom out so that he had more freedom to play without attracting too much attention. "Piss off, Shaun," he mutttered.

"Did you say something, Mr Cunningham?"

"No, Miss." I'd a firm hold on his cock by then and he daren't move "Well, pay attention then."

She droned on about cell structure or something as I squeezed, and he had to remain expressionless as I milked him to explosion. I watched him try and keep his cool as his cock surged in my hand and I felt the stickiness on my palm. He was pretty good – red, but pretty good. As we were leaving at the end of the class: "I'll fucking get you for that, McKenna. I swear it."

The same week he did indeed 'get me'. On the bus. With forty other kids present. There were always mock fights on the way home and he trapped me in the corner of the back seat, ducking under my arms and clawing my zip down. No one took the slightest notice. Once he'd succeeded, despite my struggles, in getting my cock out, the only option left to me was to prevent him sitting up and leaving me open to anyone who chanced to look. He obliged me with a very quick (painfully quick) wank, catching most of it on his hand and rubbing it off on the seat cushion between my legs. He even went so far as to partially tuck me away again before I let go the seat back in front and he could sit up.

"Told you," holding his school bag in front of distended trousers as he rose to get off. Leaving me to scramble myself back to decency before anyone looked.

Apart from a few episodes like that luck must have been with us. No one ever appeared to twig what was going on. Two years later when we left school the whole thing just died. Oh we saw each other. Kilkeel is a small town. Somehow completing school seemed to draw a line under the whole thing. I saw him at the pictures occasionally; usually he was in the company of some girl or other. We would raise a hand or say "Hi" and that was that.

Did he have any regrets? At the time I couldn't see any reason why he should. I know the only regret I had was once again being thrown back on my own resources.

5

The next morning at the hospital, as the nurse had promised, was considerably less painful. Just the slightest bit of sticking under the chin. "The Doctor will be here next Wednesday morning." As she tilted my head back. "So I think we can have these out then."

"Will it be sore?"

"A little, I expect." Disposing of the old dressings. "Now let's see the paws."

Harry had been carping on about *Dragonquest* since he'd arrived at the house and had wanted the next one in the series, but I'd put him off till he'd read *Darkover Landfall.*

"Then I guarantee you won't know what to borrow next."

"You're being cruel, McKenna." Grimacing into my face as he secured the seatbelt. "But don't you worry." Pretend anger. "All these slights are being noted down and due punishment will be meted out once you stop hiding behind those bandages."

"Oh God, I'm terrified." I squeaked. "You wouldn't really hit an invalid?"

He gave me a long look. "Mmm. I don't know." Big, big grin. "I've been thinking I might, because you can't hit back. So I could get my licks in without too much worry."

"I'm telling nurse," I threatened.

"Pooh! She doesn't scare me."

"Well she does me, particularly when she picks up those tweezers."

"Scaredy cat."

"Yeah, yeah. It's alright for you." Trying unsuccessfully to trip him up as we left the hospital.

"I warned you McKenna." Hopping to one side.

"I know!" Pretending to have a brain wave as we reached the car.

"Know what?" opening the door.

I waited till I was inside before looking up at him as he went to shut the door. "My Aunt Jean will protect me."

"That's downright sneaky, Shaun." Driving out the park. "And besides, you're supposed to fight your own battles."

"But you see, I'm a coward." Reaching over to rub the back of my bandaged hand against his cheek. "And worse than that." he smiled, but didn't try to move his head away.

"Now what could be worse than being threatened with my own Mum and finding out that my BEST friend is a coward?"

"Best friend, eh!" I couldn't disguise the catch in my voice. "Ah well, since it's like THAT. I won't call on my Aunt Jean to protect me. I suppose I'll just have to report you to the Goblin."

He laughed. "The what?" as we swung into the yard.

"Don't you worry," I threatened. "At least not yet. I'll introduce you when you take me home."

"Golly. You don't want to go already?" Deep disappointment clear as we trooped into the kitchen.

"No, no. Later, Harry. I feel so much better today."

"Good." Relieved laugh. "Sorry, no Auntie Jean today. So you see you are still in trouble." Clipping the back of my head lightly and dancing away.

"Not fair, not fair," I protested "You're just a bully." He was laying up a tray with mugs and plates. "Where is Mum?"

"Up at Nan's. The old dear isn't very well." Slicing wedges of bannock. "You want cream and all that on it?"

"Nah, just the butter." Perching half on and half off the end of the table.

He harrumphed. "I doubt very much that your Aunt Jean would protect you from anything if she saw you sitting on her table."

"Ooops, sorry." Bouncing off to follow him up the stairs (so many stairs, I counted them once, seventy-one).

"Half a dozen times up and down these every day must help you keep fit," as he put the tray on a table and fished in his pocket for the key.

"Never notice them, Shaun." Placing the tray on one of the beds. I promptly threw myself full length across the other.

"Oh come on, you lazy bugger." Poking me in the ribs. "Up, up."

"You are bullying again." Trying not to laugh. "And if you make me laugh my chin will hurt."

"Oooh, you *are* hopeless." Turning to lock the door.

"Harry? Do something for me." Sitting up and taking the mug he offered.

"Yeah, anything. What?"

My eyes were saying, kiss me, KISS ME, touch me, TOUCH ME, hug me, HOLD ME! But, all I managed was: "Teach me how to play chess?"

"Hey! Love to." Getting all excited "I haven't had a game since before Graham got married." pulling the chairs closer to the table. "No one else plays, Mum tried once but she said it was too confusing." Adjusting the pieces "Do you know anything about it?"

I shook my head.

"Right. Well the object of the game is..."

By five o'clock my poor head was reeling, my back was sore from leaning forward and I was well and truly hooked. I hadn't thought I would be.

"Just you wait." Tipping over my king. "Another hundred years and you will really be in trouble."

"It won't take you that long." Taking a standing stretch. Arms raised, back arched and pelvis thrust forward. Yesyesyes. An almost semi-hard outlined in the slacks.

"Shall we go?" Standing, hoping he hadn't noticed that I'd been staring. "I'm taking up all your time."

"And I thought we'd agreed that that wasn't a problem." Trying to look fierce. "Really, McKenna," jabbing me in the belly with a finger, "I sometimes doubt your commitment to this relationship."

"Not fair." Buckling in the middle. "I'm as com-whatsit to whatever it was you said." Dodging behind a chair. "No more," as he advanced. "Anyway, the Goblin awaits."

"Oh, alright coward." Gathering mugs and plates. "Since you're in such a hurry to leave me." Unlocking the door.

I sat down facing the door, face in hands, peeking between them. I think he was half way down the first flight before he realised that I wasn't right behind. Came back into the room to see me in apparent despair.

"Shaun?...Hey, Shaun." Setting the tray down. "Come on." Sitting on the arm of my chair. "You know I was only kidding! Come on, don't be like that." Putting his right arm round my shoulders and hugging me to him. "I didn't mean to upset you. I was only kidding." He was beginning to sound worried when I didn't answer. Instead, I poked him hard in the belly and had the satisfaction of seeing him land on the floor. It took him a little while to regain his breath, by which time I had joined him. I'd reversed the positions, sitting beside him hugging for all I was worth, face buried in his hair.

"You are one sneaky wee bastard," he told me as he lay back full length, perforce taking me with him.

"Ummm." Not releasing my hold and keeping my face hidden in his hair. Hair *so* soft, so sweet and clean. He seemed to be remarkably content. His left arm was trapped between us, but his right was free and he began gently rubbing my side and back. My right arm was under his neck and my left across his chest. I took a long breath of clean hair and raised my head. His eyes were closed and his hand kept on rubbing, massaging.

"Did I hurt you? I'm sorry."

"Nah." And an impish smile spread across his face accompanied by the merest hint of green. "I'm sorry if I upset *you*." One-armed hug. "But you knew I was only kidding. Didn't you?"

I hoisted myself onto my right elbow and gazed into his partly open eyes. "Oh yes. I knew." Left hand on his tummy. "But how else to get you at a disadvantage?" Grabbing a handful of loose flesh through his T-shirt. Now it was his turn to cry "Not fair" and dissolve into giggles as I tickled him.

"Come on Shaun." Gasping, rolling away from me onto his knees. "There'll be time enough for this when your hands are better." Taking my arms and pulling me to my feet. "At the minute" – taking my weight as I pretended to collapse against him – "I'm frightened of hurting you." Standing me upright, steadying me with hands under my armpits. Gazing into my eyes. "Take time, Shaun," grinning. "I'm not going anywhere. I'm here." Gathering me into a warm and comfortable hug. "Come on, I'll take you home."

I was returning the hug with interest and he held tight until he felt me relax a little. "Hey Harry?" I pulled back a bit to look up into his eyes. "You are something special. You know that?" Ducking my head back under his chin. "Tell me that this isn't something..." I hesitated. "It's not going to end. Is it?"

He hugged me tight and I could feel his heart hammering (or was it mine?)

"Shaun, Shaun." Holding me away and looking down. "It's only been four days, but no, it's not going to end." He stopped and his gaze became intense. "You know." He stopped again, swallowed. "I don't know what it is." He shrugged. "But I don't want..." Dropping his eyes and releasing his hold. "I don't know what it is Shaun, but I know I don't want to lose it." Eyes back to mine. "Say that you know what I mean!"

Oh, I knew (or at least I hoped I did). I just said. "Yes. I know," and rubbed the bandages lightly down his face. "Come on then, the Goblin awaits."

"Och, you and your Goblin." Picking up the tray.

"You'll see." Waiting as he locked the door.

* * *

Friday is an odd sort of day at our house and I'd been counting on that. Both Mum and Kath finish work early, come home to change and are normally out again by half five or six: Kathleen for the night and Mum till about eleven-thirty. Kath off to stay at her mate's and Mum out with the crowd from the fish factory. If I wasn't going out that left just Eileen and me to fight over the TV (she always won). Unless Dad was at home, in which case no fighting; I would read in my room and she would play the regular little housewife. Fetching slippers, tea and anything else she could think to do. Prattling all the time about school, homework and what a big bully her brother was. If it had been me, I'd have strangled her years ago, but Dad didn't seem to mind one wee bit.

As I expected, she was ensconced at the table chewing furiously on a pen as she struggled with her homework. In her place, my weekend homework has usually been cribbed from someone on the bus Monday morning. Never Padraig though; he was always in the same position.

"Ah ha" – throwing back the door. "The wicked witch of the West."

"Shut up you or I'll tell Mu... " voice dying and beginning to blush like crazy as she realised that I wasn't alone.

"Your fate is sealed, Harry Hannah! Meet the Scrogg Road Goblin." Then, on seeing that she was doing maths: "Sister, dear wee sister, meet your saviour" – bowing in Harry's direction. "Eileen, meet the maths genius from the Harbour Road."

They both said it at the same time and with almost equal levels of exasperation. "Shaun McKenna!"

"That's *me*." Twirling round. "But really Eileen, mavoureen, if you are stuck Harry will be only too pleased to help." Giving him no option but to offer. Though by the way he grimaced at me I felt sure he'd make me pay dearly for it. "I'll put the kettle on, but I'll need a volunteer to make the coffee."

I sat at the table with them for the next forty minutes as Harry coached her through her homework. Generally after she had begged me half a dozen times I would help, but there was no doubt that Harry was making better sense of the method than I ever did. By the time the back door unexpectedly opened, I could see she was under his spell.

I hadn't really been listening to them, being more intent on running the last few minutes in Harry's room over and over in my head. Oh God, my heart was doing somersaults watching his face as he smiled at Eileen. I had just about reached the conclusion that although he might not know where things were heading, he was more than willing to find out, when in walked Dad!

"Hiya Pops." Me

"Hi kids." Him.

"Daddy." Breathless delight from Eileen.

"Hello, sir." Harry springing up.

"Dad, you remember Harry from the hospital?"

"It's Harry is it? Of course I remember." Hugging Eileen. "I'm not quite senile yet, you know."

That was the end of the homework. Slippers were produced, Harry and I forgotten. He made his excuses shortly thereafter and I went out to the car with him.

"See you in the morning, Shaun." Looking a bit lost and awkward as he fished in his pocket for the keys.

"Hey!" Looking at his face in the gathering gloom. "You can't go like that." I put my arms round him. Thought he might resist, us being in the open. But no hesitation in returning the hug.

"I'm really sorry if I upset you earlier on, Shaun. I didn't mean to."

I squeezed him. "You couldn't upset me if you tried." Releasing him. "See you in the morning, Harry. Be good in the meantime."

"Till the morning," and he was gone. I watched until the rear lights disappeared over the hill before going back inside.

When I turned to go in Dad was at the window pulling the curtains. Had he seen? The rose bushes were high, but not that high. I sighed. It didn't matter who saw what. I really could not have cared less. However he said very little, apart from inquiring about my chin and hands and how often was I seeing 'Young Hannah'. The only comment he offered on that was: "Be careful about bringing that boy to the house too often. You know they're nearly all Republicans round here and it wouldn't do for the pair of you to get into trouble with them. How do his parents feel?"

So I told him about Aunt Jean, the house, hospital trips, learning to play chess and exchanging books, but not about the emotional force which appeared to be driving it all. I'm sure now that he knew anyway but preferred to let it go with the admonition to be careful. There, for the time being, the subject rested.

I left him sitting by the fire with his paper pretending to listen to Eileen giving him the run-down of the last three days at school. Went to my room and, although it was only eight o'clock, undressed and into my dressing gown before lying on top of the bed to read. Whilst undressing I became aware that I really did need a shower. I was beginning to pong, at least to myself if no one else as yet. I had no intention of asking Mum to help. I thought she probably would, but it would be at the expense of never hearing the end of it. The thought by itself was embarrassing enough. Taking my book, snugging the feet into slippers and bracing my waning courage, I joined Dad by the fire.

"Hmmph." Looking over the top of the paper at me. "Not much of a holiday for you."

"Oh, at least I'll be well rested." I closed the book. "Thought you weren't due back till Tuesday?"

"The old genny started to pack up again and we couldn't fix it this time. We really need a new one." He put the paper down and stared at me. "Something bothering you, son?" He knew me too well.

I swallowed and nodded at Eileen sitting on a bean bag at his feet. I could feel my face beginning a long slow burn.

"Eileen, love?"

"Daddy?"

"Make your old Da a cup of tea. There's a girl."

"Surely." Popping up. "Big brother, coffee?"

"Please, squirt."

Full of her own importance she stalked off to the kitchen. Dad leant over and turned the TV volume up.

"Well, son?" Looking towards the kitchen. "She won't be long."

"Dad!" I gulped, suddenly panic stricken. "I need a shower. I'm getting smelly."

"Well? Go and have one then, water's not rationed in this house that I know of."

"But Dad," I almost wailed, waving my hands at him, "I can't." I dropped my eyes "At least, not by myself."

"Jesus God, son. I must be getting old." He looked helpless. "Your Mum would…" He saw my face. "No." He grinned. "I don't really suppose for one minute that you would." He cleared his throat. "Well, I suppose that leaves me?" He reddened.

"I suppose you'd rather not." He hesitated "But Dad, there's no one else!" I was hugely embarrassed, felt small asking. Cursed all bikes and their inventors under my breath.

"Well, I've washed you often enough when you were wee." Picking up his paper. "I suppose the only difference now is that there is rather more of you."

Not the only difference, I thought.

Eileen brought in the mugs and went back for the sugar and milk.

"When your sister goes to bed then."

"Thanks Dad, you are a pal." The relief temporarily blanking the worry of being seventeen and nude before him. To my mind, there was a great deal of difference between thirteen and seventeen. Jesus Christ, why *had* I frozen on the bike? I pretended to read for the next hour and didn't take a word in. At last, after washing up the mugs, Eileen announced at 9.15 that she was off to bed. Smacked my ear quite hard (little cow). Kissed Dad on both cheeks. Went to the bathroom and gathering up her comics on the way back through, wished us both 'goodnight'.

Dad gave her ten minutes to settle into *Bunty* or whatever she was reading, before looking at me with a somewhat grim expression and nodding towards the bathroom.

"Come on then, piggy. Let's get the mud off and see what's hiding underneath."

I was totally embarrassed. Felt sure I'd shrivel to even smaller proportions than four years earlier. Dad turned the water on, aiming the jet against the back wall. I was incredibly reluctant to remove the dressing gown, but needs must. I caught a half smile as I sidled past him into the cubicle, holding my hands high to protect the dressings. As he reached past me to remove the shower head I saw he was still wearing his shirt.

"You'll get all wet," I exclaimed turning round.

He paused, the amused look on his face replaced by one of consternation. "Shit!" His turn to burn a little. "Oh well, since we're all men together..." He dropped the loo seat to remove slippers and socks, stood with his back to me as he took off the shirt and trousers. Red boxers! *Bright* red boxers, and he was forty-three. I couldn't help it. "Pretty wild underwear for an old man," I said as he turned round.

"For your information, *young* man," tapping his forehead, "in here I don't suppose that I'm any older than you are." Reaching behind me for the shower head. "And I might remind you, you're not in the best position right now to be cheeking your *old* man." Playing the jet on my chest, a soap bar in his other hand.

"Back or front first?"

I was only too aware that the hot water was rapidly undoing any embarrassment that cock might initially have felt.

"Front," I squeaked, knowing without looking that 'things' were beginning to stir below waist level.

"Front it is." Soaping my chest and under my arms, then my belly, I tensed.

"Everywhere?" Casually.

I could only close my eyes and nod, red-faced. I must have jumped six inches when he began soaping my balls and cock. Cock came alive with a vengeance at the strange touch and I'm sure my face was afire. My cheeks felt in imminent danger of melting.

"Shaun, son," as I flinched. "You'd have to be a piece of dead meat *not* to react when something like this happens. So don't worry" – my fast-growing cock held with finger and thumb – "foreskin?"

I nodded again, by now almost completely mortified. With a quick motion he rolled my foreskin back and the warm spray hit the naked head, followed by a twist of soapy hand. Then the water again. Only by holding on to the top of the cabinet with my fingertips did I prevent a collapse at the knees. And due solely to the fact that I had been practising holding back whilst wanking, teaching myself to prolong the ecstasy, I managed to avoid cumming all over his face and chest.

"Okay." Laughing a little raggedly. "That's the hard part over."

"That's the hard part." he repeated and laughed heartily.

I had to join in (from relief as much as amusement) as he soaped my thighs and lower legs, the tension slightly relieved, but only slightly. Looking down, I could see as well as feel that cock was right on the edge.

"Lift your foot," and "Now the other." Standing up from his kneeling position, as much water on him as on me. The boxers dark cherry red and protruding vastly. *Was* that a glimpse of naked flesh through the open fly's? If he saw me looking he passed no comment, rinsing the soap from the neck down.

"Those bandages must cramp your style a bit?" giving me a quizzical look. I knew immediately what he meant.

"A bit." I muttered. "Not much."

"Mmm. Thought so." Nudging my shoulder. "Turn round

now." Spray on my back then soapy hand. Now *that* felt *so* good. Kneading my shoulders and down my spine. Hot water trickling its way round my arse, sliding down the back of my legs. Soapy hand between my legs, caressing my hole, knocking the back of my balls. It was just *too too* much. All the practice in the world could no longer prevent the inevitable.

"Oooh, Jesus Dad!" I clenched my teeth. Tried to hold back. Only succeeding in splattering the back wall, as so often before. My only consolation that my back was towards him.

"That's a bit of a hair trigger you've got there, son." His voice trembled. "These things happen, son." Soaping my rear cheeks and the backs of my legs. "You know" – sounding thoughtful – "I think you're as big as your old man."

"Sorry, Dad." I was almost in tears. "Couldn't help it."

"I've told you." Rinsing my back and slapping my arse. "You'd have to be dead not to have reacted. Now, turn round" – playing the water on the slime on the wall and flushing it down the plug hole – "Can you stand it if I rinse you off there," nodding at the now semi-recumbent traitor. "Otherwise it will begin to smell again by tomorrow?"

I watched this time as he gripped the shaft full hand, squeezing out the remaining cum. Pulled back loose skin and rinsed away the residue. I also saw the end of his cock jutting out the leg of the boxers. They seemed to have ridden up his thighs and at least a third of his cock was now visible. Different to mine, looking almost sun-tanned in comparison to my milky whiteness, and threaded with protruding blue veins. Such hairy legs, I'd never had the occasion to notice before.

"Out." I stepped past him and he gave the cubicle another going over before turning the water off and replacing the shower head in its bracket.

"Stand on the mat." Taking a towel from the rack. This was another new sensation, having someone dry your body whilst you just stood there. Cock thought so too and once my back was dry I took the towel in my left hand before he could start on my front.

"Thanks Dad, this bit I can manage." Rubbing my chest, using the towel to hide the fact that 'lift off' was once again well under way.

"Okay son" – stripping off the boxers – "I'm so wet already I might as well have a shower myself." Facing me apparently totally unselfconscious. His cock, whilst not fully erect, seemed to me to be well on the way there.

"What about your hair?" turning to the cubicle.

"I'll get Eileen to do it in the morning." Frantically towelling round my balls whilst his back was towards me. Struggled into the dressing gown before drying my legs. Was he *really* playing with his cock? Surely married men didn't do that. Did they? "Thanks Dad," and I fled, towel in hand. Picking my book up from the chair and into my room. Feeling what? Confused? Certainly. Excited enough for a wank? You bet! For the first time in my life I'd been close to, and touched by a grown man. Returning cock's blank impatient stare I could see that quite a few sexual fantasies had been given birth that night.

Part Two: Alone and Together

6

Saturday morning Mum woke me early, slamming the front door as she left for overtime at the fish factory. I had a half-hearted attempt at a sleepy pull but fell asleep again before I could get into it. Waking about nine-thirty I could hear the murmur of voices from the living room. Dressing was easier this morning, with the use of the fingertips and thumb of the right hand, though it was still too painful to make a fist or splay it flat on the chest of drawers.

"Hi, Dad. Hi, squirt" – making my way through to the bathroom.

"Sleep alright, son?" Coming back to find a mug of coffee on the table.

"Thanks whoever." Having a sip, "Yes, thanks Dad. I think I died." Standing by the fireside. "I feel so much better being clean."

"Well that's good son," from behind his paper.

"Hey Frogface." Turning to where Eileen sat gazing out the back window.

"Dad! Tell him."

"I was only going to ask if you wanted to make some money." I shrugged and turned away.

"How much, and for what?" Voice hardening.

"Oooh, five, maybe ten pence."

"Get lost." Which I thought very rude.

"Now, Shaun." Over the top of the paper.

"Alright." Trying to look and sound martyred. "One pound." At the shake of the paper: "Whose side you on, Dad? Right." Very firmly. "My final offer. One pound fifty."

"What for?"

"Wash my hair. Please."

"No problem. Cash first."

"Eileen!" Her turn for paper rattling.

"You want me to do it now?" I nodded. "Let me clear the sink first then." Bustling off. "Bring a chair." I followed her into the kitchen and waved the bandages in front of her. "Honestly! You are totally hopeless." Pushing me out of the way as she went for a chair. "Dad, can't you trade him in for a proper baby?"

"Ah, but then he wouldn't be able to pay you for jobs like this."

She placed the chair and shoved me into it.

"Mind my chin," as she slung a towel round my neck.

"Baby." Pulling it tight and ruthlessly tucking the ends in.

"I won't be able to pay you if I'm strangled." Pretending to croak.

"You are the limit, Shaun McKenna." Adjusting it infinitesimally. "There, now lean forward and mind, no complaining." Pushing me. "Keep your eyes closed."

Well I couldn't not complain. So the washing was accompanied by pretend howls from me and "Big baby" from her. The chin dressing got hopelessly soaked, which I supposed would make it easier to remove. Harry tapped on the back door as we were arguing about the advisability of trying to put waves in dead straight hair. Dad made him a coffee and solemnly advised Eileen that a couple of rollers should do the trick.

"Don't you dare, squirt" – glaring at him – "or I won't pay you."

"Told you so, Daddy. You should have let him pay me first."

"Sure, and if he doesn't pay you love" – smiling – "you can get your rollers and Harry and I will hold him."

"*Dad!* You wouldn't" – as Harry hooted – "You know I always pay her."

"You'd better." Grimly, catching my ear with a vicious down swipe of the brush.

"That was really sore, you goblin. Harry, am I bleeding?"

"Don't be a silly baby. Anyway, you can always ask the doctor for another bandage." Switching off the drier and removing the towel. "Now pay up." Holding the brush menacingly in front of my face.

"Okay, okay. Let me up." Grumbling on my way to fetch my jacket. "Don't know which is worse, little goblins or big ones." I handed her three fifty-pence pieces. "Dad, couldn't you swap them for two ordinary cats?" I had to beat a hasty retreat out the door under threat of the brush, followed by Harry, still laughing. So I elbowed him in the ribs.

"You're not much help," I told him as we rounded the corner.

"She's your sister," he gasped, holding his side.

Dad was at the front door. "Are you coming back after the

hospital?"

I looked at Harry.

"We might go for a drive or something," he said.

"Did you want me for something, Dad?"

"No, no, just be careful, boys." Raising his hand as he closed the door.

"Does your Dad not like me or something?" Harry said as we got in the car. "Mind your hand" – fastening my seatbelt for me whilst I inhaled the fresh fragrance of his hair and the warmth emanating from his flesh.

"What?" realising an answer was required. "No. Yes. What I mean is, he thinks we might have problems because so many of our neighbours are Republicans."

"I thought everything was supposed to be sweetness and light since the ceasefire?" Pulling away from the gate.

"I don't know, Harry. Sometimes I think parents worry just for the sake of it."

"Ummm." Changing down at my nemesis, Scrogg Road T-junction.

"I suppose I should stop with Mrs Collins sometime and thank her."

"We could call on the way back."

"She's a nice lady."

"Yes I know, she's one of my teachers at the Tech."

"Ah ha! So, that's it, is it?" Crossing my arms.

"What the hell is the matter with you now?" Snatching glances at me. "What is it?"

"Oh, you might as well own up." I shook my head sorrowfully "I can see the whole thing now."

"See what?" he yelped. "If you don't stop being so bloody mysterious, I'm going to stop in the middle of the street and tickle the life out of you."

I held up a hand. "I know. I'm bullied at home by goblins and my Dad, now I'm being bullied by my self-professed best friend." I sighed. "I think I'll just take a bed in the Mourne and stay there."

"Mr McKenna," rolling the R's, "if you don't tell me what you are wittering on about, you won't live long enough to get to the hospital." Grabbing my leg above the knee, making me fall about.

"Alright, ALRIGHT. Let go, let go."

"Now. Talk!"

"See. Told you. You *are* all bullies."

He lifted his hand warningly from the gear lever.

"It was you and Mrs Collins," I said hastily.

"What was?" Total mystification; he almost rammed the back of the bus in front.

"Hey! You keep driving like that and we'll both end up in the Mourne."

"Never you mind my driving." He started off again. "Come on. What about Mrs Collins and me?"

"Don't pretend, Harry." Holding up a hand to command quiet. "The pair of you had it all planned. Her popping up like, like a ghost on one side and you, blaring your horn on the other. The only way to escape was to go straight ahead." Assuming my best martyred look.

He burst out laughing as we swung through the hospital gates. "I hope you're going to tell her that when we call."

"Now, don't be silly," as he held the car door. "Coming with me?"

There was a different nurse on duty that morning and she left off with the chin dressing. Just a dry dressing on the left hand and a slightly more reduced one on the right.

"Don't let your hand curl up like that." Pulling my fingers, causing the healing flesh to stretch painfully. "I know it's not pleasant," slathering cream on, "but if you don't exercise it now you'll have problems when it's healed." As I stood up, "No clinic tomorrow, come back Monday."

"Thanks, nurse."

"Remember now, you must practise stretching that hand."

"Yes nurse, thanks again." Ducking out the door, perspiration beading my upper lip.

* * *

"You alright, Shaun?" noting the sweat and no doubt increased pallor.

"Another bully," I grumbled as we settled in the car.

"But I thought you liked the nurse?"

"Different one today."

"Oh." Suddenly realising: "I can see your chin. Put your head back." And, when I did, "Eeugh! Looks horrible." Switching on. "You'll probably need plastic surgery." Driving off. "*Hey!* Come to think of it, that wouldn't be a bad idea." Grinning like crazy. "It could only be an improvement."

"See! All nasty to poor wee me." Closing my eyes. "But don't you worry. I'll get you all, my turn will come. You'll see."

I could hear the giggles bubbling under his voice. "Come on. I'll make it up to you. Let's go to Rostrevor and get some ice cream."

"Yes, let's." I perked up. "I want loads of that red stuff on mine."

"You can have whatever you want, Shaun." Generous inflection "After all, you're paying."

"In that case, two penny ice lollies please."

"Cheapskate."

"Will your mum not be wondering where we are?"

"Nah. The house is full of brothers, sisters, aunts, uncles, nieces and nephews. Saturdays and Sundays our place is like a zoo." Picking up speed as we left the restricted zone. "I'm glad to be out of it."

"Yeah! I know how you feel. I usually go out Saturdays, if Mum is at home she cleans and moans all day. It's enough to drive you batty."

"What about your dad?"

"Oh, he'll go into the garden or take the Goblin down to the harbour until tea time." My stomach turned a somersault as we popped over the little humpbacked bridge. "Hey, come on. I don't want to fly no more."

"Mmm, but it feels funny doesn't it?" Slackening off the speed. "You been up Kilbroney?"

"Where?"

"Kilbroney park." Looking. "No? Right, we'll get an ice cream and go for a walk. How does that sound?"

"Suits me, and it is a lovely day." And it keeps us together, was my unfinished sentence. Anything was fine by me as long as it meant we were together. So, twenty minutes later we ended up in the car park at the top of the Forest Drive in Kilbroney park. Ice creams eaten, car locked and a multiplicity of paths to choose from snaking away under the pines.

"Which one?" Looking to him for guidance.

"You choose." Shrugging. "Any one will do."

I decided on one that went off to the left, solely because I could hear the sound of voices in the other direction. There were a dozen empty cars scattered round the parking area and I didn't want to have to share him with anyone.

"*Aha!* Feeling fit are we." Walking beside me.

"What do you mean, fit?"

"You'll see."

To begin with the path was fairly flat, just the occasional gentle incline. Then came a rather steeper climb which left me short of breath. The aroma of the pine woods was all pervading and whether it was that or the nearness of Harry, my heart felt light and my spirit free. The path forked and he tugged on my arm to take the left-hand one, level just long enough for us to regain our breath and then almost straight up for fifty yards. Little streams bubbling on either side in stone culverts. Suddenly we were out from under the trees. A huge swathe had been cleared or maybe never planted, as the ground was covered in mature heather.

"Just a wee bit further," he gasped as I stopped to wheeze. A hundred yards on we collapsed side by side on a bench fashioned from a tree trunk.

"What do you think?" when his breathing allowed, waving an arm to indicate the view. "I come here sometimes when I'm feeling down or lonely," inhaling deeply through his nose. "Can you smell it?"

"Mmm. Oh look! You can see the patrol boat. Doesn't it look small from up here." Looking down into Carlingford Lough and over to the mountains on the southern side. "Does the border run down the middle, Harry?"

"Don't know. What's more, I don't care." Turning, he stretched full length on the bench, placing his head on my lap. "Wake me when tea's ready," closing his eyes.

My heart was glowing. I looked down into his face, the first chance I'd really had to drink it in. Round the eyes faintly bluish, little snub of a nose flaring slightly as he breathed. The full lips turned up in a sort of half smile. I'd never kissed anyone as yet, but I knew I wanted to kiss those lips. I contented myself by smoothing the hair back from his forehead and running my fingers slowly through it.

"Mmm, that's nice." He opened those truly amazing eyes briefly. Long enough to reach up and take my right hand from the back rest of the bench and tuck it inside his jacket over his heart. Retaining his grasp of my arm, his other hand outside the jacket but covering mine.

I was in heaven. My breathing ragged, but he chose not to notice. I was on the verge of tears when he turned his head and buried his nose in my tummy. Through the thickness of the T-shirt and the bandages I could feel his heart very faintly. Slow and steady as opposed to mine, tripping and lurching. If anyone had described what it was, and how to do it, I would promptly have swooned for the second time in a week. Cock never twitched, even though the weight of Harry's head rested partly on him. He knew that this was not the time for him. At that point I think both cock and I realised that both our turns were coming and, sooner rather than later. Continued to stroke his soft hair and feel the texture of an ear. I knew he wasn't asleep by the occasional pressure from the hand on my arm.

Time passed. How much? How little? It was of no consequence. Turning his head his eyes opened into mine. I slipped my hand under his head and his left my arm to clasp the back of my neck. Raised him slightly, leaning forward in answer to the pressure from his hand. Our lips met.

Mouths opened automatically, I could feel his teeth. Faint taste of mint and ice cream. Tears were dropping from my eyes onto his cheek. My heart, my whole body was soaring. I was at bursting point with joy. Reluctantly I straightened as I felt his body tense. Only to have him sit up, envelope me in an all-embracing hug and press his lips to my neck below the ear.

"Harry! I love you." Wrapping my arms round him, shaken by the force of the emotion welling within me. "I love you. I love you. I love you. I love you."

He raised his head from my neck, his face wet, and we joined our lips again. For the first time in my life everything was exactly right. The world was right. The weather, the breeze, the scent of the pines, everything seemed to be conspiring to produce sheer perfection, absolute bliss in my arms.

He withdrew fractionally in my embrace "Shaun, Shaun. God! You are my only reason for living." Relaxing now, head back on my shoulder. "You just don't know...nothing else matters now. Only you."

He was right of course. Nothing else mattered, nobody else mattered.

We cried, we kissed, we hugged, cried again and kissed. Hugging always. Damn these bandages. My lips felt slightly, beautifully bruised, when a cloud brought us gently back to earth as it covered the sun. My arse was numbed by the unforgiving bench and his left leg had gone to sleep. I made him howl when I thumped the knee to restart the circulation.

"Baby!" I taunted as he moaned. He retaliated by throwing himself at me and knocking me back into the soft heather. My arms in the air to prevent damage to the hands. His arms round my waist and his head on my chest. "Bully," I said softly, smoothing the shining black hair from his face.

"Who's got who now?" releasing the pressure round my middle.

"I think we have each other, Harry."

We helped each other up, and made our way slowly back to the car. His arm round my shoulders, mine round his waist. I know we passed some people on the path, but we were both on such a high that we took no notice.

"Another ice cream?"

"I think I need a coffee first." Letting him adjust his belt, not neglecting the chance to nuzzle his hair and ear, earning me another long sweet kiss

Coffee in a little café at Rostrevor harbour. Ice-cream cones dripping with raspberry sauce back to the car. Heavenly closeness, knee to knee watching a couple of windsurfers practise falling off their boards.

A questioning look from Harry.

"Yeah. Can we go up to Spelga dam?"

Up in the mountains he drove down the old road to where it disappeared under the waters of the artificial lake. We sat for oh, I don't know how long, and I can't remember now just what we talked about. How I wish I could! Families came into it as did Australia and the USA. What I do remember is that it was there that he first said 'I love you' and when I questioned when he realised, "As soon as I opened my eyes this morning. I suppose I really knew before that, but it was there when I woke. I must have been dreaming about you I think." Smiling and hugging fiercely. "I think about you all the time."

"Oh," I shrugged. "I think about me all the time too."

"Oh you!" laughing, as my tummy started making audible demands. "Hey," looking at his watch. "Do you realise it's after seven?" Bewilderment on his face. "What happened to the day?"

Standing up and holding him, I butted my head under his chin. "We fell in love, that's what's happened." We stood, perfectly content in this embrace, his hand stroking the back of my head.

"I suppose we'd better go." Kissing me. "Everyone will be having kittens."

"I know. My Mum will be thinking you crashed the car or something. Will I see you tomorrow? No hospital."

"I won't be able to get away till after church in the evening." Taking his time descending the narrow twisting mountain roads. "Call for you about eight-thirty?"

"How about you leave the car at home and we meet at the

70

Kilmorey at nine?" I suggested.

"I don't drink much."

"Neither do I really," I protested. "We could just have one or two, then maybe go for a walk." As he was mulling it over: "You're always driving me around, and I just want to see your eyes and talk properly. I worry about distracting you when you're behind the wheel."

"Okay, why not." Laughing. "But only one each."

"One bottle," I amended.

"It'll have to be vodka then." Mock serious.

"Whiskey surely."

"Oh, alright then, one of each," he offered.

Back on the Newry road he pulled into a lay-by outside town.

"I don't want to go home, Shaun."

"Don't want to either, Harry."

"We could run away."

"We could."

"I want to be with you," he whispered, eyes glistening awfully bright in the reflected light from the passing cars.

"I love you, Eyes." Hugging him awkwardly in the car. "But we have to go home sometime."

"Suppose so." Wiping his cheeks with his fingers. "Love you too."

Outside my house we sat in the near dark for about five minutes, listening to the tick of the engine as it cooled. Nothing to say, or rather, everything to say but no heart to say anything.

"This won't do, Harry." He turned his face to me. "I'll see you tomorrow," and I kissed his nose.

"You're right." Gulping. "You're right." Releasing my belt, waiting until I kissed his ear. "Love you," as I got out of the car. "I hope we dream about each other."

"Tell you tomorrow. I love you." I closed the door.

* * *

I waited by the gate as he drove off. Hand out the window, waving over the roof of the car all the way over the hill and out of sight. I'd remained standing for some unknown period of time staring down the road, when Dad's quiet voice brought me back. "Come away in, son." I hadn't heard the front door open, or had it been open all the time?

"Sorry, Dad." following him in. "Miles away."

"You're in luck." Noticing me peering into the kitchen "Kathleen came home with a drink on her and she and your mother had a real go at each other." He sighed. "Now your mother is in bed with one of her heads. Eileen's in bed reading and I don't know where Kath went." He looked keenly at my smudged face and, I'm sure, noted the swollen lips. "Want some dinner?" setting the microwave.

"Mmm, I could eat a horse."

"Right out of horses, I'm afraid. Mince and tatties do?"

"Dad!" as the micro hummed. Depression suddenly lifting, I felt like singing or twirling round and round, up and up and up.

"Well! What?" looking at me quizzically.

"Did I tell you I love you?" completely unembarrassed. So full of love at that moment that I had to share it with someone, who better.

His voice was dry. "I seem to remember certain problems producing that statement some years ago."

I didn't even blush, but gave him a quick hard hug. "Well, once every four years." Showing him that I remembered too. "Won't give you a swelled head then." Feeling him return the hug a little tentatively. "You are my Dad and I love you."

"Well, I love you too son." And damned if he didn't give me another dead arm.

I adopted a hurt look as the micro pinged. "Now I remember why I don't tell you too often," rubbing my arm.

"Ummm." Setting the plate on the table. "Love can be a very painful business, Shaun." Settling with his paper. "Eat your dinner son."

He *had* been in the doorway all along, I just knew it. It didn't put a damper on my spirits though, nothing could have done that night. Looking at the clock I saw it had gone nine, I'd be seeing Harry in less than twenty-four hours. My heartbeats would count the minutes.

"Thought you were hungry?" Making me realise that I was staring into the reflection of my own eyes in the window.

"Sorry, Dad. Miles away again." Waving the fork. "You made this, didn't you?" Knowing full well that when he was at home on a Saturday he always made mince and tatties. "Plenty of garlic. Well up to your usual standards."

"You're going to have to try harder than that to butter up your old man." He sighed. "Look Shaun, it's really none of my business, you're nearly a man. I want for you to be happy." He paused. "For your own sake son" – another pause – "and young Harry's as well, promise me you will be careful. Don't be acting silly in front of other people." He'd said everything without actually saying anything outright. He knew! He didn't seem to mind! Any other night I know I would have crawled under the table beet red. As it was, that night I gazed steadily at him.

"I promise." Perfectly straight and serious. "We'll be careful." I put the plate into the sink and managed to make coffee, giving him a mug. I took mine into the bedroom, back through to the bathroom.

"Going to read for a while."

"Right son, goodnight."

"Thanks, Dad."

"For what?"

"Oh nothing. Well, for dinner, but mostly for being my Dad."

"You're getting awful close to another dead arm." Smiling. "Best go to bed."

"Goodnight, Dad."

As I lay in the dark replaying the day's events cock asked a couple of tentative questions and, finding himself ignored, quite unexpectedly agreed to go back to sleep. Did Harry feel my thoughts? He would know that I was thinking about him. I concentrated hard, we were less than two miles apart. I tried to visualise him in bed. Did he sleep in the raw as I did? In pyjamas, or maybe boxers! Did he sleep on his back, front, side, which side?

As my mind recycled the day a huge soft cloud seemed to billow up under me, I was floating away. Harry was close, I could feel his hair against my face, his breath on my chest. Not a cloud, I realised, but a cushion of soft heather. His arms were round me. "Love you, Shaun." Warm, comforting, wet, pulsing. Half waking I smiled, a wet dream. Sighed contentedly, "Love you, Harry," and sunk down into the heather's embrace, into nothingness, just a warm breath on my cheek, the breath of love.

* * *

The entire Sunday until evening was a zero. I remember waking early, walking to Massforth for eleven o'clock mass, home again for lunch. Not really minding Mum droning on about getting into 'bad' company. Reading two Heinlein books without really taking them in. Tea with everyone there, Kathleen carping on about motorbikes, egging Mum on until Dad blew a fuse, banged the table and told them both to shut up. Eileen, doing her very best not to be noticed. Then it was seven-thirty, an hour and a half to go. It crawled! I was ready, sitting in my room watching the clock stand still. I had promised myself I would not leave before half past eight. By ten past, I was on eggs. Went to the bathroom, couldn't pee. Brushed my teeth and hair yet again. Wondered briefly what a wave or two would look like. Back to the bedroom, it was still only eight-fifteen. Straightened the duvet on the bed, then for want of anything else, lay down. Hugged a pillow to my face, told it I loved it. Shed a few tears for no reason other than that I felt like it. Looked at the clock. It was 8.40! Gave the pillow a beating. Out the front door on a cloud. Crashed back to earth when Dad's dry voice said,

"Do up your flies, Shaun." *Damn!* "Don't be too late, son."

"Okay, Dad." climbed back on my cloud and was wafted down to the Kilmorey.

There! Right there! Sitting on one of the bollards which formed part of the security fencing. He waved his hand, coming to meet me. Stepping into the doorway of Kennedy's building store for an all-embracing if barely satisfying hug.

"Love you," we both murmur.

"Did you dream about me?"

"Yes." I tried to look sad. "I did. It all came to a very sticky end though."

He burst out laughing and I could see the tell-tale shading of his skin. "Mine too." Pressing me against the door. "*You* are going to be a bad influence, McKenna."

"Just you wait, Harry Hannah," poking him in the ribs. "Just you wait."

We went into the lounge bar, neither of us was really into alcohol then or indeed later. We each had a double Bailey's on ice, great flavour. As he had paid I insisted it was only fair that we have a second.

We must have looked odd to the local worthies in their little cliques, a Protestant boy and a Catholic boy on such obviously good terms. Although both sides used the Kilmorey they were, in the main, happy to stay in groups from their own community. Any mingling which did take place sounding forced, false, due to close proximity rather than choice.

Harry's dream had run right to the stop in the lay-by before, as he put it, "I got off to sleep properly."

I looked into his eyes. "Don't you just mean, before you got *off?*" I had the satisfaction of seeing him blush again.

"McKenna! I'm warning you."

"Come on." Draining the watery dregs. "Let's go."

Turning down the avenue towards the sea. Walking apart until we left the street lights behind. Crossing by the tennis courts and the crazy golf arm in arm in the near dark, right to the edge of the softly crumbling cliffs. Jumped down onto the outer sunken lip. Sitting down and getting comfortable. He always preferred to sit sort of sideways to me so that he could lean back, left shoulder against my chest and braced by my upraised right knee. That way, we could see each other's faces without getting a crick in the neck. The merest zephyr of a breeze tousled our hair, whilst a quarter of a mile away, a couple of insomniac gulls were keening over that harbour entrance.

"With all my heart," turning his face up for a kiss, "and with all my soul." Another kiss, redolent of Bailey's. "I swear to you, Shaun McKenna," another accompanied by the salt of tears, "I love you."

"I can't top that, Harry," hugging him, stroking his hair, "I can only say it back." My cheek on his head. "With all my heart and all my soul, with everything I am, I swear it. I am yours and I will love you forever and forever, Harry." I felt a great sense of peace and, in equal measure, rightness and acceptance flow over me as he sighed, working his arm up behind my shoulder to clasp my neck and cuddle ever closer.

Eager as we were to carry the emotions through into action, I think we both realised that neither the time or place was right, nor indeed the mood, and we were content enough to hold together. Nuzzle each other and kiss a lot. Kiss each other's eyes, ears, noses, necks, but always back to the lips. Mouth on mouth. Learning in just over twenty-four hours how much a kiss can impart. The almost electric charge that it held. The head-swimming woolly breathlessness of a really good one, giving ourselves mutual giggles and I'm sure, improving our lung capacity no end. After an aeon or two we changed places and I burrowed into his chest like a pup on a teat. We made no plans then, content in the knowledge that we would be together the next day and the next and all the days that were to follow. After another age, during which I opened his shirt and nibbled on his hairless chest, and he slipped a hand up the inside of my T-shirt to scratch my back, a couple of puffs of cooler air induced us to leave our eyrie. His arm round my shoulders, mine round his waist, we dawdled down past the darkened coastguard station to the harbour proper. Deserted, quiet, even the gulls had

gone wherever it is that gulls go at night. The only sounds, a gentle
chafing of wood against rubber and the occasional clink from ships'
rigging. At least half the fleet was out, leaving the remainder to tug
restlessly at their moorings. Along past the fish factory, ice plant,
repair slips, all deserted. Passing his family brickyard and up the
unlit hill towards his house. Stopping in the darkness of the bottom
end of the now defunct Mourne cinema for a last goodnight kiss and
embrace.

"Shaun, love?"

"Mmm."

"Do you think we'll dream tonight?"

"Mmm. Don't know about you, but I fully intend to."

"Well then, listen." He squeezed me, something hard nudging
my thigh. "Suppose we set a time, say one o'clock," checking his
watch, "and suppose we have a waking dream. Together! At the
same time, I mean?"

"I tried to get through to you last night, Harry."

"Yes. I know that now, but I didn't know at the time."

"I'm going to be thinking about you anyway, so, yes."

"Mind, don't start till one."

"Start what?" Pretend shock. "Harry Hannah! Do you mean
what I hope you mean?"

"You know exactly what I mean, McKenna." sliding a hand
down my back and onto my arse.

"Now who's a bad influence?" Taking hold of his buttocks
and grinding my pelvis against his. Feeling his hardness pressing
against mine. "If we don't stop right now. Harry, I won't be able to
wait five minutes, never mind till one o'clock." Removing his hand
and stepping back.

"Oh *Christ*, Shaun," clutching me in a bear hug. "I want to, I
want to."

"So do I." Attempting to hold him away. "But I want to be
able to see you, you to see me all over. Somewhere comfortable,
somewhere we won't have to worry. *Please*, Harry," as he crushed
me against the wall, pelvis grinding, grinding.

"*Shit, oh shit!*" he was sobbing. "I just came in my pants. Shit!"
Then the sobs turned to giggles. "But I'll be ready again at one. Bet
I last longer than you."

"No bets." My voice quavering. "That's not fair." His hard
length against my leg. "It always takes longer the second time."
Holding him close as he softened and dampness leached through to
my skin. "Jesus, Harry! If I don't go right now I'll be taking my

clothes off in a minute."

"Go on then, prickteaser." His tension abated, he could joke. "Now remember, one o'clock. Not before." A last kiss and I walked him to the backyard gate. "One o'clock, and I'll pick you up after ten."

. "One o'clock," I agreed, turning away as he crossed the yard. Walking through the town I realised that I wasn't going to get home that easy. Cock was wide awake and straining in my pants, very disgruntled at the invitation having been refused. As he continued to threaten, I knew I had no option but to indulge him. I came to the ruin of the burnt-out Royal Hotel and stopped behind one of the pillars of the front facade, all of a foot thick, and there, totally open to anyone coming up the hill, whipped cock out and gave him the thrashing he was begging for. (Being careful! Whoever heard of that?)

Kilkeel on a Sunday bears a close resemblance to a cemetery and no one came, apart that is from me. Tucking cock away (he really didn't want to go), I hastily left the scene of the crime and the glistening evidence on the footpath. The kitchen light was on, but all was quiet when I reached home about twelve-thirty. I made a coffee, switched the light off and went through to bed.

I stripped off and sat on the edge of the bed drinking coffee as the minutes ticked by. Cock was eyeing me resentfully and twitching in time with the clicks. Stood up as 12.59 clicked over, pushed the duvet against the wall and lay down. Turned the light off and tried to remember the feel of his hardness pressing against me, his hot breath on my neck, his pelvis grinding, thought of the promise contained in the day to come! "Forever, Harry," I mouthed.

Tiredness, emotion? I couldn't feel him, see him, sense him. Light on again, looking at cock looking back at me.

"Just you and me then." Light off once more. Starting a slow squeeze, release, squeeze. Knowing that if I could hold to it, it would bring me off eventually. As I squeezed my way towards orgasm I focused on a glint of light on the wardrobe's edge. It was coming from a chink in the curtains, but I willed it, wanted it to be the moonlit gleam in his eyes earlier on the cliff top. Closed my eyes the better to concentrate. Running my fingers up my inner thighs to my balls. I was getting there purely through physical stimulation alone. Where was Harry? I cursed myself, I should have hung on till I got home. Gave cock an extra hard squeeze, balls jumping in protest. Should never have left him like that. Should have helped. Flailing round with left hand till I snagged my jeans, and worked out by touch where the damp patch would have been. Crushing them to my mouth and nose. I could smell him, the sweet slightly acrid tang of drying cum. I sucked the material into my mouth. Tasted him, convinced myself of that, the vaguely slimy texture of saliva-sodden cloth, the warm comfort of sweet body odour. The thought of seeing him in the morning, of holding him, having him scratch my back again. I writhed on the bed trying to simulate the sensation. By now I'd lost this battle with cock, like I'd lost so many before, and was no longer squeezing, rather stroking deep and strong. Tears leaking from the corners of my eyes. Sucking the jeans. Lost in love, and in lust. "Jesus, Harry!" exploding on the up stroke over my fingers, belly and jeans. "Jesus Christ." Using the jeans, out of my mouth now, to catch the remaining drops. Wiping my sticky belly. Drawing huge breaths. Looked at the clock. 1.03. Click. 1.04. Less than four minutes, too quick, he'd rib me rotten in the morning. I slung the jeans onto the floor, and sat up fumbling for the last dregs of almost cold coffee.

"Goodnight love, hope you're enjoying it." Snuggled down with the duvet over me. Asleep in seconds, tired out by emotional exhaustion as opposed to the physical.

7

I woke to the sound of rain hammering the window and wind howling round the eaves. Late, almost ten. Clean underwear and jeans. Through to the bathroom.

"Hi, Dad. Make us a cup of coffee, would you? Harry'll be here in a minute. Ta." Morning pee and shit, scrub the teeth. Heard Harry come in, talking to Dad in the kitchen, clink of spoon on china. Brush the hair and out.

"Morning, Harry."

"Well it was when I got up."

I looked him full in the eyes, Dad back in the living room. Risked a quick grab at his balls, causing him to almost drop his coffee. "Be with you in four minutes," raising an eyebrow.

He choked slightly. "Four minutes? If you can't make it in less than one..." shrugging shamefaced "...I'll go without you."

"Okay, okay," I laughed. "Let me drink my coffee first. I suppose you've had a full breakfast."

"Yup. Eggs, bacon, the lot."

"Come on through." Tugging him by the zipper tag. He pushed

my hand away but grinned.

"Thanks for the coffee, Dad."

"Okay, guys."

Bedroom door closed.

"Less than a minute?"

"'Fraid so, and it's all your fault." Pushing me down on the bed and bouncing away. Hunkering down by the bookcases "What's next in the series?"

"Which one?" Looking for my yellow T-shirt. Ah, there it was. It had even been ironed.

"Both please, Shaun."

"Aha! I knew it." Pulling two books out, then putting them back. "Tell you what," giving him another, "Try this one. It's by Marion Zimmer Bradley as well." I gave him *The Catchtrap*.

"Is it science fiction too?"

"No, no, it's about a circus. You'll love it." Pushing him out. "Come on. No time to read now, I'll be late. Come *on*. Sorry to leave you with the washing up, Dad."

"Don't worry. Just drive careful in the wet, okay?"

"I will, sir. Bye."

We ran round the side of the house to the car. "This book had better be good," he threatened, doing up my seat belt and managing to rest a hand on my cock.

"Promise you." Lifting his hand. "Come on, it's a quarter to."

"You're teasing again..." moving off " ...just you wait."

"Ooh, I'm trembling with anticipation." Holding up a hand. "Can't you see?"

"See bugger all in this rain," he grumbled as we splashed down the High Street.

"God, look at that." Both of us jumped as a huge rumble of thunder came right on top of the flash. "Shit, that must be close," peering anxiously through the windscreen as we swept into the hospital car park, spray sheeting from the wheels. Jackets over our heads we raced the few yards to the clinic and burst through the doors.

"There you are, Mr McKenna." Usual nurse. "I'd just about given up on you. Come along," holding the door of the treatment room.

I got her to wash my hands with proper surgical stuff as she changed the dressings. They really were very grubby. The left hand was almost healed, only a dry dressing needed to protect the scabbing from knocks. The right was still oozing from the centre of the palm, causing her to frown and what was worse, to poke around in it. I couldn't watch, had to grit my teeth. I thought she was going right through to the back.

"Aha!" triumphantly. "I knew it." A quick glance showed her examining the point of a pair of fine tweezers. "A thorn, young man." Slathering the cream on. "Now I know that hurt," melamine square on, "but it will heal much quicker now." Finishing the bandage with tape. "Good as new by the weekend. Now! Open it flat on the bench." Watching. "Make a fist." Frowning. "Well, you're going to have to work on that a little bit" – disposing of the old dressings – "Go on with you now, and try to be on time in the morning."

"Yes, nurse. Thank you, nurse," and I fled before she could think of any other torture to inflict. Harry was sitting by the window getting into *Catchtrap*, he didn't see me till I touched the back of his head.

"Oh, hi." Marking his place. "Long time today."

"Yeah, let's get out of here before she decides to have another go." I hustled him out the door. He was all sympathy in the car, held my right hand in his and my balls in his left.

"Harry Hannah, if you don't let go of me at once, I swear, I'll scream." So, he released my hand. "That's better," I smiled. "Can we go get something to eat? I'm starved." I squeezed the back of the hand massaging me. "Please. Pretty please?"

Mock sigh. "You and that bottomless pit." Crashing the gears. "Come on. I'll take you home and we'll both have breakfast."

"But you've had yours."

"No, I was kidding. I almost overslept. Fell out of bed and came straight over for you."

"Harry, you lied to me." Grinning at him. "Our first lie. Just make sure they're all of that order. Or else!"

"Mmm. Can't I tell a big one and find out what 'or else' is?"

"You wouldn't want to know."

"Aw come on, you're teasing again."

We kept up the banter for the few minutes it took to reach his house. The rain had eased and was only bouncing two inches off the ground as we fell through the back door.

"Where's Aunt Jean?"

"Up at Nans'. We don't think she'll last the week."

"Oh, I'm sorry."

"Don't be. It'll be a godsend for the poor old thing." Taking off his jacket. "Give me yours. I'll hang them in the hot press to dry." He came back rubbing his hands. "Now! What's it to be?"

opening the biggest fridge I've ever seen outside a grocer's shop. "Eggs, bacon, sausage, fried bread, beans or..." swooping on a bowl "fried potatoes?"

"No beans for me, Harry. And I'd rather have fried bread."

"Okay, it was just a thought," replacing the bowl. I sat watching and teasing as he glopped oil into a large frying pan. Popped it on the Aga and proceeded to lay everything out in a neat row on the work top.

"Stop sassing me and get the knives and forks and things," he ordered.

"Yes, sir." Jumping up, "Ah, excuse me sir, where *are* the things?"

"Top drawer left of sink." Rolling his eyes. "Honestly, I have to do everything myself in this house."

"Not quite everything." Grabbing him with his hands full of plates and napkins. Sliding a hand into his pocket and kissing the back of his neck.

"Not fair, McKenna. That's against the rules." Leaning back against me.

"What rules?"

"Oh, tell you later." Moving forward. "Quick, let go, the oil will burn."

"Excuses, excuses," I grumbled, unhanding him.

"No, really," moving the pan to one side. "Peace until we've eaten, okay?"

"I'm just teasing." Digging out knives, forks, salt and pepper. "Any HP sauce?"

"Next one along, Shaun."

"I promise, I'll be a good little boy," laying the table, "until after breakfast."

Even though the sausages and fried bread were a bit overdone I loved it. Clearing my plate and thoroughly enjoying the coffee afterwards. Harry had to wash and dry, but I put everything away as he dried them. Fresh mugs of coffee on a tray we trooped upstairs, sat by the chess table sipping and looking at each other. He seemed almost as nervous as I felt and suggested a video.

"All I want to look at is you."

"I know, Shaun." His gaze fell. "I'm sorry. I'm a bit frightened, I think."

Speaking no less than the truth, I assured him I was feeling more than a little shaky myself. It was rapidly coming home to me that this was not going to be a quick mindless wank in a storeroom, or the corner of a field.

"What do you want to do, Shaun?" bravely. "I'm game for anything." Face reddening. "But I don't really know what... well, I do, but I don't really..." finishing lamely.

"Same here, Harry." Very quiet, coffee forgotten. Then the sudden light of inspiration. "What I really need to do first is have a bath," looking into his eyes. "Can I?"

Relief at the delay. "Of course. I'll run it for you." Jumping up. As he filled the bath and found fresh towels, I took my T-shirt and trainers off, and walked into the bathroom in my jeans with the top button undone.

"The only thing is, Harry..."

"What?" looking up from swirling the water round.

I waved my hands under his nose.

He looked blank.

"You'll have to do the washing."

"Ooh golly. I mean yes. I mean I forgot." Blushing. "How have you managed? I mean, last week and all."

"Dad gave me a shower Friday night."

"You're joking?" He looked shocked. "That must have been a bit heavy."

"It was." Blushing myself. "I shot my load when he washed between my legs."

"Holy shit! You're not kidding are you."

"No, I'm not kidding. I could have died. But my old man's alright." grinning now at the memory "He told me I'd need to be dead not to have reacted."

"Shit." absentmindedly swirling the water, his eyes no longer on my face but fixed on my crotch just at nose level.

"Do you think..." putting a hand on his shoulder "...you could pull these off for me?"

"What? Oh sure." Turning the taps off and drying his hands. With him still on his knees by the bath I braced myself again with a hand on his shoulder. He lowered the zipper gently and eased the jeans to my knees, raised first one foot then the other as he pulled them off. I gazed down at the top of his head, hair brushing the bulge in my briefs as he wriggled the legs over my feet.

"Chuck them through to the bedroom."

I raised him up so that we were face to face. Leaned in for a kiss, placed his hands on the sides of my briefs, pushing down lightly. His tongue traced a path to my belly button as the briefs slid down. He wrapped his arms round my thighs, cupping my buttocks in his hands and pressing the side of his face against my stomach. Cock fitted snugly under his chin, sensing the soft bristles of a very occasional shaver prick his shaft. I wasn't fully hard as yet, just feeling a comfortable warming tension. Caressing his head, trying to control my increasingly ragged breathing.

"Love you forever, Harry."

Pulling back from me. "Lift your foot, Shaun. Come on, the water will get cold." Standing up, looking enormous in his chinos. "Get in." Holding my arm as I stepped in and sat down "Okay? Not too hot?"

"No, no, it's fine," as he reached for the soap. "Don't you think that maybe you're a little overdressed?"

"Yeah, right." Unbuttoning the shirt and tugging it out of the pants. Perching on the loo to remove shoes and socks. I lay back and watched as he undid the flies and dropped his chinos in a puddle round his ankles, stepping out and kicking them through to the bedroom.

"I win, I win," I exulted.

"Win what?" Incomprehension plain.

"Boxer shorts, and striped ones at that," I chortled, explaining that I'd had a bet with myself. "Aren't they coming off as well?" I complained as he picked up the soap again. "They look rather tight and uncomfortable." Trying to catch a glimpse through the flies. Foiled as he knelt by the bath.

"You can do that later." Soaping his hands vigorously, dangerously close to where cock had surfaced for a breath of air. "McKenna! Are you wanting a bath or not?" as I ran my hand down his back, playfully tugging the waistband of his shorts and letting it snap against him.

"Spoilsport," leaning forward to let him soap my back. Sheer bliss, the touch of his hands on my body. Kneading my shoulders, bumping down the spine, right to the base. Up and down each side. *Yes! Oh yes, yes!*

"I can count all your ribs, Shaun," numbering them with tickling fingers. "You really are a skinny little runt."

"Hmmph." Kissing his nose as I lay back. "You're no heavyweight yourself." Cock was rampant, straining unashamedly to see and hear all. Harry flicked him with finger and thumb. "Down, boy," as he soaped my arms and upper chest. To my utter astonishment cock retracted his head and sank below the water.

"How did you do that?"

"Oh, he won't sulk for long." Giggling, hands clasping my

belly. "A little flick stops things for a second. Gives you time to draw breath."

"Umm, what happened to you last night then?"

Blushed. "Didn't do any breathing at all," he admitted. "By the time it was one o'clock, I was so het up, I came almost before I'd done anything. Kneel or stand up now."

I stood.

He chose to wash my feet and legs first. (I doubt I could have shown such forbearance. I'd have grabbed straight away).

"I think someone else needs a flick," from my vantage point above him.

"No. I'm alright." Replacing my foot in the water and soaping my thighs.

"You certainly look alright to me," I admitted, bending a little to squeeze his shoulder.

"Turn round, easy now." Alarm as my foot slipped. Kissed both my cheeks before lathering them, running the edge of a soapy hand up and down my crack. Cock promptly came out of the semi-sulk he'd succumbed to and gave serious consideration to changing the decor from pink to white.

"Easy, Harry, go easy." as his fingers tickled my hole, causing it to snap up tighter than a duck's and cock to rear straight up against my belly.

"Sorry." Not sounding the least bit so. "Turn round now." He held my arm as I did. "See," taking in the view presented. "Can't keep a bad dog down for long." Very gently soaping balls and shaft. "You are so beautiful." Easing the foreskin back and applying a slippery hand.

"Jesus, Harry, go easy," I groaned, this not being the way I wanted things to happen at all.

"No worries," and he gave the shaft behind the balls a sharp pinch. Cock was so shocked by the rude treatment that he deflated at once and almost completely, I let out pent-up breath.

"How *do* you know to do that?" I wondered as I sat down to rinse off.

"Remind me to tell you sometime." Standing up. He seemed to have declined somewhat as well.

"Why not now?"

"Come on. Out!" He ignored me and pulled the plug. "Come on." He held out a big towel, wrapped it round me and pushed me into the cooler air of the bedroom. I got a vigorous rubdown which left me slightly out of breath and then pushed down on one of the beds. "That's mine." My middle covered by the towel.

"You cool off," pulling on his pants and my T-shirt.

"Harry!!"

"Coffee." Reassuringly as he unlocked the door. "Don't start without me." Grin disappearing round the door.

As I lay listening to the rain and cooling down I was hoping that he wouldn't revert to the indecision of before. He must have run down and back up again as no time seemed to have elapsed before the key in the lock announced his return.

"Your coffee, sir," sitting on the side of the bed. Mine disappeared as if sucked by a sponge and his mug went down on the bedside table just seconds after mine.

I slid out of the bottom of the bed and raised him up. Didn't say anything, just raised his arms to remove the T-shirt (decided to frame it) and slowly caressed his chest, prodding gently at his nipples which seemed bigger and harder than before. He sucked a quick breath as I undid his flies and followed his chinos down. His hands were clutching my head, fingers buried in my hair as I eased the boxers off.

My first surprise. He didn't have a foreskin! Second, he looked as brown as Dad did. Third, he looked so much fatter than me, even though he was only semi-hard. His balls were bigger too, but as he lengthened I decided he was a little shorter than my five and a half inches.

He quite suddenly sat, or rather dropped back down on the edge of the bed. As I stood up, having disentangled the shorts from his feet, he wrapped both arms and legs round me, butting me in the chest with his head, and heaving long dry sobs. I was momentarily dismayed until he gasped, groaned, cried: "Love you, Shaun. Love you," falling backwards, pulling me with him. "Promise not to leave me. Promise me. *Promise!*" squeezing the breath out of me. I couldn't answer, only hug back and try to control the rising tide of emotion which both threatened to break my heart and yet, at the same time to float us both up to the ceiling.

"For ever and ever and always, Harry," I managed as I coaxed him to move properly onto the bed rather than across it. He sank his teeth into my shoulder as I reached between us with my left hand and gripped both cocks where they lay together savouring the touch of their joint rigidity. Although my hand was not painful the bandages were a distinct nuisance and I was content for a little just to lay in his arms at last. Holding his cock against mine, feeling our heartbeats and breathing coincide, lose rhythm and coincide again.

I decided there and then that if heaven was not better than this (I couldn't see how it possibly could be), I wasn't going to go.

Rolling apart a little I covered his face with light nibbling kisses, then a real breath-stopper on the lips, felt both cocks twitch in my loose grasp. Moved slowly down his neck to kiss his nipples. Hard, like buttons or small cocks sticking straight out. He groaned and his cock jumped. Sighting along his body I nipped one between my teeth, and was rewarded with a major convulsion and the appearance of a glistening drop in his cock's eye. Releasing my hold I wiped a finger across the slit, smearing it with pre-cum. Licking it I savoured the taste of him for the first time.

"What is it, Shaun?" as I moaned, raising his head, eyes shining, shining fit to burst. In answer I trailed a finger across my own wet dick and smeared it across his lips, then sealed them with mine. Sat up and swung round placing my head by his cock.

"I want to see," as he protested the move. I slipped a hand under his legs groping for his balls. Obligingly he opened his legs, letting them drop into my hand. Cursing the discomfort I took him between finger and thumb of the right, marvelling at the supple silkiness covering bone hardness. My palm was screaming, my face close to him, why *not*? I kissed the purple head.

"Shaun, *Shaun!*" his body jerking wildly as I kissed my way down the shaft to the balls, which seemed to be trying to burrow into his stomach. I ran my tongue slowly back up his length to the head, now tight against his belly.

"Jesus Christ, Shaun!!" as I lapped at my new lollipop. "Oh, *fuck!*" It sounded as though he were crying, and yet not. Spurred on by his twitching and the incredible sensations building within myself (partly due to his fierce two-handed clutching, now at my head, now at my cock and balls) I opened wide and took the head into my mouth. His whole body seemed to buck off the mattress and he let out a wail of pure astonished ecstasy.

"I'm cumming. I'm *cumming.*"

So was I, and he was holding my head and not my cock.

I could feel the jolt as it travelled towards the head through the back of my hand pressed against the shaft behind his ball sac. Feel it coming, in the expansion of the head in my mouth. I lapped at it with my tongue, forcing it against the roof of my mouth. Clamped my lips tight and sucked for all I was worth. He slid further in and with another sobbing wail drained himself into me in about two seconds. Unassisted, I covered his cheek and neck.

He continued to hold my head as the tremors lessened and I

kept him in my mouth, savouring his taste and alert to every twitch as he gradually softened and shrunk. How *can* I describe it? How can anyone really? I was alive to every facet of the whole experience. That unique flavour, the consistency as it slid down my throat, the bitter sweetness, the feel of his flesh in my mouth, on my lips. His balls relaxing back down into my hand. A first, never to be forgotten, rivalled maybe but never forgotten.

"Shaun, Shaun, love," exerting gentle pressure with his hands. Reluctantly I let him slide out of my mouth, opening my eyes to see him glistening and still pulsing with the afterglow, slowly but inevitably diminishing.

"Shaun," urging me to turn round, gazing with tear shiny eyes into my face.

"Sorry, Harry," indicating the bandages. "No hands. Somehow it just seemed the right thing to do."

"Oh my love, don't talk now. Hold me, let me hold you." Crushing me to his side. "I never knew!!!"

"I didn't either."

"But we do now," in chorus.

"What now, Harry?" using a tissue to remove his tears and my cum from his face and neck.

"Can we get into bed properly for a while?" running his fingers through my hair. "I want to hold you."

"And I never want to let you go." Creeping under the duvet with him.

"Ooh, this feels *so-oo* good," snugging his head in the angle of my neck and shoulder. The initial awkwardness of what to do with feet and hands dissolved in seconds as we sprawled on and around each other like puppies in a basket.

"God! How I love you," whispering in his hair.

Gentle pressure from his hand cupping my sleeping cock and balls. "Love you too," he concurred.

I traced the line of his arm from shoulder to fingertips in my groin, whilst he contented himself with a sigh and cuddled even closer, holding my legs between his. This was how we were meant to be, I thought. Repeated it aloud.

"But Shaun, it will get even better, you'll see."

"Mmm, I don't know which is best."

"Which what?"

"Oh, the sex, or like this afterwards."

"Why try to decide when we have both?"

"You're right. It's all part of the same thing anyway."

"God!" A sudden catch in his voice. "What if we'd never met?"

"It was meant to be, Harry. We did meet and to prove it, here we are." Encircling his shoulders. "And I don't want to be anywhere else."

"Me neither."

We lay listening to the rain for what must have been over an hour, not talking much, just revelling in the situation. My heart so large I felt sure I'd burst with the joy of it all. The high, instead of lessening, grew more intense as time passed. I shed a few tears, snuffling in his hair, but he knew I was happy, comforting me with a squeeze and: "Hush now. It's alright. Everything is alright."

The encroaching drowsiness, which was promising to turn into the sleep of the innocent, was interrupted when Harry stretched.

"Fuck it," in a ruefully resigned tone.

"What's the matter?" feeling him tense.

"Got to go pee." Sighing as we disentangled. "This cock of mine is never happy, always wants something."

"Come with you. Can I?"

Pausing a-straddle my stomach, the warm moistness of his arse heating me between belly button and pubes. "Anything you want." Grinning. "Bet I last longer than you."

Crushing into the bathroom side by side over the bowl. "No cheating then. No stopping halfway through." We aimed our streams to mingle just above the water. He beat me, still going strong when I was reduced to milking the last drops. To my nose, the scent of his urine and the sweet body odour emanating from him was like spring flowers (no, that's not quite right), more akin to the heavy musk of some of the older roses in our garden. Loo flushed, we sat in one of the armchairs, me on his knee nibbling on an ear.

"Jesus, Shaun, but your arse is all bones." Wriggling under me.

"Stand up then. Come on." Pulling him out of the chair. "Everything went so fast earlier, I've not had a chance to look at you properly."

He did a mock pirouette, arms above the head. "There, that's all of me. Satisfied?"

"Don't be silly, Harry. I mean it." Tugging him over to the bed. "Lie down and just let me look. Please. Please."

"You're not kinky or anything, are you?" pretending to be worried and falling back with a grin as I swiped at his head. "Front or back view first?"

"Back first, Harry, and as far as you are concerned, I *am* kinky."

"Oh good. That's alright then." Burying his face in the pillow. "Let me know when to turn over."

"Umm." Leaning across to push the hair away from the back of his neck.

He had a mop of really thick blue-black hair, dead straight. Not quite as fine in texture as my reddish blond, but he seemed to have four times as much. He kept it short at the back with a straight line razored across the neck, the top longish and flopping down over the forehead and eyes. No parting like me, but an absolutely beautifully defined crown, almost like a miniature bald spot. The skin under the hair was startlingly white in contrast, not milky white, rather a pure blank whiteness graduating down his neck into not so much a tan, more a healthy warm honey glow. The bones on the points of the shoulders, and the shoulder blades themselves, were not attempting to pierce the skin, unlike mine which were almost visible. But then, he was almost three inches taller and two stone heavier. It made him look smooth, finished round the joints, whilst I looked to be all angles and sharp points. The texture of the skin of his shoulders and upper back was firm silky smooth. There was a little patch of barely visible black hair between his shoulder blades and running down his spine. Like the rest of his body hair, it would come into its own over the next eighteen months, changing him from near hairless youth to even more desirable man. The only blemish (if you could call it that), a large deep brown patch or over-grown freckle below his right shoulder. The fuzz of hair topping the points of his spine faded out midway down and recommenced at waist level, to continue all the way into the crease of his buttocks. Small and firm globes, of a whiteness rivalling that of the head. They snugged close together even in his presently relaxed state. I parted them gently to follow the hair line round.

"Hey!" sleepily. "I thought this was just looking?" One green eye evident.

"It is. It is." Slapping a cheek lightly. "Just be quiet."

"Mmm, I feel like a bull at a show."

"If I were the judge, you'd get first prize."

"Oh, that's alright then. But I've never seen the judge look at the bull's arse before."

Holding his cheeks apart, fascinated by the change in skin colour from white to brown faintly shaded with blue around his hole. The hole itself, tightly puckered, edged with a growth of coarser black hairs. The urge to kiss it, lick it, was almost my undoing, nearly breaking my 'just looking' resolve. But I did promise myself

I'd explore those possibilities soon and released him. The rear upper thighs shaded from white to near brown and had only the lightest fuzz of hair all over. The backs of the knees, fine skinned and threaded with delicate blue veins, swelling out from there, firm strong calves with well-defined hair growth. Hair fine and smooth with lack of years lying flat on his flesh. The ankles (and later the knees) were the only knobbly bits of his anatomy. Slim, blue veined and attached to small exquisite feet (size six to my eight and a half), the arch was beautiful and the toes, miniature delights.

"Okay, turn over." Tickling the sole when he groaned and showed a reluctance to move.

"Yeow! Not fair," scrabbling his feet away and flipping over. "You promised, just looking." Green eyes wide awake and shining. Settling again, hands clasped on stomach. "What *are* you looking for, Shaun?" Curiosity in eyes and voice.

"I've been thinking..." I glanced at his face and took in the still sleepy cock lolling on his thigh... "that this must be the best dream I've ever had, and I want, I need to see all of you so that I remember when I wake up."

"This is one dream you're never going to wake from." Sitting up, folding me in his arms. Kissing me hard, stroking my back. "You hear me!" staring me straight in the eyes. "Never, never, never."

I pulled him to me, kissing the soft flesh behind his ear, hands wandering down his back...and the phone rang!

"Shit and corruption." He leant across my knees to pick up the receiver.

"Skyhutch here."

....

"Oh, hi angel."

....

"Okay, five minutes."

....

"Yes, he's right here."

....

"Okay, Mum," replacing the phone on the cradle.

"Your Aunt Jean commands your presence at the tea table." Pushing me onto the floor. "Get dressed." Slinging jeans and T-shirt from the tangle on the floor. "All kinky tours abandoned due to inclement conditions." Rooting in a drawer, coming out with a black T-shirt. "Don't dawdle." As I had the usual difficulty with shoelaces, "Let me Shaun." Dropping to his knees in front of me. I kissed his hair as he bent over my trainers, and then long and full on the mouth as he straightened up.

"Umm." Breaking off. Running a hand up my thigh. "We'd better go." Tinged with regret as he cupped me in his hand. "Now, where's the bloody key?" Searching his pockets and gazing round. I crossed to the door and turned the key where it sat in the lock.

"Now, that's all your fault." Grumbling as he picked up the tray. "You're making me forget things already."

Locking the door behind us, I tucked the key into his pocket, foiled by the bandages from pushing it all the way down. Even so he grinned.

"Watch it, McKenna, watch it." Starting down the stairs.

8

Entering the kitchen. Continuing rattle of rain and the lights on against the early gloom.

"Hi guys. Just pop them in the sink, Harry." The table was laid for four and there was an unusual spicy smell coming from the Aga. "How are the hands, Shaun?" Opening the oven door, closing it again.

"Much better, Aunt Jean, thanks." Sitting down opposite Harry at her insistence.

"Sit, sit," she smiled. "Good, good. And what have you guys been up to today?" She caught the look we exchanged. Harry blushed, I giggled and he began to laugh. She looked from one of us to the other and I later interpreted the look on her face as one of knowledge and slightly baffled acceptance.

"Oh well, as long as you're enjoying yourselves and... " interrupted by the back door opening to admit a small fat man. I realised in seconds that he wasn't small, more like Harry's height. But he did look small beside Jean as he swept her into his arms.

"How's my wee girl then?" giving her a resounding kiss at the top end and a light thwack at the other.

"John Hannah! Leave me go this instant." Really girlish tones. I was dazed, slightly awed by the level of love in their eyes and behind the bantering tones. "We have a guest." Struggling, but even I could see not too hard, to get out of his grasp.

"Tush, woman." Throwing a wink in our direction. "They're only children. Close your eyes, children, whilst I attend to my girl," he boomed, gave her another smacker on the lips and a smack on her bottom before throwing himself into the chair at the top of the table.

"Harry, son. Get your hair cut before you come back to the hotel." He thumped the table. "Food, woman. Food. Can't you see I'm failing here? Fading away." Ignoring the tart rejoinder of "Good" and turning to me.

"So! You must be Evil Knievel." Keen eyes taking me in. "Must say I thought you'd be more impressive." Looking at Harry. "From all we've heard this last week I'd been expecting a cross between Elvis and Jesus Christ."

"Really, Bear. You're embarrassing the boys." Placing a big bowl of rice centre table. "Take no notice Shaun, he's nearly all bark." Returning to the cooker.

"Just as well you said 'nearly', woman." Grinning, the eyes retreating into little folds of flesh. Harry's grin. Harry's hair, longer if anything than Harry's. "She's right, kid. Don't mind me, I'm very pleased to meet someone Harry thinks so highly off." Placing a hand on my shoulder and giving it a warm squeeze.

"Hi, Pops." (Harry.) "I'll go with you to the barber's when you're getting yours cut."

"*Aha!* Mutiny in the lower ranks is it?"

"Quite right too," from Aunt Jean, placing more bowls of food and a plate of oversized crisps (well, that's what they looked like to me) on the table. "There's nothing wrong with his hair." Ruffling it in passing. The bowl came round to me, and I spooned a mound of rice onto my plate. "Hope you like curry, Shaun."

"Oh, I'm sure I will." Not sure at all, despite the great aroma which had me salivating like mad.

"You've never had a curry?" from Harry, breaking bits from one of the crisps and popping them into his mouth. "Oho, are you ever in for a treat kiddo." Accepting the bowl of rice from Jean.

"It's very mild, Shaun," as she made a hole in the rice on my plate and spooned chunks of meat dripping with sauce into it. "Have some of these," scattering diced onion, chopped eggs, pieces of white stuff (coconut), sultanas and mandarin segments over the top of the whole thing. "And, you must try some of this," dolloping two huge spoonfuls of mango chutney on the side of the plate.

"Have a pappadom." John holding the plate of crisps towards me. "How's Mother today?" to Jean as she sat down and started filling her plate. No one had started eating yet (apart from crunching pappadoms) and I realised from Harry's nod to my questioning look that we wouldn't until Jean was ready. I thought it very odd, in our house you started once you got your grub, never mind anyone else.

"Sinking fast, love."

"Who's with her?" as we all started. Me, using a fork very awkwardly, unable to trap any of the sauce. Harry noticed, and changed from a knife and fork to a spoon. It was with some relief that I followed his example.

"The twins are taking it in turns tonight, and of course the nurse is there."

"Glass of milk, boys?" holding out the jug. "Or would you prefer a cold beer?"

"Milk please, Dad."

"Milk's great, Mr Hannah."

"The name's John." Pouring for me. "Not Mr. Hannah, not even Uncle John. Too many damned nieces and nephews as it is." Pouring for Harry "John! Okay?"

"Yes, sir."

"Told you so," from Jean.

I was petrified, I couldn't go round calling Harry's father by his first name.

He laughed at my evident discomfort. "Oh, alright then. I don't suppose one more nephew will hurt."

I was glad of the milk. Mild as my first curry may have been, about two minutes after starting little beads of perspiration were popping almost audibly from my forehead. There was a glow on my tongue which the milk was barely keeping in check. A surreptitious look at the others revealed no signs of discomfort. I was regarding the mound on my plate with some trepidation when John rose, went to the fridge and came back with half a dozen lagers and glasses.

"Here, lad." Handing me a foaming glass. "This works best, and take it slow. We're not in any hurry." He poured for Harry and himself.

Jean had neither milk or beer, just enjoying her curry, and really, it was very good. At home the whole idea seemed to be, eat as quickly as possible, then go wherever. Here, there was a lot of talk, lots of pauses. Lots of laughter. Here was enjoyment in both the food and the company. My mind's eye was rapidly being opened to the probability that not all families were the same as mine.

Although what with sisters and school I'd never really thought of myself as lonely, I was realising now that I had been lonely for years. Not allowed to bring schoolfriends to the house or play with other kids after school hours, I'd been brainwashed until I left school.

Then, work and daring to go into pubs and the like had, over the last year, slowly been breaking the conditioning. Meeting Harry had been the last blow to an already crumbling dam. Watching him at the table, finding myself equally included in the conversation, my opinions asked for and then not ignored when given, joining in the teasing (secure in the knowledge of our love), I felt as if I was coming alive. Really being alive for the first time. Something of what I was feeling must have gotten through to him as, looking up from my plate at the end of the meal, I found him gazing at me. Eyes full of love, slow smile spreading. Me responding in kind. Locked like that for long seconds. Unaware of the silence from the other two, or the looks they exchanged.

"Aye! Well," wearily from John. "That's it then." Pushing his plate aside. "Come on you two. I've got something for you." Scraping his chair back.

"Go on with your Dad, son," from Jean as Harry protested and started picking up plates. "Go on with you now."

We followed him through to one of the front rooms. "Sit you down," waving us towards a large comfortable looking sofa. He opened the front of a big cabinet, revealing rows of bottles and glasses. Popped ice into two glasses, filled them and handed us one each.

"I'm told you both like Baileys?"

"Thanks, Dad. Yes."

"Thank you, Uncle John."

He poured himself a large brandy, and sat opposite us in an equally large armchair.

"Do you know, I heard that at eight o'clock this morning," he sighed. "There is nothing you can do in this town but everybody knows it." He sipped his drink. "You do realise, don't you, that the two of you are going to be, at the very least, a major topic of conversation for as long as you hang out together?"

I felt Harry shrug. "My Dad said much the same thing," I admitted.

"Aye! He would at that. You have the look of him, except round the eyes."

"From my Gran, his Mum."

"Aye, a good woman that." He gazed into his glass, swirling the liquid.

I suddenly wanted to take Harry's hand. I felt an awful premonition as he looked at both of us in turn, his face both thoughtful and resigned.

"I know, without asking, that if I were to forbid you to see each other it wouldn't work." He held up a hand as Harry drew an indignant breath and my heart plummeted like a stone. "I said, I know!" shaking his head. "But you must realise. Ceasefire or no ceasefire, you are both going to get a lot of abuse at the very least."

"I don't care about that" – Harry.

"Yes, I'm quite sure you don't, but that's hardly the point, is it?" Turning his gaze on me. "How about you, Shaun?"

I could feel Harry's eyes on my face, but looked John straight in the eye. "I'm concerned for Harry." Patting his knee as he tried to interrupt. "But I can't see why we can't be friends. I'm sorry, but I couldn't agree not to see him, even if both you and my Dad said I wasn't to." I took a breath. He remained quiet, watching me. "Sorry, Uncle John." My voice suddenly and unaccountably trembling, but knowing what I had to say. "I love him" I looked down into my glass. Harry slumped, all the wind taken out of his sails.

Silence, for maybe half a minute. I didn't dare look either up or sideways, convinced now that everything was going to end right here and now.

"Harry, son, what do you say?"

He coughed, cleared his throat. "I agree with Shaun." Pausing for breath, clutching my arm "Sorry if I'm a disappointment Daddy, but I love Shaun."

I had to look then, hearing him say it. My eyes were burning, his equally full. In that instant I became convinced that we would win through, no matter who, no matter what.

"Aye! Well, my girl said as much." Heaving himself out of the chair. "Well, drink up, I expect you need it." Going back to the drinks cabinet. "I know I do." He filled our none too steady glasses, poured another Baileys and a brandy for himself. Went to the door. "Jeannie!" He sat down as she came in drying her hands. She saw her glass, took it and sat down in the other armchair.

"You were right, Lass."

"That's what I thought, Bear." Confirming that I had indeed heard her aright when I thought that was what she'd called him earlier. There was a tension round the eyes which the smile she bestowed on both of us could not quite dispel. She sipped her Baileys.

"Maybe it will be alright this time. Times have changed."

"Not that much, Lass. And not for the better either." His gaze was unfocused, mind obviously far away.

I looked to Harry, what were they talking about? But there was no help there, he looked equally mystified.

John sighed, his gaze sharpened and he rejoined us.

"Look boys, Lass and I, we have been through something similar before." He sipped his brandy.

"Not Charlie!?" Harry's eyes fairly goggled.

"No. Not Charlie." Jean was grim. "I think that he thinks it was just put there as a convenient way to get rid of all the beer."

"Mind, once he cottons on to you two, he'll be an even bigger pain than he is now," cautioned John. "I admit, I was glad when Graham got married." I sensed Harry tense. "You should have asked for a lock on that door long ago, or rather, Graham should have."

"You *knew!*" Harry's voice was a squeak.

"We didn't *know* anything." Jean interposed. "But we thought there might be something between you." Turning her head to John. "That's one marriage that won't last, and I blame Charlie for forcing him into it."

"We'll see, Lass. We'll see, give it time. Give it time." Reaching over to pat her knee.

I raised an enquiring eyebrow at Harry, who only shrugged and mouthed "Later." I took a sip of my drink. I was slightly confused; it suddenly appeared too easy. My heart had yet to regain its normal rhythm. I'd been convinced that I was on the point of being thrown out, at the very least.

John leant forward and tapped Harry on the knee,

"Your brother John, shortly after he left school, started going round with a wee girl from Castlewellan. They met at a dance one Saturday, and it seems, like you two, they more or less clicked straight away."

Now I was totally lost. I'd never heard of this one. I knew there was a Charlie, who for some as yet unspecified reason was 'that bastard'. There was Graham, who had married within the last year, and now it appeared shouldn't have done; Robert, who had Downs syndrome and lived in a home; and Alan, who was at university in Belfast, a rabid Orangemen who didn't come home very often. Then there were three sisters: a pair of twins, both married with young families, and the third, single and a senior nurse, also in Belfast. But a John, this was a revelation.

"You two wouldn't remember," Jean interposed. "But things round here were pretty bad at the time. You" – looking fondly at Harry – "would only have been eighteen months." She sighed.

"They'd only been going together eight months." John shook his head. "He's never gotten over it you know, nor for that matter, have Lass and I."

"That was the girl that got shot. Right?" Harry held tight to my wrist.

"Aye! But you wouldn't know the carry-on. What they went through." The tone of her voice matched the sadness in her face. "It was just one thing after another that week. You couldn't be sure when you left the house, that you'd come back in one piece, or that the house would still be standing."

"But why, Aunt Jean? What happened?" I could not begin to see the connection.

"You probably never even heard about it, son. You're even younger than Harry. In fact," as he stood to refill his glass, "you're just about the age Avril was at the time. You see, Avril was a Catholic." He took our glasses.

"We'd all received warnings, hadn't we, Bear?" looking to him for confirmation. "Dreadful phone calls, stones through the windows, dog's dirt in the post, car tyres slashed at night. They burnt her father's hay barn, covered their house in orange paint. Things were so bad towards the end, they were planning to leave Northern Ireland."

"And things were very bad generally at the time, boys." He sat down again. "A policeman who lived at Grahamville had his legs blown off one morning when he opened his garage door. Eleven soldiers were killed just up the road by a bomb. The Royal was firebombed and the UDR station mortared. Not forgetting the postman who was shot or the young lads Clellan and O'Rielly who just disappeared one night... They were great pals too."

"But Dad...That was years ago."

"Harry, son! And you too, young Shaun." Jean was solemn. "Listen to what I'm telling you. Listen to what your father is saying. And you know fine well it's only a couple of months ago that those two young men were pulled out of a crowded bar up the country and shot dead in front of everybody there and all for the sole reason that they were friends despite one being Catholic and the other Protestant."

"You see, boys, ceasefire or no ceasefire, these so-called 'punishment beatings' haven't stopped. Things remain the same as the night they shot young Avril dead as she made a cup of tea, just ten minutes after John dropped her off at home. Him, they ran off the road at Tollymore. Left him tied to a tree with two broken legs and a broken arm. I know now I should have put my foot down and insisted they got out of the country sooner. But they wanted to go in their own time and it was getting very close to Christmas."

"Bear and I have been thinking that maybe if we'd talked to them the way we're talking to you two now, it might, just might have been avoided. But we left things too long and I don't think either of us have forgiven ourselves." Her eyes were very bright with the memories called up.

"You know, boys." John was thoughtful. "How you feel about each other now quite often turns out to be just a stage in your sexual development."

"Dad!" Harry reddened. "I know, Shaun and me, we haven't known each other very long and maybe..." He hesitated, squeezing my wrist. "Look Mum, Dad. I really don't know how to say it, but I can't agree to stop seeing him... Please don't ask me that... I can't, I won't do it...I've never disobeyed you... Please Mum, Dad?" A hint of desperation creeping into his voice.

"Please, Aunt Jean, Uncle John." Adding my plea to his, unsure now how this was going to turn out. I felt poised on a knife edge.

"Does your dad know what is between the pair of you?" John sidestepped a direct answer.

"I think so, in fact, I'm sure of it." I grinned. "He knows me too well."

"What did he say, Shaun?" Harry interjected.

"Just that we shouldn't be silly in public. Really, almost what your dad is saying."

"Why didn't you tell me?" he protested.

"Well I would have, Harry, but I really haven't had a chance."

"Now guys, no squabbling. You know the two of you are going to have to be very careful," John warned, "and not just because you are... ah...." groping for a word, "'friends', but even more so because you are from different sides."

"God forbid that anything should happen either of you," Jean sighed. "I do sometimes wonder why we stay in this God-forsaken country."

"Here, guys." Handing us the bottle of Baileys. "Lass and I, we have some talking to do, and I'm sure you have a lot of thinking and talking to do as well. So, off with you. Go on," ushering us out the door. "Don't be worrying about getting home, Shaun. My Lass will drop you off." Smothering Harry's protest. "You and I have had too much to drink, young man. Now, off with you." Closing the door on us.

* * *

98

We made our way to the top of the house in silence, not breaking it even when we perched side by side on the bed. I knew his mind, like mine, was working overtime but I didn't know what to say to him. Everything had happened so fast, so many things changed in the space of just one day. I couldn't begin to adjust myself. Mostly I couldn't imagine my parents being like that; not quite true, I couldn't imagine my Mum being in the least like Jean. What if she found out? If what Jean said was true, and with sinking heart I realised it was, some kind busybody would be sure to plant a seed in her mind. With a sigh I lay back across the bed, legs dangling, gazing at Harry's back as he continued to sit, silent. I couldn't let this silence go on, already it had lasted too long. Gently I stroked his back.

"Harry? Tell me about Charlie."

"What do you want to know about that bastard for?" Jumping to his feet and round to face me, voice angry, face red.

"Harry?" Sitting up. "Are you mad at me?" His head was down and his breathing harsh. "If I said the wrong thing to your parents, I'm sorry." I took his unresisting hands in mine. "But you know, they knew anyway." Tugging him lightly till he stood between my legs. "I couldn't, I wouldn't lie to them about you and me." Encircling his waist and pressing my face against his abdomen. "Please Harry. Don't be mad at me. I couldn't take it."

His hands left his sides and wrapped round my shoulders. I could feel his chest heaving.

"Not mad at you. Not mad at anyone." Letting go and sitting down with a bump. "It's just everything." Waving a hand distractedly. "Everything."

"Can you call your mum on that phone?"

"Yeah, sure. Why?"

"Why don't you call her and ask her to take me home... "

"*No!* You can't. Not yet."

"About eleven o'clock," I continued. "If that's not too late for her, that is."

"Don't you ever give me a fright like that again, McKenna." Giving me a serious prodding below the ribs and leaving me gasping as he dialled.

"Hello, Skyhutch here."

....

"Yes, well can we book a taxi for eleven, or is that too late for Mum?"

....

"Thanks, Dad."

....

"Okay, Dad. Thanks a lot." He replaced the receiver.

"He's going to bed soon, but Mum will ring through at a quarter to eleven." He looked at his watch. "That gives us nearly four hours." Looking expectantly at me sprawled across the bed.

Bracing myself, I said, "I wonder what we'll find to talk about till then?"

Some few breathless minutes later we were undressed and under the duvet cuddled together, spirits almost fully restored.

"Know what you mean about 'everything'," I whispered into his ear. "It's all happened so quick, it's a bit scary."

"A *bit!*" he responded. "When you said to Dad that you *loved* me, I nearly died." Smacking vaguely at my bottom. "Then, when he didn't throw us both out and I realised that he knew anyway! Well, I was totally flabbergasted." He shook his head on the pillow. "It was Mum! But how did she know?"

"Harry, I hate to tell you." Cuddling ever closer, becoming aware of something prodding my thigh. "But if she can't see in your eyes, what I see, she would have to be blind."

"Oh, pooh! You give just as much away as I do." Hand inching its way down my belly.

"The unstoppable force meets the immovable object," I whispered as his fingers came to a halt on my cock head. "Go ahead," encouragingly. "He won't bite. No, wait a sec." His lonely cock was threatening to bore a hole in my leg. I pulled him over on top of me, my cock warmly trapped between our bellies. Forcing a hand down, I straightened him up so that cocks lay side by side. "Up on your elbows," I gasped. He weighed a ton.

At that angle our cocks were gripped tight, as in a sandwich of flesh. Reaching round him I grasped a buttock in each hand and pulled him up a little. The idea clicked in his mind straight away and he commenced an up and back motion, massaging both cocks at the same time. I traced lines up and down his back and tried to get into his crack, but his little mounds clamped together, Indeed, they squeezed tighter every time I touched them. I gave up on his back and concentrated on trying to tease my way into his crack, increasing his muscle tension and making him groan. As I felt a warning tremor in his legs trapped between mine, I brought both hands to his head and pulled him down for a kiss. Whilst it may not have been a great kiss, given the amount of panting going on, it acted just like a trigger.

His cum provided extra lubrication, and within a few seconds I joined him in making the sandwich very wet indeed. He collapsed on me, head buried in the pillow beside mine. Two hearts racing in concert, legs trembling, sucking in great gulps of air. Now he didn't seem so heavy.

"Look, Ma," I giggled in his ear. "No hands. For the second time today."

"Oooh," he groaned, rolling off me and onto his back. "Don't you dare make me laugh. I think I've ripped a muscle in my stomach." I reached over and rubbed his tummy with my fingertips, massaging the cum into his flesh. "We should clean up."

"No! Mine's staying where it is until tomorrow. In fact," I declared, "I may never wash my belly again."

"Filthy little beast." Slipping an arm under my neck "Shaun, lie on your side... no, the other way," as I rolled towards him.

"But I won't be able to see you," protesting as I turned away.

"It'll be dark soon anyway, and we can still talk." He brought his other arm round my waist, hand on my chest, cuddling up tight to me. Fitting himself like a shoe on a foot, knees behind mine, feet entangled and his softening warmth trapped in the crease of my arse. We lay like spoons and it was undeniably comfortable, his warm breath tickling my neck.

"Love you, Shaun."

"Love you, Harry." Taking his hand in mine, bestowing a kiss on his arm.

We lay in a cuddle for maybe half an hour. The light slowly waning and the wind increasing in force until it seemed to shake the entire house. Protected by each other's presence, truly at home for the first time.

"Do you *really* want to know why Charlie is such a bastard?"

"Only if you want to tell me," I murmured.

He lay quiet, his hand massaging my chest for a long time. I thought maybe he wasn't going to tell me after all.

"Graham and me... " he tried again. "Well, Graham started it... " Another pause. "I suppose I did really... " He gave me a hug. "Anyway. I always shared this room with Graham. Alan shared with Charlie and I think Robert shared with John before he went away. You know, I really don't remember John at all, shows how small I was at the time." He sighed and hugged again. "I know *now* that it was a kind of hero worship, the feelings I had for Graham. In fact, in some ways I still do. When I got to ten or eleven I used to try and stay awake until he came to bed. Particularly if he'd been to the pictures." He laughed softly in my hair. "He used to like all the horror movies, and if I'd managed to stay awake, I'd beg him to tell me the story. He always pretended to be tired, or cross because I wasn't asleep, but he always told me in the end." Again a soft laugh. "Now, when I think on it, I'm sure there were some nights he had scared himself witless, and was only too glad to sit on the bed and try to scare me."

He rolled onto his back, pulling me round and tucking me into his side. I bent my knee to rest a leg on his thigh, arm encircling his tummy.

"I must have been, oh, twelve or thirteen. My cock had been getting hard for ages. Anyway, one night as he was sitting on the bed with me tucked in beside him, just like you are now, I saw his cock sticking straight up out of the front of his pyjamas."

He shrugged. I was enthralled.

"I just reached over and took it in my hand. I really only wanted to see if it felt the same as mine. He stopped the story for a little while, but he didn't get off the bed. He didn't push my hand away or tell me not to. He just started the story again from where he had left off. My hand was sliding down his cock, but it wasn't slipping, the skin was moving with it. He isn't circumcised like me," reaching down to cuddle my sleeping cock in his hand. "In fact, he has a much longer foreskin than you and I had to let go twice and start over again before it stopped going back, I could see then that he looked just like me, only much bigger."

"How much bigger?" I interrupted.

"Oh, come on Shaun. I was only thirteen or so and he was older then than I am now. I suppose, much the same size as I am now."

"Umm. Go on. Then what happened?"

"I was fascinated by all this loose skin, like an extra coat. So, I pulled it back up to see the head disappear and then down again."

I could feel the grin even if I couldn't see it. Hear it in his voice as he continued.

"We both know what happens when you do that a few times. He'd stopped talking by then and suddenly he moaned and this white stuff shot into the air. Well, I made the connection between the rubbing and the white stuff pretty quick and moved my hand even faster, but it was already over. After a couple more strokes he held my hand still and said, 'That's it, Sprout, all over.' He wiped my hand with a tissue and cleaned it off his pyjamas, made me promise not to tell anyone. 'Our secret,' he said. He'd be in trouble otherwise, and there'd be no more stories."

"What did you say?"

"Well you know, I can't really remember, but I do remember him telling me that I'd soon be able to make the white stuff too. So I must have asked him about that." He sighed and stretched hugely, absentmindedly rubbing my chest with his hand.

"Was that it?" I urged. "Just the once?"

"What? Oh, no." Giggling. "He stayed up late the next few nights, to make sure I was asleep. I suppose he was terrified I'd blurt it out, and I'm sure now he had a wank downstairs every night before coming to bed, so as not to betray himself. But then one night, I don't know how long after the first time, he got into his pyjamas in the bathroom and came and sat on the side of the bed. I doubt he'd even started a story before I was into his pyjamas. After that he stayed away again. Felt guilty I suppose, but he always came back. I learnt very quickly not to argue about it with him, because then he wouldn't for even longer. I suppose after a while I used to get him once, maybe twice a week, and for a while after I started to spunk up it was every other night."

"How did that happen? Your first cum, I mean?"

"Oh, I used to rub myself under the bedclothes as I was rubbing Graham and one night I felt this terrific jolt, just like a shock, my hand got all sticky. I showed him what had happened and after that he had me lie on top of the bed with him so that he could see me cum."

"Didn't he ever... you know... do it for you?"

Harry shook his head.

"When I asked him, he said something about him being the older, that it would be wrong. As I said, I'd learned not to argue with him and, although I was disappointed, I wasn't that upset."

"And Charlie caught you both at it," I guessed.

"Yes. The bastard!" Venom in the voice. "You know how the door opens outwards? Well, one night Graham was just wiping my belly, he always did the cleaning up, never let me. We heard him laughing, and when we looked, he was standing in the doorway. He said something like 'What a pair of wee poufs' and went downstairs laughing his head off. I could have killed him. I still could and that was over three years ago."

"So, where is he now?" I asked. "Charlie, I mean. Is he in England too?"

"I wish he were dead." Resigned tone. "No, worse luck. He

skippers one of Dad's boats. They're out at the moment, due back next week sometime."

"But, he didn't tell anyone, did he?"

"No, or at least I don't think so. Gives me a fucking hard time though. Touching me up, calling me 'darling' when no one's around. I hate the fucking bastard." Crushing himself into me, seeking my lips.

"How did Graham take it? Did you carry on afterwards?"

"No. He wouldn't. Said it was all wrong anyway. We had a blazing row one night and I thumped him."

"Wow! What did he do?"

"Went to sleep in the twins' room. He slept there until he got married. Never even asked me to be best man, got Alan to do it."

Silence.

"Harry?"

"Mmm."

"If I'm being too nosy, just say so."

"It's okay, Shaun. What is it?"

"Well I mean, after Graham, didn't you... you know?"

"Find someone else?"

"Did you?... God, I'm sorry Harry, I must sound like the inquisition."

"No, it's alright, really. It's just so good to have someone to really talk to. I've been bottling everything up inside me for so long, there have been times I thought I'd explode."

I kissed the point of his shoulder and hugged him to me.

"Mmm. Really, truly love you, you know."

"I know. Love you too."

He was quiet for a few moments.

"After the row with Graham, I got to thinking, you know, that maybe he was right. Maybe what we had been doing *was* wrong. At that stage I wasn't as certain as you about what I really wanted."

"But, you're sure now?"

"Oooh yes! How can you even ask?" Squeezing me. "I've never felt so right. So sure of anything before. This is where I want to be, and I don't mean here in Kilkeel. I mean *here*, in your arms. You know..." rubbing my side "... like Dad said, everything just sort of clicked into place when we met. All of me seemed to come together in one piece. Before that, I felt as if I were... I don't know, how can I put it... almost as though I was made of several different bits that wouldn't fit, and now, quite suddenly I'm complete, you know?"

"Yes, love."

We slid down in the bed a little and rearranged ourselves to lie facing each other, noses all but touching. I lay inhaling his warm breath, flavoured by curry and Baileys, with relish. Within me there were still the giddy knife-edge feelings of an hour before, but paradoxically I was growing more and more certain that nothing could part us now despite a combination of fears. What would John and Jean do? What would Dad do? I shuddered to think what Mum might do. I couldn't bring myself to believe that anyone would shoot us, that was just too ridiculous to even contemplate. All that, mingling inextricably with my love for Harry, the feel of his body, here in my arms. His quiet confidences in me as he began to speak again had my emotions, my mind, my whole being in a state I find almost impossible to describe. I wanted to laugh, laugh loud, long and free, just for sheer joy. I wanted to cry, again from the joy of it all, but also from the fear that someone or thing should succeed in taking this from me. I wanted him to be physically part of me, as close, closer if possible than Siamese twins. I wanted that particular moment to last for ever and ever, and yet, I wanted us to be five, ten, twenty, fifty years down the road. I was *so* young. *We* were so young. I wanted someone, God, Dad, his Dad or Mum, anyone, to prove us right, to say *yes*. I was, we were in heaven. There was too, an incredulity, almost as if the whole thing was some vast mistake. I – we – surely could not be so lucky. I even felt in a weird way that I should be apologising to someone, something for daring to accept this entire mind-blowing, heart-bursting package which, in such a short time had grown from sexual attraction, to become an all-encompassing reason for life itself. Rampant teenage hormones, combined with being tossed headfirst into an ocean of emotion, made for an irresistible combination, and I gave myself wholly to their power. I felt I was on board the greatest roller-coaster ride in history. Come what may, there was no way I was going to get off. The euphoria just kept fizzing and bubbling like freshly poured Coke, leaving me holding on tightly as I struggled to control the welter of feelings and emotions surging within me.

"I know. I know, love. I feel it too." Returning my embrace till we were touching from nose to toe. Both cocks asleep, this was not sex. This was the urge to meld into one, to bond into an indissoluble unit. We wanted to be like two little globules of mercury meeting, merging into one. Complete.

"You don't really have to say anything at all." Kissing his nose. "What matters is now. What matters is us."

"I know that, Shaun. But I don't think you know just how

good it is to be able to share things at last. And anyway I don't want to have any secrets from you."

His fingers were gently tracing the knobs of my spine, short fingernails lovingly scratching up and down.

"Graham and I had the row just before I left school. Dad didn't want me to leave, nor did Mum. It was her who got me to go to the tech part time. You know Shaun... I always thought there was nothing I wouldn't do for them. But one thing I won't do for them, or anybody else, is give you up."

"I know that now, Eyes."

"Anyway, I went to work for Dad at the Hotel. As I said, I really didn't know what I wanted. I guess I was felling guilty as well, I don't know. I'd been there a couple of months, hadn't really made any friends, got a reputation as being stuck up because I was the boss's son. But really, I was just so mixed up about everything, I was terrified of letting anyone get too close. Graham was still living here, and I suppose, deep down I was hoping that we'd get back the way we were. Then, Mum told me he was engaged to be married! I'm not sure how I felt at the time. I was angry, angry that he'd got engaged, angry that he hadn't told me himself, angry with myself for having been so stupid. At the same time, I felt lost, let down, cast off... sorry, I'm not very good at explaining my feelings."

"You're doing fine, Harry."

"There was a girl who'd started work in the hotel just about that time. A little shrimp of a thing with the most enormous tits. She scared the wits out of me, she was real sharp, had an answer for everyone and everything. She had a way of looking at you, as if she could see right through you, could see painted on your face the things you weren't saying. I think I only asked her out to prove to myself that I could do whatever Graham did, or maybe it was to try and make him jealous. I was never in love with her, you do understand?"

I nodded in the darkness.

"We went to movies, local dances and all that. Arranged to have the same days off. Pretty soon everyone assumed we were an item. Dad was pleased, so was Mum, she was forever slipping me a tenner and telling me to 'get the wee girl something'."

"How did you feel about it all?"

"To tell the truth, Shaun, I was terrified. I was getting in over my head and I didn't know what to do, I couldn't cope. The easiest thing to do was to let it carry on. I didn't know what she expected, I hardly even touched her for the first couple of months, except when we were dancing, she liked all the slow ones. The head on my shoulder, tits squashed up against me, that sort of thing. My heart was in my mouth the whole time, she was so soft, everywhere."

"What was her name?"

"Colette Henning. Everybody called her 'collywobbles' because of the way her tits bounced up and down all the time. I knew after a couple of months that it wasn't going to work, that it wasn't what I wanted. The first night she made me kiss her, I felt really sick. When she put her tongue in my mouth I wanted to run a mile. Don't know why it should be so different when I kiss you. Then I don't ever want it to stop, I can't get enough of you."

Following up that declaration with a demonstration just to prove the point, which left us both panting and grinning in the dark.

"She said I'd learn. Seemed quite pleased by what I think she took for shyness on my part. I couldn't see a way out of it, didn't have the guts to tell her I didn't want to see her again. I felt like running away. I dreaded going into the restaurant, having her come over for a hug as soon as I walked through the door, squashing herself up against me in front of everybody."

"How *did* you end it?"

"Well, I didn't, she did."

"She found somebody else?"

"No, not that. Though I wish it had been." He sighed. "You know, I was even more confused afterwards than I had been after the row with Graham."

"You had a row?"

"No, not really."

He was quiet for a while. I didn't pressure him, he'd either tell me or not. I realised it didn't matter either way.

"I don't know why it should be so difficult to tell. It's not as if it matters now. I found you, and I know now what I am, what I have always been and what I want."

"Mmm, and what's that, pray tell."

"Och, you. You know what I want! You!"

"I know, I just like to hear you say it."

"Let me get this off my chest, Shaun and I'll never stop saying it."

"If you feel you must, and as long as that is a promise."

"I must, and yes, it's a promise."

He pushed me onto my back and fitted himself to my side, head half on the pillow, half on my shoulder.

"I never knew just how much experience she'd had with other boys, certainly it was more than I'd had with girls, that's for sure. Well, after the first kiss, she started to teach me. Just a little bit at a time. She'd put my hand on her tit and encourage me to squeeze it, rub it. At first, outside her clothes, then it was inside her blouse, her hand on my bum, then on my front. I couldn't *do* anything, there wasn't even a twitch, never mind getting hard. Then, one night, she had no bra on, Jesus, she felt so squashy, everything was soft, including me. She insisted on getting my dick out. Said I'd never learn if I didn't play, honestly Shaun, I just wanted to be somewhere, anywhere else. We'd been going out together for something like six months by then and I was beginning to hate her, hate myself. I felt so inadequate, you know? Anyway, she had no intention of giving up, I think by then she was seeing herself as Mrs Hannah. One evening we went for a walk up Donard park, I was trying to pluck up the courage to tell her it was over, that I didn't want to go out with her anymore. We stopped at one of the lookout points and were lying on the grass when she got up and sat astride me. I suddenly realised as she put my hands inside her blouse that she had no knickers on, and she was all hot and wet. I should have got up and left then, it's what I felt like doing. But, at the same time I had a queer feeling, half fright and half expectancy. She had got herself pretty excited, got my dick out and was rubbing herself backwards and forwards on me. She kept saying 'help me, help me'. By which time all but one part of me was petrified. She had french letters in her bag and she tried to get one on me, then get me inside her. I don't know to this day whether she succeeded or not. All I could feel were her nails digging into me. Then, quite suddenly she started to shake all over, her fanny was pressed tight against me and for a second I thought she was peeing on me. She was so wet, and the smell from her! I almost threw up. She moaned and moaned then got off me and lay on her back with her hand up her skirt playing with herself. My cock was all slick from her, and round my balls. The front of my jeans were all wet, and I felt... as though I'd been raped... can you understand that?"

"Yes. I rather think I can, Harry." And indeed, really did understand. When he'd told me about him and Graham, I'd found that quite natural, something I could have done myself, probably would have done in a similar situation. But my feelings on hearing about this Colette were very different. A revulsion bordering on disgust. The same revulsion and disgust as was evident in his voice.

"I got up and got myself back together. I had to take my sweater off and tie it round my waist in case anyone noticed the stains. She was still lying on the grass fingering herself, her eyes closed, blouse open and she was squeezing her tits with her other hand. I said that I never wanted to see her again and left her there. She shouted after me that I should 'come back when I was a man' though she 'doubted I ever would be'. "

"You *are* a man, Harry. Just as I am. This is where we both belong and what went before doesn't matter a damn."

"I know. I know, I just feel relieved to have been able to share it at last. So! Now you know mine, what about your sex history?"

So I told him about my first cum. The whole thing. Bursting foreskin, shorts round the ankles and Dad trying manfully not to laugh. Padraig and the wilder episodes in the science class and on the bus, his split foreskin. Keeping it light until he was choking with laughter and I had to join in. Cock decided at one stage to join in the fun. Harry's however, at a tentative touch, remained deeply unconscious.

"Sorry, Shaun. Don't think I can manage again so soon. That's three times today, almost a record for me."

"Hey! No problem." Not wanting to appear greedy. Then, after a quick mental calculation "You little sod! So *that's* why you were nearly late this morning."

"Yeah, well," sheepishly. "I felt that something was sure to happen today and I just couldn't not do it. I was so uptight wondering if everything would go alright, I had to do something to release the tension."

"Well, I suppose I'll have to forgive you this time Harry. Just remember in future," wiggling his willy, "this is all mine now and everything that goes along with it."

"Sorry, Shaun." Failing miserably at being penitent.

"Your Mum will remember to ring, won't she?"

"Why? Do you want to get away from me that quick?"

"No, of course not. I just thought it would be nice to fall asleep in your arms for a while." I yawned hugely, causing him to do the same. "It's been a very tiring day, what with one thing and another."

"Yes, it has, Shaun McKenna." Wriggling round and getting comfortable. "And the next time you decide to make public pronouncements, consult me beforehand, okay?"

"Okay Harry." Meekly. "Still miffed at me?"

"Oh, don't be a silly sausage." Smacking at my arse and catching his wrist on my hip bone. "Yeow, shut up and go to sleep."

"Yes, boss."

"That's more like it."

Minutes of silence.

"Harry?"

"Mmm, thought you were going to sleep?"

"Forgot to tell you something."

"What?"

"Love you."

"And I love you too. Now, go to sleep."

Another short silence.

"Harry?" I couldn't stifle the giggles.

"I'm sleeping."

"When did you get it cut off?"

Giggles from him. "You're hopeless, and anyway, that's another story for another wet night. Now, will you go to sleep?"

"Okay, boss."

Lengthening, drifting silence. Warm dark, warm flesh on warm flesh. Faint salty flavour from his skin where I touched his shoulder with my tongue. Deep, deep, deep contentment.

9

The phone must have twert, twert, twerted itself to exhaustion before Harry roused himself sufficiently to answer it. It was his departure from the bed and the glare from the bathroom light which woke me

"Time to go," as I stumbled into the loo and edged in beside him at the bowl. "Wish you were staying, Shaun," shaking his last few golden drops. "Come on now." Bedroom light on. "I said we'd be down in a jiffy."

"How long's that?" pulling half heartedly at my jeans.

"Never mind that now." He was already fully dressed, and shoving my feet into the wrong trainers.

"Now who wants rid of who?" I was sleepy and disgruntled, didn't want to go.

"*Never* want you to go. Never want to leave you. Don't want to sleep by myself." His voice shaking with emotion, waking me right up. I grabbed his woebegone frame in my arms.

"Sorry, Harry. Sorry. Sorry. Sorry." Feeling the hug returned. "I'm sleepy as hell, I didn't mean it to sound that way."

"I know." Sighing. "I'm a bit by myself as well. You ready?"

Holding me at arm's length, giving me a critical look. "Your hair is a mess." Running his fingers through it. "It'll have to do."

Jean had coffee ready and her mac on by the time we entered the kitchen.

"Tut, tut." Shaking her head. "Even the cat would have left you two outside." Picking up a bunch of keys. "Drink your coffee. I'll get the car out." Closing the door.

"Harry! Don't come."

"Why not?"

"Now don't get mad. It's just that I want a kiss to take to bed and I'm not brave enough yet to kiss you in front of your Mum." I slid onto the seat beside him. "So, can I have it now, please?"

He took me in his arms. "You don't have to beg for what's all yours."

We kissed, and again.

He stood up and smacked my arse, caught his wrist again. "We'll have to do something about that. Silicon implants I think." Smiling at my mystification. "Tell you tomorrow." Opening the door. "Goodnight, love."

I gazed into those never to be forgotten green, gold and black pools. "Night, angel."

He stood on at the door as I got into the car – a huge Audi.

Looking back at him and raising a hand I realised that where we had been in the kitchen was fully visible from the car and Jean must have seen the kiss anyway. Hand out the window, waving as we pulled out of the yard.

"Thanks a lot, Aunt Jean. I could have walked and saved you all this trouble."

"Hold your wheesht, man. It's no fit night for man nor beast to be out." Swinging the big car down past the Royal and the scene of the previous night's spasm. I blushed, thinking that at least the rain would have washed it away.

"Mrs Hannah?" correcting myself at a look. "Sorry, Aunt Jean, I hope you're not mad at Harry and me. I know, it must all have been a bit... " I hesitated. "Well, a bit of a shock. You know?"

"Well, after that business with John, I must admit, I kept a close eye on all the boys and Harry was the only one I was concerned for. He worshipped Graham. Did you know?" She caught my nod.

"Yes. He told me."

"Has he told you how upset he was when Graham got married? Or just how depressed he was after the break-up with Colette.

I still don't understand that."

"Umm."

"Oh well, I don't expect you to betray any secrets." Flicking on the wipers as the rain came down again. "This past year, he practically never went out at all. Bear and I decided, after he'd passed the test, that a little car might take him out of himself a wee bit." She sighed. "We made sure that all the kids knew the difference between right and wrong but we've never been ones to live their lives for them."

"Do you think we're wrong? Harry and me I mean?"

"As God is my judge, Shaun, I can't see anything wrong in loving each other, no matter what form or combination it takes."

"Thanks, Aunt Jean," as she pulled up at the gate.

"This is the right one? Harry said yellow roses."

"Yes, thanks again, Aunt Jean." Undoing my own seat belt (I could mange it easily, I just liked to have Harry do it).

She put an arm round me and kissed my cheek. "You're both so very young. I worry. I wish the two of you were somewhere other than here."

"We'll be alright, Aunt Jean." Kissing her cheek twice. "One for you and one for Harry if he is still up. Goodnight."

"Goodnight, son," as I closed the door. "I'll say a wee prayer for you both." Raising a hand as I looked back from the gate.

Dad opened the door as she drew away and I hustled in out of the rain. "My, that's some car. Hang your jacket in the hall, son," as I went to sling it over the back of a chair.

"Mmm. My new girlfriend." Twitting him just to see his eyes widen. "No, really it was Harry's mum. She wouldn't let me walk."

"Something the matter with Harry?"

"No, no. He's fine. We had a curry dinner with his mum and dad, and his dad is a bit heavy- handed with the Baileys. So, they wouldn't let him drive."

"Aaah, I see, and what does his father think of the pair of you?"

"Much the same as you do, I think. Concerned that we might get into trouble. Worried that we might make fools of ourselves." I followed him into the kitchen. "Oh goody. Cocoa. No one makes it like you do." Drawing back in pretend fright as he raised a fist towards my arm.

"Watch it, junior."

"Seriously, Dad. Harry and me, we're going to be 'friends'... " hesitating slightly over the word "... for a very long time. I promise,

we'll be good, ah, I mean, careful. Oh shit! *You* know what I mean."
Colouring up at his grin.

"Alright, son." Whipping milk and cocoa together. "But be prepared for squalls when your mother gets wind of it. I may not be here to referee." Shrugging and pouring thick cocoa into mugs. "I expect you're big enough to fight your own battles now, but I want a promise from you. Shaun, look at me, son." I raised my face from the mug. "Promise me, no matter what she says, no matter how loud she shouts, that you'll keep your temper and not shout back. Promise me."

"Alright Dad, I promise. Mind you, it might not be easy."

"I know, son. She's a tartar when she gets going. Nevertheless, you have promised and I expect you to keep to it."

"Okay, Dad, okay."

As he turned for his cocoa, I deadarmed him beautifully and scarpered for my room, calling out goodnight.

"You little bugger." Then, as I closed the door, "Goodnight son, sleep well."

"Night, Dad."

He does make the bestest cocoa. I've been trying for years and never got it quite right yet.

I stood surveying my little kingdom, particularly my lonely bed. Visualised Harry and me cuddled up together. Thinking wryly that it would have to be a tight cuddle. It was only two foot six.

I set the mug down with a sigh. Pulled the curtains and bounced on the side of the bed. What a difference half an hour and two and two-tenth miles made (Harry measured it on his tripometer). I wondered if he was still in the kitchen talking to his mum. He was. I followed him with my mind's eye up the stairs, sipping cocoa as he shrugged out of his clothes. Savoured the view of his firm little cheeks as he struggled out of the pants (must remember to ask what silicone implants are). Could see him having a pee. Scrubbing the white, white teeth, taking a running jump onto the bed and rolling onto his back. Taking a couple of experimental pulls on his cock.

Would he? Wouldn't he ever! I knocked back my cocoa, and stripped in seconds. "Oh, wait for me. Wait for me." I could see him already erect, whilst I was still limp. Come on. Come on. Wait for me, Harry. Please wait. Cock normally responds almost as quickly as switching on a light, but tonight he was showing a distinct lack of enthusiasm. Even so, I could feel the welling in my balls. Closed my eyes in frustration, could still see Harry. See his leg trembling, tongue licking his lips. His cock, swelling, shooting.

His eyes, those great green eyes, snapping shut. Screwing up with the physical sensation as another stream struck his chest/my chest. *Oh God!* I was rock hard, pumping great gobs on my belly. Right where we had mingled our cum earlier.

"Harry, Harry." Panting, milking, cumming again. "Oh sweet Jesus Harry, love you, love you." Feeling the ghost of his warm breath on my neck, eyes bursting open. But I was alone. Alone with my sticky belly and sticky hand. I crawled into bed, switched off the light and cried Harry and myself to sleep.

I woke early next morning, heard some passing noise and a door closing. Felt at peace with myself and the world. Yawned happily, "Morning, Harry," cuddled the pillow and went back to sleep.

Woke again at ten – Harry would be here soon– and saw an envelope pushed under the door. Opened it to find a sheet of paper with unfamiliar writing and, my God, a fifty pound note.

> My Dear Son,
> Hope I didn't wake you. Gone to fit a new genny, then sailing. Back next week sometime. Be good (or whatever).
> Remember your promise. Don't mention the money to the girls.
> Take care son,
> Luv, Daddy.
> PS I owe you one for last night. So, look out.
> PPS Regards to Harry (Baileys?).

I wasn't exactly short of cash, but he knew that Mum had had most of my holiday money and that things were a little tight. "You are an angel," I breathed over the money. "Ta, Dad," tucking it under the pillow. Wrapped a towel round my middle and through to the bathroom. Harry tapped on the back door just as I was passing it.

"Come on in. Nobody home but wee me."

"My God, but there's a sight for sore eyes." Grabbing the towel and ripping it off me.

"Help, help," I whispered as he advanced on me. Hugged him hard, slid a hand between his legs. "Been a naughty boy again this morning? No!" Feeling him twitch and lengthen. Pushed him away. "Unless you want to watch me crap." Smiling at his pout. "I'd go and make some coffee if I were you."

"Ugh. I'm not into that," pulling back, "yet."

As I closed the door, cock reared straight up. "Down boy,

down." Flicking his head. "It was a joke, I think." Shit heavy and overpowering, must have been the curry. Teeth cleaned, belly wiped clear of dried spunk, face rubbed with a wet sponge and I was ready for the world again. I avoided severe sexual molestation only by pleading that if we were late, the nurse would dig more holes in my hand as revenge. When he said "You owe me one," I had to show him Dad's note (well, he was in it too) and the money.

"Whooee, I've got a rich uncle." Grabbing the money and waving it round. I just grinned and got on with dressing, feeling safer once the zip was up.

"Come on, Goldfinger," stinging his arse with a swipe of the towel.

"That's assault and makes two you owe me." Tucking the note into his jeans pocket. "Now, when you want it you'll have to try and take it." Taunting me as we walked round to the car. Automatically he leant over to do up my belt and I took great delight in sticking my tongue in his ear and swirling it round.

"You little sod." Rubbing the top of his head, having banged it on the rear view mirror as he jerked back. "That makes three," and we were off down town, whooping with laughter.

I savoured the relief of a bandage-free left hand, wiggling my fingers delightedly as we left the hospital. "That feels *sooo* good." I was reduced to a pad on the right palm. All the minor cuts were pretty well healed and even the palm had scabbed over and was beginning to itch slightly as the new skin formed.

"Where shall we go today?" Starting the engine. "The twins and their yaps are at the house, Mum is up at Nan's."

"I'm hungry."

"Okay, fatso." Doing up my belt, even though he knew I could do it myself. Well, it gave him a chance for a quick feel. "Let's go to the Wimpy in Newcastle." Letting out the clutch.

"I've got a better idea. Why not go back to Kilbroney? There's a café there and I want to finish what you started on that summer seat."

"What if it rains?" Eyeing the clouds chasing each other.

"Nah! They're too high and anyway, we'd only get wet."

"Okay, then. Kilbroney here we come, I mean *cum*."

"We soon will be," I agreed. Settling back, head turned towards him, drinking in the profile. From that angle his nose was slightly ridiculous, but lovely from any angle as far as I was concerned.

He insisted on paying for the sandwiches, crisps and Cokes,

asking as we started up the path,

"Are we *really* going to? On that bench, I mean. What if somebody comes?"

"Somebody had better cum," I panted. "Besides, we can pretend to be nudists doing yoga or something."

Harry's laugh died as we entered the clear swathe in the pines. There, on *our* bench, a white-haired old lady and an even older man. "Shit!" was the joint remark, giving Harry the giggles and me a fit of coughing as I choked on some phlegm.

"Are you alright?" He thwacked my back over-enthusiastically.

"Jesus." Getting my breath back and dodging another blow. "I'll be black and blue tomorrow. Lay off, will ya," as he connected again. "Are you sure you're not a sadist, or is it masochist?" I shook my head. "I never can get those two right."

"Come on, Shaun. Let's go further up." Encouragingly. "We're sure to find somewhere."

"And if we don't find 'somewhere' soon. I won't be able to wear these jeans back to the car. You'll have to go home for another pair."

"Oh come on, you're not that randy," he scoffed.

"Oh no, Mr Sexpert? You're the one that's already cum in his pants as I recall." Nodding to the two oldsters in passing.

"Having a picnic, boys?" she yodelled.

"Fine day for it," says he.

"Well, see and enjoy yourselves." Mother hen.

"We will," we chorused.

It must have been grey day out in the Mournes. We passed two more elderly couples on their way down, came to another bench to find four old hens cackling away and overtook an old boy with a stick, who looked as though he belonged six feet underground and not fifteen hundred up a mountain side.

"It's alright for you young ones," as we raced past. "But I think this is far enough for yours truly." Leaning on his stick and turning to admire the view.

A couple of hundred yards further on Harry abruptly turned right, into the trees. "This way."

"Where?"

"Look. There's a path here. Come on."

"You call this a path!" I snorted. "If this is a path, it was made by the wee people or, more than likely, rabbits." Grumbling as I followed.

"Oh, do stop moaning and mind these low branches."

"Come on, Harry." I bent double under the closely packed trees. "This isn't going anywhere."

"Isn't it now?" Triumph just in front. "What about this then?"

'This then' was a little saucer-like dell, some twenty-five or thirty feet across, completely surrounded by trees. Bathed in warm sunlight, grassy and untouched, apparently unknown.

"Never saw it before, honest," Harry pleaded when I accused him of having been here some other time. "Just sheer luck" – pulling at his shirt – "Mmm, feel that sun." Kicking jeans aside and stretching out on the grass. "Great bronzy spot." Shading his eyes against the glare, still squinting as he looked at me, sitting down, chest heaving. "I can see you need some exercise to toughen up those excuses you've got for muscles."

"You wait till I get my breath back, I'll show you who's got muscles." Swatting at his head.

"Oh pooh. Promises, promises." Rolling over onto his tummy, propping himself on his elbows. "Thought you were going to be the nudist round here?" Fixing his gaze on my still fully clothed body. "You want to eat first or, afterwards?" Grin broadening as I started to undress.

"I haven't got the breath for anything strenuous yet," I protested, hopping round on one leg to peel off my jeans.

"Oh well, you know what they say about exercise on a full stomach." Reaching for the carrier bag. "Goody. The Cokes are still cold." Fishing around. "Sandwich or a packet of crisps?"

"Crisps please, plain ones." Sinking down beside him. He hadn't removed his boxers so I'd kept my briefs on, figuring that he could do the removals when we got to that stage. By the time we had found the dell my cock had become as limp as the rest of my body and only now was he beginning to perk up again. His interest increased remarkably when Harry turned over and it was glaringly obvious that his was searching for sunlight or something.

"We'd better take the rubbish back with us," I said as I saw Harry casting round for somewhere to dispose of his crisp packet. "We might come here again and we wouldn't want it all messed up."

"Okay, Mum."

"Watch it!"

"Or what?"

"Or this." Throwing myself at him, almost missing as he rolled to the side. Just managing to snag him with an arm round his waist.

Turning back, he succeeded in knocking me flat, landing astraddle my belly, where he bounced up and down a few times, quite winding me.

"Now, where's these muscles?"

"Big bully," gasping. "You're killing me."

He rolled over, giggling with a relaxed delight that was infectious. Holding me against his chest, arms pinioned to my sides and legs trapped between his

"Now what are you going to do?"

"Bully. I hate you." Laughing. Then, seeing an opportunity, I took his right nipple in my mouth and nibbled none too gently.

"Oh," he shivered. "Not fair. No teeth, no teeth," as I rolled the hard little lump round, flicking it with my tongue. He felt enormous, trapped against my thigh as I endeavoured to reach the other nipple and dish out the same treatment. Relaxed his hold slightly to assist, protesting about teeth all the while. Shivering with delight when I found it at last. Quite abruptly groaning in genuine agony and pushing me aside.

"Jesus, I thought it was going to break in two." His cock, on release from what had obviously become a painful entrapment, tented his boxers. I was alright; mine, being quite accustomed to making his own way past the waistband of the briefs, lay on my stomach pulsing in the warmth of the sun.

"Oooh, that's better." Skinning out of the shorts and flinging them aside. "Come on, what's keeping you?" as he saw me lie back, cock half visible.

I smiled, closed my eyes and placed my hands behind my head. "You're in charge, boss." I waited, but not too long. He started with my nipples, making me jump. But mine weren't quite as sensitive as his and, although his tongue was pleasant, the sensation was never on a par with how he said this made him feel. I opened my eyes when he stopped, to find him propped on one elbow, regarding me with an expression filled with love and yearning.

"Oh, Harry." Taking my arms from behind my head, I slipped them round his waist.

"Love you," simultaneously melting into a kiss, with the thrusting of pelvis's and tongues.

"Let's get these off." Tugging at my briefs, nudging me to raise my bottom, slinging them after his. "Lay back, Shaun," pressing me flat. He started with the nipples again, doling out little kisses, then down the breast bone to the edge of the rib cage and over the soft flesh to my belly button. Pausing there to wipe it round with an inquisitive tongue – now that was a sensation I felt worth many repetitions – a little way beyond he came to a halt, jabbed in the cheek. "Now! What have we here?" proceeding to kiss its length from quivering head to twitching base where it sprang from the ball sac. Balls too, they each got a kiss, then he popped one right into his mouth, rolling it around with his tongue. I was groaning, moaning, then he sucked the second one in and started tugging with his mouth, in effect, wanking me off. I gasped and clutched the back of his head. "Jesus, Harry, nearly, nearly!" almost screamed with frustration when he immediately released them, giving each a pleasurably painful squeeze as they popped out. The air felt cool blowing on the moisture and the sudden change from warmth to cool wetness staved off the imminent explosion. Before I could do more than moan, he enveloped cock's head with his lips.

"No! Jesus Harry. Stop!" pulling at his head. "Oh *please* stop a second." Forcing him to sit up, disappointment writ large on his face. "Turn round Harry, please." Tugging at him. "Oh quickly." His face cleared into a grin. I've never seen anyone move so fast. Within seconds he was in my mouth and I was safely back in his.

The multiple sensations! Warm flesh pulsing on my tongue, the musky, bittersweet flavour. Warm, wet clasp on my cock, massaging it squeezing it, sucking on it. Oh my God, may heaven be one tenth as enjoyable. It was too much, I clutched frantically at his side, feeling it gather. Knowing that he was close too by the balls climbing tight to my nose. Even with a mouthful of lovely thrusting cock, I still managed a squawk as I came in his mouth for the first time. Either the force of the flow or a slightly deeper thrust from me caused him to gag, but I had no time to worry about that, by then I was struggling to cope with a gush which was threatening to overcome my ability to swallow. I managed somehow and, as the flow diminished, regretted only that it was all over so quickly. We continued to hold each other as the tension drained away with the cum and cocks slowly softened, lapping up the last traces of bittersweet liquid. He slipped out of my mouth into the cool air, but carried on sucking, trying, I think, to keep me hard by suction alone. Cock resisted the temptation manfully having decided that he needed a rest. I withdrew sufficiently to leave Harry with just an end of soft foreskin in his mouth. He let go with a marked reluctance and lay back breathing heavily.

"Oh, *wow!*" as I turned and lay my head on his chest. "Oh, *wow!*" He put his arms round me. "When you did that to me yesterday," hugging, "you almost scared the shit out of me." Hugging again. "But, oh wow, I never knew it could be so good." Stroking my hair. "Where did you learn that? With whatisname, Paddy or whatever?" He pulled my hair teasingly. "I think I'm jealous. I'll kill him."

"First time yesterday, Harry." Kissing a nipple. "It just seemed right." I crawled up level with his face and its big, big smile. "Honest."

"I know. I'm only teasing." Kiss, kiss.

I knew that of course, but it was fun pretending to be worried.

We lay in the sun, at ease with ourselves and the world until nature called. We indulged in a competition to see who could pee highest and furthest (I won both). Got partially dressed in knickers and T-shirts as I was beginning to feel the sun on my shoulders and Harry's little nose was turning bright red. Lying back, side by side, watching the clouds. Making up stories about them, pretending they were faces or animals (Harry won that; he was much better at stories) until a big one came to a halt right in front of the sun. The temperature dropped noticeably, encouraging us back into jeans and shoes.

"I know." Taking my hand as we rejoined the main path.

"What?"

"Let's go for a swim." He paused. "You can swim?"

"Oh yes. A little. But not today, Harry," waving my right hand.

"Shit! I forgot." Trying his best to look grumpy. "You're no fun at all."

"Actually I'm not a brilliant swimmer," I admitted. "The waves knock me down and scare me a bit."

"Oh, I didn't mean in the sea," he explained. "In the pool at the hotel, and afterwards..." squeezing my hand "...in the jacuzzi."

"In the what?" Then, not giving him time to explain, "That reminds me, what *are* silicon implants?"

He whooped with laughter and the walk back to the car was taken up with the story of breast enlargement and – what sounded even less likely and positively stomach-churningly painful – penis enhancement.

"You have GOT to be joking!"

"No, no. I've got it on video." Grinning. "Mind you, it's a bit gruesome, and it doesn't always work."

"Yeah, I bet." I shivered. "I'm quite happy with what I've got." Poking him. "Come to that, with what you've got too."

"Oh, me too, Shaun, and besides, we haven't stopped growing yet." Teasing, straight-faced. "I expect, like me, you've grown about four inches since you were thirteen, so you've got a few more years before you stop growing." Working sums out with his fingers. "That should equal, oh, another four or five inches." Finishing cheerfully and trying not to laugh at the expression on my face.

"But, that would be, nine, ten inches." I was aghast. "What will I do with that?"

"Oh, I'm sure I'll think of something." Patting me on the back.

"But that means you're still growing as well. I'll never get my mouth round that!"

"Oh, your mouth will grow too, I'm sure we'll manage somehow."

Eventually I got him to admit that it was unlikely we should reach such staggering proportions and would probably end up with another inch to an inch and a half. (I stopped dead on six, though it did get much thicker.)

* * *

Swimming being out of the question for me, we settled on a paddle. Drove down to Newcastle and went walking on the beach. Out past the Donard with its golf course and on round the bay. The tide was out and, tying our shoes round our necks, we walked hand in hand at the water's edge. Enjoyed the sandpapery feel of the sand between our toes and the cool rush of water up the ankles, soaking the bottoms of our jeans. We walked for miles, and hours, before returning to the car. Buying ice creams, we sat on the retaining wall to let the sand dry on our feet. By then I was ravenous again, my belly rumbling in discontent.

"Come on. Let's go to the Wimpy." Brushing the sand from between my toes. "I'm starved."

"Nah! I've got a better idea." Hopping of the wall. "Let's go begging."

"You're joking. How do you mean? We've plenty of money." He'd given me back the fifty, and as usual, when I had money to spare, it was burning a hole in my pocket.

"*Begging.*" Firmly, doing up my belt, having his ear licked. "You'll see." Pressing lightly on my crotch. Starting up, U-turn in the middle of the street and out past Donard park.

"We must go for a walk up there someday," he mused. "Apparently there's a path right to the top."

"How high is that?" Cautiously.

"Oh, about twice as high as today, maybe a bit more."

"I'm going to need a lot more *exercise* before I even think about attempting that." Caressing his knee and getting my hand in the way as he reached for the gear lever. "Sorry, Harry," as the gears crunched and we lurched through a pillared gateway.

"'s okay, love."

"Where are we?" and "Oh!" as we swept up the drive and pulled up at the front of the Arrandale Hotel. "I cant go in there looking like this."

"Oh pooh. You're fine." Undoing my belt, waiting, waiting, till I realised and pecked at his head. "Huh! Is that *it?*" he snorted.

"Ohh, I'm sorry Harry, *really.* But we look so scruffy, and it's so posh."

"*Do* stop fussing." Opening his door. "Come on. Scaredy cat."

We didn't go in the main entrance, but walked along the front to the bar entrance, which made me feel a little better but, not much. Trepidation turning to near panic as we entered the dimly lit room to be greeted by, "Who let those tramps in here? Come and throw them out somebody."

"Now, Dad!"

"Oh. Is it *you*, son? Then, that must be Evil Knievel with you." We saw John sitting at a low table with some other men, all grinning hugely at our discomfort. "You'd best come away in, then. You're blocking the door." Swivelling round to face the bar. "Theresa, give the guys whatever they want. Only one, mind! Then find them a dark corner to hide in."

"Sure thing, boss."

"Where are you guys heading?"

"We're just on our way to the Wimpy..." Harry, all innocence "...and thought we'd drop by."

"Are you now?" Very bland. "Well, go and sit down for ten minutes and *try* not to lower the tone of the place too much." Tturning back to his conversation. All the men now grinning openly at us, he shook his head. "Kids!! What can you do?"

"Baileys, Theresa, please." Glancing round to make sure John wasn't looking. "And, make them tiny triples as we're only getting the one."

"Harry Hannah, you'll get me sacked." Smiling fondly at him and upending the bottle over half-pint glasses with a couple of ice cubes in each. "Now, introduce me to your friend." With the formalities achieved, she nodded towards the far corner. "Go way over there and, for God's sake, don't let him see how much is in those glasses."

Sitting down by the window, I asked, "What time does the Wimpy shut?

"We won't be going to any Wimpy, Shaun. Just be patient a wee while, you'll see." Pressing my foot with his under the table.

"My belly button is pressing against my back bone," I complained.

"Well, it does that all the time." Which was most unfeeling of him, I thought. "Drink your drink and stop complaining."

"It's pretty quiet tonight," in answer to my query. "Friday and Saturday can be frantic." He nodded towards the window. "Dad wants to extend the car park but the council are being awkward because he needs to take out some of the trees."

"What kind are those?" pointing towards the two big ones arching over the drive.

"Lebanese cedars, I think."

"They're so beautiful, it would be a shame to kill them."

"Oh, not those. It's the trees to the side, over there." Pointing. "You can't see them properly from here," as I twisted round to follow his finger.

"So! You're old man's grub not good enough for you. Eh!" John, pulling up a chair.

"Your prices are a bit steep," quipped Harry. "Us just being poor working lads and all."

"And if that's a hint about a pay rise," darkly, "forget it."

"Oh well. No harm in asking." Harry sighed theatrically. "Come on Shaun, drink up, let's go."

"Sure, and it's full of flannel you are Harry Hannah," as he turned towards the bar. "Must be your mother you get it from."

Harry winked at me.

"Theresa, get Tony to lay up for three in the sitting room. Steak, eggs, chips, mushrooms and peas all round." Turning back. "You like yours medium, Shaun?" seeing me look helplessly at Harry. "You will." Back to Theresa, who was on the phone. "One well done, two medium. Tell him, some of that fillet." Holding up his hand, finger and thumb two inches apart.

She waved in acknowledgement, as she repeated his instructions.

"Well, and where did you get to today, kids?" resting his elbows on the table and pretending to see our glasses for the first time. Swung back to the bar. "Theresa Sloane! Remind me in the morning, I just fired you."

"Yes, boss." Cheeks creasing in a grin.

Whilst awaiting our meal we filled him in on most of the day's events, including the old people on the mountain.

"Huh! Just you wait, my lads. You'll find out, just because you've got years, it doesn't make you feel any different. It's just that the old body can no longer do as much as you want it to. Let me see your hand, Shaun." Examining it under the table lamp. "Still looks pretty raw, and the other one?"

"Dressing should be off by Friday."

"And the stitches?"

"Tomorrow morning." I shivered.

"Tush, lad. You won't feel it..." pause "..much." Laughing at my grimace, Harry joining in. "When's your holiday end?"

"This week."

"I doubt you might have a week or two yet." Nodding at my hands. "Can't see you handling much with those. Especially sharp bits of metal, screws and that. It *is* the stores you work in?"

"How did you know that, Dad? I don't remember telling you."

"Ahh," laying a finger alongside his nose. "My spies are legion." Noticing some signal we had missed. "Come on, guys. Grub's nearly ready." Pushing back his chair. "And I've no doubt that by this time tomorrow, I'll have had a full report on the day's activities in Kilbroney." He laughed richly at the look we exchanged. "Well, maybe not the gory details, but I'll hear about it, don't you worry none on that score." Leading the way through Reception, nodding to people right and left. "Ach, you needn't look so worried." Opening a door and revealing a sitting room with dining table all laid up. "Those oldsters, they're from Richmond House. The retirement home on the front, they come in for their glass of sherry or port nearly every day." He tried to pitch his voice high. "Oh Mr. Hannah, we saw that lovely son of yours in the park yesterday with his friend." Pausing. "Now, we don't know him, some relative no doubt?" The effort of the high pitch too much, he reverted to his normal bass tone. "I don't know who's worse, the ould wimmin or the ould men. Ah, here we go," as the door opened and a tall willowy man entered with a tray piled high.

I'd had steak before, but not often. I'd quite liked it, but thought it a bit chewy and nothing to rave about. But compared to the flat brown objects I'd previously encountered, just the aroma when Tony removed the covers from the plates made my mouth water. The steaks! They were about two inches thick, criss-crossed with what looked like burn marks and literally oozing juice. The eggs were spot on, the yolk soft and the white solid. The brown squidgy things I realised must be mushrooms. Peas are peas. The chips, in a separate dish, were golden, dry, crisp and piping hot.

"Let Tony give you some chips," John urged.

"Sorry," I muttered, sitting back, looking up at the waiter hovering above me. Startled by the fluttering of what appeared to be purple eyelids. His eyes dropping from my face to my crotch, mouth making a little moue of disappointment because my hands were crossed in my lap.

"Thanks," I managed as he piled chips on the plate.

"Careful, you might trip over your tongue, Tony." dryly from John. "And there's a great big sign somewhere, says don't even think about walking on the grass."

"Well! Whatever you say, boss, I'm sure," wafting round to put a mound of chips on Harry's plate. I'd never heard anyone talk like that before, the high-pitched lilt, the batting of the eyes, the sinuous way of walking. "The cat can look at the queen, can't she?" loading John's plate.

"True. No harm in looking. Now, back to work before I smack your legs."

"Oooo. Promises, promises." Picking up the tray and waltzing out the door.

"Take no notice, Shaun. Do you need Harry to cut your steak?"

"I think I can manage, Uncle John, thanks." Picking up the knife and fork, expecting to have to saw at least a little bit. But it parted at the merest touch of the knife, releasing a little puff of steam and an irresistible aroma. The meat literally melted in my mouth, the flavour was intense, really gratifying the taste buds. The chips were very crisp, but on the inside, soft, delicious, perfect. Even the unfamiliar mushrooms, although strange in texture and flavour, seemed a perfect complement to the meal. Silence reigned for several minutes as we all tucked in. I refused mustard when Harry did, not even needing my usual dollop of brown sauce with this.

"Tony's getting worse." At last, from Harry, taking a break.

"Ach, he knows just how far to go, that one." John waving a fork with a cube of steak smothered in yellow mustard on the points. "Shaun being here took him by surprise, that's all. He would have been expecting your mother. You do realise," popping the meat into his mouth, chewing, "that by now every member of staff will know that quiet, shy Harry is dining tête-a-tête with his Father and a 'friend' ?" Turning to me. "How's your steak, Shaun?"

"Oh, it's brilliant. I've never tasted anything so good."

"Good, good. I thought fillet would be easier for you to manage." Back to Harry. "I wonder that he never tried it on with you?" I thought I'd caught the gist of what he was saying. Tony, the waiter, was homosexual, like Harry and me. Well, not like Harry and me, but still, homosexual. I was fascinated and almost forgot my steak listening to Harry (I said, almost).

"But, he did, Dad." Blushing a little. "The only thing is, it took me weeks working out exactly what was going on." Nibbling a chip. "It wasn't till he invited me to his room for a drink, that I realised just what he was after."

"So?" John.

"I'm afraid, I probably wasn't very nice." Looking down at his plate. "He'd made me so nervous, I laughed at him, I couldn't help it."

"Well, you may be sure, if he thought he'd made a mistake then, you've set him to rights now. You've got broad enough shoulders." Wiping his lips with a napkin. "I'll expect you to take all the jokes and the ribbing in good part when you come back to work. Don't be going all quiet and sulky with me or the staff. You hear me?"

"Yes, Dad." Sounding the tiniest bit subdued.

"Now, if we're all done, we'll have one normal-sized drink. Then you two had better push off up the road before they set up a breathalyser."

As he picked up the phone I looked at my plate and realised that there wasn't even a pea left. My stomach was pressing very comfortably against my waistband and I felt completely relaxed. Looking at Harry, I could see he felt the same.

Tony came in with the drinks and caught my eye. I couldn't help but blush when, from behind John, he pursed his lips in a kiss. Harry saw of course and a look of chagrin fleetingly crossed his face before he burst out laughing; even I giggled.

"Tony Donnelly, remind me in the morning you've just been sacked."

"Yes, boss." Once again behind him, and this time leaning over to almost, but not quite, plant a kiss on the top of his head.

"Did you bring the chit?"

"Yes, boss." Taking a slip of paper from his pocket and placing it on the table. John signed with his fountain pen. Gathering up the tray and chit, Tony waltzed out the door.

"When did you say you see the doctor, Shaun?"

"He takes the stitches out tomorrow and I think I'm supposed to see him Friday."

"Right then. What I suggest the pair of you do is this. *After* you've been to the Wimpy on Friday evening you call in here about eight o'clock. I may have something for the pair of you." Standing up. "Come on now, boys, it's a quarter to ten, and I don't want you speeding up the road, Harry." Cuffing his head gently. "You hear me?"

"Yes, Dad. And, thanks for dinner."

"Yes, thank you sir, Uncle John, it was the best ever."

"Away wi' the pair of you." Pushing us out the door, calling, "Somebody come and throw this pair of bums out." Catching sight of Tony and Theresa in earnest conversation over the bar "Sloane!, Donnelly! No work to do? By God, we'll see about that." Striding purposefully off, and flinging "Goodnight, guys" over his shoulder. Tony streaked off and Theresa curtsied behind the bar. At least, she bobbed down and up again, and from the grin on her face I gathered that it wasn't because her knees had given way with fright.

We called out "Goodnight" and left.

"Now I wonder what has he got up his sleeve?" Harry mused as we shot up the road.

"You're not supposed to be speeding," as the car drifted a little going round a corner.

"It's only sixty-five." Blithely.

"I'll lose all that lovely dinner if you don't slow down."

"Moan, moan, moan," he sighed, slowing down nevertheless to a more reasonable forty-five. "I do wonder."

"What was that about the Wimpy on Friday?"

"Oh, he doesn't mind having his arm twisted once in a while. That was just to let us know not to try it twice in one week."

"Oh, I see." My tummy settling down again. "Was I seeing things, or was that guy Tony wearing eye shadow or whatever it's called?"

Harry laughed. "Yes, he does. He had a stand-up row with Dad about it. He told Pops that if the girls could, so could he." Catching his breath. "He threatened to sue Dad for sexual discrimination."

"What's that?"

By the time I thought I understood a very garbled version of a law I hadn't even known existed, we were nearly at my house. Harry pulled into the Manse Road and turned the lights off.

"I'd invite you in, but there will be a hen party in the kitchen."

"And I'd invite you in, but Mum will make a point of sitting up since Dad's away."

"Oh! I'm *so* full."

We gave each other a hug and a Baileys-flavoured kiss.

"I suppose we'd best go?"

"No use prolonging the agony," I agreed.

He did a very neat three-point turn. At the gate I held his crotch as he undid the belt, and blew in his ear to be rewarded by a squeeze just above the knee.

"Ten o'clock, Shaun?"

"Ten it is, Harry." Getting out.

"Dream about me?"

"Only if you promise to dream about me."

"Love you Shaun, love you forever."

"Love you angel, don't make me cry."

"Goodnight."

"Goodnight." Waiting and watching till the rear lights popped over the hill.

10

I knew she was still up, the light was on in the living room. I sighed as I walked round the house, she must know something by now. I had a foreboding, even before I tried the back door, that this wasn't going to be pleasant.

For the very first time that I could recall, the back door was locked. That would be so that if she fell asleep on the settee, not unknown after a half bottle of port, I'd be unable to sneak past her as I'd managed on previous occasions. I considered going round to tap on the girls' window, but she'd been awake and heard me at the door. The kitchen light snapped on and the door flew open.

"Oh, so it *is* you, is it." Which, from the half satisfied, half vindictive tone didn't sound too promising. "In the name of the Sweet Jesus just where do you think you've been till... "

"Hi, Mum. There in a minute." Squeezing past and into the bathroom. Finished, I grimaced at my reflection and stepped into the kitchen.

"Out with your swanky new friends again? *Eh!*" Sneering, arms crossed, leaning against the door frame. "You're heading for big trouble, my man." An expression of distaste on her face, eyes bulging dangerously. I started to make coffee. "Oh, aye. Can't even look me in the face," as I filled the kettle. "You're turning out no good, may the Blessed Virgin be my judge, I always said you would." She seemed to take great satisfaction from that. "Your own wee house not good enough for you any more? It didn't take the Divil long to get his claws in you. Hard-earned grub I put on the table not to your taste anymore?" She'd registered the involuntary dismay on my face when I'd seen the dried-up fish and wizened chips on the plate under the grill.

"Now I hear your own sort's not good enough for you either." Short forced sarcastic laugh. "I'm surprised you're not wearing the sash already."

Unwisely I interposed, "Left it in the car. Sorry."

"Don't you cheek *me*. You ungrateful little bugger," she flared. "And don't be fancying yourself too big for the trashing you so richly deserve. *Aye!* And don't think for one minute I'd lift a hand to stop it either. Oh aye! They'll get you my man, you'll have more than a wee scratch on your chin when they do. Aye. You will that."

Strangely, I wasn't afraid this time. Before, when she'd given me a tongue-lashing accompanied with wild swinging blows to whatever part of me she could connect with, I'd been terrified. Now, looking at her dumpy little figure, sagging cheeks, the loose flesh of her arm quivering, spittle flying and eyes bugging, I felt... distaste? There was also a growing anger, a barely repressed urge to scream back as she was screaming at me, working herself into one of her frenzies.

"And don't be bringing any more of those blackguards to my wee house ever again. *You hear me?*" Volume increasing all the while. "Do you think I don't know what's been going on here? Just because I'm out working my fingers to the bone. *Do you?*" Drawing breath.

I wondered whether it would be worth pushing past and going to my room, but knew from long experience that once she'd started, there was no way of stopping her until she either ran down or got a migraine.

"That, *that* blackhearted wee *get* of an *Orangeman* has been in my wee house every day. Don' think I don't know it." Holding up a clenched fist. "Wheesht! I don't want to hear none of your lies."

I had no intention of denying it, but wasn't given a chance to either confirm or deny.

" There's them that see. *Aye!* And see a damned sight more than that and all. *Aye!* And make sure and tell me and all, so they do." Thumping the door with her fist. "And *what* did you think you were doing? Skulking round the harbour in the dead of night, *arm in arm*, if you please, with a *Protestant get*! What have you got to say for yourself? *Eh! Eh!*" Her chest heaved and she had to stop for breath, wiping the specks of spittle from her mouth with the back of her hand.

I was tired. I'd had an emotionally charged forty-eight hours. I wanted this to be over.

"I can see you intend making Harry as welcome as any other friend I ever wanted to bring to the house."

"Friends! Friends!?" She nearly exploded. "No snot-nosed tramps from Newry Street are ever going to darken my door. Aye! Nor any more of the swanky scum from the Harbour Road neither. You mind *that*, my man."

Alerting me to the fact that she *had* known of my friendship with Padraig.

"Next thing you know you'll be getting drunk in the Kilmorey and making a spectacle of yourselves before the whole town. *Then*, no doubt, yous'll be going out and getting some poor wee girl pregnant, just to try and pretend that it's men that you are." The venom and contempt was rich amongst the spittle. *"Men!!"* she almost choked *"Men!* You're just like your Father. The two of you put together'll never make one good man as long as grass is green."

"Leave Dad out of this." I was really stung. "At least he loves us."

"Och aye," very dry. "Loves you?" Breath. "Surprised he doesn't fucking sleep with you. He might as well for all the use he is to me. Had to get nine sheets to the wind before he could keep it up long enough to father any of you. What kind of marriage do you call that? Eh? Eh?" Her breathing was very rapid now and I honestly feared that her eyes would pop any second.

"Dad's got nothing to do with any of this." My own face was getting warm.

"Och aye! You *would* say that, wouldn't you? Like Father like son. Another fucking wee shirt-lifter. It must run in the breed of the McKennas. He *used* me. He wanted *me*. And for *why? Eh! Go on. Tell me why? Och aye!*" not waiting for an answer. "Aye! You think your Father's such a saint, Such a *pal*." Investing the last word with an ocean of sarcasm. "Aye but you're well matched, the pair of you." Stabbing me with a glare filled with enough loathing to kill.

"But God has punished me for my sin, may the Blessed Virgin bear witness to that. I'm an ould woman before my time. I've scrimped and gone without as a penance to raise three useless mouths, brats! Snot-nosed, shitty little brats the whole fucking lot of you."

I was more taken aback by her continual use of the F-word than by anything else she'd said up till that point and, although I'd heard most of it before, I was nailed to the workbench, hypnotised, unable to move. I heard the girls' door open, then Kathleen's voice.

"What in God's name is going on here? You'll waken the whole bloody road."

"Aye! Aye! There it is." Whirling round and screaming, arm stretched, accusing finger pointing. "My sin. The *curse* of my life."

"Been at the bottle again, you ould bitch?" Kathleen sneered. "Been at the port again, have we?"

She was ignored, Mum turned on me again as I tried to inch past into the living room.

"I thought he loved me. I thought he was shy. One night when he'd had a drink he started pawing me, and that Man up on His Cross has never forgiven me for letting him. How was I to know that it wasn't me he was after? Oh no! It was my *brother* he wanted. Aye. It was Seamus, may his wee soul burn for ever." Gasping for breath.

"You're sick, Mum. You don't know what you're saying." Appalled, yet fascinated at the same time.

"Och aye! You think so? You would. He never came near the house for six weeks after. By then, I knew I was carrying that, that fucking spawn of the Divil. That hoor sitting thonder." Spinning to shake her fist at Kathleen, calmly lighting a cigarette.

"Sounds like you're the whore round here," through the smoke.

I finally managed to escape into the living room, as the rant resumed. "Aye, and I've been paying for it ever since, all these fucking years. My Father and his dragged him to the altar, and for what? Eh! *For what?* Nivir in all these years has he been a man to me, except when he got drunk enough, and then I had to end up with you and the other hussy." Now she was shaking her fist in my face. "He was nivir bothered about me, him and Seamus were for *Australia* if you please. Going to leave me with my sin for all to see. *Well,* I put a stop to that, I can tell you."

"Sounds like you should have taken your own advice and kept your legs closed." Kath casually flicking ash on the floor.

"You, you, you, you pox-ridden little bitch! I know all about

you and the Kenmuirs and the Rooneys and the McCartans and the Greens. You've been spreading yourself pretty thin, my girl. What halfway dacent man will look at you now, eh?"

Whirling on me, knocking me against the sideboard, spilling the remains of my coffee. "And you. *And you! Another fucking wee shirtlifter.* What *do* you *do* for your wee Orangeman? *Lick his arse? Eh? Eh?*" glaring bug eyed into my face and shaking me by the arm. *"Well?"*

"No, not yet," I heard myself say. "But maybe tomorrow."

She lurched back as though I'd slapped her, her face contorting and blackening with sheer spite and rage.

"GET... YOU... OUT... OF... MY... SIGHT... YOU... FUCKING... PERVERT." Screaming and flailing at me with her fist.

I ducked and she connected with one of her many pictures of the Blessed Virgin, garnered from some shrine or other, knocking it to the floor in a tinkle of shattered glass.

Kathleen was laughing fit to burst.

"You fucking queer wee bastard." Sinking to her knees. "Look what you've done. Och aye. The Divil's surely got you now. You'll burn, my lad, och aye you're going to burn forever." Picking at glass splinters. "May the Blessed Virgin be my witness, but you, him and that brother of mine'll make grand company for ould Nick."

I was trembling, rage mixed with long repressed hatred and a barely suppressed urge to kick her in the face as she scrabbled on the floor.

She hadn't finished, her voice suddenly filled with equal amounts of glee and malice. "Don't be running away with the idea, any of you, that he cares one whit for any of you. He just spends the days and years pining for that brother of mine. I call the Blessed Virgin as my witness, I was *glad. Glad.* I laughed when I heard that he was dead."

"You're a disgusting, drunken, evil, sad old cow and you've only got yourself to blame." Kathleen coming over, casually kicking the picture frame across the floor, taking my arm. My whole body was shaking as she gently pushed me through to my room, closed the door and pushed me down on the side of the bed. She leant against the door lighting another cigarette.

"Is it true?"

I nodded.

"*Does* Dad know?"

I nodded again.

"His parents?"

I nodded.

"Well then... take my advice. Clear out of here. Out of Northern Ireland, the pair of you. Believe me, your lives are not going to be worth that." Snapping her fingers under my nose, spilling ash on my jeans.

"It's not true what she said about Dad," I burst out "He *does* love us."

"Oh yes, he loves us. *We* all know that." She shrugged. "The rest of it probably is true I think."

"But I didn't know she had a brother, that we had an uncle!"

"Och aye. Granny McKenna told me a little years ago. He did go to Australia sometime before I was born and apparently nothing was ever heard from him until the day his death notice arrived."

"I don't know what to do, Kath. I didn't think anything like this... " I trailed off. "God, but I hate her. Not once, *not once* has she ever shown any feeling, any love. Only nag, nag, *nag!*" My temper rising again.

"Hold on, little brother," as I stood up and tried to move her from in front of the door. "I would bet you something?"

"Let me go, Kath. What?" as she braced herself against the door.

"I would bet that Dad made you make a promise." Releasing me as my shoulders slumped. "I knew it. Well, you've been better at keeping it than I ever was." Pushing me back to the bed. "So, go to bed. Think about what I've said." Turning as she left. "Oh, and jam the chair under the door handle. She'll probably simmer away for a couple of hours and then decide to have another go. Goodnight."

"Goodnight, and, thanks, Kath."

Even through the closed doors of the bedroom and hall I could hear their voices. Kathleen's high and taunting, Mum's lower and less distinguishable. Repetitions of *whore* or *hoor* seemed to have special favour. I was still trembling, I felt cold and totally exhausted. Propping the chair against the door, I undressed and tumbled into bed wrapping the duvet round me. I tried to get warm. I missed Harry's arms round me, the stir of his body against mine. My mind was jumping. Why, if she didn't love him, was she complaining about the absence of sex? Why had he not left her when he'd gotten older and gone out to Australia, to Seamus? Had he *really* been as friendly with Seamus (in love even) as I was with Harry, as she implied? Why couldn't she have been more loving to him, to us? Was she really as bitter and vindictive as she sounded, or was she maybe a little bit mad? How much could I ask Dad? Should I even mention it? Who'd seen us at the harbour? Why should anyone want to hurt us for being friends? What could I tell Harry? (No problem there. Everything, of course. Could I continue to live here? Where else to go? I knew Harry would say with him, but I didn't think that that would be either easy or safe, although I couldn't tell him that. (Yes I *could*. I could tell him anything. I knew he would understand.) How *could* all this have happened in one week? One short week! Why *had* Dad stayed with her all these years? I wished he was at home. I wished Harry was beside me. I fell asleep around that point. How late was it? I had no idea.

I woke up to daylight edging the curtains and the banging of a fist on the door accompanied by a rattling of the knob.

"You keep away from them Orangemen or don't you darken this door ever again. *You hear me?*" More thumping and rattling.

"The whole fucking road hears you, you crazy bitch," I grumbled.

"*What* was that you said to me? You're no son of mine." Continuing to thump the door. *"You arse-licking wee shit! You hear me?"*

Promise forgotten, I raised my voice. "I fucking hear you. Now, *piss off* and leave me alone."

"Get out of my wee house this minute, you hear? Run to your swanky new friends. Get them to take you in... I don't think" – now at screaming pitch – *"Get. Out. Of. My. House."* It sounded as though she was kicking the door.

"Jesus *Christ!*" Kathleen's voice. "Close the front door, you stupid ould cow." I heard it bang "You *want* the whole town to know your business?"

"And sure and why not? They know all about you, you slut, and now half of them know all about him." Door bouncing off the wall, open again. *"Let the whole bloody world know. What the fuck do I care?"*

The gate clanged on the wall and, peeking through the curtains, I saw the bun bobbing on the other side of the roses. The front doors of the houses opposite, McGonigle and Rooney, ajar.

"She's away now, Shaun," door closing, "I'll put the kettle on."

I looked at the clock, seven-thirty, took a mug of coffee from Kathleen as I came out of the bathroom.

"Won't you be late for work?"

"Huh! I'll phone in sick later. Ould 'Jelly Belly' won't mind."

We sat sipping coffee.

"You'll go out to Granny McKenna till Dad gets back?"

"Why, yes! Why didn't I think of that?" I cheered up a bit. Gran and Mum hadn't exchanged a word for years as far as I knew.

"Here! You'd better take this." Reaching into her bag and giving me some notes. "Go on. Take it. You know she only has her pension and you eat like a horse." Stuffing the money into my hand. "Give her twenty-five and hang on to the rest. You never know what's going to happen."

"Hi, Goblin," catching sight of Eileen peering round the door.

"What was all that shouting?" She'd plainly heard the lot. How much she understood was impossible to say, but she'd obviously been crying. "What's going on?" Her bottom lip trembling.

"Come here, pet." Kath reached for the hairbrush on the window sill. "Let me do your hair."

"Mum and I had an argument."

"Was it about Harry?" Suffering the tangles being loosened. "I like him."

"So do I, Frogface, but Mum doesn't." I bit my lip. "So I'm going to stay with Granny McKenna until Dad gets home."

"Can I come?"

"Now, you know she only has one spare room, Frog, and it's only for a few days."

"I'm going to be late for school."

"No. You're not going today, pet." Tying her in a pony tail. "You and I are going to sneak a day off and go shopping in Newry." Tweaking the bow experimentally. "How does that sound?"

"Can I get a new blouse to go with my black skirt?" All eagerness.

"We'll see what we can find. Now, run on and get dressed. As for you, my lad, you'd better pack some things in a bag. You can't be wearing the same clothes all week."

She made us all cheese on toast whilst I crammed clothes and shoes into a bag.

"Don't forget washing gear." Handing me a wash bag.

"What if she says no?"

"Don't you be worrying none about that. You and Dad are the apple of her eye. It's us women she can't stand." Sliding a plate of cheese on toast across the table. "Have no fear. You'll be treated like a lord."

"Kathleen," I hesitated. "Make sure she doesn't damage my books."

"Well now, I can't sit here twenty-four hours a day, but I

wouldn't think she'll bother with them." Cocking her head. "Unless you have any 'funny' ones?" Glancing at Eileen.

"Oh pooh. He doesn't read comics. No pictures at all, they're all reading." Scooping up another slice of cheese on toast. "I like to see the pictures."

"What time does your friend usually pick you up?"

"About ten."

"Well then, if this little pig ever stops eating, you can both help with the washing up and we can get a lift to the bus station with you."

An hour later, just as I was forcing another pair of shoes into the bag, Harry arrived. Waving to him through the window I saw the doors of the houses opposite open. Mrs McGonigle and Mrs Rooney came out the front, ostensibly to stand chatting over the fence, but watching hawk-eyed as Harry sauntered round to the back door.

"Oh, hello." Shyly, startled by Kathleen's presence.

"Hello, brainbox." Grinning at Eileen. "No school today?" Pretending to grab her pony tail.

"Oh you." She blushed, smiling up at him.

I brought the bag through from the bedroom.

"What's all this?" Anxiety dawning in his eyes.

"Tell you later." Nodding warningly towards Eileen. "Can we give the girls a lift to the bus station?"

"Surely." Looking ever more bewildered.

"Handsome is as handsome does," smiled Kathleen. "Must say, I love the eyes."

Harry blushed furiously. I've never seen him go such a deep red.

"Now, Kath!" I stopped. "Shit. Nearly forgot." Diving into the kitchen for a shopping bag and scooting back to the bedroom to bundle the Darkover and Dragon books into it.

"Harry," calling him through. "Can you take these for me?"

"What *is* going on, Shaun?" taking the bag. "Is that your wallet on the drawers?"

"Shit. Yes, thanks. You just saved my life. Come on, tell you later after we drop the girls."

Out at the car, Kathleen *would* call across to the neighbours. "Well, heard anything juicy this morning, girls?"

Mrs Rooney just sneered, but Mrs McGonigle couldn't resist the bait.

"Having a party, were you? In your house last night. Keeping dacent God-fearing folk awake into the wee hours." Noisily clearing her throat, spitting a gob in our direction. *"Slut!"*

Kathleen wasn't at all put out. "That's right, I do hear that you get ould Arthur Kenmuir to show you the meaning of the word twice a week." Turning cheekily to Mrs Rooney, leaving the other one red-faced and choking with venom. "I also hear that your ould man took quite a liking to sheep some years back." She paused to give the ugly sneering face a long look. "Can't say as I blame the man."

"*Kath*-leen!" I was mortified. Eileen was already in the car and Harry had managed to jam the bag into the boot. "Get in. for God's sake. Before they start throwing things." I followed her into the car, wedging the books between my feet. Harry made no comment when I secured my own belt, just a little pout of disappointment, which I decided to ignore for the moment. At the bus station I heaved a sigh of relief, sinking back into my seat after the girls got out.

"Now, will someone tell me just what the hell *is* going on here?" Harry complained as he did up my belt and had his ear nibbled.

"After I get the stitches out. *Please,* Harry. I promise."

Sighing, he put the car into gear and pulled away. "I take it, it's trouble?"

"With a capital T," I agreed. "But please, let's get this over with first. Okay?"

"Okay then."

* * *

Being so uptight and not having slept very well left me particularly vulnerable to the pulling and tugging. The sight of tweezers and scissors disappearing under my chin had me wishing that I hadn't had the cheese on toast. Tears formed in my eyes and I squeaked when two of the stitches proved reluctant to part company with me. I felt sure that the whole thing was opening up again.

"Aye well, that's done. It'll be a neat wee scar. Somebody did a fine job there." That was the doctor's brisk voice. "Right, nurse, let's look at the hands please." Pulling and stretching the left as the nurse removed the dressing from the right. Turning his gaze on it next and, as I feared he would, giving it just as thorough a mauling. Sweat popped out on my forehead.

"Mmm. Better than I thought it might be." Sitting back.

"Good. Just a dry dressing I think," scribbling on a chart. "Then make an appointment for him Friday evening, about six o'clock," capping his pen. "Now, young man, are you working?" I nodded. "Well you'll need a certificate."

"I'm on holiday."

"When are you due back?"

"Monday."

"Well now. No, I don't think so, lad. But we'll make a final decision Friday." Turning to the nurse. "That will hold him till Friday you think?" I nodded when he asked if I could keep it clean until then.

"Good, good. Well then, you won't need to bother the nurse again. Now, don't forget, six o'clock Friday at the surgery."

"Thank you, doctor, nurse." I escaped.

"Where are we going, Harry?" Tongue in his ear.

"Back home. They've all cleared off, and I thought you might need a bath or something," wrinkling his nose and sniffing delicately in pretend disgust.

"That was a low blow, Hannah. I'll get you for that."

"Goody." Giggling. "Now give. What happened last night?"

I waited till he turned the corner on the crest of the hill. "Mum threw me out."

"Jesus!" The car swerved, causing an approaching lorry to blare its horn and flash its lights. "Jesus. Because of *me?*"

"No. Because of *us*, Harry."

"Holy shit! I don't believe it." Coming to an abrupt halt in the yard. "You're kidding me?" Staring straight ahead at the blank wall.

"I'd never do anything like that, especially not about something like this, Harry." Hefting the bag of books in my left hand. "No, leave it," as he went to open the boot.

"But! Where will you go?" Stopping in his tracks. "You can't go without me, Shaun." Catching me up, grabbing my arm. "Not without me, I won't let you."

It was on the tip of my tongue to say that I was on the three o'clock flight out of Aldergrove, but the lost, hurt look on his face killed that idea half-formed. Instead, I dragged him into the house, dropped the books on the table and wrapped him in my arms, unwilling to see him look so miserable for even one second.

"Oh, Harry. You didn't really think I'd leave you?" Feeling him gulping as he tried, vainly, to hold back the tears. "I truly love you, and I'd die first."

"Shaun." Drawing a great ragged breath. "Don't frighten me like that again. I don't know what I'd do now if you weren't here." Snuffling on my shoulder. "I think I was nearly cracking up when we met. You are everything to me now. My heart would break."

"Hush, Harry," I chided him. "You're not listening. I'm not going away. Not leaving. Never going anywhere unless you go too. Please Harry, don't make me cry too." Kissing the top of his bent head, rubbing his back. "I've had a very rough night. Only knowing that I'd be seeing you stopped me thumping her, or running away or something. Please Harry," as he clutched me tightly, tears coming in a flood. Now I began to get worried, very anxious. Something was the matter, something more than my being thrown out. "Please, Harry. Tell me." Pushing him away, wiping his face with a tea towel. He shook his head blindly, crushed me in his arms, hiccuping as he tried vainly to stem the flow. I could only hold him and sway back and forth whispering in his ear: "Love you. Never going to let you go. Love you, never let you go. Talk to me, Eyes. I love you, I'll never let you go. Please talk to me Harry. You're breaking my heart. I love you, only you. Nobody can come between us. I need you, I want you all the time. Be good Harry, okay? Say you love me. You haven't said it yet today."

"Have, too." Strangled whisper.

"Haven't."

"Have so."

"Not so." Risking a tickle of his ribs.

"Not fair, Shaun," and I felt the tension drain away as he slumped in my arms, snugging his head on a very wet shoulder. "Sorry, Shaun. Guess I'm not as strong as you."

"Everybody is different Harry. I'm learning that very fast." I kissed the back of his neck. "You, I wouldn't have any way other than as you are. No changes, just to get to know you better and better every day." I gently lifted his head. "Harry, I can't love you any more than I do today. My heart is full to overflowing." Gazing deep, searching his tear-swollen eyes. "There isn't the tiniest bit of space left and, even if there were a little corner somewhere, when I find it, it'll be like the rest of me, drowned by your eyes, your love, my love, *our* love."

He nodded, mute.

"Make some coffee, Harry and let's go up. Okay?"

"Okay."

I managed the tray, he carried the books. He locked the door and we sat side by side on the bed drinking the coffee. At last he got up, went to the window and closed the curtains. Not thick enough to make a full blackout against the midday sun, they brought a pleasant dimming of the light.

"Let's go to bed for a while." Taking his trainers off.

"What about the bath?"

"Later, Shaun, please?"

"Okay." Nothing loath, I started to skin down, then realised that he was standing beside me. Stopping after freeing the T-shirt from my jeans, I reached out and slowly, very slowly undressed him. I didn't hug him, kiss him or even touch him very much. Just made him naked. Then, standing relaxed, let him do the same for me. He turned to the bed and pulled back the duvet.

"Behind me, Shaun."

I climbed over and lay down, slipping an arm under his neck as he drew the duvet up. Right arm round his waist. Knees tucked in behind his. His buttocks nestled into place in my groin. Both my hands held in his. Feet warmly entangled. He breathed a great sigh of relief.

"Now, I'm home."

I didn't say anything. He'd spoken for the both of us.

I don't know how long we lay before he began to talk, very low, but, loud enough. Almost as though talking to himself, but by the pressure from his hands, I knew he was talking to, telling, me.

"I've had a very rough couple of years. Right up till last week. Mum and Dad have been just about crazy with worry, I know that. I knew I wasn't alright but, up to last week, I just couldn't snap out of it. I thought I was in love with Graham, you see, it nearly drove me mad. Then, Colette! It was all almost too much for me... when Graham cut me dead after Charlie had walked in on us, I couldn't understand it. We had the row and it wasn't very nice, he wasn't very nice to me. At the time, I couldn't understand why he was doing it. He told me it was wrong, that if we didn't stop, we'd both go to hell. Told me he would continue to love me as his brother but not in any other way. I remember I did a lot of crying then too. Then I began to think it was *me*. That there was something wrong with me, to want this thing *so* much. I blamed myself because I'd started it that first time, and every time after. He would never do it for me. Oh, an arm round the shoulders when I was old enough to cum, that and the cleaning up afterwards. He never would get into bed, always half sat, half lay on top. Most times, he'd carry on with whatever story he was telling, almost as though nothing else was happening, right up to the last moment. Then he'd take up the story again as he was cleaning up. He'd never talk about it, never let me talk about it. And then, when it stopped after Charlie came in, I thought he'd only been letting me because I was his brother. Then the months with Colette! Especially when I couldn't perform, couldn't even begin to get hard, felt little other than a revulsion. I felt *so* alone. I stopped going out, just went to work and home again, spent all my time reading or watching videos. I even tried to stop wanking, I pretty well convinced myself I was sick in the head, began to despise myself. I brought a knife up here one night, I was going to cut my dick off. I thought that would cure the whole thing."

He carried on in a steady monotone as I hugged his body to me.

"But I'm not very strong, I couldn't do it. Then, after Graham's wedding, on my birthday, Mum and Dad gave me the car. I loved it from the start and it got me out of the house. I'd just drive for hours, or maybe drive somewhere and sit in it for hours. Not doing anything, not even thinking, just sitting. I found the bench in Kilbroney that way. Drove up, sat for I don't know how long and then thought I'd find a high place and just throw myself off."

"Oh yes," as I hugged him hard. "That was five weeks ago, but my legs got tired and I couldn't find a big enough drop so I put it off for a while. Then one day I thought I'd drive up the dual carriageway towards Newry and crash it into the bridge. I was sure I could do that and if I was doing ninety at the time it would all be over in a flash, no pain, I'd be free. I didn't think about heaven or hell or Mum and Dad, just doing it! And then, you happened. Almost did it for me. A couple of seconds later and you'd have been in the front seat with me. I was very upset that you should have stopped me when I'd made my mind up, I think I really went back to tell you off. Then when I got in the field and saw you lying so still, I thought maybe you were dead. I thought I'd go and see what death looked like, what I would look like. I really, truly did think you were dead. All that blood coming from your neck and your poor hand! I looked at your face. So incredibly peaceful. I wanted to look like that, to be at peace. You looked so very young, so beautiful. I felt an enormous sense of loss, even though I didn't know you from Adam. Then Mrs Collins arrived and wrapped your hand, and I got down on my knees beside you as she was padding your chin."

He moved abruptly in the bed.

"Roll over, Shaun."

We reversed positions, him now spooned in behind me. I couldn't speak. He stroked the scar under my chin very gently. I was in floods of tears.

"Then you were looking at me and you said quite clearly 'such amazing green eyes' and shut your own again. I was lost! That instant, when you looked into my eyes, something I thought was dead woke up inside me. I think, really I fell in love right then. I certainly realised that I'd never been in love with Graham, that all those months with Colette had been the biggest mistake of my life. I didn't know what the word love meant until I looked in your eyes and saw it staring back at me. Oh, I had doubts. Even following the ambulance up to Newry I thought to myself 'You're mad'. It wasn't till the day we went to Kilbroney and you picked that path. Then I knew, really knew, that everything was going to be alright. Alright for you, alright for me, alright for us. But I got nervous, especially alone here in bed at night. What if all you felt for me was the same as I felt for Graham? What if you only thought you were in love with me? When I saw you this morning with that bag! I knew you were leaving home. Oh yes, I knew, even before you told me, I knew. I thought, this is it. It's all over. I should have rammed the fucking bridge instead of following you all the way to the hospital. I thought you'd been making a fool of me. I just couldn't take it, Shaun."

"Harry?" My tears were running in a river over the hand cupping my jaw and onto the pillow.

"Shush, Shaun. Let me finish." He was silent a little while, his lips pressed to my shoulder "When I came in last night, after I'd dropped you off, Graham was here. He wanted to come up here and 'talk'."

I must have tensed in the bed.

"No, I didn't let him. We went into the dining room and I sat across the table from him. Word about you and me being together all the time this last ten days had gotten to him. He said that he wasn't happy, he realised he should never have got married, he blamed Charlie. Said that he loved me."

"What?"

My voice must have been pretty shrill. Harry held me very close, kissing the bony point of my shoulder.

"Exactly how I reacted. I screamed at him. Told him what he'd been responsible for over the last two years. Nearly driving me to suicide. Making me think I was sick or mad or, both. I told him I'd never been in love with him, just enthralled by his dick, that I hadn't known what the word love meant till the day I met you. Told him he was a coward and a liar. I must have been pretty loud.

He just sat there, saying over and over, I'm sorry, I'm sorry. Mum and the twins must have heard most if not all of it, but she waited till I ran out of steam before she came in. She told him he had a wife and a home to go to, so go. That he'd made his own bed and would have to lie in it till he plucked up the courage to be himself. He went, tried to say something to me as he left, but Mum told him he'd already said more than enough and to just go. She asked me if I was alright, then told me to go to bed, otherwise I'd be late picking you up this morning."

I wriggled round in his arms, glued my lips to his, realised that he was crying again quietly. We couldn't kiss properly, too much emotion, too many tears. I strained to hold him close, butted my head under his chin, tried to wrap him completely round me. Envelope him completely within me. Protect him, shield him. Shield me, protect us both. Shut out the whole fucking world.

Twenty minutes of cuddling and hugging must have passed when cock decided that enough liquid had been spilt at the top end. He wanted to get wet too. I wasn't sure it was the right time, still shaken by Harry's confidences in me, but I needn't have worried. Something was prodding me in the thigh, leaving little wet kisses as it struggled to straighten up. But, just to be sure. "Harry, bath?"

"Mmm, not just yet." His arm sliding between us, hand grasping semi-rigid cock, caressing him lovingly.

11

When we did bathe later, we squeezed in together. Made a huge watery mess of the floor, managing to lose the soap an extraordinary number of times. Much as it proved a waste of time, I loved brushing his hair, seeing it bounce and shine under my hands. There were a number of distractions, though. We were nude, Harry sitting down, me standing between his legs, and he would insist on brushing my hair at the same time. My pubic hair that is.

Eventually and reluctantly we climbed back into our clothes. He drove me to Ballymartin where Gran had an old cottage almost like ours but with only two bedrooms and a tiny patch of garden.

"Come ye away in, son." When I told her about having a row with Mum, not going into any detail, she snorted, "Yon hoitytoity bitch would try the patience of a bunch of saints," obviously pleased that I'd come to her. "Stay as long as you like, son. I'll nivir know why your father nivir took a strap to her." Peering out the window. "Will you not be bringing thon chile in for a cup of tay." Shaking her head as I waved Harry in. "Thon Mother of yours! Aye, she was a bonny enough wee thing once but somebody has long needed to bring her down a peg or two."

She took Harry by the arm. "Stand here in the light, chile. These ould eyes are not what they used to be." Gazing at him shrewdly. "Ye have the look of a Crawford about ye, wi' them black Irish brows."

"My Mum was Crawford."

"Aye! *Now* I've got ye. That must be the wee girl that married Hannah. Now, let me see," looking at me. "Your Da must have jist started the school, the wee soul. Well do I remember all the photays in the paper. Real proper do that was." Suddenly brisk. "Aye, well that was long ago. Now, don't jist stand there Shaun, show him where to put that bag. I'll put the kettle on." Calling over her shoulder as she made her way to the kitchen. "You'll be in the front room, too noisy for me now. What did you say the chile's name was?"

"Harry Hannah, Gran."

"Aye, that'll be after your great, or would that be your great-great grandfather? Good stout Protestant that he was. Always one to have the time of day for a body, aye, that he was. Now, away and sit down the pair of ye."

Within the hour, what she didn't know already, I'm sure she guessed. Putting two and two together and coming up with something not far short of the mark. I almost choked when, on hearing about Harry's Nan, she remarked, "Aye! Well, but sure she must be full of years yon wan, pon my soul she must be ninety-four if she's a day."

"Ninety-six in August."

"Well there you are then, aye, well and sure and she's had a grand life." This, from a little dried-up old woman who wouldn't be seeing eighty again.

"Aye well, thank you chile," taking the money I gave her. "The ould pension goes nowhere these days." And as she gathered up the cups, "Away wi' the pair of ye. I'm needing no help with a couple of cups." She looked at Harry. "Don't be making a stranger of yourself, son. Shaun will no doubt be wanting his friend wi' him, and there's not wan round here to be bothering the pair of ye. And if you don't want to be driving thon wee motorcar round in the dark, there's plenty of room for the both of ye in that big bed so there is. Aye, I must put a bottle in it, give it an airing."

144

"Thank you, Mrs McKenna."

"Yes, thanks Gran."

"Aye well, I can see ye're in a rush to be away, so away wi' ye. Shaun son, you'd better take a key, I'm not as young as I was, like to get to bed early. But don't you be worrying none, you won't bother me no matter what time ye get in. I'll leave a pot of brown stew and spuds on the cooker, jist help yourselves."

"We're away, Gran."

"Bye, Mrs McKenna."

"Where are we going, Harry?" as we sped through Annalong towards Newcastle.

"It's a surprise, but we'll have to get a move on."

"What is it?" I wheedled. "We can't be going begging again and besides, Gran's leaving that pot of stew for us. She'll be awful upset if we don't eat it."

"Do you think she *knows?*" adroitly changing the subject.

"Well, maybe not what your Dad calls the gory details, but she's not soft and, if only half of what Mum said last night was true, she must be well used to boys hanging around together."

"Do you think *all* families are like ours? Yours and mine?"

"To be honest, Harry, I've never given it a thought but you know, it wouldn't surprise me too much."

"You never did tell me exactly what happened last night." Rueful smile. "Not that I gave you much chance." Pushing himself straight-armed against his seat. "But oh, I feel *so* much better having told you all of it."

"You only really scared me for one instant."

"When?"

"When you said that Graham was waiting to talk to you last night. I had the horrible thought that you were about to tell me you and him were getting back together and that it was all over between us."

"*Never!* Not in ten thousand years, Shaun. You must know that."

"Yes, I know. I was just being silly, but it did make my heart jump. I can tell you that."

"I think Shaun, maybe, we should have one rule."

"About what?"

"About us." Pausing as he whipped past a bus. "Not really a rule, what I mean is, we shouldn't be worrying about what either of us might be thinking." Glancing at me. "I'm sorry, I'm not explaining this very well, am I?"

"Go on, I think I see what you're getting at."

"Well, if you are worried by anything I say or do, don't keep it to yourself, tell me or, ask me and I promise not to lie. *Ever!*"

"And vice versa." I nodded. "I like that, I promise too."

"Well?"

"Well what?"

"*Is* there anything bothering you right now?"

"Well, not bothering me. But I do worry a little."

"About what?"

"Well, you don't feel like jumping off cliffs or crashing into bridges any more, do you?"

He didn't answer immediately.

"*Do* you?"

"That's not easy, Shaun." He sighed. "I've been down so long. To be truthful... " He shook his head. "Remember when I asked you the other day what you were looking for?"

"Mmm."

"You said you thought you must be dreaming. Well, I feel as if I'm in an even more fantastic dream and, somewhere inside my head is a little me, sitting absolutely terrified. Waiting for someone or something to wake me up. Then I'd find you never were, I was still on my own."

"But Harry!"

He patted my knee, then gripped my hand. "I *know* it's not a dream. *Really*, I know you are here, that we *are* real. It's just... I think it's going to take a little while longer for it all to sink in. To convince that little me in here," tapping his forehead, "to relax, to get happy."

He slowed down as we entered Newcastle.

"Well?"

"Well! I think Harry Hannah, you are not fit to be left on your own. I think," as we crossed the end of the Castlewellan Road, "that you should stay in Ballymartin tonight, so that I can be sure you don't go sleepwalking off the end of the pier. At least, not without me. So there. What do you think of that?"

"Okay."

"You *will?*"

"Of course. Did you truly think I wouldn't?"

"Yes. I mean *no*. What about Aunt Jean and your Dad?"

"Oh, we'll call in with Dad on the way back and get him to let Mum know where we are."

"Golly! I mean, okay then."

"Happy now? Good. Now, tell me, what *did* your Mum say last night?"

He kept glancing at the clock on the dash as the miles passed, listening as I regaled him with the detail of the row in the Scrogg Road. Interjecting at one point, "You said *what?*"

"I said, not yet, but I might."

"Shaun McKenna, if you ever dare to try, I'll scream." But his face was at odds with his words. "Oh good," as we entered Ballynahinch. "We've still got ten minutes."

"For what?"

"You'll see." Pulling into a car park. "Come on. Quick."

We watched one of the best movies I've ever seen, 'Interview with the Vampire'. It was so real. Scary in parts, funny in others, but real, believable. We both admitted later, that having Brad Pitt who played Louis sink his teeth into our necks, or wherever, might well be worth dying for. I had to qualify that by saying that on second thoughts, I wasn't too sure about him. I only liked small firm arses and I had thought his a bit on the big side.

The rejoinder I got was, that at least Brad Pitt had got an arse, whilst I just had bones! Very nice bones, beautiful bones even. But, still *bones.*

Movies we had seen, those we wanted to see and various actors and their attributes (or the lack of the same) occupied the run back to Newcastle and the Arrandale. John didn't seem too surprised to see us, but did let us know that the kitchen wasn't taking any more orders.

"Actually Dad, I wanted to phone Mum and let her know I won't be home tonight." When an eyebrow was raised: "Staying with Shaun at his Gran's."

"Mum and I have had a difference of opinion and it seemed best. At least, till Dad gets back."

"I see! Well, go and phone then. Tell her I'll call later." Turning to me as Harry went off "Shaun, I take it this 'difference' is pretty serious?"

"Well yes, sir. It is."

"Mmm. We'll see. Now, don't forget, you two are to come down and see me tomorrow evening. Okay?"

"Okay, Uncle John. But we're both dying to know what the big mystery is."

"Hmmph, you're as bad as he is," nodding at Harry making his way back towards us." Away with you now. I've got work to do. Mind, tomorrow now. Goodnight."

"Night, sir."

Gran was in bed when we got back and closing the kitchen door we reheated her stew and potatoes. We lingered over the table afterwards with tea, talking softly, doing the washing up, going to the loo separately as Harry announced he needed a sit down. We left the hall light on, unsure whether she usually did or not. The old iron bedstead looked as high as a mountain. On climbing in we seemed to sink forever into the centre.

"You could get lost in here and never be found." Harry had an attack of the giggles.

"God! How many blankets *has* she got on this thing?" Struggling to roll some of them back, squeaking when my foot contacted mildly warm stone. We had to get out again and rearrange the bedding, draping four of the blankets over the end of the bed and removing the stone water bottle.

"Wait a sec." Harry tugging his jeans on just as we were about to assault the mountain for a second time. Out he went, reappearing in seconds with a wad of toilet tissue. "Don't want to leave stains on the sheets." Throwing himself at the bed and me.

Feather mattresses are a bit like sleeping inside a duvet as opposed to under one. We were almost totally cocooned, the mattress moulding itself to our bodies. The amount of give in it forcing us together as we sank into it. Following the tensions and the emotions of the day and, given our surroundings, we were reluctant to experiment or indulge in any horseplay (Gran was just on the other side of the wall). We contented ourselves with a rather sleepy mutual wank, drifting into sleep afterwards arms, legs, minds entwined.

* * *

We woke late, having slept long and dreamlessly, what need of dreams when we were together, my eyes opened to the sensation of cool air on my chest and the intense scrutiny of those truly amazing eyes.

"Morning, sleepyhead," briefly kissing the tip of my nose. "My turn to look." He'd pushed the blankets down to waist level and was involved in the study of my upper body. "I suppose you *will* fill out sometime," sounding doubtful as he trailed a finger over my ribs.

"Built for endurance, not comfort." I yawned deeply. "Time is it?"

"Breakfast time. I can smell bacon."

"Oh goody." Snapping wide awake.

"*Hey!* Don't I get a cuddle or anything?" Pulling me back as I made to scramble out of bed.

"But, if I don't eat I'll never get cuddly." Struggling feebly in his grasp, allowing myself to be pinned back. Surrendering to the embrace and joining in the kiss as enthusiastically as I knew how. "Now, can we go eat?" some minutes later. Massaging his rock-hard cock and nibbling on an ear.

"You can't leave me like this." Thrusting against my hand.

"Can. And *will*." Tickling his sides and managing to escape from the bed.

"Not fair, Shaun McKenna." Pulling on his shorts. "You are one cruel guy." Trying to tuck his cock away, looking down helplessly at the bulge as he zipped up the jeans.

"We'll just have to wear the T-shirts loose," I suggested, being in exactly the same predicament myself. "Come on, you can borrow my toothbrush and comb."

"Morning Gran, morning Mrs McKenna," as we dived into the bathroom and flushed the evidence from the previous night down the pan.

"Mornin', childer. Thought I heard you talking," when, after a very sketchy wash we trooped into the kitchen. "Did you get a good night's sleep?"

"Yes, thanks."

"Sit down. Sit ye down." Placing plates of eggs, bacon and fried bread on the table followed by a pot of tea, mugs, sugar and milk. "Don't be letting it get cold" – heading for the door – I'm away for my pension. Aye, and I'll be needing to have a word with that Lizzie Charlton. Them spuds were not right good." Voice echoing from the hall. "Too many eyes. Aye." Sound of front door opening and closing.

We ate in companionable silence until, pushing his plate away, Harry sat back.

"Do you realise something, you skinny little runt?"

"I realise you're in for a thick ear, fatso."

"No, really Shaun?"

"Really." Menacingly.

"We've just spent our first night together. I've never slept with anyone before."

"Me too. Or is that either or neither?"

"Who cares? Does this mean we're official now?" Cocking his head.

"Till death do us part," I avowed solemnly, watching the de-lighted grin spread across his face "I mean it, Harry. You've no way out now." Grinning back at him. "Come on," as he continued to sit, eyes shining at me. "Let's get the dishes done."

"You know, Shaun," as I was drying the plates. "I don't feel much like doing anything today. I mean, going anywhere. So, why don't I go in and see Mum, I'll borrow the wee mower and the strimmer and we could do your Gran's garden." Pulling the plug. "What do you think?"

"Don't know that I should let you out of my sight that long," I growled. "Oh, alright then," at his laughing pout. "But help me make the bed first."

* * *

"Aye! Poke up the fire a wee, bit son. These ould bones feel the damp something terrible." Settling herself. "You wee pal gone, has he?"

"He'll be back soon, Gran. Will I put the kettle on?"

"Don't bother yoursel', son. I had a cup wi' ould Ellen down at the post office. Ould gossip wanted to know what I was doing, starting a new family at my time of life. Och aye" – seeing my look – "word doesn't take long getting round."

"Gran?" I hesitated, changed slightly what I was going to ask. "What was Dad like? At my age, I mean."

"Sure, and you're just his image, son. Maybe not so skittery as he was, and you take after me wi' the eyes and nose. But for all that, as like as twin lambs." She sighed, pulling herself out of the chair. "Wait there a wee."

She came back from her bedroom with an old shoebox tied with string.

"Come over to the table, I can't see right in this light." She placed the box beside me. "It's in a knot, your fingers will be more nimble than mine." She sank into the chair opposite. "Aye, but it's a terrible thing to get old enough to start feeling your age. I'll be thankful when the good Lord sees fit to take me. Aye, I will that. There's been nothing but bother all the days of my life and I'll be glad to be done wi' it." Putting her specs on the end of her nose. "I'll away and get the scissors, son."

"No, it's alright Gran, I've got it now." Unravelling the last of the tangle. "There we go," pushing the box across the table.

When she took the lid off I could see it was full of photos, most of them brownish and old looking. Some were torn or had corners missing. She rooted through them with the occasional "Aye" or "God rest her soul."

"Aye! Here's one," passing me an old yellowed photograph showing an old woman propped up in a bed. "That's your great-aunt Maggie, a sister of mine. You won't mind her. The TB took her afore ye were borned, but aye, what a bonnie lass she was. Your Da was always her pet, climbing in behind her with his comic. She'd feed him on barley sugar and lucozade till he couldn't stomach his tay. Aye, well, God rest your soul, Maggie darlin.'"

I passed it back without comment as she started taking photographs from the box and laying them on the table.

"Aye, here it is. I knew there was one here somewhere." She handed me another about the same age. It showed the same scene but with the addition of a young boy of about nine or ten also on the bed. Solemn faced, introverted even. "Aye, that's your Da. My wee Shaun."

I looked with renewed interest, but for the life of me, I could not see the slightest resemblance. Either between me and him, or between the boy in the photograph and the man that I knew. Did everything, everybody, really change so much with the years?

Harry came back just then and, leaving her sorting through the box, we went to make tea.

"What gives with the old photos?" he whispered.

"History lesson," I whispered back. "I'm getting her to tell me about Dad."

"Oh," loading a tray.

"What's that?" I pointed to a paper bag he'd put on the table.

"Mum sent out a bannock."

"Can we have some?" Unwrapping it. "Mmm, still warm. Gran will love it. I don't think she bakes any more."

"Sure, but don't butter it till we get in."

"Och, son. Your mother shouldn't have bothered," she exclaimed "Mind you, I haven't had a dacent bit of bannock for years." Moving ornaments into the window. "Does a lot of her own baking, does she?" buttering a slice. "Mind, them 'lectric ovens are no good, dry everything up so they do."

"Harry's mum has an Aga, Gran. A big coal-fired range. Just like you had in the old house."

"Och aye! You can taste the difference." Nose and chin almost meeting over toothless mouth. "Aye, but she's a right good baker, your mother. You make sure to give her my thanks now.

You hear?"

"Yes 'm. "

"Aye. Now look here young Shaun," thrusting a picture at me. "That's your Da and Seamus Young when they were altar boys for Father Sweeney." It was a bit disappointing, they were so far away in it, it was practically impossible to make out any detail. "This one was taken at the Mourne Festival down at Kilkeel harbour."

They were about fourteen. A good close-up, both laughing, arms round each other's shoulders. I recognised Dad in that one alright, and as for the other boy! Fresh round face, shock of almost white curls, angelic beam. Harry looked from the photo to me and smiled; we were both thinking alike. Another photo, the two of them perched side by side on a rock on a beach somewhere. It looked to me very like the Ballykeel shore. Again, arms round each other, and surely that was the outline of a hard-on in Dad's shorts.

"Lived in each other's pockets did those two. If he wasn't with us at the weekend, your Da would be at his house. They used to practically live at the shore during the summers. They had an ould tent, just came up to get fed. Your grandfather, God rest his soul, took them photays. He was forever worrying that they'd get up to some divilmint down there on their own." Another picture. The two of them in front of an old round tent, dead campfire to one side. In swimming trunks, both sets of ribs like washboards. Slightly out of focus, tantalisingly blurring the fine detail.

"What happened to Granddad?" Just to spur her on, as she was staring blankly out the window.

"My Shauny?" Laying butter thickly on another half slice of bannock. "Aye. Fell off his bicycle one night on his way back from the pub. Split his skull open. Just down by the bridge it was. Lay in the hospital for two days. Aye. God rest his soul. You could see the brain moving through the hole. Then, he just up and died. Aye." Lapsing back into silence, studying for long seconds a photograph held in both hands. "Look here." She handed it over, and we leant close together to look. The same two boys, maybe a little older, between them a girl. Smug faced, eyes popping even then, hair a mass of curls just like her brother only much darker. A much, much better photo. Harry looked from it to me,

"Like peas in a pod," he wondered. The other boy's face was very clear. His skin looked very white and there seemed to be an almost total lack of colour in the eyes.

"What colour were his eyes, Gran?"

"Blue they were. Aye. But very light, very fey. Like a changeling he was or, maybe one of the wee people growed big." She laughed. "Aye. A proper scamp that one," sipping her tea. "Always covered in muck the pair of them. Rolling round, pretending to be fighting all the time, but you could see it was all a put-on. When they were wee you'd go in of a mornin' and like as not each would have the other's thumb in his mouth. Aye. Rogues they were, but good boys."

"How come you only had Dad?" I wondered.

"Aye. Well he gave me a powerful hard time did your Da, being borned, and I was nearly forty at the time. I had the last rites before he'd come into this world. I still make a novena for him every year on his birthday. They took me into the hospital after and cut me away to stop the bleeding. After that I couldn't have any more. But sure an one was enough to bring into this vale of tears."

"What happened to Seamus, Gran?" Edging round the real question at last.

"Aye!... He went to Australia... Just like my brother Arthur did... and just like him the only word we ever got was years later to tell us he was dead. Aye."

For a minute I thought she wasn't going to say anymore. I was resigning myself to never finding out when she drew a couple of deep breaths. Her face looked both awfully grim and sad at the same time.

"Aye well... May God forgive me, but I blame your mother for it all." She leafed through the photos and handed us one. "That was taken the day he left." The boys in the picture were older than Harry and me. Nineteen, maybe twenty. No arms round each other here, no laughing. Immense strain evident on both their faces. Both wearing uncomfortable looking suits with collar and tie.

"Aye. That would have been in Southampton, I think that was where the boat sailed from." Shaking her head. "Och, they were forever running round wi' heads full of nonsense. One day they'd be for joining the navy, then it would be America or they were going to be pilots. Not a titter of wit between the pair of them. Then your Granny Young up and died of a heart attack. Your Granddad Young, may the ould shite burn for eternity..." she'd taken the photo back and was gazing grimly at it "...he wouldn't have your mother in the house on her own. Wherever her brother went, he had to take her. Och. It was alright for a while. Her and me, we'd do the cooking or a bit of sewing, but she always wanted to be with the boys. Even wanting to sleep at the shore in the tent. Aye. Well I saw to that you may be sure! A young hussy of her age in a tent wi' two strapping lads. I tell you she wasn't right pleased. But then as they all got older I had no control over her. She'd paint her face, and her just sixteen, and go away after them. It didn't matter where they were or what they were doing, always getting between them. Sulking and threatening to tell her Da if they tried to get rid of her. Your Da was fair annoyed, much as he might try to hide it. If she couldn't have her own way she'd make fun of them, about them always being together and all that. Aye, she was a born wee trouble-maker thon one."

I refilled her cup, seeing that now she had started, she wasn't about to stop till there was no more to be said.

"Aye. Thank you, son. Well your grandfather, he started taking the boys down the pub of an evening. I've nothing agin a drop of the hard stuff you understand, I find a wee nip of brandy helps a body off to sleep at night. I told her she was too young, but she was having none of that and down she would go. I don't know where she got the brass neck at her age, and her not seventeen. Going marching into a smoky room full of men. Not another woman in the place, excepting Mrs Trainor behind the bar, and she was no great example to be taking after. Drunk as a lord every night and making a fool of herself wi' any that had the wit left to ask. Oh aye! There's many a man in Ballymartin larned all they know up against the back wall of the pub of a Friday or Saturday night. My Shauny? He couldn't see anything wrong, mind, a couple of whiskeys inside him and he couldn't see much of anything anyway. Nothin' wrong wi' the wee girl being in the pub, he said. Said I was narrow-minded and a scandal-monger, just like the rest of the wimmin."

She was rubbing the photo with her thumbs, tea forgotten.

"Aye well," she sighed. "I let it go. May the good God forgive me. I doubt I could have stopped it anyway. God surely works in mysterious ways. They went down the pub one night for the other fella's birthday...." tapping Seamus in the photo. "He was eighteen, your Da three months younger. Little madam would trail along as usual. I can only suppose they all had more than normal. I nivir heard them come in, but all three of them were suffering the next morning. She was sick a dozen times. I knew from your Da's face there was something wrong, and the other fella's face was totally washed out, he looked more like a ghost than ever. Aye. Well the two of them went home after Mass and we didn't see either of them till the Thursday or maybe it was the Friday mornin' Seamus turned up at the door and said he was off to Belfast, to the Australia office, he was going to emigrate! I could see by my fella's face that there was no point in arguing. Where one went, so would the other, and though it broke my heart to know that he would go, I didn't try to stop him. They got their sailing papers or whatever about a month later, though they would have to wait about four months for a boat. Your granddad and me, we had to sign papers to say that he could go, what with him being under twenty-one and all. God, I dreaded the day coming when they would leave."

She took her glasses off and rubbed her eyes.

"It was the mornin' after their papers came, your Granddad Young, he came bursting through the door yelling his head off, saying it was all my fault, mine and your granddad's for taking her down the pub. She was pregnant! Your granddad was nearly as bad, both of them shouting at my wee son. Just out of his bed, so he was, sitting by the range. When he saw me looking at him he just smiled and shook his head. Then he started shouting back at the two ould men. 'Well then, I'll marry her. That's what she wants, isn't it?' and again, 'It's what you want too, so just effing shut up'. They didn't shut up of course, but it took the wind out of their sails and that was how it was settled. The two ould men went down the road to get drunk and I asked him if it was true, was it *his* child she was carrying? Your Da laughed, but I could see his heart wasn't in it. 'She says it is. Just leave it at that, Ma.' He wouldn't say another word about it. Seamus turned up very down in the mouth and the pair of them took themselves off God knows where."

She raised her old head from studying the photograph and stared out the window for a while. We kept silent. I was totally involved in the story she was telling, Harry was holding my hand almost painfully tightly under the table.

"They were married six weeks from that day and I nivir saw nor wanted to see that wee girl from the day and hour they walked out of St Joseph's. Aye, but there was a fine scandal, whispering behind hands and all the rest of it. But like everything else it was a nine-day wonder. Then, aye, then came the day they were due to leave for Australia." Covering the picture with both her hands. "They both turned up at my door... just as you see them here. I thought he was going to go after all and my heart was glad. But one look at their two faces and I knew I was wrong. They left for England on the quarter to six bus and for a week I prayed every day and every night that he would go, that he wouldn't come back. When I did see him at my door, I lost my temper with my son for the first and only time in my life. Told him what I thought of him in no uncertain terms, I can tell you that. Aye! Told him I knew the only reason he'd married her was because she was carrying her brother's bastard. I could tell from the look on his face I was right. I'd thought so all along."

Drawing breath, looking at the two of us grimly.

"Call me an evil ould woman if you like, but I knew my son, and him, too well. Aye. They were just like the two of you sitting there." Harry squeezed hard. "Och aye, I'd long years realised what it was between them. You think maybe because I'm an ould woman I know nothing of what goes on?" She snorted. "Aye well, enough of that I'm sure." Gathering the photographs together and repacking the box. "She was a bitch in heat thon one, and my guess is, when the boys got drunk she saw her chance and tried it on with your Da. He was either too drunk or just couldn't. Too drunk I should think, otherwise he surely would have stopped her when she turned to her brother. Him! I *hope* he was too drunk to know what he was doing, or maybe he thought it was your Da he was fooling with. However it went, she got what she was after."

She sat silent for some time.

"Your Da only married her to protect Seamus from the bigger scandal. He probably would have got the jail for it. I'm sure now, that's how she held onto your Da, by threatening to tell someone, either the priest or the polis." Retying the string round the box. "I told him he was a fool not to have gone and he just looked at me and said, 'Ma, I know.' Well, she had no satisfaction out of him for years. Aye. I don't believe he touched her in over seven years and that must have been like hell on earth for a hussy like her. You," nodding at me, "you were born nine months to the day after your Granddad's funeral, he got drunk at the wake. Your full sister Eileen was born just about nine months after we got the news that Seamus had been killed in a car accident somewhere in Australia."

Holding onto the table with both hands she pulled herself to her feet, picked up the box and moved to the door, turning round before she went out. "Too many memories! Though not a day but passes that it's not on my mind. But you two," as we looked at her, "you heed this ould woman's advice. Times have changed for the worse in this country since Seamus and your Da were young. Get ye both out of here. Go to Australia like your Da should have done years ago. It's not just that the pair of ye are like what he and Seamus were, but it's the fact that ye are from opposite sides in this God-forsaken land. Listen well when I tell you. They will nivir let you get away wi' it." She held her box of memories close. "I know, you think I'm a silly ould woman. God knows, maybe you're right, but my heart and soul tell me you'll nivir be allowed to prosper in this country... now, I've managed to talk myself into a dither, so I'm going to lie down a wee. Make yourselves at home."

"We thought we would do your garden, Mrs McKenna."

"Aye well, the grass could do wi' a cutting." Calling back from her room. "Think long now. Think long on what I said, childer."

I held Harry's hand blindly, lost in thought. Had my mother known what she was doing the night Kathleen had been conceived? I had to believe so. What had she been thinking when she turned to Seamus, that it was a way to keep them both? Were women really as randy as guys were? Was sex always on their minds too? How did I feel knowing that but for a funeral and some booze, I probably wouldn't exist, Eileen probably wouldn't either. I shivered, sure only that I didn't like having come into being as the direct result of a death. Harry got up and stood behind my chair, crossing his hands on my chest, chin resting on my head.

"I wonder how he felt when he got the news of Seamus's death?"

"I don't know, love. It must have been twelve, thirteen years after they parted. Eileen's what, nearly thirteen?" Pulling me to my feet. "Please Shaun, let's not get morbid today." Hugging me from behind. "Look at the bright side. How could you ever have managed to be on the Scrogg Road last week if you'd been born in Australia?"

"Don't be silly. If he'd gone, I'd never have been born at all."

"Exactly what I'm saying." Turning me round, tilting my head up. "You know very well, I needed you to be born just where and when you were. So Shaun, as far as it directly concerns us, it was all meant to be."

I kissed him very softly then rested my head on his shoulder, revelling in the clasp of his arms, his breath on my neck. I ran my hands over his bum, feeling him tense, then relax. "Like Gran, I think I'm in a bit of a dither." Looking up into his face. "Maybe we should go and lie down too?"

"Oh no, McKenna! You are not getting out of the gardening that easy." Grabbing my arm and hustling me out the door. "Come and help get the things out of the car."

We cut the grass, Harry mowed and I grabbed the strimmer, we weeded flower beds in the warm sunshine, deadheading roses and tying back those that were falling over. We trained the little heavy-scented clusters of red ones up the side of the door to stop them from catching legs every time you entered or left. And we talked. Talked about the future, talked about how we were to manage once we returned to work. Discussed Australia with some ambition and a gleam in our eyes. Where would we go? I didn't much fancy sheep farming and Harry didn't want to be in a city. We decided we'd better get a map and we wondered whether there was still an Australian office in Belfast.

There was a sudden mini panic about four-thirty when Gran called us in for tea and I remembered that I was due at the clinic at six.

"Plenty of time," Harry said. "I'll drop you off, take the mower and that home and come back for you."

"Gran, don't leave us any dinner tonight, we're going to the Wimpy in Newcastle and then round to see Harry's Dad."

"Aye. Alright son, I got a wee bit of fish but it'll keep till mornin' ." Refusing help with the washing up. "Go on wi' ye. Ye'll be late for the doctor and you know they don't hang on waiting these days."

"Right. Bye Gran, bye Mrs McKenna."

"Did you take your key, son? And don't be forgetting young Harry, thank your mother for me. You hear?"

"Yes Gran."

"I will, Mrs McKenna."

12

"Guess what?" Getting into the car outside the surgery. "Your Dad was right. Doc gave me a certificate. Two more weeks off work. How's Aunt Jean?"

"Oh, she must be at Nan's. I just left a note to say hi. You are a lucky dog, just as the weather's getting better too. Are you hungry?"

"Nah."

"What say you we go straight down and see the old man?"

"Sure thing."

"Sure you don't want to call in with your Gran?"

"We'd better not. She's not expecting us and she'd only start fussing with tea and stuff. We'd never get away."

"Okay."

We did go to the Wimpy in the end as Harry decided we were

too early. I do love the Wimpy milk shakes, almost thick enough to eat with a spoon. I had two to Harry's cup of coffee and we continued to speculate about Australia, though I had developed a hankering after New Zealand. Don't ask me why, I knew as much about one as I did the other, meaning practically nothing.

Harry was very thoughtful on the way round to the hotel. "Maybe we could take a spin to Belfast next Saturday and get some information on both."

Being a Friday evening, the hotel was pretty busy, Harry's dad was nowhere to be seen and after leaving a message at reception we got ourselves a couple of Baileys, found a corner and sat people-watching. Harry knew many more of them than I did and gave me a thumbnail sketch of what he knew about each, also giving me titbits on the various staff members flitting about. The discussion had turned to Canada (too cold we thought) when John showed a young couple out of the sitting room and espying us, waved us in.

"Another wedding, Dad?" as he shut the door behind us.

"Yes son, but I don't think we'll be getting that one." Motioning for us to sit. "They're not prepared to pay for what they want. How's your Gran, Shaun?"

"Fine, sir, fine."

"Good, good. Well, as you can see, I'm busy, I don't have a great deal of time. So I'll put it to you straight." Sinking into a chair. "My Lass and I, we had booked up to go away for a week, but with my mother on her last legs, we can't go now. Now it was nothing fancy. We'd taken a cottage outside Sligo for a week, it's all paid and we'd lose the money if we tried to cancel at this late stage. So what we've done is ring the agent and told them to expect you two instead."

Harry and I looked at each other.

"Here." He handed Harry an envelope. "That should see the pair of you through. Now, you'd better get home and get packed. You'll need to make a reasonably early start tomorrow."

"But Dad, I'm due back at work on Monday."

"Och, I've given you another week," grinning. "Without pay of course, and I know without asking that the doctor will have put you off for a while."

"What?" I was dumbfounded. "Oh, yes. Sorry sir, two more weeks. But I can't take this, I mean it wouldn't be right."

"Don't be silly, boy." Standing up. "My Lass and I, we had a talk. We would have lost the lot in any event and, with all the talk going on about you two, we both think it a good idea that you should have some time on your own far away from here. And Shaun, I'm sure your Dad would agree, I'll have a word with him when he gets back next week. It will also help you sort yourselves out, one way or the other. Now, what's wrong with that?" Urging us towards the door. "No more arguments now. You'll find directions and everything else in there," nodding towards the envelope. "Away now. See and enjoy yourselves and I'll see you next Friday or Saturday. Yes, make it Saturday. Come down for lunch about twelve-thirty, okay?" giving each of us a quick hug and seeing us out the door. "Drive carefully now." Turning away. "Mr McCombe, good to see you, and this must be your daughter, come in, come in," raising a hand as we called goodbye.

We were both so startled that neither of us said anything on getting back to the car, just sort of stared at each other. It was dawning on me that we had just been given a whole week together. On our own! And at a time when I had been trying to resign myself to the fact that we would mostly be apart when Harry returned to work.

"I surely love your dad."

"More than me?" His face relaxing into its normal smile with addition of an impish gleam in the eyes.

"Well, maybe not *that* much," I admitted. "But I do love him."

"Let's see what we got here then." Opening the envelope.

"Holy shit," I breathed. I'd never seen so much money all at once in my life. "How much is there Harry?"

"Oh," riffling through the notes. "About three hundred I guess."

"Shit."

Reading the enclosed letter. "It's a three-hour drive and we have to meet the agent before four o'clock. He will change the money into Irish punts and take us to the cottage. We have to vacate it again by two the following Friday afternoon." Turning the page. "There's a list here of what we should take. Oh, and some addresses. Must be pubs and things. He says here to see Mum before we go." Looking at me. "A whole week together!"

"Alone!" I added. "We'll have to call with Kath in the morning."

"What for?"

"Well, Dad will be home midweek, he'll want to know where I am."

"Your Gran will tell him, won't she?"

"Och aye, but he'll see Kath first."

"Okay."

"Oh golly, we'll have to be up early. What do you want to do, go and see your Mum or call with Gran first?"

"We'd best see your Gran first. She goes to bed early, remember?"

"Right."

Gran didn't seem at all put out, except to say, "Isn't that where they kilt that, Lord... what was his name?"

"Mountbatten."

"Aye, that's the one. Now, have ye had any dinner, boys? No, well away and see your mother and I'll cook that wee bit of fish. No, no, childer," at our protests. "It's too much for me and it'll only go to waste. I'll put the oven on low and ye can have it when ye come in. Wait ye now." Shuffling off to the kitchen, returning with a paper bag outlining a jam jar. "Give that to your mother, son. Blackberry jelly, last year's and I've got another ye can take wi' ye in the mornin. Now, I'm up wi' the screigh, can't sleep once the light dawns, so I'll call ye at eight o'clock?"

"Thanks, Gran."

"Aye well, ye'll be in need of a proper breakfast afore ye go. Away wi' ye now."

Aunt Jean said much the same as John had when we tried to thank her, and: "Don't be buying anything before you come to the house in the morning. I'll have a box of things ready for you."

"Aye Harry, your old Nan's not too good. She seemed a wee bit brighter today, but I don't think it'll last long. It'll be a blessing for her when it's over. Now, get a good night's sleep the pair of you," as we both gave her a hug. "It's a long old drive and the roads are none too good in places."

Gran was in bed as we tucked into her pan-fried fish and potatoes. My mind wasn't on my food, what with the excitement of going on my first ever holiday and a growing pressure between my legs, it could have been anything on the plate. Harry wouldn't believe me when I told him I'd never been anywhere, except for two one-day trips to Dublin with the school and last year when I'd gone to Belfast by myself to do my Christmas shopping. He laughed his head off when I told him how I'd got totally lost within five minutes of leaving the bus station and had had to do the shopping in Newry the following day.

I was frankly envious as he told me about holidays in Majorca and Madeira with his Mum, Dad, Alan and Graham, not forgetting a couple of trips to Spain.

"I feel like the village idiot," I said ruefully.

"Don't take it like that, Shaun," as we cleared up the kitchen. "Before we're through, we'll see the whole world together."

"Do you really think we should go somewhere, leave, emigrate?"

"Everybody this week certainly seems to think it might be a good idea."

"I've noticed that too, and, I'd love to go, as long as we are together." I hesitated. "But I'm a wee bit nervous. I've never been anywhere."

"Shaun." Catching me in his arms. "An igloo at the North Pole will do for me, as long as you are in it too."

"That's alright then." Stroking his bum. "But I'd as soon settle for somewhere a wee bit warmer, thank you very much."

He pushed my hands away. "Bathroom, then bed." Very firmly.

"I thought you'd never ask," giving his arse a resounding thwack as we entered the bathroom.

"You know, McKenna," eyeing my cock as we peed. "I think you just might be in trouble this night."

"Ooh, is that a promise?"

My mind, which had been buzzing with visions of Donegal, kangaroos, polar bears and hot sandy beaches (could I learn to surf?) was soon engrossed in the taste of Harry on my lips, in my mouth, the warm wet enveloping my cock and the rising, rising surge of exquisite release. I crawled back up beside him, blissfully relaxed. Loving every inch of his body, mind seemingly attuned to his. Comfort and all-pervading peace in his arms. Kissed him thoughtfully, mingling the taste of our cum. All thought of the future banished in the utter contentment of the present.

"Love you," we murmured, as sliding down a little, I chose his chest as my pillow, soothed to sleep by the beat of his heart and the rise and fall of his breathing.

* * *

Waking was not the slow languorous affair of the previous morning, but coming abruptly as the room flooded with light to reveal Gran throwing back the curtains. "Come on now, childer. Bacon and eggs in ten minutes." She shuffled to the door, pausing to look at the two of us wrapped in the bedclothes and each other. "Aye. Just your Da all over the world." The door closed.

Harry was still a bit muzzy-headed, so I nibbled a little on a nipple before shooting out of bed before he could trap me.

"Shaun McKenna, if you are going to do this to me every morning, I don't know what I'll do." Swinging his legs out of the bed, hugely erect.

"I don't doubt you'll think of something." Grinning as I stuffed myself into my jeans. "Only I wish you'd hurry up about it." Evading his grasp by streaking out the door.

"Coward." Joining me in the bathroom "I'm so hard, I can't even *pee*!"

"It'll keep till after breakfast." I wasn't in the least sympathetic, having had great difficulty managing myself.

Gran had boiled herself an egg and sat with us dipping her toast as we laid into bacon, eggs, sausages and fried soda bread. She insisted on returning twenty pounds of the money I'd given her. Which meant, what with my own money (very little), Dad's fifty, and the money Kath had given me, I had about one hundred and twenty. Allied to John's three hundred and the cash Harry had on him, we were rich, rich, rich.

I repacked my bag whilst Harry went down to Quinn's to top up with petrol and check the oil and water.

"We'll see you sometime next Friday, Gran," as we got a hug each at the door.

"Don't be cooking anything for us, Mrs McKenna, we'll get something on the way back."

"Aye, alright then son, if it's sure that ye are." Closing the gate. "Thank'ee for tidying up my wee garden and mind, drive thon wee car carefully, boys."

"We will, Mrs McKenna."

"Bye, Gran."

We stopped at the factory so that I could drop in my certificate, then on to Haughian's dress shop for a word with Kath. Harry turned the car whilst I went in.

"Goodness! Early bird this morning, I've only just opened. Gran not tired of you already?"

"Honestly Kath, you are the absolute limit sometimes."

"Mum's working this morning if you need to call in for anything." When I had explained what was happening: "Well, okay, I'll tell him. Mind you, I hope I'm not there when he gets hold of the ould bitch."

I realised I was staring when she demanded to know whether she had a smudge or something, diving into her bag for a mirror.

"No, nothing, Kath. I'd better be off. Bye." I left rapidly. I'd actually been looking to see what similarities might exist between her and Seamus, but she looked too much like Mum. Taller, slimmer, and her eyes didn't pop, but she certainly had none of Dad's features.

"Okay, Shaun, all sorted?" as I nuzzled his hair.

"Fine, angel."

Aunt Jean was all set to provide another breakfast and was put off only after we agreed to have something before we left. Up in Harry's room I ran a bath as he packed; he finally managed to pee as I lay in the bath laughing and flicking water on his bum.

"McKenna!" he warned, shaking the last few drops before lowering himself into the bath between my legs, back towards me. I soaped as much of him as I could reach, which was quite a lot, then we reversed positions. After the bath we washed each other's hair in the sink, mine to the usual accompaniment of howls about soap in my eyes. My heart wasn't in it this time however, I was more interested by the inquisitive nudging lower down at my rear.

Why is it that when you get out of the bath, you sweat? I would have thought the cool air would have switched all that off straight away. As it was, we had to lie down to cool off. The lying down didn't really help, neither of us being strong-willed enough to ignore the other's waving flagpole. Harry wanted to try something different, getting a bottle of baby oil from the bathroom and slathering my cock with it to wank me off. He gripped very loosely and allowed the friction to do the job as opposed to the strength of his hold. I was in ecstasy, it felt so ghostly, so teasing. I couldn't take it for long and forced my foreskin right back. "Tighter, Harry, for fuck's sake, tighter. Put some more juice on it." Moaning with pleasure as I slid into and almost out of a tight slippery hole. It really was incredible.

"Oh *God!* I'm cumming." Moaning as the unstoppable force gathered in my balls. "Tighter. Please. Tighter. Oh, please," and cock erupted. I left red imprints on his arm, I was holding so hard.

When my breathing returned to something near normal and my vision cleared, I could see that he wasn't far from letting go himself. His breath was decidedly shaky and a pulse was hammering in his throat. Coating my hand in oil, I teased him a little by running it up the inside of one leg, giving the merest flick to his balls, then down the other leg, before reversing direction and repeating the process.

"*Shaun McKenna!*" as I knocked his hand away from his cock.

"If you don't do something *soon*," this through clenched teeth, "I swear I won't talk to you for at least five minutes." Relenting, I trickled oil onto his shaft, making him twitch alarmingly. *"Now, Shaun, for fuck's sake, now!"* Six slippery strokes were all that was needed to leave him panting. "Oh, oh, oh," drawing in great gulps of air after each "oh".

"I'm going to tell Mum how cruel you are to me," pushing my hand away as I went to towel him off. "Not yet. It's too sensitive, give me a minute." Relaxing as I wiped his belly and fingers, then my own. "Jesus, I think we need another bath, Shaun," as his nerve endings stopped jangling and he gingerly wiped his cock free of the oil and cum mixture.

"Ah, no. You'll do now till we get there." I stood up somewhat shakily.

"*See!* Cruel. Come on, then. Let's get the stuff in the car. Come on, get dressed."

"Umm. Cuddle first, please," standing beside him. "Please, please."

"Oh you! You're insatiable." Taking me in his arms. "Come here."

"Love you, Harry." Arms round his waist, cupping a buttock in each hand.

"Love you, monster." Tensing as I slid a finger along his crack. "No funny stuff, McKenna, this is just a cuddle. Remember?"

"Spoilsport." Pretending to be miffed and slowly releasing him with a kiss for his nose.

Jean was twinkling away when we came down loaded with Harry's bag and an armful of books.

"Hmmph. Thought you two had gone back to sleep." She dimpled when Harry reddened.

"We had to have a bath." He protested lamely.

"Mmmm. Well no doubt you did that too." Setting the table. "Now, away and put the things in the car, then come and have a bite."

"Auntie Jean," I groaned. "We'll never eat all that!" I looked with dismay at the piles of cheese and tomato, egg, beef and salmon sandwiches, plus bannocks, buns, chocolate cake, cream and jams.

"Never mind now," pouring coffee. "What you don't eat I'll pack up and you can take it with you. It'll do for tonight whilst you're settling in." She filled her own plate with a selection. "Harry! Have some sandwiches," when he seemed more inclined towards the chocolate cake. "Now mind, you won't have to buy anything, the agent will have the basics in for you. I would suggest you go out for dinner tomorrow, then you can shop for yourselves on Monday. Shaun McKenna!" looking reproachfully at me and my plate, "that wouldn't fill a sparrow."

"Honestly, Aunt Jean, we've not that long had bacon, eggs and sausages with Gran, I'll burst."

"Nonsense! All boys your age have hollow legs. Mind you have some of my chocolate cake before that gannet eats the lot."

"Mum. That's not fair," round a mouthful of cake, lips flecked with cream.

"And don't speak with your mouth full."

"Mum!"

Between us we made surprisingly large inroads before I, for one, had to refuse another bun. I was absolutely stuffed.

"Aye well, let me wrap these for you, then you'd better be getting under way. Just leave the dishes," as she rose. Within five minutes a box of food joined the bags and books on the back seat. Jean gave us a hug apiece. "Did you pack your toothbrush and washing things?"

"Yes Mum, yes Aunt Jean."

"Aye well, away with you then. Have a safe journey, oh, and there's a wee something for you in the bottom of the box." Raising her hand as we went to pull away. "See and enjoy yourselves... And don't get too drunk."

"Mothers!" Harry in exasperation tried to wave out the window, steer one-handed and change gear all at the one time. The car gave a couple of abrupt jerks and the engine cut out. I nearly laughed myself silly as he swore, then banged his funny bone bringing his arm back in. His Mum walked back towards us again. "Harry Hannah, if you're going to drive like that, perhaps Shaun would be safer thumbing it."

"Oh Mum! It's all your fault," as the engine picked up again. Off this time and away. I'd given myself the hiccups with laughing and only stopped when Harry made a grab at my balls.

"Hey, hey. You could wait till we get there."

"Just getting rid of your hiccups, Shaun."

"Come on! You're just a sex fiend, why not admit to it?" But the hiccups had indeed stopped.

"See! Oh ye of little faith."

He had made me navigator and I surprised us both by only managing to get him lost twice. As we neared Sligo the sky darkened relentlessly. We could feel the rising wind occasionally rock

166

the car and we entered the town accompanied by short sharp wind-blown blasts of rain.

"No bronzy today, Shaun." Taking in the leaden and ominous sky. At the estate agency a pleasant lady by the name of Norah changed our money. She followed us into the gathering gloom and had us tail her as she drove out of town along the coast road.

Norah slowed down and turned right so unexpectedly that we almost rammed her. "Bloody woman got no indicators?" as we slowly and bumpily followed down a steep curving track towards the sea about a quarter of a mile distant. We ended up practically on the pebble beach, with low cliffs rearing seventy or eighty feet either side. Seemingly buried in the one to the left, presenting its gabled end to the sea, was a small whitewashed stone cottage. It looked for all the world as though it was either growing out of the cliff or being hammered into it – I never could make up my mind as to which.

"It was all renovated a few years back," Norah explained as we followed her across the small patch of tough grass to the door. It had an old-fashioned half door much like Gran used to have on her old house and basically consisted of just two rooms, a living room combined with a kitchen and the bedroom. The walls were at least three foot thick and the ceilings low. Lighting was by bottle gas, as was the fridge and cooker. Hot water came from a gas geyser in the bathroom, which was a tiny and new afterthought tacked onto the back of the living room and practically buried in the ground, as we discovered the next morning. In fact, from the rear, the whole thing looked like nothing more than a slate roof resting on the ground. The only natural light in the bathroom came from a small skylight. The living room had two small deeply recessed windows and the bedroom one. A huge open fireplace took up two-thirds of the wall dividing the living area from the bedroom and was laid ready for lighting. Norah put a match to it and to the two gas lights either side.

"You'll be needing a wee glede tonight with that breeze blowing up. Now, I'll show you where the coals and gas bottles are" – a very low lean-to with its bottom actually in the pebbles. "There's a radio, the batteries are fully charged and usually last about ten days. Now I'll away and let you get settled," wrapping her scarf round her head. "The fridge is full, but if there's anything you need tomorrow, McFaddens in the High Street is open till two."

We waved as she turned her car and ground back up the hill, then rushed to get everything into the house. There was no missing the long black line advancing across the sea.

"Do you not think you'd be better parking it up the hill a wee bit?" I looked at the sea rolling in and crashing on the rocks just below.

"I suppose I'd better really," as we made our second and last trip. "If it gets really rough it might start chucking the stones about."

"Right then, you move the car and I'll put the kettle on, then we can unpack."

13

Half an hour later, we had just found Jean's 'wee something' when we both nearly jumped out of our skins. An enormous burst of light was followed almost at once by a deafening roll of thunder and a sudden percussion of heavy rain on the windows and roof. Another flash and the crackling roll of thunder all round induced us to pull the curtains on the windows and across the inside of the door.

"Jesus! That must be right on top of us."

"I hope the car will be alright," looking at him holding Jean's note.

"Well there's neither of us going out in that to see."

"God, just listen to those waves." They had become much louder, and the breeze had risen to a full howling gale. For all their thickness, the old walls seemed to be shuddering under the combined assault of wind, waves and rain. Inside, the hissing of the gas jets, their yellow glow, the crackling of the fire (now picking up nicely) and the sheer solid age of the place gave us a comforting sense of impregnability.

"Well, what is Aunt Jeans 'wee something'?" cuddling up beside him on the big sofa in front of the fire. "Oh golly! More money," as Harry took sixty punts from the envelope along with the note.

> Hi Guys,
> You are booked for dinner at 8 p.m. tomorrow in Declan Murphy's.
> Follow Dads directions. This one is on me.
> Have fun,
> Mum/Aunt Jean
> XXX   XXX

"Well, I'll give you yours if you give me mine" – and I popped three quick ones on his cheek. Harry wasn't having any of that, and started trying to tickle my tonsils with his tongue. Coming up for air I pretended to be shocked. "Harry Hannah, are you going to tell me that your Mother kisses you like that?"

"Stop complaining and come back here."

"Hey, hey. Leave some for tonight." Though in truth it was already so dark outside, even though it was just six, you might have been forgiven for thinking that night had already fallen.

"Tease," he growled as I managed to wriggle free. "Just you wait, my lad."

"If that means that I'm likely to be involved in *hard* labour later, we'd better eat first, don't you think?" I went over to the fridge.

"Open the Baileys too, love."

A bottle had been in Jean's box along with a chess set and Scrabble. We made a meal from the sandwiches and cake washed down with coffee and Baileys, ending up playing Scrabble for a couple of hours. Later, as I was putting the Scrabble away and he was washing up, Harry commented that northern Canada might not be such a bad idea if it meant long dark evenings together.

"Aren't you worried that you might get bored," I paused, "after the first ten years?"

"You only going to allow us ten years?" He played along. "I didn't know that this was a short-term contract." Arms encircling me from behind, cupping me in his hands. "I'd better make the most of it then," caressing suggestively and successfully.

"Dry the dishes first, bath next, then coffee," removing his hands and passing him a tea towel.

"Slave driver, these could wait till morning, they'd be dry then."

"No. Let's do them now."

He convinced me to defer bathing in favour of the coffee and turning the lights out we sat in front of the fire. Lighting courtesy of the flickering flames, sound effects provided by the storm. The thunder and lightning had moved on, leaving us with the howling of the wind and the ceaseless beating of rain or windblown spray rattling the windows. With the booming tremors from the sea assaulting the beach, the absence of TV, the knowledge that there was no hurry, no possibility of interruption, this all served to imprint our first night alone together so deeply in my mind that I needn't even close my eyes to recall every nuance, every touch, every glance. I put a cushion on the floor and sat down resting an arm on his knees.

"I can hardly begin to believe we're really here, Harry." He started to stroke my hair and the back of my neck. "Two weeks ago I had nothing on my mind, not even sex really. I was happy enough playing with myself and, I suppose if I thought about it at all, I just assumed that one day I'd be a man. Married with kids, like Dad... Mmm, that feels good," as he swung a leg over my head and pinioned me, my head resting on his crotch as he traced the contours of my face and neck with his fingers. "What I mean is, I've never been with a girl, never felt any attraction to them. Always it's been boys who've aroused my interest but apart from Padraig I never did anything about it till I met you."

"I'm glad about that," fondling my ears.

"Oh, me too," hugging his legs to me and undoing his laces. "From the first time I saw you, really saw you in the hospital, I knew my life was going to change. No! *Had* changed."

"Regrets, love, doubts?" raising his feet as I eased the trainers off.

"No. Not now, not one," removing his socks. His hand inside my T-shirt, fingers tracing circles round a nipple. "I think I knew we were meant to be, and my only worry in the beginning was would you feel the same way."

He leant forward, giving me an upside-down view of his face, his eyes in the reflected firelight glinting more golden than green. Brushed my nose with his lips. "And now?"

"Now?" running my hands from his feet up his legs and behind my head on up to his waist. "There is no 'now', Harry. Only forever." I loosened the T-shirt from his jeans, as he was doing for me. "I can't see another future, I don't want any other future. I just see you, just want you. Now and forever."

"I love you, Shaun. I never knew what love was and even though I can't properly put into words what I feel, I *know* this can only be love."

He pushed my shoulders gently until I moved forward a little, then slid to the floor behind me, keeping me between his legs. Eased my T-shirt over my head and settled me back against his chest, my head on his shoulder. I had an arm round each leg, slowly rubbing my hands up and down his inner thighs as he stroked my chest and numbered my ribs.

"Do you really think I'm too thin?"

"No. You're just right, and besides, you'll fill out as you get older. However you are you'll be alright for me."

"What if I get fat?"

"Won't let you."

His turn to nuzzle my ear, trace its contours with his tongue, give it the occasional nip. He could have eaten it right off my head if he'd wanted. His fingers now busy with my zip. "No, let me," as I went to help.

I returned to rubbing his thighs as he undid me and slipped a hand inside the top of the briefs. His fingers tangled in my hair and touched the root of cock who, though awake to all that was happening, remained relaxed and unhurried as he was brought into the firelight.

Oooh, I don't think he loves me any more." Looking down my body to where it nestled in its little bush.

"Never mind, Harry, if he doesn't, I do." Sliding my hands as far up the inside of his jeans as I could. "But honestly, he tells me he's just taking his time and loving every minute of it."

"Rise up a bit, love," pushing my jeans and briefs together down and over my knees. I helped then by removing them from my feet, leaving me naked in the stuttering firelight. Secure in his arms, I turned my head and caught the corner of his mouth with my lips.

"What about you?"

"There's no rush, Shaun." Guiding me with his hands till I lay stretched out in front of the fire. "I want to look and touch for a little, and cuddle every now and then." Laying himself down and doing just that. Sitting up again he moved all the way down to sit beside my feet. Cock thought he was going to get some undivided attention, getting the idea that now might be a good time to wake up. However, we were both wrong, cock disappointed and even drooping a little as Harry picked up my foot and kissed it. All over! It was a strange sensation, and as my feet aren't particularly ticklish, I could savour the feelings without flinching. He drew each toe into his mouth one at a time, lapped the sole of my foot with his tongue, kissed the top from toes to ankle, then kissed the shin bone from ankle to knee, using both lips and tongue as he inched his way up. Cock began to get over his earlier disappointment as the kissing and licking continued above the knee, concentrating on the more sensitive flesh of the inner thigh. Again however he was crushed when, with just the merest flick of the tongue for his dependants, Harry moved all the way back to the other foot. I caught the wicked smile

171

as he did so and cock must have seen it too. He wasn't about to be fooled, after all, there are only two legs.

I must admit I groaned (or perhaps cock did) when again he was ignored, the balls receiving the littlest flick of the tongue before I was encouraged to roll over and he was trapped between belly and floor. The second exploration of the legs went much more quickly and stopped with a kiss to each buttock. I could hear Harry's breath quicken but continued to lie, eyes closed, head cradled on my arms, knowing that he would indicate when he needed me to participate. I heard the removal of his clothing after the kiss to the second buttock and felt his nakedness stretch out alongside me. Opening an eye I looked at him, propped on an elbow, his hardness pressed to my thigh.

"Hi, beautiful."

"Hush, love."

His hand glided smoothly all over my back and down to my arse. His lips and tongue followed its path down my spine and on right on into my crack. If I yelped at the first tentative touch of the tongue on my hole, cock positively screamed. My hole snapped so tight I thought I might never shit again.

"Jesus, Harry! What are you doing?" Jerking up onto my elbows and twisting my head to look back at him.

"Now just lie down and be quiet," pushing firmly on my back. "This was your idea. Remember?"

"Well, I can't promise to be quiet if you do that again." I lay back down. He parted my legs to kneel between them, a hand on each buttock. "Cock will get spitting mad in a minute," I warned, tensing as I felt the gentle wind of his breath on my cheeks.

"Don't worry about it, I'm sure he has plenty more for later."

There was no question of tentativeness this time. Straight in with a broad-tongued lapping right on the fissure. I was jerking and howling in seconds. I tried to relax, but my whole arse tensed automatically, though all to no avail. Strong hands held my cheeks apart and the tongue would have its way. Now broad and lapping, now pointed and probing, seeking a way through. Lips clamped tight to me, sucking hard as the tip narrowed and burrowed like a rabbit excavating a new hole.

"Harry! Jesus. I'm cumming," I screamed, but there was no let-up on the assault on my arse, and cock exploded with a force that left me totally breathless, extra strength engendered by that hot wet tip trying to screw itself into my hole.

Then my arse was twitching to the assault of nothing but air.

172

I looked over my shoulder to see him kneeling between my legs, eyes tightly closed, fist flying. Reaching back, I took his free hand in mine, interlocking fingers and holding tight as he reached his climax.

"Oh yeah. Oh yeah." Eyes snapping open as he drenched my back and arse. "Oh yeah... Shit, I'm buggered." Laying himself down on my back and sliding his arms under mine. Blowing hard and the sweat dripping from his nose.

"Jesus, Harry. That was wild." I struggled slightly under him. "Let me turn over."

"Oooh, that's better," as he subsided on my chest and I could get my arms round him, his head over my heart, ear pressed to my breast.

"Shit, Shaun," he murmured. "You having a heart attack?"

"You should have been listening when I came."

"Nah. Too busy for minor details."

"Harry Hannah, you do that again and I'll probably explode."

"Didn't you like it?"

"Like it! You nearly drove me crazy."

"Oh goody."

"Listen Harry, you've got to promise me something."

"What?"

"Not more than three times a day. Okay?"

"Okay," giggling. "What did it feel like?"

"You just wait till I get my breath back and cock gets over the shock. I'll show you just what it feels like."

"Oh goody." Raising his head, grinning into my face and reaching round to give poor old limp cock a squeeze. "Do you think there's any danger that that might be soon?" All innocence.

I rolled him off me. "You great fat lump. First you nearly gave me heart failure. Then you try and crush me to death. Now you want things to happen to a timetable!" I smacked his arse, hard.

"Yeow. What was that for?" Standing up and rubbing his cheek.

"For making me cum too quick." Kissing his nose and smacking the other cheek lightly.

"Oooh, just you wait McKenna," as I dodged out of his way round the sofa. "I'll tell Mum how you beat me." Heading towards the bathroom, a protective hand on both cheeks.

"Harry!"

"What now?"

"Don't clean up." His cock twitched a little. I smiled.

"Okay, I'll just have a pee and clean my teeth. Does this mean we aren't having a bath tonight?"

"Yeah. I want to be able to taste and smell you as well as touch and see. Leave it till morning."

"Mmugh." Sounds of tooth brushing and the toilet flushing.

* * *

"Go on. I'll make coffee when the kettle boils," giving me a minty kiss and, dropping to his knees, bestowing one on cock as well. "Go *on* then."

He made the coffee, poked up the dying fire and placed all the cushions from the sofa on the floor. We sat together watching the little blue and yellow gas jets from the coals erupting like miniature volcanoes, sipping coffee and Baileys. Finished, he washed and dried the glasses and mugs. I put the cushions back and placed the wire-mesh guard in front of the fire, then lit the little oil lamp that provided the only illumination in the bedroom.

"Fire safe enough, you think?"

"Yes, it'll be okay." Lighting our way through the door into the coolness of the bedroom.

"Did you put the bar in the door?"

"Shaun! Who on earth do you think is going to be coming down here on a night like this?"

"Just asking."

He placed the lamp by the window where it gave about as much light as two candles, soft, mellow and warming. We could almost have been transported back in time, most of what little furniture there was looked very old, heavy and dark. The wood seemed to have a glow. The walls were lumpy, coated with plaster and yellow wash, the ceiling very low, painted white between four huge brown beams. With the door to the living room closed it seemed quieter here, though the thud of the breakers was somehow more noticeable.

Harry stretched out on his tummy, arms under the pillow, green eyes flashing at me. "Leave it for a while, Shaun," as I went to blow out the light. "Come and cuddle."

I stood by the bedside drinking in the sheen on his skin in the golden light until he lost patience, reached out and tugged on cock. "Come on." Cock thought he'd been uprooted and promptly went into full retreat. I yelped and smacked his arse. Within seconds a full-scale wrestling match developed; inevitably, I lost. Flat on my back, arms pinioned above my head, his weight on my stomach.

174

"Big bully." Struggling to regain my breath.

"Kiss my arse," grinning.

"I will. I will." Cock had quite forgotten the insult and was trying to nudge his way between Harry's legs with considerable force.

"Now?"

"You'll have to let go then."

"You promise, no more fighting?"

"Umm, I'm not promising anything."

"Oh, *you*. Okay then." Sliding off my tummy onto his belly beside me on the bed, one half-open green eye watching as I raised my hand as though to smack him again.

"Shaun!" warningly. So I brought it down gently on his hair. "Mmm," as I stroked the length of his back.

Leaning over I kissed his ear, then his neck and shoulders. He gave a little shiver as I followed the indentation between the shoulderblades with my tongue, savouring the faint saltiness and clean body odour all the way down to the mound of his buttocks. "Move over a bit," pulling him towards the centre of the bed. I nudged his legs apart to kneel between them, held each of the firm globes in a hand and kissed the cleft. He shivered again as I tried to reach his hole with my tongue; not quite making it, he was so tightly tensed. He moaned in frustration and used his hands to assist me in reaching the prize.

"Put the pillows under your tummy."

That helped a little, but even so, I could only just flick the hole with the tip of my tongue. The effort was such that poor tongue was beginning to feel somewhat detached from its roots.

"Sorry, Harry. Tongue not long enough."

"Christ! Do *something*, Shaun. Use your dick or something. I'm going fucking crazy here."

I scrambled out of bed.

"*Now* where are you going?" plaintively as I climbed over his leg.

"Just a sec, Harry." grabbing the bottle of baby oil from where I'd placed it next to the talcum powder on the old chest of drawers. I jumped back into bed and, with trembling fingers, poured a little into his crack. He jerked in the bed.

"Jesus, Shaun, that's freezing."

Ignoring him, I decided, what the hell. Cock was pretty slippery from his own juices already but I slathered oil on him anyway. Lying face down on his back I reached between us and positioned cock's head against his cleft, pushed. Cock shot straight up his crack and ended up trapped between my belly and his back. Another try, lower down this time, he slipped the other way and lay snug under Harry's balls. By this stage we were both trembling from frustration and I was nearing the point of not being able to hold back.

"*Fuck, Fuck, Fuck!* Jesus, I can't stand this. *Do something, Shaun.* Anything for Christ's sake." Almost weeping into the bedclothes.

"Right! Up on your knees," tugging at his waist. "No. Keep your head down." I knelt behind him looking at the globes of his arse. Taking cock firmly in hand, I pushed gently into his crack.

"Oh God... I can feel you... Right there, that's it... push, *push!*"

Cock's head felt as if it was being slowly crushed between two bolts of warm wet velvet. I didn't know quite how far I should go with this, I didn't want to hurt him and I wasn't sure that he had intended for us to do this. So I stopped. He almost cried:

"No! Don't stop *now*" and thrust himself back against me. Something amazingly tight, warm and velvety slowly gave way. Cock's head was inside him! I will never be able to give an adequate description of that first fuck. Who could? The sheer *warmth* of him. The tightness, and yet, the slow yielding of his flesh. That smooth, total, all-round embrace which *pulsed!*

"Oh God. Oh God!" He *was* crying.

"I'll take it out."

"Take it out. Oh, take it out, I'm splitting." Then, immediately, "*No!* No, keep going Shaun. Keep going. *Oh God!*"

I took my hand away from cock (who no longer needed guidance), looked down, watched in total amazement as I slowly disappeared into Harry. With the pulsing of his insides, I felt as though I were being sucked in.

"Stop, Shaun. Oh *stop.* I don't think I can take it."

I held his buttocks with a thumb either side of cock. Pressing with the thumbs parted his cheeks, and suddenly, cock slid another half inch into him.

"*Yes.* Yes. *Yes.* Do that again." Both his hands coming round to assist. I left him to do that part and strained to reach round to his front and straining cock. With a half-strangled sob, he parted his cheeks and thrust himself back onto me. I was *all* the way in! The muscle around his hole kept trying desperately to close, giving rapid constrictions round the base of my cock, almost like a high-speed tremble. His flesh inside enfolded me completely, giving intimate little pulses which travelled all the way from cock's head down the shaft to the base where it was gripped by the anal muscle.

He straightened up with a cry, half pained but deeply self-congratulatory and triumphant. Put his hands behind him to hold me close. His entire back drenched and running with perspiration. Now I was able to reach his cock and balls, the former drooling a thick rope of clear pre-cum.

"Alright, Harry?" Even my voice was trembling.

"Wait, Shaun. Wait," he begged. "Don't move for just a minute."

"Don't think I can hold off." My voice was increasingly quivery, the sensation building rapidly.

"Jesus, Jesus. You feel so *good* in me. So *fucking good*." Holding me motionless, he pulled away slightly, then jammed himself back onto me. I got the idea straight away, withdrew an inch or so then pressed myself home again. Pulled out a little further and in a little faster. Again and again. One or both of us was kind of growling and, as I speeded up, cock was ringing all his alarm bells: 'Make way. Make way.'

"Cumming Harry, cumming." A veritable host of tiny stars were dancing and sizzling madly in the yellow light. His cock was bucking in my hand and, wonder of wonders, inside I could feel his cum spurting up the tube of his dick past my cock. I couldn't hold any longer. Cock's head seemed to expand enormously within him.

His voice was quiet, exultant, if somewhat shaky. "I can feel you cumming, Shaun," then he groaned and filled my hand. "It feels *hot*" – wonder in his tone. Though he might be drained, I could still feel great gouts of cum spurting into him. My stars were whirling like crazy and I felt sure I must pass out any second. I had to hold onto his shoulders as the last spasm shook me, I was trembling like a leaf and racked with sobs. I was vaguely aware of the alarm in his voice. "Shaun, you alright? *Shaun?*"

I held onto his shoulders desperately, sinking my teeth into his neck as the last plug raced to its destination.

"Shaun, love. What *is* it?"

"Minute, Harry... minute." The threatening darkness slowly, reluctantly fading, likewise the stars.

"Can you keep it in if we lie down?"

"Think so."

Gently he eased forward, using one arm to lower us with the other behind him holding me close. It was sheer relief to rest full length on his back. Cock remained in situ, softening slightly, having his retreat slowed by the constriction of Harry's anal muscle. My leg muscles continued their violent trembling unabated. Poor old heart had had to find a new gear, something akin to changing from two- to four-wheel drive, and now was finding difficulty in returning to normal service.

"Shaun! You okay?" Twisting his head round. "*Talk* to me."

"Okay, Harry. Really. Okay." Cock shrunk a bit more and Harry's arse, sensing it was fighting a losing battle, wrapped him back in his foreskin and released him.

"Oh." A note of regret in Harry's voice as we finally parted company.

I rolled off him onto my back, totally exhausted, totally happy.

Harry hugged me hard and then popped out of bed.

"Harry?"

"Back in a minute, love."

I heard the loo flush and a few seconds later the clinking of glass. He returned with two glasses of milk and a warm wet cloth. Having set the glasses down he wiped cock's shaft and head without raising even a twitch. I was still having slight leg tremors as he slid an arm under my shoulders and raised me to a sitting position.

"Drink this," handing me a glass. "That was thirsty work." Matching me as I drained it almost in one. Taking the empty glass he laid me down, climbed in beside me, pulled up the duvet and wrapped me in his arms.

"Shaun, you know, you really had me worried. I thought you were having a heart attack! Is it always going to be like that for you?" Stroking my back, full of love and concern.

I reminded him of the story of my first wank, the little stars and the almost fainting feeling. "I think tonight was the same. And, like then, it will probably fade as I get used to it."

"Mmm. And who said you were going to have the opportunity to get used to it?" Smile in the voice. I just hugged him more closely.

"I don't know what to say, Harry. That was truly indescribable. I know, no matter how long I live, I shall never forget tonight. Are *you* alright? How do you feel?" Wanting to know, knowing I wouldn't be satisfied now until I'd had the same experience. The idea gave me a delicious shiver of fright. His cock was a good deal thicker then mine. It might be just a little shorter but, would I be able too? Another shiver of anticipatory fear.

"Are you cold? Are you sure you *are* alright, Shaun?"

"Mmmm. I was just thinking, your cock is thicker than mine."

He was so surprised that he laughed. "You wee *goat!* Let's get some rest before you start planning the next bout." He snuggled

178

down so that my head was on his chest.

"Are *you* alright, Harry? *Really?*"

"A wee bit sore, and I couldn't keep it in," he admitted quietly. "But I feel like a new me. Now, go to sleep," caressing my face.

"We can get some cream at the chemist. I know what Dad uses, and I think we're both going to need it, at least to start with." I was rapidly returning to normal and my heart was beginning to sing. He was *mine*. He was *mine*.

"Umm. Go to sleep."

A minute's silence.

"Oh, Harry!"

"What now?"

"The light is on your side."

"Oh. Shit and corruption."

He was back in bed within seconds. Blissful dark. The howl of the wind dropping, thunder of the breakers now a dull booming.

"Mmm, Harry?"

....

"Harry?"

"This had better be real good, McKenna."

"I was just thinking. I must be in love with you."

"Ahh that's funny. You know, I was just thinking the same about you, little goat." He patted my ass. "Now, go to sleep. Goodnight."

"Goodnight, love." Sighing with utter contentment as I let the darkness waft me away.

14

Some time the next day I slowly came too, aware of a warm welcome weight on my chest and legs, the feather-soft touch of breath caressing my shoulder. I lay on, savouring the gradual return of consciousness and sensation. His arm across my chest, a leg thrown over mine. The full length of his body in contact with my side and his head half on the pillow, cheek pressed to my shoulder. My right arm under his neck, hand resting on his upper arm. The room was dim as my eyes opened and, though I did wonder, I was pretty unconcerned as to whether it was morning or afternoon. This would have been my description of heaven.

I lay content in his nearness and touch, aware of the need to pee but, not just yet. Like Harry, cock too was sound asleep, not

179

raising his head in normal morning fashion. I assumed he was still as stunned by the events of a few hours previously as I was. In the end, I had no option but to go to the bathroom. As I didn't want to wake him it took an age to extricate myself from our embrace. But I needn't have worried, he slept on as though poleaxed. Only a low mumble, too indistinct to make sense of, showed any awareness at all as I pulled the duvet up to his shoulders. I stood a long while just looking at his face. Long lashes forming two perfect crescents either side of the ridiculous snub of a nose, tousled hair as ever falling over the brow. Lips curled in a secret semi-smile, breathing slow, regular and faint. I felt tears pricking. "Jesus, Harry, how can I have been so lucky?" I leant over and kissed his hair.

I made my way to the bathroom closing the bedroom door very gently. A sense of stillness all round, only greyness visible through the skylight. The wind had gone and I could neither hear nor feel the sea. Leaving the bath to fill (a process which looked likely to take an age), I made coffee, re-laid the fire and turned into one huge goose bump when I opened the door to put the ashes out. I couldn't see ten yards. Dense clinging grey mist obscured practically everything. What I could see of the beach bore no resemblance to the gentle slope it had shown on our arrival. Within feet of the house there was a three-foot drop where the pebbles had been scoured away by the breakers, and brown seaweed lay thick on the grass in front of the door. I could sense rather than hear the susurration of the water and knew it was a long way off, low tide.

I thought of having a shave after the bath, imagining a fuzz on my upper lip, then abandoned that idea after considering the possibility of catching my chin scars with the razor. I made another coffee instead and picking up a book, settled myself on the sofa wrapped in a bath towel. I was on my third coffee and half way through chapter two when the bedroom door opened and a tousled head appeared round the corner.

"Afternoon, lazybones."

"Where's my lawyer? I'm suing for divorce." The rest of his naked body followed the head and he climbed onto the sofa, putting his head on my lap. "Abandoned in the middle of our first night! Bet I even win custody of the books."

"Well, I might allow visiting rights every sixth Tuesday of the month."

"Oh yeah?" grumbling, and at the same time, slipping a hand under the towel.

"Filthy little beast." Slapping his wrist and sliding out from under him. "Go run the bath, it takes ages. Brush your teeth and I'll make you a coffee."

"Spurned," he wailed. "Rejected again." Trying so hard to look dejected as he trailed into the bathroom. His cock however gave the lie to that, being jaunty enough for both of us. "How long you been up, Shaun?" Water beginning to trickle into the bath.

"Hours," over the sound of the toothbrush. "Fire re-laid, ten mile jog, beach rearranged, bathed, two books read, etc. etc."

"Yeah, yeah. That'll be right." Sounds of the toilet flushing and seconds later I was sans towel with him tight behind me. "Don't I get a good morning kiss and cuddle?"

"You already did," turning in his arms, "but you were asleep. What kind of lover is it that sleeps through a passionate embrace?" Kissing him anyway, and running hands down his back. "Off. Off," as he began to get ever more amorous. "Go on with you," pushing at his chest. "Coffee and bath, in that order."

"You're being cruel again."

"I know. I just love the sensation of power. Now come on, drink your coffee and, if you promise to be good, I'll wash your back." Pouting. "I had to do my own this morning."

"Oooh, you *have* done the fire."

"You mean you didn't believe me?" flinging open the top half of the door. "And look, beach rearranged as well."

"Jesus Christ, I'll catch pneumonia or something. Close the door."

"Not till you admire my handiwork."

"Oh, alright sadist." Looking out. "Holy shit! That must have been some storm."

"Any closer, my lad and we'd have been afloat." Shutting the door.

"Put a match to the fire, Shaun," exaggerating his shivers.

"But it's the middle of summer!"

"Don't care what it's the middle off." Pouting. "I can see I'm not going to get warm any other way."

"How's the bum this morning?" I struck a match and evaded his one-handed grasp.

"McKenna! If you don't hold still for once, I swear... I'll have to give myself a wank."

"Mmm." I slipped round the side of the sofa furthest from him. "I've never seen you do it for yourself. I might learn something."

"You really are being a total tease this morning."

"Have your bath first."

"Only if you promise to wash my back and things."

"Back, yes." circling the sofa. "'Things', we'll have to think about."

"Brute," flopping down on the sofa. "I'm going to hate you for five seconds." Holding up a hand. "Not a word. OneTwoThreeFourFive. *There!* I hope that's taught you a lesson. Now, come here and be forgiven. Oh. And the bum's fine if you really want to know," as I slid cautiously into his one-armed embrace. "How's yours?"

Looking down over his chest and belly my arse clenched tight, tight, *tight.* He looked enormous, fat and twitching gently, a glistening drop of pre-cum sitting in the eye. God! Could I do for Harry what he'd done for me? I'd surely split in two.

"A bit nervous."

"If you feel the way I did last night, you won't be nervous for long," holding me tightly and finishing his coffee. "Jesus but you are beautiful. I can't believe it's been just two weeks. I feel as though we'd known each other all our lives."

I leant down and transferred the little glistening drop to my closed lips, then up and onto his lips. The kiss was long and tender. Cock, who'd been asleep all this time, finally shrugged his hood aside and emerged into the air to see what was going on. One look convinced him it was time to get up.

"Harry, bath," I murmured.

"Oh! Do I *have* to? Now?"

"Yes you do," springing up in alarm. "Fuck! The bathroom's probably flooded. Quick, let go." It wasn't, of course, but the alarm was sufficient to win my release and dampen his ardour slightly. In the bath I washed his hair and his back, then each of his legs, chest and stomach – steering well clear of 'things'.

"I'm going to have to hate you again," he announced, kneeling in the water and soaping his cock and balls.

"Now, now. Temper, temper," I cautioned. I soaped his crack, lightly fingering his hole, and made him flinch.

"McKenna!"

"Sit, sit. Get the soap off."

I loved drying him after a bath or shower. Caressing his body with a soft towel, inhaling the clean scent and heat of his skin. I finally relented as I was drying his thighs, caught him with my teeth and eased him into my mouth while continuing to dry the backs of his legs and bottom.

Bending slightly at the knees he braced with one hand on the wall, the other fondling, holding the back of my head.

"Yes, yes. Oh *yes*," as I flicked the sensitive underside with my tongue. I discarded the towel and took his balls in one hand, pulling and rolling them together very gently, with my other hand kneading his arse. Practice obviously makes perfect, I could get more of him in without gagging. My nose was touching his hair and my jaws seemed able to open wider and encompass him more easily. Leaving his balls, I grasped the root behind the ball sac and wanked him in time to the movements in my mouth. He was beginning to get erratic and I could feel the onset of tremors in his right leg.

"Shaun. Shaun." The breath hissing through his teeth. "I'm gonna cum. Jesus, Shaun." With that, I pulled him to me by the arse and felt my lips touch his hair. His balls were rising, the tremor more pronounced. Both his hands on the wall. Shuddering gasps as the juice welled up his shaft and flooded my mouth. I had to swallow rapidly to accommodate him, the swallowing motions driving him wild. Both his legs threatened imminent collapse. "Shit, oh shit." His hand falling to my shoulders. He pulled out abruptly and sank onto the side of the bath, his cock giving a last spurt in protest which landed on my neck. His forehead resting in my hair, gust of breath rushing past the end of my nose.

Resting my arms on his thighs I let him recover somewhat before picking up the towel and removing the perspiration beading his body. Raising his head up to wipe his face, I was rewarded with a huge exuberant smile.

"I take it all back," cupping my face in his hands. "I could never stop loving you, not even for one second," taking a corner of the towel and wiping my neck. He kissed me long and deep, fingers buried in my hair. "Love you. Love you. Love you."

"Love seems such a tiny wee word." I was still kneeling between his legs. "Somehow it's not big enough to even begin to describe all this."

Standing, he raised me with his hands under my arms. "I know," folding me close. "It's not just the fantastic sex, is it? I feel as if in a way, I wasn't really complete, whole, until we met."

"Mmm. We really are one, now that we are together."

Slipping a hand down he positioned my cock between his legs. Cock tried his hardest to regain his upright stance. Iron hard against the root of Harry's dick, surrounded by warm flesh. Harry tensed and relaxed his thigh muscles, rocking back and forth, just a touch.

"I just dried you off," I protested giddily. It wasn't going to take much bring me off.

"Well then, you'll just have to do it again." Sealing all further talking with his lips. Hands on my buttocks holding me still whilst he milked, using just his thighs and the downward pressure from his pelvis to do it. Soft silky flesh moving on me. Light contractions from his thighs embracing me. Tongue questing in my mouth. Not enough air reaching my lungs. I pulled away to sink my teeth into his collar bone. Only the grip of his strong hands holding me up as, with a helpless squeak. I pulsed and smeared his inner thighs. With a judder, again. Keeping up the movement and muscle tensing as, with diminishing force, I added another pulse.

"No more, Harry," panting and hanging on to him. "Let me go, please."

With a final cramping of the muscles he moved his legs apart sufficiently to let cock get some air. Releasing his hold on my bum he sat me down on the loo seat to recover whilst he attended to himself. When I was more or less back to normal he wiped me as well, first with his mouth then the towel.

"I reckon that makes us more or less even now, little goat," pulling the plug. "How about some breakfast?"

"How about lunch, you mean," following him into the bedroom.

"Whatever," shrugging. "Lunch, brunch, munchies." Dragging on clean clothes. "Come on, get dressed. Or are you starting your nudist colony here and now?" Then, seeing the pensiveness on my face as I sat on the edge of the bed, "What is it love?"

"You know Harry, sometimes I'm a little slow on the uptake, but things are just beginning to click in my mind." I threw a pillow at the arched eyebrows and quizzical smile. "No! Really. You think about it. Didn't your Dad seemed pleased, relieved even, to be getting us out of Northern Ireland? And you know, everyone who knows about us has said the same thing. Dad, Gran, Kath, your Mum and Dad, even my Mum. We are going to get into trouble because of who and what we are."

He stood looking keenly at me then sat beside me, an arm round my shoulders.

"I could say, don't borrow trouble, Shaun, but I think they are probably right. You're right too, and I must admit I'm not looking forward to going back home."

"I hope Dad's back when we do go home."

"Now that you've brought it up, I think my Dad must be

planning something. He wouldn't have invited us for lunch on Saturday just for a report on the holiday."

"God, Harry," turning my face into his neck. "We can't be parted now. I don't know what I'd do." Holding tight.

"Hey, little goat! Come on. *I'm* supposed to be the one with gremlins in his head." Mouth in my hair. "Come on. You've got to be the strong one for both of us. At least until my gremlins get happy." He gave me a squeeze. "Come on, Shaun. Please? Don't do this to me."

Drawing a shuddering breath I straightened up and drew the back of my hand across my eyes. "Sorry, Harry. Really." Sniffing. "Don't know what got into me."

"The after-sex blues?" Joky smile.

"No more sex for me then. Not if I'm going to get like this." Trying to lighten the mood and shivering at the same time.

He chuckled derisively. "We'll see how long you hold to that."

"That's all very well, Harry Hannah." I started to get dressed. "But if I'm in charge round here, we are damn well going to see to it that nothing and no one comes between us."

"Yes, boss." Meekly but with the merest suspicion of a giggle. "Excuse me, boss, but you wouldn't happen to have another pair like that would you?" pointing to my feet.

For one moment, an instant only as I looked at my feet, one yellow and the other white, everything threatened to collapse. My vision blurred; it was so nearly the last straw. I knew then that I had a gremlin all of my own. I could even envision it – small, plump, angry face and bulging eyes. It attacked with all the venom it could muster. 'Fucking wee shirt-lifter, you're going straight to ould Nick. You don't know what you're getting into. You're going to suffer, my man. Get out now! Walk out. Go back to your own life, finish it here. They're gonna get you. Sure, you'll be miserable, for a while. You know you're committing a mortal sin, you'll burn for ever and, what are you going to do when he drops you? It might be next week, next month or five years from now. What will you do then? You're too young. Get out now before it's too late.'

This all takes a thousand, no a million times longer to tell than the nanosecond during which doubts, fears and nerves almost gained the ascendancy. Harry's infectious giggle acted as the catalyst which set the pattern for my life. Kicking the gremlin back to whatever hole it had been hiding in, I joined the swelling laughter, knocked him back on the bed and gave him a merciless tickling. Tickling bouts I always won, he was much more sensitive that way than I ever was. Having reduced him to a quivering hulk on the bed, I dangled the other white and yellow socks over his nose.

"New style, just introduced today. These are for you, get them on."

"Oh God! I can't move," flapping a hand at me as I pulled on my jeans.

"And if you don't want more of the same, you'll move."

"Cruel, cruel... Oh *no!*" as I poked him in the ribs. "I'll tell Mum." He changed his socks. "What *is* for breakfast? I'm absolutely starved."

"Egg, bacon, sausage, beans, fried bread or... me?"

"Oh, pooh. You're just the starter. Mere fruit juice." Gggling and flipping himself over to the far side of the bed when I threatened to start in again. "Peace, peace. No more, Shaun, I'll be sick."

"Oh, alright then. I'm ravenous as well, come on."

* * *

As we ate, the sun finally succeeded in completely dispersing the fog, so it was in bright sunshine we drove the few miles into Sligo town. We only found one supermarket open but it was enough. Pushing the trolley past the medicines, I spied Preparation H and in grabbing a tube my eye was caught by KY lubricating jelly. I was on the point of asking Harry what it was used to lubricate when a twitch in my jeans made me ashamed of my own naiveté. Blushing furiously, I dropped a tube into the trolley.

"Shaun! Here." Waving "Should we take a box?" They were selling cut logs by the box-full.

"Sure. I haven't seen a log fire in ages."

"Do you want a paper?"

"Nah. But you get one if you want."

"Nah, got everything?"

"Think so."

"What's that?" peering into the trolley.

"Throat lozenges for bums," I whispered. Delighted to see him colour up.

"I'm not even going to ask what the other stuff is."

"Well," I said solemnly. "It's just like baby oil. But especially for grown-ups."

"You can pay her. I'll pack the bags." Cheeks pink as our turn came at the checkout.

"Sorry, Harry," neatly passing him. "Left my money at home."

"Oooh McKenna, I'll get you for this." All pink and uncomfortable as he placed the items on the belt. He tried to look as though the shopping had nothing to do with him, though in truth the shop was almost empty and we had the checkout to ourselves.

"How's the throat, Harry?" keeping my face, not very straight, as the girl picked up the Preparation H. I laughed at his mortified expression and deepening colour. Revenge was writ large in his eyes and I pretended to cower away, letting him carry the logs back to the car. I reckoned that he couldn't punch with both hands full and that he'd have calmed down by the time we got there.

"You rotten little goat," he hissed as we left the store. "I'll get you for this."

"What's the matter with your voice?" dodging a kick to the shins. "Throat still sore?"

"Just you wait, my lad. You'll have more than a sore throat by the time I've finished with you."

"Promises. Promises." Looking sideways at him. "Not before dinner though, I wouldn't want to have to stand all the way through it."

"Too bad."

"You wouldn't?"

"I just might." Good humour reasserted. "So, watch your step Shaun."

We were so busy exchanging banter and mock threats on the way back that we missed the turn into the lane. The high good humour prevailed all afternoon and into the evening. I almost beat him at chess, with a little bit of cheating, which he blandly ignored. Neither of us had had the foresight to bring anything dressy in the way of clothes, so it was with some relief that we found Declan Murphy's was really just a pub, the small dining room being a relatively new development. Only four of the twelve tables were occupied, giving us a corner to ourselves.

The menu was horrendous, I didn't know what ninety per cent of the things were. In the end I got Harry to order for both of us, drawing a very firm line when he wanted to order escargots. Having him explain that we were going to eat *snails* made me feel green.

"No way, Jose," very emphatically. "Maybe you'd better just tell me what everything is and I'll do my own order."

"Come on, Shaun, let me. Please, I want to." Seeing my doubtful look. "Honestly, no snails. But you don't know what you're missing."

"Well, as long as you promise, nothing weird."

"Look, how about if we stick with fish? We can't go wrong with that."

"Okay then. Mind, if I can't eat it, you have to."

"Where's your spirit of adventure, man?" looking from the menu to me.

"I said okay. What are we having?"

"Whitebait, with brown bread and butter to start."

"What's whitebait?"

"Give me a break, Shaun. You'll love it. Deep fried."

"Okay, okay."

"And lobster thermidor as main course. What veggies do you want?"

"Do I like lobster whatever it was? I've never had it."

"Of course you will. Now, broccoli and sauté potatoes?"

"If you say so," more than a little embarrassed. "I'm feeling like the village idiot again, Harry."

"Why? There's no reason to. Everybody has a first time for everything. Want some wine?" He scanned another menu – sorry, 'wine list'.

"Don't know. Never had that either. Are we supposed to?"

"We'll just have half a bottle and see how it goes. Sherry before we start?" as the waiter approached.

"Don't know," I whispered, looking at the table and wishing I was somewhere else.

He ordered two schooners of sweet sherry and gave our order for the food and wine. The sherry was good and I took a crusty roll to nibble on when he did. When the whitebait arrived, I was totally aghast. They were whole! Eyes, guts and everything!

"Harry. I *can't*."

"Rubbish, Shaun. Look, squeeze the lemon over them, have some ground pepper and a little vinegar," ministering to my poor dead baby fishes. "Now, go on, try it. I swear, you'll love it." His face was encouraging. "Honestly, Shaun. Please try them for me."

Much as my gorge rose, I had to try them. Actually, they weren't too bad and I felt quite pleased with myself when I managed to clear the plate. As long as I didn't think too closely about what I was eating, it was okay.

"There now. That was easy, wasn't it?"

"Not too bad. Mind, it'll take a bit of getting used to."

"Rubbish man, forget all your prejudices, enjoy yourself."

The wine was sharp and tangy after the sherry but very moreish. We'd finished the half bottle with the whitebait so Harry ordered a bottle to go with the lobster.

"Will you be alright to drive?"

"Don't worry till you see me fall out of the chair. Okay?"

Lobster thermidor I fell in love with at first smell. I just love cooked cheese, and the combination of fishy flavours with cheese knocked me out. What had looked like an impossibly large lobster each steadily disappeared until I was left scraping the shell with the last of the broccoli and potatoes so as not to leave any of the sauce. I sank back in my chair and raised my glass.

"You know, the broccoli was just about perfect, the sauté potatoes crispy and light. The brown bread and butter was superb and this wine's not half bad either."

"Shaun McKenna, you wouldn't be looking for trouble this night?"

"What?" trying to look and sound hurt.

"Listen, little goat... ."

"Oh! Sorry. Did I forget to mention that lobster whatever it was is now my very favourite meal and that your poor dead wee fishes were not too bad either?"

"That's better. Now next time, you can try the snails." Refilling the glasses.

"If you don't want me to lose that lovely dinner, I'd lay off that subject if I were you."

"Alright, alright. You want some dessert?"

"I'd love some ice cream."

"Not want to try a crepe suzette?"

"Nothing more new or startling tonight Harry. Just plain old ice cream please." The wine made me want to pee. "Back in a minute."

"Don't be doing anything I wouldn't enjoy," he hissed as I got up from the table.

When I came back the ice cream was waiting, floating in a sea of emerald green!

"Now what?"

"Just a creme de menthe, good for the digestion."

"Why do I get the feeling you are trying to get me drunk?"

"Don't be silly. We've both had exactly the same."

"Ah! Then you're trying to get us both drunk." I sighed.

"Now what is it. You are not getting the miseries again?"

"No, no. I just sometimes wish I could play the piano."

He showed surprise "Whatever brought that on?"

"Nothing really." grinned at him "There's a piano in the bar and I just thought it would be nice to be able to play."

"Hmmph" shrugging "Eat your ice cream before it gets hot."

"Yes Mum."

"How about a coffee?"

"Not just now, Harry. Is there any more wine?"

"About half a glass each I think."

"Thanks," as he topped up the glasses and upended the bottle in the ice bucket.

"Let's go sit in the bar so that the waiter can clear away."

"Okay."

The bar was pretty empty, only about a dozen people clustered round the bar itself and of those, three appeared to be staff.

"Where shall we sit?" as Harry plonked his glass on top of the upright piano.

"I'm sitting right here." Pulling out the stool and raising the lid to reveal the keys.

"Harry! What are you doing?" as he sat down.

Eyes dancing, he just said "Listen," and began to stroke the keys.

I was enraptured as he played a kind of music I'd never heard before. His eyes sometimes closed, some of the time fixed on me, his face reflecting the mood engendered by the music.

"Harry, what *was* that?" when he rested his hands on his knees and looked enquiringly at me. "I never knew you could play."

There was applause from the bar, bringing a hint of pink to his cheeks. "It was a piece by Franz Liszt called 'The Sigh', one of my very favourites."

"Give us another one, son," from the bar.

He grinned and ripped into a medley of pop songs and traditional Irish tunes, surprising the life out of me when he began to sing 'Danny Boy'. Before he was half way through someone had got a fiddle, someone else a bowron and we were in the middle of a ceilidh. The barman brought us another bottle of wine. "On the house, lads," as Harry sang 'The Mountains of Mourne'. His voice was a very light tenor with a little tremor (I've come to treasure the tapes I subsequently made). 'The Old Spinning Wheel' was followed by the fiddle unexpectedly striking up with 'The Sash My Father Wore' then 'The Minstrel Boy'. He knew the words to them all, being joined in the chorus by a number of voices. The pub had filled as if by magic and another fiddle, then a flute appeared from nowhere. I was utterly enthralled by these new facets to Harry. The voice, the twinkling fingers, the laughing eyes. His face sported an ear-to-ear grin and his whole posture spoke of total relaxation and of being at ease with himself and the world. When he came back from a visit to the loo the girl with the fiddle put some sheet music on the piano and asked him if he could play it. He nodded and turned to me.

"Shaun, will you turn the pages for me?" Then, seeing I was more than a little nervous, "Just turn them when I give you the nod. Okay?"

"Okay, Harry." Thrilled to be able to participate in any way, any way at all.

Everybody quietened down when the girl readied her fiddle, and nodding at Harry, began. The boy with the flute had sheet music too and the three of them played a piece by Mozart, I think. I turned the pages in obedience to Harry's indications, carried away by a type of music I'd known existed but had dismissed until that night without even giving it a thought. I could hardly join in the applause, gazing at him, as he smiled back at me and closed the piano lid.

"Harry! That was... well, it was just terrific. I didn't know you could sing as well."

"Well?" his cheeks pinked.

"Well, I think maybe I'll let you sing for your supper and mmm, 'things' in future."

"Come on now, lads, it's way past closing." Looking round at the call, we saw two Gardai at the bar, each with a pint of Guinness in hand.

Harry paid for dinner and got a slap on the back from the manager. "Come back any time lads, that was a great bit of play-ing." Waving as we left.

* * *

Harry explained as we drove slowly back in the brilliant moon-light, that he hadn't played much in the last year, in fact since he and Colette had split.

"There was no fun in it any more, or perhaps, there was no fun left in me any more," he mused, "until tonight." Resting a hand on my leg. "Tonight my gremlins either got a little happy or went to sleep. *You* are good for me in more ways than one."

"The more I get to know you, Harry, the more you amaze me. Knowing all about the food and wine like that, the singing, the piano." I shrugged. "I feel like a totally uneducated idiot. No, no," as he went to interrupt, "It's no problem. It's fine, really, because you are going to teach me and I intend enjoying every minute of it." I laughed. "I was a total idiot at school you know, couldn't wait till I was sixteen and could leave. I see now, I've done nothing since, the last year has been a total non-event."

"But not now?" he protested as we turned into the lane.

"No, not now," I agreed. "I've said it before, but that doesn't make it any less true, life began the day I came off the bike." Blowing in his ear as he undid the belt. "Do you think we might have to frame it?"

"What? The bike?" locking the car. "We might take a photograph and frame that," linking arms as we crossed the pebbles, "with us either side of it," yawning vastly. "Mmm, I'll sleep well tonight."

"Last to get out of it. Now first to want back in. Be truthful," as he made protesting noises. "All you want is bed."

"Not quite all, little goat," patting my rear. "Mind you, I don't think I'm up to any major exertion tonight."

"Aren't you now?" I fumbled with the door key. "Well that's good," striking a match and making my way towards the light. "Because you'll remember, I said this morning, no more sex for me."

"Ach, that was yesterday," enfolding me from behind. "And, I love you."

"Love you too, my little singing angel."

"Less of the 'little', little goat." Hands descending my front to where my jeans bulged strongly. "Oh ho, my lad. No more sex is it?"

Reaching behind me I stroked his hardness, then pushed him away. "Make the coffee, Harry, I need the loo."

"Okay, but don't be long."

"Same length as this morning."

"Very funny I'm sure. You'd better take the oil lamp, there's no light in there." Then, as I went into the bedroom to get it, "Oh, and you'd better open the skylight, let all the hot air out."

I shook my head as I entered the bathroom. "And there you are, I thought you loved *all* of me."

"Give me time, little goat. I'm working on it. In the meantime just open the window."

Feeling a good couple of pounds lighter I washed myself thoroughly before joining him for coffee. The fire was dead, but the night, (as Gran would say) was 'powerful close'. We opened all the windows and just drew the bedroom curtains.

The unaccustomed wine had relaxed me to such an extent that

I no longer had qualms about being fucked for the first time and I welcomed his naked embrace eagerly. Exploring each other anew with our mouths only served to heighten the anticipation. Again the wine helped when his tongue found my hole. The previous night had all been a bit of a scramble, not exactly comfortable, I hadn't been able to see his face at the climax. So, when it became evident that we were both ready and more than ready, I placed the pillows under my lower back and raising my legs invited him between them, on his knees facing me. I could just reach his balls and tugged gently as he applied the KY, managing to give me a foretaste by slipping a finger part-way in, then slathering his dark cock generously.

"Easy now, little goat." Positioning the head against my hole. "Tell me if I'm hurting you." Slowly bringing his weight to bear.

I flinched, more in anticipation than from any other reason, as I felt the muscle being parted from the 'wrong' side. I really hadn't thought I'd be able to take him, at least, not on the first attempt. I could only continue to thank the influence of the wine as I felt myself stretching to what I was sure was beyond the ripping point, yet was able to accept it with the very minimum of squeaks and very little real discomfort.

"Jesus God, Shaun! It's *so* tight." Face suffused with love and lust. "Are you okay?" Stopping with what I could sense was supreme effort.

I was surprised to discover tears streaming from my eyes. "Fine, Harry. Really. Just too much love and happiness," pulling gently on his hips. "Keep going, nice and slow. Fuck, but you *are* the most beautiful thing I've ever known. Do it, Harry. Do it *now*." Raising my bottom slightly to engulf more of him. Taking his hands from my calves and bringing him forward on top of me, the change in position plunged him to the hilt inside me.

I gave a half-strangled scream: *"Oh shit!"* as I felt my gut stretch. I thought its head must be sticking out my belly button. "No. No, Harry. Stay. Don't pull out." Reaching under to grab his balls, holding him down by the back of the neck when he made to withdraw. "Stay for Christ's sake. Give it to me. *All* of it." My cock, which had shrivelled to a piece of shrunken flesh, regained his former jauntiness when Harry came off his knees. Bracing himself against the bottom of the bed, supported only by feet and hands on my shoulders, he started a slow thrust and withdrawal.

Having his root massaged internally was a new experience for cock. He rapidly decided that he didn't just like it, but adored the whole thing, so did I. I held onto Harry by the back of his neck with one hand and with the other fondled his balls, stroked his root and occasionally managed a finger on his hole when he buried himself in me. His face was a picture of desire and his eyes never left mine. The wine had had its effect on him as well and he was able to keep going much longer than I had the previous night. On one exuberant lunge he slipped out completely, causing my cock to give a little shudder of dismay and plant a single blob on my tummy. Putting Harry back where he belonged was accomplished in an instant, with little help from either of us; his cock seemed to know instinctively where to go.

After that things speeded up; I could feel his pre-cum tremors, his balls contracting against the root. With a major contortion I managed to get a finger inside his hole and worked it vigorously, making him gasp and strive to drive ever deeper. Sweat dripped from his forehead and nose, hair sticking damply. He gripped my shoulders roughly, face screwing up with the final rush to the finish. I felt him expand in my gut and his left leg began a violent tremor as he gushed inside me. I could feel it, hot and driving as he poured forth. He sobbed helplessly as he thrust again. *"Shit. Oh shit!"* shuddering all the time as he continued to pound and pour into me, his arse contracting like a vice on my finger. *"Shit, shit, shit!"*

My own balls were boiling, cock jumping, jerking, triggered off by the final plunge and neatly depositing his first shot on the underside of Harry's chin, before landing the remainder on my chest and belly. Absolutely exhausted, I pulled his head down for a damp kiss, wrapped my legs round him and turned slowly till he was lying facing me on the bed. The effort to keep him inside, indeed the whole technique, was something we would obviously have to work on as, despite my best attempt, he slipped out. Raising him to remove the leg he was lying on I drew him to me in the biggest, most all-embracing hug that I could manage.

"Dear, *dearest* Harry. I love you. I thank you. I adore you. You are my life, my God, my breath, my heart, I am yours till all time ends."

"God, Shaun." Voice still quavery. "That was incredible. You were incredible. I could die happy right now."

"Oh no, my lad. I've got other plans for you." Stroking his wet back. "And they extend for at least the next hundred years."

"*Shit!* If we go like this, I don't think I'll last a hundred days."

"Oh, pooh. You'll be ready for action again in no time, and you know it." I crawled out of bed to stand shakily – we were definitely going to have to get better organised. "Wait there," taking the lamp through to the bathroom. I cleaned myself up and taking a warm wet cloth did the same for him. "Milk?"

"Oh yes. Please."

The night was so warm that we had to remove the duvet and just use a sheet for cover. "Spoon me, Shaun," settling down, knitting ourselves together, to awake next morning in what was to be the familiar pattern. Me on my back, his head half on my shoulder, an arm across my chest and a leg trapping mine. As was also to be the norm, I woke long before he showed any signs of doing so. His little sperms, apparently fighting a full-scale civil war in my gut, eventually forced me to move. When I reluctantly parted company with them (comforting myself that I'd soon have another batch), I ran a bath, did the fire, made coffee and after bathing, settled down with my book to await the resurrection. When over an hour had passed with no sound or sight of life, I decided I'd had enough of being on my own. Setting the bath to fill, I went back to wake him. He looked so peaceful, so innocent, I didn't have the heart to shake him awake. Instead, drawing back the sheet I surveyed his totally relaxed abandon for a minute or so before leaning over to take his semi-flaccid cock in my mouth, slowly and gently bringing him to full rigidity and consciousness.

"And a good morning to you too," came sleepily, at the same time a hand caressed my head, subtly urging me to continue with a little more dedication. "Oh golly. What a way... oh, oh!" tummy muscles tensing as he filled my eagerly questing mouth. "God! What a way to meet the day," as I crawled up beside him, inhaling the musk of his body and the odour of stale sex.

"Awake now?"

"Mmm." Eyes still closed. "I think I just had a wet dream."

"Wet certainly, but no dream," laying my head on his chest. "Talking about wet, the bath is filling, the kettle has boiled so, move your delicious little arse."

Rolling over, he cocked his bum in the air. "My little arse is feeling sadly neglected." Mirth and seduction warring in his voice.

Slapping him lightly, I got out of bed. "Later, love." He made a moue of disappointment. "That's a promise. Now come on, it's far to nice a day to spend indoors. Let's find a mountain or something and then we'll see about giving you some attention. Won't we?" looking down and flicking cock, who couldn't see any reason to defer enjoyment.

"Oooh, the willpower," mockingly. Walking past me into the

bathroom. "You've promised, so don't try wiggling out of it."

"I'll be wiggling alright, but it won't be out, I can assure you." Tucking cock away as I dressed. I washed his hair and back, resisting all attempts to disrobe me. "In the open air, Harry. On a bench or up a mountain somewhere, come on now. Go and get dressed." Pushing him. "Boiled eggs alright this morning?"

"Okay boss, not too hard."

"Just take them as they come."

"Brute."

That evening, back at the cottage, we took the small table outside and had dinner in the open. The second bottle of wine was broached as we washed up and finished in front of a blazing, snapping log fire. After it was empty we hit on the Baileys, ending up more than a little woozy by the time thoughts turned to bed.

"Cuddle?" as I prepared to blow out the light.

"Mmm, please," I muzzily agreed, joining him. Sleep, fuelled by alcohol, overcame us before anything more strenuous ensued.

We never did go back to Declan Murphy's, but spent the remainder of the time walking Sligo bay, talking, fucking and talking some more. I never knew that there was so much to talk about or, that there were so many ways of having sex. The books, chess, Scrabble, all took a back seat as we discussed sex, religion, the planets, sex, Australia, religion again and, more sex, just how much we loved each other, the next fifty years and more, much more. That week in Sligo was our bedrock, our foundation. By the end of it, even our respective families had to take second place to the one which we were building day by day. Any lingering doubts I might have had were firmly squashed and, even if one still did lurk in some dark corner of my mind, it was no more troublesome than the fear that I might be hit by a falling plane.

Harry's gremlins were not quite so passive, but then, he had been hurt in ways I'd never experienced. Even so, he would sing a little every day, I learned to recognise that as a sure sign that he was planning some sexual ploy or other. You may be sure I didn't protest too much. His growing self-confidence, his almost constant smile, the harmony between us, the sheer fun of being young, being in love and together, remains fixed indelibly in my mind. As does of course, Friday morning coming so quickly that the entire week seemed to have been compressed into about ten minutes.

All too soon we were packed up and waiting by the car for the agent to turn up. We drove away in silence, a silence barely broken until we crossed the border and stopped in Newry for something to eat.

"Home, Shaun, or your Gran's?"

"Gran's, I think. Dad may have been delayed and she is expecting us."

"Okay," sounding relieved.

"What's the matter, Harry?"

"Well, I wouldn't be able to stay with you at your house and I still feel kind of uncomfortable sleeping together at home. Sorry," blushing slightly.

"Don't be. I understand, but won't Aunt Jean be upset?"

"Maybe. But Shaun," snatching a glance at me, "though I'd be sad if she is, I've decided I'm never going to sleep again unless you are beside me. Okay?"

"I second that," stroking the back of his head.

"We'll see what Dad has to say tomorrow and we'll call in with Mum first. We can put the dirty washing in the machine." A grin replacing the pinkness.

"Okay, love."

Part Three: Flight and Freedom

15

If on reflection, we were to consider that the events of the previous three weeks had taken place at a breakneck pace, the rush with which our lives changed in the following three days left us slightly battered, dazed, dizzy and not a little bewildered.

The apprehension with which we both viewed our return home received a boost on turning into the yard at the back of Harry's house to find it almost full of cars.

"Oh, damn." Harry swore, braking hard. "Sorry," as we lurched against the belts. "Nan must have passed away."

"Oh, I'm sorry Harry."

"I'll bet the house is full of drunks." Looking at me. "Maybe we should come back later?"

"Nah. We'll have been seen by now. Your Mum will be awful mad if we don't at least say hello."

"I guess you're right," sighing as he undid the belts. "There could be some nasty comments."

"I'm a big boy now," licking his ear.

"Mmmm, you are that," giving cock a squeeze.

All hell broke loose the moment we opened the kitchen door.

Jean was struggling mightily in the grasp of a man who, for one shocked instant, I thought was Harry's Dad. One arm round her waist from behind and the other hand clamped tightly over her mouth. One guy was being forcibly restrained in his chair by two others. Half a dozen more pounced on us and only the fact that all were in an advanced state of drunkenness saved us from a really severe beating.

"No fucking pope here."

I was knocked back into the yard when a wildly swinging fist connected with my ear.

"Fucking Fenian arse-licker."

I was in the middle of a melee, my back against one of the cars, trying desperately to cover myself against the blows. I suppose I was lucky that they were so drunk. They kept getting in each others way as they tried to get at me.

Harry gave vent to a wordless roar that I was only ever to hear once again after that day. Drunk and stumbling or not, a few too many blows were landing. I was experiencing, not so much fear or pain but, a sick realisation that this *was* happening to me! To us! Harry was pinned against the wall of the house being repeatedly punched in the stomach by a boy who looked remarkably like him; in fact his brother Allan. Charlie, who had been the one restraining his mother, appeared toadlike to join the fray, but he'd made a mistake in letting her go. She grabbed a frying pan and dealt with the two that had hold of Graham in the kitchen. Like an avenging angel out of some old tale, trailing Graham in her wake, she shot out of the door into the yard. Swinging once, twice, with deadly aim at the two beating on Harry then, into the middle of the scrum surrounding me. They were lucky (though I doubt if for one minute they thought that) that the first pan to her hand had been one of her light omelette ones and not one of the cast-iron variety. Charlie was amongst the first to feel its weight.

"You *excuse* for a man." Thwack on the back of another head. "Don't you *ever* darken my door *ever* again Ian Forsythe."

Thwack.

Thwack.

Thwack.

I was leaning up against a car struggling to draw breath as they scattered before her blazing fury.

"Your father will be having a few words for you two," she called after Charlie helping Allan, who was holding his head, through the gate.

"That's enough, Mum." Graham ducked hastily as she swung at him. "Mum, it's *me!*"

Her face was dripping perspiration, bosoms heaving mightily.

"Och son. Och son!" and she reeled up against one of the cars. "Aye. To think on it. I should have lived to see. Two of my own sons! To turn on their *mother!*"

As Harry and I helped Graham get her back into the kitchen, my heart was thumping madly, little stars skittering at the edge of my vision. I, me, I had been the cause of all this, my stomach threatened to rebel any second, I felt *so* cold. Graham's left eye was closing rapidly. Harry's face was unmarked, but he looked white and sick and we would both have a colourful set of bruises on the arms and ribs come morning.

Graham fetched a bottle of brandy and, after a couple of swallows, Jean pulled herself together, coming over to the sink where I was bathing Harry's face with cold water.

"Sit down boys, before you fall, go on now." Pushing us into chairs. "Gray, son, get the boys a drink whilst I phone Bear."

From outside we could all hear loud yelling. Indecipherable for the most part, except for the constant repetitions of 'popery', 'fucking shirt-lifters', 'wee cunts' and 'you'll get what's coming to you'.

"And make sure the bar is on the front and back doors. Charles has keys."

Tears of rage and frustration spilled down Harry's cheeks as Jean went to the telephone and Graham left to secure the doors.

"Why *us?* What did we ever do to them?"

"It's because of me."

"What's that got to do with anything?"

"Because I'm a taig. You know it! I don't think we'll ever be safe."

"Shaun! You stop that, stop it right now. I'm sick, sore and scared enough already. Don't you dare let go now."

"I'm sorry Harry. None of this would have happened but for me. Your mother must be ruing the day she invited me in. God, what *are* we going to do? They'll kill us."

"Nobody's killing anybody just yet." Graham returned with a bottle of Baileys. "But you're right" – looking at me through his one open eye – "it *is* because of you and the fact that you're Catholic. If you weren't, well, there would have been a few sniggers and dirty comments, but I doubt it would have gone beyond that," pouring the drinks. "*Jesus Christ!* Couldn't the pair of you have been a wee bit more discreet? The whole fucking town knew about you within two days. Laughing at the pair of wee queers. Every single one of them waiting for the likes or today, or worse, to happen. And, believe you me if we don't come up with something, it *will.* You can be sure of that."

"I'm warning you Gray." Harry glared at him through the tears. "Lay off him." Fierce grip on my hands. "You said more than enough last time. I don't want to hear any of it again. We will *not* be parted by them, or you." Shaking my hands in his. "Don't let him get to you, Shaun. You know what it is, apart from sheer jealousy? Gray always was full of 'if I was you' except that is when it comes to taking his own advice."

My heart was trip-hammering in my throat and the bottom

seemed to have dropped out of my stomach. I didn't have a clue what to do. I couldn't stay here for long and the continual yelling outside showed that I daren't go out. Harry was still crying, glaring at Graham through the tears. Graham had a set mulish expression on his face.

"Go away Gray, don't start with the preaching now."

"But, what happened?" My throat was very dry. "How could this happen. *Was* that your *brother* hitting you?"

"Aye," Jean returned. "God help me. Where did I go wrong?" She sat and sipped her brandy. "Son against son. And sons to treat their mother so. I'll not be getting over that in a hurry, I can tell you that!" prodding Graham. "Take that look off your face and away upstairs, see who is still outside. Go on now," pushing him lightly. She sighed. "I might have known there would be trouble this day, and we only buried your old Nan this morning. God, what a country." Sipping again, her eyes on the both of us. "I would say, your wee holiday did you both good, confirmed things. Yes?"

We both nodded.

"Aye. Well, Bear and I thought it would be one or the other. You'd come back as one, or else unable to stand the sight of each other." She sighed. "And, God's truth, I don't know which I wanted it to be."

"Mum!!!"

"Mum nothing! *We* knew, even if you couldn't see it, what was likely to be in store for the pair of you. Now Shaun, no guilt. No guilt from either of you, you hear me? I won't have it. The only thing is, we didn't expect it so quick, nor from this quarter. I should have known when they sat on drinking, long after everyone else had left. Something was up. Just you wait till those devils Charles and Allan try creeping back in here after they've sobered up." Her smile was grim. "That's two who are in for a shock. Well son?" as Graham came back into the kitchen.

"Can't see any of them. But Ian Forsyth's car has gone. They could be anywhere."

"Aye." She was thoughtful. "Bear was right. We'll give them a couple more hours on the beer."

"Mum, what if they come back?"

"Don't worry your head about that son." Ruffling his hair as she came round to me. "There'll be some of the lads from the blockyard arriving at the gates any minute." Raising me by the arms to enfold me in those expansive breasts. "Shaun, son, it's not your fault." I couldn't hold the tears back any longer and Harry came round to join the hug. "Blame the old enmities and the vested interests that want to see the divide remain as wide as ever, but don't blame yourselves." Hugging us both. "You're only young. Don't let anyone take that away. Be strong for each other."

"Mum, what can we do?"

"Right now?" holding us at arm's length. "You get your things out of the car, and then go and have a bath. I've no doubt it'll ease the... ah... bruises."

"I should go, Aunt Jean. Whilst there's no one outside."

"I'll not be hearing of it. I daresay, they're not too far away. In time, we'll all go, but for now, just do as I say. Okay?"

"And besides, I told you, McKenna. Where you go, I go, or had you forgotten?" Harry was glaring at me, colour returning to his face.

"Sorry, I'm sorry." I felt really miserable. Lost, and apart from Harry, very alone. "But, they'll come back if I stay here."

"For Christ's sake!" Graham was exasperated. "Do as Mum says, the pair of you, honestly one is as stubborn as the other!"

Jean laid a finger on Harry's lips when he went to retort, shaking her head. "Car! Then upstairs with the pair of you. And you, young Shaun. This is *my* house. I wouldn't care if Paisley himself was at the door. You stay! Now, scoot. I've got work to do and so does Graham" – who, it must be said, looked highly surprised at that statement. We scooted. Out to the car. Back with the bags. Upstairs when Jean chased us. "I've spent a lifetime sorting boys' dirty laundry. Believe me, there's nothing new in that. You hear me?"

A couple of hours later, we'd had a bath, gently rubbed Olbas oil over each other's darkening lumps and were cuddled under the duvet. Quiet, yet wondering what to do, when the phone went twert, twert.

"Hi."

... ...

"Okay. Five minutes, Mum."

He shrugged. "She just says to come down."

"Bear has problems at the hotel. Nothing to do with you," she assured us. "Water plant type problems. He's had to move the guests to the Donard and make arrangements for a do that was to be held tonight. The hotel is empty and he wants us all to go down there. Graham has gone to tell his wife... Ahh, that will be him now." She went into the hallway. "Everything is okay," she reported when she returned. "You take the Mini. There's no sign of any one as far as Maghereagh. No stopping now. Straight to the hotel. Graham and I will follow on behind in a wee while."

"Shouldn't we all go together, Mum?"

"Better if we follow. That way, if by any chance you do get held up, we can put the fear of God in any that dare. I've still got my pan. Now, go on, we won't be far behind you."

"What about my Dad, and Gran, and the Goblin?"

"Shaun, son, don't worry. It's all been taken care of. My promise on that."

With a quick hug each we were bustled out to the car. My nerves, like Harry's, were on edge as he nosed out into the Newcastle road.

"I'm shit scared, Shaun."

"So am I. But we are going to be okay," putting as much conviction into my voice as I could muster. It couldn't have been much.

"Yeah! Sure." Very dry. "If you say so, boss."

"I wish we could call in with Gran."

"Now Shaun, we don't want to be bringing trouble to an old woman."

"I know. I know. But, what's going to happen to *us*? We're not going to be safe anywhere. Your house, my house, Gran's house."

"Shush, Shaun... Fucking sand lorries." Changing down as we crawled through Ballymartin.

We couldn't see or be seen from the top of the Old Cottage Road leading to Gran's, until we were practically level with it. That proved just as well, four or five guys were sitting on the corner wall drinking bottles of beer, a sight unusual enough to cause me to look back as we passed. Harry cursed when he saw them, and slamming into third gear overtook the lorry even though we were on a blind bend. There could be no doubting that they'd been on the lookout for us. A half-dozen empty beer bottles crashed onto the road behind us along with some stones, and I watched in open-mouthed disbelief as a couple of the guys stood in the middle of the road making exaggerated wanking motions. The rest of them ran off down The Old Cottage Road before they all vanished from view as Harry whipped the Mini in front of the lorry, fractionally missing a bus coming in the other direction.

"*Jesus!* What's going on?" sinking back into my seat as Harry put his foot to the floor "Do you know those guys?"

"Yeah, Charlie's mates. The bastards." White-faced and sweating.

"I think some of them went down the road, I hope Gran is

alright."

"They wouldn't dare touch her, Shaun. More than likely they have a car parked."

My stomach flipped as we hopped over the dip at the Valley Road. Needle climbing past sixty.

"Harry?"

"If Ian Forsythe was there with his BMW, just pray we don't get held up behind anything."

"But, they can't *do* anything, can they?" needle nearing eighty.

"Try and run us off the road, I expect." The steering wheel jumped in his hands as the little car almost bounced its way along the Annalong straight. "Shut up, Shaun. Let me drive. Keep watch for a red BMW," concentrating fiercely on the road ahead. He slowed to just under seventy as we flew through Annalong village and down to about fifty for the corner at the top of the hill. Even that was almost too much, the car seemed to float towards the ditch on the nearside, stone flashing past awfully close. "Come on baby," driving his foot flat to the floor again. Two miles outside Newcastle, as we crested the rise from the Bloody Bridge, I caught a glimpse of red on top of the hill behind.

"Red car, Harry."

"Should be okay now, we'll make it."

I felt very cool, unafraid, belief totally suspended. This was ridiculous, all a joke, wasn't it? Nothing more was going to happen to us. Was it?

He didn't slow down as we passed the harbour and entered the thirty mph zone, instead, using the slight descent to push the needle up even faster. Braked hard, leaving rubber on the road as we turned into the one-way system, still over sixty-five. Down to a seeming crawl but still around fifty as we lurched into the Castlewellan Road. Red BMW visible entering the system as we left it. A minute later we screamed to a halt in a cloud of dust and rubber smoke at the main reception entrance.

"Quick, Shaun," as we piled out. "Into the sitting room." We burst through the swing doors as the BMW slid noisily and none too gently into the back of the Mini, shunting it forward several feet.

The lobby was not quite deserted. Harry's Dad stood behind the desk, and I also thought I could see several shadowy figures through the part-open door of the back office.

"Brought company, I see." Very dryly, waving us towards the sitting room. "Lock the door. *Go!!!*" and, as we hesitated, raising a double-barrelled shotgun from under the desk. *"Go!!!"*

We went.

Drunken curses and the sound of breaking glass followed us.

"You're fired, Forsythe," we heard through the door. "And your share should just about pay for the door."

"Fuck you." Two or three drunken voices. "Gi'us the wee papist get and you'll have no trouble."

"There'll be no trouble here anyway, boys," and I surmised from the momentary silence that the gun had come into view.

"Fuck you, you ould shite!" Roar of approval. "You wouldn't dare use it, we'll take them both. *Right, lads?"* Another drunken shout and I began to think, for the first time, that we could really be in serious trouble. All thoughts fled at the overpowering blast from the shotgun. I almost shit myself. Harry scrabbled the door open. *"Dad!"*

"You are *all* fired." John's voice was very calm in a suddenly quiet reception. "None of you will ever fish out of Kilkeel again. You're finished." He was backed by four burly looking figures wearing balaclavas, only nose and eyes visible, all holding hockey sticks. "Leave now and I will not involve the police. Stay..." and he looked at us, then his backers, "...and I'll call you an ambulance."

The one who Harry later identified as Ian Forsythe spoke up.

"Oh we'll go, *Mr Hannah.* This time. You fucking ould shite. Just remember, you can't keep your nancy boy nor the romish spawn here for ever. They're both gonna get what they deserve, one way or another. You and all your guns and bully boys won't stop it." Turning to look at me, real venom and relish in his eyes. *"Fucking Fenian pervert. You'll never sleep easy in your bed again. I promise you that. No matter how many fucking Hannah's you spread your legs for."*

They moved towards the shards of glass which was all that remained of one half of the entrance doors.

"Oh, boys." John pitched his voice higher, but was still calm. "I say, *boys!"*

The five stumbled to a drunken halt and faced him.

"My friends here..." indicating the four silent masked figures. "They know you all well and, should anything happen to Shaun's family," nodding towards me, "or mine," looking at Harry, "They *will* come to see you." Motioning them out with the gun barrel. "And you'd better tell my two idiot sons who put you up to this, that that includes them as well. Now, don't forget, you are all fired. Do have a nice day."

He waited by the door as they piled into the car, then as they pulled away let them have the second barrel over the roof. We followed him out as he surveyed the damage to the doors, the upended planters and the poor little Mini. There had been little apparent damage to Forsyth's car, but the Mini's back end was a wreck. Looking back I saw the four guys removing their face coverings; one of them was the waiter who'd served us dinner. Catching my eye he flipped me a wink and, though his face was dead white, raised a rather tremulous smile. Harry's face dropped when, after a nudge from me, he saw they were all hotel staff.

"Dad! What can I say? I'm sorry." Reaching to touch my arm. "We're sorry."

"Och aye. And what have you got to be sorry about, you pair of wee rats?" sounding strangely cheerful. Breaking the shotgun and ejecting the shells. "Think your old man got where he is without being able to handle a parcel of drunks?"

"Uncle John, I don't understand." Looking round helplessly.

"Aye well. Never mind son." Then, looking at Harry, "What speed did you get out of her?"

"Don't know, too busy driving to look."

"Just over ninety as we passed the harbour," I volunteered.

"Och aye, it's a fine enough wee car," coming back to the door. "I'll away and phone the Lass, just to let her know you're both alright. Then we'll get you settled and have a wee chat."

We had just succeeded in rescuing the few bits and pieces remaining in the car when a big chap came out. "Your dad says to see if it'll move. If not we'll give you a push round the back."

With some terrible sounds from the back end Harry managed to drag the car round the hotel, parking its rear end to the wall by the bin area, out of sight to the casual glance. All the time since we'd come out of the hotel his face had been whitening and tightening, the eyebrows lowering into a straight rigid bar across the nose.

"Bastards, Bastards, Bastards. Fucking drunken slobs! Brothers? Fucking *bastards!*" His voice rising from a flat monotone to a vicious sarcasm. As we made our way round the side of the building, I was still not quite comprehending the danger we'd been in, indeed were still in if we were to believe the threats.

"Harry, I'm sorry about the car."

"The *car!*" stopping me with a hand on my arm. "The fucking *car* doesn't matter," searching my face. "All that matters is us. You and me! And what damage they may cause to that – may already have caused "

Looking at him I could see a gremlin looking back at me

through his eyes.

"Harry," touching the side of his face. "Send your doubts back where they came from. Not for all your brothers, your parents, my parents, not for the IRA or the UVF, the pope, or anyone else am I ever going to be anywhere other than I am right now. Nor do I want to be, okay?" repeating "Okay?" when he failed to respond.

"Shaun," clearing his throat. "Shaun, I'm so fucking angry, I can't think straight. When I think that they were after *you!*" clutching my arm. "Jesus. If I'd had that gun, I wouldn't have fired over their fucking heads."

"Harry, you don't really think that if they *had* caught up with us again they would have ignored you? I doubt it somehow."

John met us in reception. "I'm expecting company in a few minutes, you two best shoot off and get settled in. You'll be in 210, or why not go for a swim? You've got the whole place to yourselves." Two police cars came up the drive. "Go on now," heading for the door.

"Come on Shaun, Dad will be alright."

"I wish I could be sure about Gran," I said as he pushed the health club door. "I wonder if my Dad's back yet?"

"We'll talk to Dad once he's got things sorted," giving me a much needed hug as the door closed. "In the meantime, how about that swim?"

"Okay."

* * *

I'd never seen an underground pool before. It was astounding and looked all of a hundred feet long when he switched on the underwater lighting. Close by a small pool twelve by twelve also lit up, then started bubbling and frothing.

"Jacuzzi," seeing my puzzled expression. "Come on.". In the changing room he fished round in a locker bearing his name, and slung a pair of briefs at me. "Try these, they're getting too tight for me." On his assurance, I followed his example and bombed the still waters of the pool, to come up swearing at his laughter as he stroked away from me.

"It's *fucking freezing. You sod!*" – splashing vigorously while not getting anywhere very fast – my usual style, I'm not a great swimmer. From a point of safety on the other side he continued to laugh at my face.

"Honestly, it *is* heated."

"Well, it doesn't fucking feel like it," spluttering my way across to him. He had a quick thrash up and down a couple of lenghs as I splashed and spluttered back and forth across the width. Catching me up he tried to improve my almost non-existent technique – without, it must be said, much success. I'm nervous in water and, though I trusted him implicitly, I could not relax as he wanted me to. However, I enjoyed his hands on me in the water supporting, guiding, helping my progress the length of the pool. At the shallow end I caught him off guard and managed to give him a ducking, bringing the swimming lesson to an abrupt end. A wrestling match in and under the water came to a swift conclusion when I swallowed one too many mouthfuls and began to retch. He helped me out and guided me towards the jacuzzi.

"I suppose you're going to tell me this is heated too?"

"Try it, doubting Thomas."

It was almost hot to my hand. Climbing in I found there was a moulded bench-type seat all the way round under the water. Sitting down left just the head above water level. A strong jet from the corners was like very soft invigorating oil on the skin, sensuous, and – I realised, positioning myself so that the full force played on the groin – arousing. He giggled, knowing exactly what I was feeling.

"It's even better if you take the trunks off and get closer."

"I'd cum."

"That's the general idea."

"But it would be floating round. Other people wouldn't like it."

"The water changes every few minutes."

"Oh."

At that juncture, the complex door opened, and in walked my Dad.

"Dad!" arousal reluctantly lessening. "What is going on?" looking plaintively at Harry. He just shook his head, his surprise as great as my own.

"Aye well, boys." He seemed to be, not upset, but dejected, even sad. "We need to have a talk, son," looking at me.

"Right, Dad." climbing out along with Harry. "We'll get changed."

When he followed us into the changing room I saw his eyes take in Harry's body, gleaming skin, bulge in the trunks. I *know* I saw a wistful look cross his face and knew inside me that Seamus had never for one instant been forgotten.

Taking one of the fluffy towels offered by Harry I proceeded to dry his back. He flinched away, hissing, "Shaun!"

"Shaun nothing," I hissed back. "Just your back, and you do mine."

"No."

"Yes. It's important. Okay?" rubbing gently. *"Okay?"*

"Okay," grimacing. "But later, goat."

He kept his back to Dad as he stripped before picking up a towel and drying my back. Me? I didn't bother, he'd seen it all before.

Dressed, he slung his towel round his neck. "See you upstairs," heading for the door.

"No," raising my head in surprise and stopping him in his tracks.

"We need to talk, son."

Harry gripped the door handle and I could see him trying to maintain an impassivity.

"No, Dad. If we're going to talk... Harry, I'm begging you... no, not begging, asking you to stay." I turned to Dad. "What you want to talk about is Harry and me and the situation today," pulling on my T-shirt. "Well, we can't talk about any of it unless Harry is included."

"Son, I... "

I cut him off. "Sorry, Dad. I'm not going to be the one left on the quayside whilst Harry sails off into the sunset." Walking over to join Harry, I could see that that had hit him hard. I did not want to hurt him, I loved him, but I loved Harry more and had no intention of taking part in any discussion involving him in his absence. "Sorry Daddy. *Really!*" looking him in the eye. "We know that you know exactly how and what we feel for each other. And though the circumstances may be different, we don't intend to be split now by anyone or anything." Taking Harry's arm, looking into his face then back at Dad. "Nothing else matters and I think you know that."

"Damn her. *God damn her.*" Quiet resignation. I was never sure after whether he was referring to Gran (who must have been our source of information) or Winnie (his wife and my mother). Rising from the bench, "What about your parents, Harry?"

"Same thing, sir." Smiling at me. "We *are* together and that's the way it's going to stay," opening the door for us.

"I suppose we'd better join them then. Harry, son, you lead the way, I'd only get lost again." He pushed us gently forward.

"Is Gran alright?"

"Hopping mad. Boiling pans of water to throw round anyone coming to the door." He chuckled. "You've never seen her in a temper. Much as I could do to stop her going to the top of the road and tackling them herself."

"You were there?"

"Harry's Dad suggested it. A couple of the young Greens will stay with her tonight. But I don't think anyone will bother her."

Harry opened the sitting-room door. Aunt Jean was there, Graham also, eye now totally closed and almost black. John was pouring drinks as we entered and asked Dad what he wanted – lager – before pouring a Baileys each for us. Jean smiled as we sat side by side, towels round our necks, on one of the sofas. Graham looked grim and rather sad, nursing what appeared to be a scotch and lemonade.

"What about the door, Dad?"

"A couple of lads from the yard are on their way down with new glass." Settling himself beside Jean. "Well, who wants to start?" glancing from us to Dad and Graham.

"Perhaps," clearing my throat, "someone would tell us..." I looked sideways at Harry "...just what has happened. We're both at a bit of a loss." I looked to Dad.

"I think John had better fill you in. I only got back yesterday."

John didn't speak immediately, staring into his glass instead and swirling the golden liquid. Looking up he took a sip and held Jean's hand.

"My Lass," favouring her with a smile, "and your Dad, Shaun," smiling at me, "we all I think had hoped you'd be given more time to settle down with what's between the pair of you." Taking another sip. "You know, I think you'd be surprised if you knew the number of young guys, and for that matter girls too, who develop sudden overpowering crushes for someone of their own sex." He waved his glass towards us. "Understand me well! None of us here take what you have, what you feel for each other lightly. But we would do you less than a service if we weren't also to say that the vast majority of these crushes never reach a sexual stage. Even then, those that do, the majority of them end as abruptly as they began."

"Dad! You can't... "

"Let me finish, son." Getting up to refill his glass. "Anyone else?"

Taking Harry's glass I joined him at the cabinet.

"Help yourself, son." He resumed his seat and continued. "I would say that over ninety-five percent of all crushes are an integral part of growing up. I honestly believe it when I say, those who don't ever admit to having felt it during their teens, are either liars or ashamed of something perfectly natural. In your case none of us knows the future, and we had hoped that you'd be given the time, to either let things develop and die or continue to grow into whatever. Hopefully something you could both take pride and joy in."

"I think you'd better count us as being in the minority who grow with it." Harry took my hand in his as John paused for a sip, I looked at Dad, but he was concentrating on his drink. "I agree with that," I said.

"You may very well be right" – Aunt Jean. "For myself, and despite your youth, I think you probably are and we all here wish you all the very best with the years to enjoy it. That's mainly why we are here today" – turning to John.

" *We* realised" – looking back at her – "from the very start that you were going to attract trouble, just by the mere fact of who you are. And with the open regard you have been showing each other, it wouldn't, and didn't take long for people to put two and two together and come up with the right answer." He sighed ruefully. "Discretion and youth don't generally go too well together. Within a week, snide remarks were being made where your mother or I were likely to hear, or were reported to us by so called 'friends'. "

"Aye. And to me too." Dad cleared his throat.

"And not only from people we know, and not just face to face either." John was very serious. "I've had, as your mother has, a number of very disturbing phone calls, from the extremes on both sides. I know these people, by reputation if not by sight, and in some cases I can make a good guess as to just who they are. Never mind that though, the upshot is, you are no longer safe here. Even if you were to break up... I know, I know..." as we both reared back, "I'm saying, even if you were, I don't think I could guarantee the safety of either of you. It has, rather, *you* have become too big an issue in some minds for the whole question to be settled so easily."

"By God, John Hannah, you keep some very dubious company." Dad's eyes were narrowed.

"And by God, Shaun McKenna" – he meant my Dad – "it is not from choice! Think you it doesn't cost me every time me and mine drive up and down this road unmolested? Doesn't cost me to see that my Catholic staff, here in the hotel and in the building trade, are free to live their lives peacefully, cost me to insure that the hotel, aye, and doubly cost me to see that the hotel remains in one piece? In the thirteen years since we opened for business, I could have built two more like it with what it has cost me. Almost twenty years ago I refused to pay. That cost the life of an innocent wee girl and earned a son of mine four months in hospital. I will not risk that again, more to the point, they don't want money this time. This time they will only be satisfied with blood. Your son's blood and our son's blood."

"Dad, I... we're sorry. We didn't know... "

"Forgive me John, Jean. I'm very tired. I appreciate what you are doing for my son, believe me. If I have offended either or both of you please, put it down to tiredness, and worry."

"No offence taken, Shaun, I'd be as doubtful as you were I in your position. But, you must accept that what we decide here to-day, we decide in both our sons' interests, not just for the benefit of one over the other." Though Jean smiled, her eyes were saddened.

"Aye, I grant you that and thank you again."

"But what about today? Charlie and Allan. Surely they can't be... ?" Harry tailed off, a fine tremor in the hand holding mine. "They wouldn't... would they?"

John shrugged. "Charlie docked Monday morning, by evening he had heard, whatever. He should take a look at himself and young Forsythe. Living in each other's pockets since Forsythe joined the boat. Of course they'd deny it, but it's there, sublimated in boozing and wenching. If this whole thing wasn't so serious I'd laugh at the transparency. I saw Allan in deep conversation with the two of them the night of your Nan's wake, so I assume he was in on to-day's event as well." He shook his head. "A real black wee Orangeman we've reared there," looking slightly bewildered. "We tried not to prejudice any of you. I don't know where he gets it from."

"He's a miniature Ian Paisley," Graham volunteered.

"Well, if he's like that at University, I don't know how he hasn't had it knocked out of him by now," Jean grumped.

"Och, Lass. If someone did duff him up, he's the kind that would consider that sufficient proof he was right." There was a knock to the door. "Come in."

"Mr Hannah, Bob and Peter are here with the door."

"Thanks Haydn, tell them to get on with it. You know what to do tonight?"

"Aye. That I do."

"Good lad. You'd better get all the exterior lights on and make sure the chain is across the drive."

"Right, boss."

"Tell the others to get themselves something to eat, anything they want. Tell them not to worry about us, Lass and I will lash something up later. Got your walkie talkie?"

"Yes, boss."

"Okay. Off you go, and Haydn," as the door started to close, "call me if you see or hear anything. Anything at all."

"Okay, boss."

"Now..." turning back as the door snicked shut, "...I'm not expecting any trouble tonight, from any quarter. I doubt if many know you're back yet, and as for today's 'heroes' , no doubt they will go drown their sorrows with Charlie and Allan. I don't think that they'll be fit for anything in an hour or two."

"But we can't go on like this," I protested.

"No you can't, son, either of you." Dad handed his glass to Graham. "I'll have a drop of what you're having." He turned back to us. "There is really only one option. I've talked it over with John and Jean."

"But not with us," Harry's brow lowering. "Are we to have no say in our own lives?"

"Let me point out a couple of things, boys." Jean was brisk. "One, Shaun is not yet eighteen, and therefore still a child legally subject to his father. Two, and perhaps more important legally," looking us over in turn, "a sexual relationship between the two of you is illegal until such time as Shaun does reach eighteen. Three," holding up her hand as we both made to interrupt, "and three, what happened today was at best a drunken escapade. Tomorrow, when the realisation hits them that they've lost their jobs over it, not only would you have the worry over extremists, you wouldn't know the day, time or the person who would turn on you."

"Okay, Mum, okay. But we would like to be involved in any decisions made about us, not just told."

"I'm sorry boys, but there isn't really much to decide." Dad was looking at me. "You either spilt and take your chances, or you leave Northern Ireland."

John took over. "If you were to split, I'd do what I could to pacify the hotheads, but mind you I can give no guarantees."

Harry didn't even bother to look to me for confirmation. *"Never."*

"And amen to that," I added.

"Well then. You'll have to leave." Graham raised a tired grin.

"You always were a stubborn wee beast."

"We were thinking about Canada or..." I hesitated "...Australia."

Dad flinched.

"Aye well, maybe in time," John said. "But that's long term. We need to get you out tomorrow to ensure your safety."

"Where will we go?"

"We rather thought..." Jean looked composed, but I could see she was steeling herself to Harry leaving "...you would go to your brother John in London. Bear phoned him and he's all for it, jobs and all arranged for the pair of you."

"*God!* I feel like a five-year-old being told it's time for bed," Harry sighed. "I know, I know, I do believe you. I only wish it didn't have to come to this. I feel as though we are running away."

"Or, like we're ashamed, or had something to hide," I added.

Dad spoke up. "There's no shame attached to any of this, and, as for running away! Do you really want to end up in adjoining hospital beds with broken bones, shattered kneecaps, or worse? Because believe me, you mustn't think this a one-sided affair." He smoothed back his hair. "I had Father Sheridan in the house yesterday afternoon. He was carrying on about sodomy, and various other mortal sins. You know how he is. I think your *biggest* sin, in his eyes, was to pick a Protestant boy! Apart from that, you well know that over the years he has acted as mediator and messenger for those lunatics in the IRA. His main message was, renounce this relationship now, or suffer the consequences. I was left in no doubt as to what they would be and that was one reason for getting together with John and Jean."

"I'm sorry, Dad. For all the trouble. Are you, the Frog and Kath going to be alright?

"Och aye. If you're not here there is nothing for them to fulminate about, and Harry, I don't for one minute think you'd be safe from them either. What a God-awful country we live in, ruled by thugs and killers."

"You'll have to sack Charles from the boat, Bear." A statement from Jean as opposed to either a suggestion or question.

"Aye. And we'll have to trim Allan's sails too."

"They're going to love you for that, Pops."

"I can handle those two, never fear." He smiled at Graham. "Now, we have to work out the logistics of this operation. You'll fly from Belfast tomorrow evening. We couldn't get seats on an earlier flight, so it'll have to do."

I was bewildered by the speed with which things were going. Still strongly disbelieving any of it, the same frame of mind which had enveloped me during the fight in Kilkeel and the chase down the road. People threatening us? With what, a beating, or death? And for what reason? I couldn't believe it was just because we were 'queer'! It had to be because on top of that we were from different religions. I could tell that Harry's gremlins were in full cry by the way his hand gave an occasional tremor in mine and the set paleness of his face.

"Look! Sorry if we seem stubborn. It's just that all this has happened so quickly. Of course we'll do whatever you think best." I pulled gently at Harry's hand. "Do you mind if we go for a little walk? We won't be long."

"Stay inside the hotel, boys." John got up and passed me the bottle of Baileys. He walked out the door with us and put his arms round us both. "Be strong for each other, guys. Shaun, thank you for bringing him back, and Harry, have faith in yourself." An extra squeeze and he returned to the sitting room.

* * *

"Where shall we go?" linking an arm through Harry's and looking round.

"The bar should be clear."

We couldn't see much, the room being very dark. Not wanting to turn any lights on I urged him over to the window seats, placed the bottle on a table and took him in my arms. I felt his encircle me, a fine tremor running in spasms from his arms down his whole body. I rubbed his back soothingly, resting my head against his neck and shoulder.

"I'm shit scared, Shaun," he muttered low.

"So am I." I stopped rubbing to hold tight. "But not half as scared as I would be without you."

"They'll catch us, I know it."

"*That* is a gremlin talking." I was very firm. "Not my Harry."

"Why am I such a cowardly shit, Shaun?"

"Everything is happening so fast, it's hard to adjust."

"I feel as if I'm poised on the edge of a huge drop, and I'm afraid you will let go. I'm sorry." He hugged desperately, cracking my ribs. "I'm sorry, Shaun, I'm sorry." Tears threatening.

"Hold up a little longer, love. One more day. This time tomorrow we'll be in London. We'll be free! Free to live as *we* want, free of problems, free to be together without fear. I love you, Harry. I'll never let you go. You're safe with me, I won't ever turn away from you, nor deny you. You must learn to accept the truth of that and stop tearing yourself apart like this."

He buried his face in my hair, inhaling deeply, bringing a hand up to clasp the back of my neck.

"I *do* love you. I *do* trust you. I know that. I'm just so frightened that it's all going to end somehow, that you'll be taken away from me. I love you, I truly love you Shaun, I love you." He sighed "God! I think, even if we weren't being forced to go, we would have had to go soon anyway. I need to, I *have* to have you to myself. All to myself until I get over what Graham, what Colette, did to me. What I did to myself, I suppose. I need to convince myself that we're really real." He sighed again, moving his mouth to my ear. I gave him an encouraging squeeze and started rubbing his back again. "Don't get me wrong, Shaun. I know we *are* real. I really do know it. Ninety-nine-point-five per cent of the time I know we love each other, and that nothing is going to change that. But all the time this little niggle is there, sometimes I forget it for a while, but it won't go away. All this carry-on today just gives it fuel, and I'm scared it'll get the upper hand. Maybe make me do or say something that will offend you, or worse. I'm sorry Shaun, I'm not much good in a crisis."

"Mmmm. I thought you were pretty good this afternoon coming down the road. As for doing or saying something? You couldn't put me off if you tried. But I think I know what you're really thinking. You're wondering if one day, a week, a year, ten years from now I'll walk out on you. Wondering if it's just the sex that attracts me, wondering if maybe, just maybe we really are too young for all this." I took his face in my hands and kissed the end of his nose. "Well, you can stop all the wondering." I kissed him properly, slowly, deeply, felt him respond. "I'll leave you when I die and not one day before."

"Sounds as if you've had similar thoughts?"

"Of course. Did you think you were the only one to have had doubts? But Harry, my gremlin was a very small one, about the size of a fly. And, you know what happens to flies that become annoying?"

"Yes."

"Well, we may have to swat yours a couple of times. But you be sure of one thing. We *will* kill it, and sooner rather than later." We held each other silently in the almost dark for long minutes. As

217

we broke apart I raised the bottle: "Death to all gremlins." I drank and passed it over.

"Death to all gremlins." He swallowed deeply.

"Don't you dare get drunk tonight, Mr Hannah."

"Okay, Mr McKenna," lowering the bottle. "I guess we should go back?"

"That might be a good idea."

Passing back into the lights of reception, we looked at each other. I gripped his arm. "Okay, love?" pleased to see some colour back in his face, the eyebrows relaxed and the merest hint of a smile tugging at the corners of his mouth.

"All thanks to my little goat." His eyes glowing, and regaining somewhat their normal mischievous glint. "But you promise to hold me tight tonight?"

"And every night to come, Harry."

They all looked as we re-entered the room.

"Alright, kids?" Jean.

"Yes Mum, we're fine."

"Good. Well, in that case Harry..." getting up from the settee "...come and help in the kitchen, it's getting late and we must eat." He raised a hand, and a smile, as he followed his mother. John stood up too.

"Come on Gray, we'd best check with Haydn, make sure everything is secure."

Which left Dad and me alone. I don't know how many whiskeys he'd had, but he didn't look quite sober.

"Are you *really* alright, son?"

"I feel so, so... " struggling to put it into words "...so, unreal. The whole day has just been... I don't know..." I sank into a chair "..like a bad dream in a way. I'm having difficulty in accepting, or even believing any of it. Everything seems speeded up, just like the old movies, all out of step with reality."

"Are you sure you want to go on with this whole thing?"

"Oh *yes*, Dad. You know I love him, he loves me. I really don't think I could live without him now."

"Nevertheless, you could you know. Believe me, I know it."

"Yes. I know that you *do* know." I paused, aware that he might not want to talk about the past. "Can you tell me truthfully, that if you had it all to do again, that you still would let Seamus get on that boat on his own?" I could see the pain in his eyes before they dropped to his glass.

"You realise that if I had gone, you would not be here now?"

"Aye. And that's the only good thing that seems to have come out of it all."

"Well, Eileen too."

"Dad, I've only known Harry a very short time, but, I can no more see the future without him than I can fly. It's not just a crush as John implied; Harry said it, and I believe it's true. We are only truly whole since we've been together, we are the two halves of the same thing. Isn't that how it was for you and Seamus?" looking at his bowed head. "Maybe you'd rather not talk about him? I'm sorry."

"No. That's alright, son. You know... I look in the mirror... see myself, see the changes the years have brought. I find myself wondering what he would have looked like now... It's over twenty-five years since I saw him and I know that it wouldn't make any difference. Inside... inside we'd still be the same boys that we were then." He gulped his drink. "I told you not so long ago, love hurts! Well, I pray you and Harry never face the hurt that I've had to live with all these years, and all for a lie... You, you have been my only consolation. I've seen so much of myself in you as you grew. In a way I seemed to relive my childhood and teens through you. I prayed that you wouldn't develop an interest in boys, and yet at the same time I desperately wanted you to experience what Seamus and I had had. But always, always with a happy ending. The only thing is, I never foresaw it taking this end."

"But it's only beginning for us, Dad."

"Yes. For you, but not for me. Jesus son, you don't know how hard it is to let you go!"

"In a way Dad, I don't want to go. But I want to be with Harry, and since it seems we can't be together here, I'd agree to go anywhere rather than be parted from him."

"I think maybe I'm a wee bit jealous of your Harry."

We sat in silence for a while. All the time something was nagging me.

"Dad? What did you mean when you said it was all for a lie?"

"Och, son. The whiskey must be loosening my tongue." He shifted in his chair. "When I got in yesterday morning, Eileen was still at home, I thought you were back at work. That wee girl is going to miss you almost as much as I will, I reckon. Anyway, she told me about the row, and how you had left, and that you were at my mother's. I got pretty mad. No, not at you son, I had a fair idea of how things would have gone. I went to the shop and had a word with Kath, which only confirmed what I had already guessed. I was going out to your Gran's to see you, but Kath told me you were in

Sligo. I'm afraid I let my temper get the better of me. I walked down to the factory and dragged that bitch outside." He held his glass out for a refill.

"Sure you're okay, Dad?"

"What? Oh, yes. It's alright, John said I was to stop the night, I'm fine. Really."

"So, what was the lie then?" He didn't answer directly, his gaze unfocused, far away.

"It's been twenty-five years! Twenty-five years, and I only slipped up twice, and *now!* Now to know it was all for nothing, all the sacrifice, all the heartbreak, for fuck all!" Eyes focusing on mine. "I hit her. The first time ever, I hit her twice there in front of the factory, the whole harbour looking on. You know, Seamus went to his grave believing he'd fucked his sister. He never got over it. I don't believe he lost control of the car like they said. He killed himself. And now? Now I find out it was all for nothing!... Kath's father was your Granddad Young." He drew a great breath. "That evil old man... he must have been laughing inside fit to burst when I said 'I do'. *Christ!* We were so fucking naïve, Seamus and me. So fucking young and frightened. We believed him, believed her, and all the time they'd cooked it up between them to hide the truth. If only we hadn't got so drunk that night. You should have heard the story she spun the next morning. Pretending to be sick, going to commit suicide, going to tell the priest, going to tell the police. I had to promise to marry her if it turned out she was pregnant. *God!* What a performance she put on, and all the time, all the time she knew she was carrying her father's bastard."

"*Jesus!* Dad, you'll have to tell Gran. She couldn't believe it of either of you, but I'm sure, she never suspected Granddad Young. How *could* he?"

"Och, son. Theresa, his wife had died unexpected, maybe she found out what was going on and that killed her. I would guess he was drunk when it happened, he usually was, you know, and your mother bides her time, I'll vouch for that. She has an itch which I don't think will ever leave her. Twice in twenty-five years I let her get to me. Thankfully you and Eileen were good kids. As you say, the only good things to come out of the whole sorry mess."

"But why, why didn't you leave her?"

"I wouldn't leave a dog to be raised by her, let alone you or Eileen, or Kath for that matter."

"What will you do now?" I couldn't imagine being able to go on living that kind of vast lie.

"Oh I'll carry on a while yet son. Eileen is still young. I'll use your room though. Kath will probably be disappointed, she'd like not having to share. But I think she might move out soon. The whole of the town must have heard your mother screaming about 'her sin' yesterday. It wouldn't surprise me if she doesn't crack up altogether."

"Dad?" I stopped, then plunged in. "Dad, how could you live all these years without..." hesitated "...without sex?"

"I promised myself, when I married your mother, I'd never touch her. I almost succeeded." His voice was quiet, distanced. "The first two or three years after Seamus left were a nightmare. I had no interest in anything, including sex, it just seemed to have switched off. Always, I was wondering what he was doing, how he was... he never wrote you know." Shaking his head. "I wrote to him at the hostel a few times, then one came back marked 'address unknown' and I never heard any more until he had been dead and buried for three weeks. I remember being surprised that I hadn't felt anything at the time he had died. I thought I would have... we were *so* close... A letter came to my mother's, from a lawyer in Woolongong, to say that he had died, naming me as sole beneficiary in his will... He'd been working in a steel mill at Port Kembla, practically since he'd arrived. He can't have spent much. He'd bought a house, and the car he died in... That was about it... I couldn't bring myself to touch his money...I wrote to the lawyers and told them to invest it... got them to send me the press reports and the transcript of the inquest. The verdict was accidental death, but I know better. And now... now, to find that he needn't have died at all! I'll never forgive her for that. Her own brother! Never forgive her." His head was bowed, drink forgotten.

"I'm sorry, Daddy. *Really* so sorry. And sorry I have to go. I love you very much, you know that."

"I know, son. I love you too." Raising his head. "My life lies in a cemetery in Woolongong. Take my advice. Live every day as though there was no tomorrow. Love him, take care of him, and yourself. And always, always look out for yourselves first. *Everything* else must come a long way behind that. Make your priority each other." He stood up and stretched. "As for sex?" He shrugged. "It's undoubtedly better with someone to share as opposed to depending on yourself. But without love, it's just a physical release. Without the emotional content, well, it doesn't really *mean* all that much."

"And have you?"

"Now you are getting personal." But he smiled. "Yes, I'm no monk. I usually find something when I'm away."

"Never felt like falling in love again?"

"*No!* Now, if the inquisition is over, I'm going to the loo and then, if we can find the kitchen, I'm starved. Coming?"

"Okay, Dad."

Crossing reception on the way back from the loo, Harry intercepted us, taking us to the main dining room where Jean and Graham were placing loaded plates on a table. John was outside talking to the two guys who had hung a new door whilst we'd been talking. Harry tapped the window to attract his attention and pretty soon we were tucking into huge steaks with all the trimmings. During the meal John outlined the programme for the following day. Dad and I would go up to Kilkeel with Jean and Graham so that I could pack. Harry would go with his Dad for the same purpose.

"What about Charlie and Allan?" I was more than a little worried.

But John was grim-faced. "When I've finished with those two, son, they at least won't be bothering anyone here again." Jean nodded approvingly. Following the packing, John would bring us all back to the hotel, from here we would go to Aldergrove Airport. Harry's brother John in London would be at Heathrow to meet us and take us to our new home. "He'll explain what's being proposed when you get there, but you are under no obligation and in any case, I think you should take a few weeks to get settled in before making any major decisions. And *boys!*" making us both look up. "That includes all thoughts on emigrating." Nodding at Dad. "I think both your Dad, Shaun, and Lass and I, Harry, would like you to give London at least a year before you decide to stretch your wings. Can we ask you that?"

Harry looked at me "Okay with you, Shaun?"

I nodded.

"Good. That's settled then." Pushing back from the table. "Now, I think we've all had enough excitement for one day, and morning comes early."

Jean refused all help from everyone except John.

"Bear and I have some talking to do. So goodnight to you all. Don't you two..." looking at us "..spend half the night... talking." She laughed as we both blushed. "Go on with you!"

At the top of the stairs we said goodnight to Dad and Graham as they turned for their adjoining single rooms. Dad muttered something and, when I stopped to ask what, very neatly gave me a dead arm. "For earlier," he chortled, moving smartly off – leaving me dumbfounded, Graham looking puzzled and Harry giggling madly. "I'll see *you* in the morning," I called after him

16

Graham came in to call us next morning, and by the wistful expression on his face, I gathered he had been in the room for some time before I eventually swam into the light. We were in our usual morning cuddle.

"Better wake him. Breakfast in an hour." He left.

Jean was twinkling away as usual when we wandered down late. "I trust you both slept well?" Eyeing Harry, who didn't even bother to try and hide a jaw-cracking yawn.

"Like logs, Aunt Jean." For both of us.

"Mmm. Well, sit down. Get some fresh coffee inside you. I'll get your breakfast."

Dad looked decidedly under the weather, Graham was glumly stabbing a sausage to death and John was his usual imperturbable self. Harry woke up enough after the first cup of coffee to ask, "Who are we flying with, Dad?"

"British Midland, leaving Belfast at seven-thirty this evening, that will put you in London about twenty to nine."

"Looking forward to your first flight, son?"

"I think so, Dad, but I'm glad I won't be on my own."

Harry grinned at me.

* * *

The front of our house was a mess. I couldn't get over it. There was yellow-orange paint all over the walls and windows. I felt my face burn when I made out the word 'queer' daubed across my window. Jean tut-tutted and said to Dad, "You see? I think we made the right decision after all, and not a day too soon by the looks of things."

"Will we be alright?" I was worried about Harry even though he was with his dad.

"Don't worry, son. See the police car up the road? John had a word, they'll stay till we leave and Jean, you were both right, I'm sorry to say. Well, see you in a couple of hours." Dad waited till Jean and Graham drove off before giving full vent to his feelings.

"Fucking cowardly bastards! Great strong men when they're in a bunch. No doubt covered from head to toe so that no one recognised them. If they've harmed one hair of the girls' heads... "

Inside we found a note on the fireplace.

> Eileen and me at Gran's.
> We are OK. Love Kath.
> PS Mum in Kennedy's.
> Good luck.

No one seemed to have entered the house, they had been content this time to throw paint around.

"Nothing to be worrying yourself about, son," Dad replied when I apologised for all the trouble I was bringing him. "And don't you be worrying about us. You know how much I wish you could stay, but they'll leave us alone once you've gone."

I was standing in my room for the last time, looking helplessly at my books, when he appeared with a couple of large suitcases.

"Those are Kath's, she'll go mad."

"Not this time, son. Now, pack all your clothes, don't worry about your books and things. I'll pack those and have them shipped over with Harry's. John and I, well, actually Jean suggested it."

"Good for Aunt Jean."

Watching my rough and ready methods of packing made him sigh and send me to make coffee. So I ended up watching as he folded, smoothed and filled the suitcases. Then he gave me an envelope.

"I know Harry has plenty of money. No, don't open it now. Put it in an inside pocket and on Monday, I want your promise that you'll go to a bank. Harry's brother will take you. Open an account and Shaun, don't blow it, son."

Packing completed, we sat in the living room waiting for John and Harry.

"Shaun, I know you're growing up fast. In many ways you're more mature than I was at your age. But son, I worry about you going to London."

"We'll be alright, Dad." I was panicking inside. The thought of leaving the old familiar life. Fear of the new. No time to get accustomed to the idea of change. Oh, I *wanted* to go, was longing to be gone. But at the same time, a feeling of fright at the imminent and complete change now thrust upon me had settled in my stomach.

"Oh I know I'm probably worrying without cause, but do be careful son, don't get involved with drugs."

"Dad! Honestly!"

"I know, I know. But remember what I said. It's too easy. Before you know it you could be in worse trouble."

"Come *on*, Dad. You know we hardly even drink. I wouldn't know what a drug was."

"You'll find out soon enough in London I expect. They won't make things any better between you and Harry. That I *can* tell you. Anyway Shaun, as I said, you'll soon be a grown man. You must decide these things for yourself." Taking the mugs to the kitchen he made more coffee. "Harry has come to depend on you a great deal. Am I right?"

"Well yes, sometimes. We depend on each other really."

"John and Jean told me a few things about him. The problems with him and Graham, and that wee girl he had been seeing. You know about that?"

"Yes, Dad. He told me all of it."

"It would seem they've been pretty worried about him this last year or so. Do you think he is going to be alright?"

"Yes Dad, I do." Positively.

"I think you'll find that Jean is placing a lot of trust in you to look out for him as well as yourself. It wouldn't surprise me if she doesn't have a quiet word with you before you go."

"That's alright, Dad. You know he comes first in every way."

"Aye. Well son, just take care of yourselves." Reaching over to pat my knee. "I'll get the phone in so as I can call you. Eileen, and Kath if she's still here, will want to hear your voice occasionally."

"Are we calling with Gran?" Sudden pang as I realised that I might never see her again.

"Och, aye. We'll spend a wee while with her and the girls on the way down the road."

There came the sound of an engine and a couple of toots on the horn.

"Well son," and he hugged me hard as we stood up, kissed the top of my head.

I hugged just as hard, my voice shaky. "I think I'm due another dead arm."

"Aye well, maybe later." Releasing me. "Come on, we'll take one each." Hefting a suitcase, I followed him out through the gate to where a Ford Galaxy sat idling, John standing by the open rear door. There was of course a furious twitching of lace curtains all round. A number of doors opened as the curious, the idle and the downright evil came out to look on.

Kennedy's front door flew open, banging off the wall.

"Look at my good fucking wee house!!" Mother shrieking, spittle flying and the eyes bulging dangerously as she stormed down the path and across the road. *"You shit- licking wee pervert! I telt you, did I not tell you nivir to set foot in it again? Spawn of the fucking divil! That's what you are."*

I put a hand on Dad's arm as he went to intercept her. "Don't, Dad. That's just what she wants you to do."

Stopping a few feet away she licked the spittle from her mouth and sneered with evident satisfaction.

"Och *aye*! Father and son, is it? Well, your fancy friends, their fancy cars and the polis sitting up the road! They don't impress me one wee bit, so they don't." Hugging herself with delight and crowing. "I telt you what was coming. Didn't I? Didn't I? Aye, I did that, and don't you go thinking it's over, my man. Oh no. You'll live to rue the day you first drew breath. Aye, that you will, see if I'm not right." She recognised the suitcases. "Where the fuck do you think you're going with them? Put them back this minute. You hear me? Fucking thieving wee bastard. You hear me?"

I moved to block her as she tried to grab a case.

"I'll have the polis on the lot of ye. Fucking orange scum!"

"Shut up! You lying vindictive bitch." I surprised myself as much as her by the intensity of my anger. "You want me out? Well, I'm out, and I hope to God I never set eyes on you again. Okay?"

She cackled. "Aye, aye! That'll be right. It's fine thanks I'm getting for the pain of borning ye, and the years of scrimping to raise ye. Didn't take long, did it, for your fancy 'friends' to turn a mother's son against her?"

"Oh no. *You* managed that all by yourself."

"I'd have been a damn sight better off dropping ye on yer head the day ye were borned, and what are you going to do about my good wee fucking house? *Eh! Eh!*" Eyes narrowing over my left shoulder.

I felt an arm circle my waist. Harry, bless him.

"Och look!!" No doubt this will be the other wee shirt-lifter. Don't the pair of ye look sweet?" Recrossing her arms, hugging herself.

Harry's arm tightened fractionally as he felt me tense.

"Not much to look at, either of ye. I *do* hope he's more capable between the sheets than your father ever was."

"You twisted evil cow!" Dad exploded. "Leave the boys to go in peace."

"*Go!* Go? Och aye! And where is it ye think ye might be going? There's not one place where ye'll be safe." Grim satisfaction. "*And,* ye're not eighteen. Ye need my permission. I'll have the polis after ye."

"He's got all the permission he needs."

"*Aye!* That he would have. I wonder now ye don't go wi' them... or, could it be they don't want to share a bed wi' an ould man?"

"*Mother!!*" Catching her attention, putting an arm round Harry's waist, gratified to see her lip curl. "We're going to put flowers on Uncle Seamus's grave... That okay with you?" Her face whitened and stilled. "Harry, Dad. Let's get out of here." I raised a hand to all the onlookers and called out, "Hope you all enjoyed the show." I kissed Harry and followed him round to the door.

"Ye'll burn. Ye're poor wee black soul will burn. Ye'll burn forever." She was recovering fast.

"I do hope not, Mother," looking her in the eye and summoning all the scorn I could muster. "Wouldn't want to spend five more minutes in your company, never mind eternity."

Dad was visibly shaking as he sank into his seat. Jean's face was set and grim as John got us under way. Mother was still screaming imprecations and I was half expecting stones as we gathered speed, drawing a sigh of relief when we dropped down over the brow of the hill.

"You okay, Shaun?" Harry gripped my hand.

"Yeah. I'll be fine, Harry. You okay?"

"Mmm." Squeezing gently.

Their house and the yard wall had received the same treatment during the night. Along with 'Fucking Queers' was 'No Pope Here' and 'No Surrender'.

"God, Harry! I'm sorry."

"It's only paint, son." Jean was grimmer than ever. "It'll wash off."

* * *

Gran's door opened as John reversed up to her gate. She stood in the doorway puffing furiously on a cigarette.

"Oh shit," Dad mumbled as we got out. "She's started smoking again." He raised his voice: "Alright, Mother?"

"Aye! Well, we'll see about that." Squinting through the smoke. "Bring them away in. They're not sitting outside my door like a pack of gypsies." I could see Eileen behind her in the hallway, making faces at me.

"How's my favourite Goblin then?"

"Dad! You said you'd tell him to stop that. I'm too grown-up for baby names."

Behind us, Gran was at the gate, refusing to take no for an answer. You could sense the gentle twitching of lace here too as Harry, Graham, John and Jean followed her in. From the kitchen Kath inquired as to how many for tea.

"Ah," I gloated, advancing on Eileen. "If you're grown-up, then that makes you an Ogre." Catching her round the waist and tickling.

"*Dad!* Stop him!" Shrieking.

"Childer, childer. Away into the kitchen with ye. Help your sister. You too child," giving Harry a push. He bent over and kissed her withered cheek.

"Thanks, Gran."

"Och. Away wi' ye. Ye scamp." Patting his face lightly then turning from us. "Shaun McKenna... John Hannah... I've got a few words for ye both!" The living-room door closed on them.

"Hi Kath. You'd better hold off on the tea. Granny's either about to read the riot act or deliver a sermon."

"Well, we can go ahead." Pushing her hair back. "Hello sexy," to Harry, anticipating a blush, and getting it. She laughed. "Sit down, there wouldn't be room for us all in there anyway."

Eileen was full of questions over tea and cake about where we were going, what we would do, where we would live, when were we coming back and so on. Kathleen just asked, "*Did* you see her?"

"Yes. The whole Scrogg Road saw her, and heard her as well."

She sighed and shook her head. Harry was teasing Eileen and Kath murmured, "I think she's going mad. You've heard the story of my real father?"

"Yes. But that doesn't matter, you're still my sister."

"Matters to me though. She apparently shouted loud enough for the whole town to hear before he socked her one. *Jesus!* He should have done that years ago."

"Yes, he should. But, you know, he couldn't."

"He should have done it anyway. Things could hardly have been worse."

"I know, Kath, but until yesterday, he thought he was covering for Seamus."

Jean came into the kitchen. "Need a hand?" Eyes twinkling again and the face broadly smiling. "Och, you should see them in there, like wee boys all sitting in a row." She shook her head, chuckling. "I haven't seen Bear so chastened in years. Now, you must be Eileen and you're Kathleen, what pretty girls." Rounding on me. "Where is the other one then?"

"Sorry, Aunt Jean?"

"The Goblin of course." Winking at Eileen. "Where is she? You *can't* mean this pretty girl." Smiling at her. "Shaun McKenna!" swatting the back of my head none too gently. "Don't ever let me hear you calling your sister that again."

Kathleen hid her smile by making more tea, Harry was having the devil's own job keeping his face straight. Eileen? She was glowing. "Now! Apologise at once."

"Sorry, Aunt Jean."

"Not to *me*."

"Sorry Eileen, really."

"Promise you'll never call me that again, or the other one."

"What other one, child?"

I cowered up against the wall, foreseeing the possibility of another swatting.

"He said, if I was grown-up, then I must be an Og... Og... something, Mrs Hannah."

"Call me Aunt Jean, child." She turned to me with a twinkle. "Well, young man?"

"Ogre."

"Well then, you'd better apologise for that too, and then promise."

"Sorry Eileen, and I do promise. Truly."

"Good, that's settled. Now you girls, take the tea in whilst I sort these two idiots out properly."

Pouring herself a cup of tea she sat down beside us. "I'm not going to preach at you boys. I expect your father has spoken to you, Shaun, and I know Bear has had words with you." Smiling at the both of us. "I ask the two of you for only one thing, and believe me, nothing is more important." She took one of Harry's hands and one of mine in hers. "What I want from the pair of you is not a promise, it's more an understanding. To my mind it is more important than any promise you may have made to your respective fathers. It may not sound very much, but it's how I've run my marriage for over thirty years." She shook Harry's hand. "Now, don't you be going and telling Bear I said that."

"What is it, Mum?"

"I want to know that you will never go to bed any night, *any night*, with the slightest disagreement between you. If either of you becomes too stubborn to apologise, you will not survive, boys. So, even if you *know* you are right and the other is wrong, if he won't say sorry, you do it." She put our hands together and covered them with hers. "Do the three of us have an understanding, boys?"

"Yes, Mum."

"Yes, Aunt Jean."

"You stick to that. You remember that and you'll be alright, boys. God knows, but it's a terrible thing in this country, folk not being able to live their lives in peace." Pressing herself up from the table she turned to the window. "One other thing and I'm through." Her voice was very gentle. "Don't be afraid of tears. Never be ashamed to cry. It's a great healer."

I urged Harry by the hand and we joined her at the sink. She was crying silently, great big tears rolling down her face.

"Mum, please don't cry." We put our arms round her.

"I know, I know. I'm a silly woman." Hugging us both. "But there you are."

Harry's bottom lip was trembling and I felt very weird.

"Now, don't you two start, otherwise your Gran will be on to me."

"I could never do that, child," Gran's voice from the door. "God knows but it is a difficult thing to give up a child. Now dry your faces, it's time and past time ye were on the road. Ye'll all be better off far away from here." She turned. "Shaun, son, come with me, I've a wee thing for ye." I followed her into the bedroom where she gave me a small loosely wrapped packet. "I don't have much to give ye and I'm an ould woman. I don't expect I'll ever see ye again. They would probably be lost or destroyed, but I know the two of ye will want to keep them." On opening the wrapping I found the photos of Dad and Seamus.

"Gran! Has he told you the truth about Mum and Kath?"

She straightened up her old back and looked me in the eye.

"The both of them?"

"No, Gran. Neither of them. She taunted him with it yesterday"

"Mary and Joseph... *Mother of God!* Not, not her own *father?*" I nodded, her shoulders slumped and she sank onto the side of the bed. "God in his heaven! How could I have been so blind?... *Her father! Damn him. Damn him.* I was so sure in my own mind." She sighed. "Ach, my poor wee son. After all these years, she could not have hurt him more. Ach! But she knew that, she's been biding her time, waiting till it would cause most hurt. By God, she must have spent the years regretting the marriage she forced on herself."

"Gran! Are you going to be alright? He'll be mad at me for telling you."

"Aye. Don't ye worry none, son. He'll never know that I know, unless he tells me himself." She patted my arm. "Come now son. Time ye were all away from here. God take care of ye both, ye'll have this ould woman's prayers every night that God sends me. Come ye now. No tears, there's my wee boy."

There followed a general leave-taking. Eileen predictably in tears. Me with a huge uncomfortable lump in my throat. Kath pressed a smallish weighty parcel on me. "Don't forget to hoover afterwards, Shaun," pecking me, then Harry on the cheek. "I may see you sooner than you think. God speed.". Gran had a private word with Jean at the door and the two women embraced before Jean joined us in the car.

The run to Newcastle was uneventful and very quiet. Jean and John prepared a meal whilst Harry and I sorted out the gear we already had at the hotel and added it to the bags in the car.

The airport was a new experience for me, and had it not been for the circumstances, I expect I would have enjoyed it more. As it was I felt miserable and tense, I wanted it over, to be on the plane. Away! That hour until we boarded was the longest I've ever spent. There was nothing, yet everything to say. The call for the flight, I think, came as a relief for us all. The last round of hugs and kisses seemed interminable. Of us all, it was Graham who completely broke down, and to my surprise, it was Dad who comforted him. I followed Harry blindly onto the plane, accepting the window seat he prodded me into.

"Be strong, Shaun. *Please!*" Shaky voiced as he fastened the seatbelt.

Out of habit I kissed his hair and ear. "Love you, Harry."

"I know. Love you too," taking my hand. "Love you forever."

The take-off came as something of a shock. I wasn't prepared for how noisy, how bumpy it would be. I held tight to Harry's hand. Surely this thing would never get off the ground? Suddenly, my stomach dropped away. Looking out I found myself holding my breath as everything grew smaller and smaller. The plane tilted over on its side and I squeaked, grabbing Harry's hand in both of mine.

"It's okay, Shaun, we're only turning." My ears felt as though they were going to burst. "Hold your nose and blow gently." Following his instructions, there came a little popping sensation, and hearing returned to normal. I couldn't eat when the meal came round but managed a couple of cups of coffee. Harry didn't eat either, saying he wasn't hungry.

Coming down over the lights of London was, if anything, even more nervewracking than the take-off. I hadn't known that there were *bumps* in the air. I had also thought that wings were *solid*! I grabbed at Harry when I saw them flex.

"It's really okay, Shaun," attempting a feeble joke. "Birds do it all the time."

I let out an explosive gust of relief when the wheels kissed the ground. Silently promising myself, never, never, never, ever again! My poor legs were still trembling as we disembarked.

"God, Harry. Don't you ever expect me to do that again. I've never been so terrified in my whole life."

His whole face lit up. "Go on. You're kidding me." Punching my shoulder playfully. "We're here! We're in London! Come on, let's find John."

"How long is it since you saw him?"

"Och, I don't remember him at all. But Dad said just to look for a younger version of him. So it shouldn't be too hard."

That optimism lasted but moments, until we entered the main hall of Terminal One, which was absolutely heaving with people. There were moving staircases going off at all angles; some up, some down. I was bewildered, Harry almost as much so, deciding in the end to follow the 'Baggage Reclaim' signs.

John eventually found us there, watching bags going round and round on the carousel. "Well, there can't be two more like you anywhere else in this crush." Big smile and a warm hug each. On standing back, he was in truth, a slighter version of his father. "Thought you were coming in on British Midland?"

"We did," panted Harry.

"You guys should be over there," pointing to an adjacent carousel. "This one's for British Airways. No wonder I couldn't see you."

"Ooops."

* * *

Within minutes we were following John out of the building to the car park. The emotions engendered by leaving home were rapidly dying, being replaced by the sights, sounds and bustle all around us. I stumbled more than once trying to look in all directions simultaneously. Harry laughed like a drain when I missed one kerb completely.

"I'll get you for that, see if I don't." Staggering under the weight of the suitcases. Happiness, almost giddiness, welled suddenly strong and sure within me. I put the cases down and with a whoop, which turned a few heads, grabbed Harry round the waist, making him drop his cases. I swung him completely off his feet.

John turned and laughed. "Boys, boys, boys, I'm not sure London is ready for the two of you. Now get the bags, the car is just over here."

David and Nu were incredibly good to us; long-time friends of John's, they welcomed us into their home and lives and took great pleasure in proving to us that we were not some kind of freaks but members of a huge segment of the human race. The first couple of weeks in London we did all the touristy bits, got lost every time we turned a corner and enjoyed ourselves enormously. We stayed with them in their flat over the off-licence for about two months before finding a large studio to rent in Streatham. It did come as something of a relief to have our own front door. With Dave and Nu being incessant party-goers, we'd been reaching the point where we seemed to have no time to ourselves. We didn't turn into hermits, no way, we never turned down an invitation to accompany them to the Albert Hall or the Barbican. Nu was mad on Opera and didn't find much difficulty in converting us. We went to work for them in their off-licence with the long-term idea that if we liked it well enough, we would take on one of our own in about a year. We didn't disillusion the pair of them, or John, who we saw several times a week. But we had by then firmly set our hearts on Australia and were saving every penny we could towards that end. Also with that in mind, we had both started night school in IT, wanting to be qualified in something.

Our time together in London, some fifteen months in all, I relive every day, with its details of precious memories to be hoarded, treasured and constantly reviewed. Amongst my most precious possessions from those days are the tapes we made in the flat. Sometimes jointly and sometimes unknown to each other until later.

Dad had had the phone put in and we used to call our families about once a week. I soon learned to be wary of Dad and Harry chatting, when he gave me a dead arm one night after putting the phone down.

"Your Dad said to," he chortled, from what he appeared to think was the safety of the far side of the bed.

"Ooooh," rubbing my arm. "Just you wait, Harry Hannah. You're going to need an extra dose of 'throat' medicine in the morning."

"Mmm. Is that a threat or a promise?"

The flat is small, so he wasn't left long in doubt as to which it was.

Remembering those days would be incomplete without a mention of dear George and his lover Dessie. They were dancers with a well-known company, and together with Dave and Nu they were our closest friends and inevitable companions on nights out. But I'll get to them later.

Christmas swept up on us unexpectedly. I was worried about Harry, as he was about me. But we resolved that one cold night, whilst walking home along the Brixton Road.

"I thought you might be homesick, always having had a big family do?"

"And I was worried about you too," he admitted.

"We are all the family I need, love."

"Mmm," hugging me. "I'll miss them, but given a choice, I'd choose you every time."

"I'd choose me too."

He laughed and kissed my cheek. "Big head."

Harry's Dad had had the Mini repaired and shipped it over to us the week before Christmas along with a slew of presents. For ourselves, we had decided on just one main present each, settling on identical rings set with a small emerald. Harry liked green and I loved it because of his eyes. David raised his brows when he saw them at Christmas lunch and Nu, well, he thought it all terribly romantic, almost to the point of tears. George and Dessie just hugged us, though Dessie did slyly ask if it was 'Mr and Mrs Hannah' or ' Mr and Mrs McKenna'.

We'd exchanged the rings during the midnight service at Westminster Abbey, and if our kiss of peace was more intense and prolonged than most, we didn't care. This was *us*. *Our* life. I lay awake long that night in his embrace, counting my blessings, stroking his hair as he slept.

David and Nu went to Mauritius for the New Year to visit Nu's parents, leaving us to run the store with a little help from Des and George. We saw the New Year in amongst the crush in Trafalgar Square and decided that once was probably enough.

All our books and the things we hadn't been able to carry were shipped over at the same time as the car. With them in place, our little flat really took on the aspect of a home, our home! Early in the New Year I passed my test and we took to venturing ever further afield on days or weekends off, developing a great love of Weymouth, despite the distance, with its faint echoes of Kilkeel. Shortly after Christmas, Dad rang to say that Mum had gone completely round the bend. She had apparently begun seeing the devil everywhere. The previous Saturday she had finally cracked, in Dunne's store, screaming about 'her sin' and 'ould Nick'. She'd removed most of her clothes before being restrained and was now in the Downshire Hospital with the prospect of an extended stay. With Mum in hospital, Kath became more settled, even bringing a steady boyfriend to the house, something which previously would have been an absolute no-no.

Dad was now skippering the 'Mary Jean' for Uncle John, with Graham as mate. Both our brows rose at that tit-bit. Could it be?

On Harry's side, Allan's allowance had been severely cut and he now never went home at all. Jean was sure he would end up in prison, or worse, as word filtered back of his growing involvement with the most extreme Loyalist organisations. Charlie continued to live at home, silent and morose, working in the brickyard to keep himself in beer money. True to his word, John had blacklisted all those involved in the fight and car chase that day.

Mostly though, we were uninterested in anything other than ourselves, we were still fascinated by each other. I suppose we almost became an exclusive world of two. Over the months we both filled out and grew a little. Harry became chunkier and developed a mat of chest hair – such fun to play with! – which, along with the thick line of silky hair growing down his spine all the way into his crack, taught me why his Mum had nicknamed his Dad 'Bear'.

I put on a padding of flesh which helped hide my bones, but I'd never be chunky. Cock had stopped growing at just on six inches but he had thickened considerably. Whether that was due to natural growth, or the continual exercise he indulged in, I can't be sure. Harry's both thickened and lengthened and some nights I'd ignore him completely, devoting all my conversation to his cock. I swear, it could lip-read, always nodding sagely at whatever I said. Unfortunately I don't remember one of those conversations reaching a conclusion. Sooner or later, and it was usually sooner, it and I would be forced to act on my words. But it was great fun and we were in a continual state of euphoria.

I could, and still can, describe every facet of his body. Every crease of his skin. The ever and always amazing green eyes which were gradually developing more and more golden splinters. I never tired of looking at him. His body, that elegant cock, the floppy hair, that ridiculous nose and those eyes! Those eyes never leave me. I see them in my sleep, I feel their gentle pressure following me wherever I go. See them glinting and half closed with laughter when he pulled a successful trick or cracked a joke. See them misty and running with tears, as when we first heard *Tannhäuser*, the sublime Pilgrims' Chorus! I see them in my mind, focused on me, clear and limpid as we cuddled in front of the fire on a cold night. Unfocused and far away as he caressed the keys on a piano, or blazing with love and lust, as his cock slammed into my arse and his seed filled me with his love. See the eyes dance with mischief as we prepared to entertain David and Nu, or George and Dessie, or maybe John and his current girlfriend to dinner, both of us in perfect harmony in the tiny kitchen. If I could only see those eyes just once more, particularly as they were of a morning when I woke him! Hazy, warm, and pools of quiet, his arms rising to encircle me. Drawing me down into the safety and warmth of his embrace, his love. How could life be any other way? This, this was what we were born to be, and I was content in my adoration. Content in the surety of love, and life.

If only...

17

His birthday – nineteen this year – was the twenty-fourth of March, and I booked us for the weekend on the Isle of Skye without telling him. We went up by sleeper on the Thursday night and back on the Sunday. That really was a weekend to remember. David, Nu and John phoned on the Saturday evening during dinner, then John and Jean, followed minutes later by Dad and Graham from somewhere in the Irish Sea. After dinner, a party reminiscent of Sligo developed in the bar, with him on the piano. But possibly the best came when we got home Monday morning. I'd found an old upright piano going reasonably cheap and over the weekend Dave and

Nu had moved it into the flat. It took up more space than I thought it would. However, the look on his face when he turned to me after opening the door was worth it. Tears were streaming down his face when he turned.

"You?"

I was delighted by his response and nodded.

"How could you know? I've wanted one *so* much." I'm sure my ribs cracked during the ensuing hug. "Shaun McKenna, I swear, I love you to pieces."

"Love you too, Harry. Why don't you try it? I'll put the kettle on."

He ran up and down the scales listening to the tone then played Liszt's 'The Sigh'. I stood in the kitchen area, focused on his face, and coming back from wherever the music took him he caught my eye. "Love you. Come here." I stood behind him, hands on his shoulders, as he played a little Chopin for me. Closing the lid he turned and buried his face in my stomach, arms tight round me. I stroked his hair as he held me. "Love you Shaun, love you for ever and ever."

"Love you, Harry." My voice quiet. I hadn't thought it would affect him quite so strongly. "Is it alright? I mean, is it in tune and everything?"

Standing up, still holding me, he looked down into my eyes (by then he didn't have to look quite so far down): "It's fine, Shaun. Perfect as far as I can judge, but Shaun love, darling little goat, it's not the piano that's in tune," briefly kissing me on the lips, "it's us who are in tune. Jesus Shaun, just when I think it can't possibly get any better, it suddenly does. Thank you. Thank you for the very bestest birthday ever." Tears were spilling over again and, brushing them away with my thumbs, I decided the whole thing needed lightening up.

"I wouldn't get totally over-excited," I warned with a smile.

"Oh, and why not?"

"Well," I kissed him. "You have to teach me how to play it."

Next morning I woke to an empty bed and the gentle notes of a softly played piano. I lay silent, watching him. Naked on the stool, head bent, fingers gently caressing. It was like watching someone make love to themselves all unaware of the watcher. His fingers stilled.

"You're awake!"

"Yes."

"You okay?"

"Yes. How did you know?"

"I felt your eyes."

"Maybe we're developing telepathy."

"Maybe."

"You coming back to bed?"

"Mmmm."

We slept for another couple of hours, wrapped in each other, my head on his chest this time, the rhythm of his heart lulling me back into the warmth and comfort.

John and Jean, on their way for an early break in Madeira, stopped over for a few days staying with John. We had them to dinner every night and Harry brought tears to Jean's eyes, playing up a real storm on the piano. She hugged me fiercely, whispering, "Thank you, son." Neither of them seemed able to get over how much we had grown in the ten months since we'd left Northern Ireland.

"Lass and I, we're so happy to see you both looking so well."

Harry hugged him. "It just goes on getting better, Dad."

We went down with them on the Gatwick Express to see them off and in the airport John gave me a thick brown envelope.

"Your Dad asked me to give you this, with the strict instructions not to be opened till your birthday. So no peeking. You hear me?"

"Okay, Uncle John."

"Bless you both, my boys." Jean hugged us as their flight was called.

"Have a good holiday Mum, and don't spend too many nights..." looking at me, eyes shining... "talking," I finished for him.

He whooped as she dimpled and coloured.

"Shame on the pair of you," John grinned. "We're too old for all that."

"You speak for yourself, Bear," she turned to us with an exaggerated whisper. "He wasn't too old last night."

"Shame on you too, woman," slapping her ample bottom. "Bye kids, see you soon."

On the way back to Victoria, I sat looking at him through narrowed eyes until at last he lost patience.

"Well, what is it?" Kicking me under the table when I began to laugh. "Come on then, what little light has switched on in there?"

"Oh, a couple of things really."

"Well?"

"I was wondering if you would be too old at sixty?"

"Honey, as long as you are there, I'll never be too old. Now, what's the second?"

"I was wondering if you knew whether there was a mile-high club, or its equivalent, for trains?"

Grinning, he followed me from the seat. "If there isn't, there soon will be."

My eighteenth, on April 30th, fell midweek, and he took me by surprise the Sunday morning before when he woke me.

"Come on sleepyhead, breakfast as soon as you have a shower."

"What's up, Harry?" Still half asleep, but awake enough to see that he was fully dressed.

"Never you mind. It's a surprise. Come on, get a move on."

By eight that evening we were tucking into Dover soles at 'The Captain's Table' on Weymouth seafront. He'd taken a caravan at the holiday park on Chesil Beach for the week. We had our first legal fuck (his words) on the morning of my birthday. Technically, I suppose we had jumped the gun, as my birth certificate showed that I'd been born in the afternoon, but who the hell cared? Afterwards he gave me a gold bracelet with my name on the front and, 'To Little Goat, Love Eyes' on the reverse. I held him long and tight, savouring the aroma of my man, my love, my life. Words were inadequate to describe the emotions which gripped me.

"Harry... Eyes, I feel... I *know* I'm the luckiest guy in the whole world... I have you."

"And I have you," he whispered in my hair, hands roving, caressing and rekindling the fire of an hour before.

"Love you, Harry."

"Love you, Shaun."

That evening, after dinner, he produced the envelope his dad had brought from mine. Inside was a long letter from Dad and an old, fat, brown envelope postmarked 'Woolongong Australia'.

"Read your Dad's letter first, Shaun," as we looked from the postmark to each other. Moving round the table I spread the letter between us.

Hi Guys,

    I'm pretty sure you'll be reading this together. I know Seamus and I would have. First things first, I'm so glad your first year has been so good to you both. If I was a praying man, I'd pray for you both. However I'll just wish you all the very best for the years to come, and you can be sure, this comes from the very bottom of my heart. I miss you son, in fact, I miss both my sons (I know you wont mind Harry). Despite talking to you both on the phone I miss seeing you. However guys, I may see you later in the year. More of that anon. Now, to the essence of the matter in front of you. You Shaun, will remember our talk in the Arrandale and I don't doubt Harry, you know all of it as well. (He did). I never could bring myself to touch anything that Seamus left. I felt it wouldn't be right, not having made a contribution. Ideally it should have represented our joint efforts, been the product of a life shared, instead of the hurt and division engendered by a spiteful lie. I admit to you both now, had I become aware of the true nature of the deception before you Shaun were born, in all likelihood you never would have been. I'd have dropped her, as I suppose, with the benefit of hindsight, I should have done anyway. I'd have been on the first plane, boat, camel or bike to Sydney. Where I know my welcome was assured, but then, I always knew that. You will see why when you open the inner envelope. I have debated long with myself before deciding to send every thing to you both and, although I will never change inside, I cannot change the past. You have no conception of the depth of my wish that I could do just that.

Sorry, that is unfair to you both. Recalling the depth of the emotional bond between Seamus and myself at nineteen, I'm sure your union is just as deep if not more so and, you are both capable of realising how we felt. How I still feel for him. I am and have been physically sick when I think of all that we have gone through, all because of one, maybe two warped minds. I daresay I can appreciate the old mans thinking. He must have been horrified as well as (I suspect) terrified by his actions and the result. To him, if not at first to her, the availability of two naïve boys, who already had one guilty secret (which, on reflection, he knew all about) must have been a God send. How well things turned out for them in the end.

Neither Seamus nor I, had any memory of leaving the pub that evening, never mind what was supposed to have taken place afterwards. I'm sure now, that it was her idea to place the blame on Seamus, as a method of ensuring that he would leave. The added bonus that he elected to go quite so far would have been the icing on the cake. Her biggest worry I think, may have been, that once married to her we might have just carried on as before. If there is something she could never countenance, it is competition for something she considers hers. No matter that she got little joy out of her ownership. In that respect, the only things I gave her, were you and Eileen. Your presence I'm sure, is the only reason I hung onto my sanity, particularly when I received the letters etc., which are enclosed. I've told you already that I have through you Shaun, and even more now that you Harry are with him, relived my childhood and teenage years. You kept me going through the bad times when I learned that Seamus was dead.

You wont remember you were only little, but had it not been for you, I probably would have joined him then as I'd been unable to do before. Your little face before me was my only lifeline, and in the end, I learned to live with my grief for your sake.

Time does heal in some respects and I'm no longer suicidal, though I can never forget, just as I can never forgive. One of my many regrets is that he never knew you or you him, especially now that your life, both your lives have taken a roughly similar path. Of course it would never have been in the realms of possibility but I know he would have loved you both, just as I do, and I'm sure you would have come to love him too.

That's really why I have arranged for the two of you to receive the inheritance he left me. It isn't a fabulous amount and I wont accept any arguments, as neither will I accept any of the money, I just could not do it boys. So please, from Seamus and I, take what we have to give with love. Live your lives to the very fullest. I know he would agree, that much I can sense, I knew him as well as you know each other. When you go on to the enclosed documents, you'll see that I'm right. You will ask, why did I not tell you all this face to face? I just could not relive all this again, except on paper. Even as I write the tears never cease to flow for what might, indeed, should have been. Live the life that Seamus and I should have had, full of love and each other. I confess I envy you boys, both your love and, your youth. Forgive me for that, know that at the same time, I wish only the very best that life can provide for you both.

My love is yours and will go with you, where ever

you go. Should you by chance or design, come to visit him in Woolongong, put some roses (you know which colour) from me on his grave. Give him my love, not that he ever needed any reminders of how I felt.

I must close this now, I'm becoming maudlin. Accept my apologies for landing this on you on your birthday, but I needed to share, have needed to share my feelings for years. Now that you are both men, I'm sure you wont mind, too much. It eases the burden a little, as well as presenting the ideal solution to a problem I've had for the last fourteen years.

May you both have many, many, many happy birthdays in the years to come.

With all the love in my heart.
Your Father and, Father-in-law.
(Can I say that now in these days of sexual equality?)

PS. Oh yes! I'll be in London in early July
(With a FRIEND)

"I'm sorry, Shaun." Harry's voice was trembling, face white, eyes enormous and dark, dark green. "Should have left it at home till we got back." He handed me a paper napkin, and as I sat holding it, took another and began wiping my face. Only then did I realise that my cheeks were wet with tears.

"No. No Harry, it's alright, really it is alright." Taking over from him.

"What about the other, Shaun?" indicating the still unopened old brown envelope.

"In a minute. Put the kettle on, would you? How could he live with that all these years?"

"Don't know, love, but I do know he had no business dropping this on you today. Today of all days. Oh, I love him, but this was not well thought-out on his part."

"Please Harry, don't be mad at him. I think we should be proud that he thinks us old enough and secure enough to feel able to tell us both. He's kept it to himself for so long! It must be, have been, awfully difficult to share it with anyone." I kissed him long and slow. "I wonder how many times he wrote that letter before he felt he had it just right?"

We opened the brown envelope after Harry made the coffee.

Inside were three hand-written ones addressed to:-
Shaun Peter McKenna,
C/O Mrs. Elizabeth McKenna,
Ballykeel,
Ballymartin,
Newry,
Co. Down, N.I.

None were stamped or franked, but they were marked on the back in ink 1, 2, 3. There were also three official-looking brown envelopes. The first to the same address and the other two to the Scrogg Road. Finally a note in Dad's handwriting:

Guys,
As you can see, he never posted the letters. They came with the copy of his will.
They are yours now, as is everything he left me. Use it well, but mostly, use it with love.
Dad (in-law)

"Legal or personal ones first, Shaun?"
"Oh, the personal ones I think. Don't you?"
"Okay, love."
The envelope marked '1' contained, besides a letter, two photographs of Seamus, one very obviously aboard the ship. On the back he'd written 'Cape Town'. The second showed him wearing the same short-sleeved shirt and baggy white slacks with the addition of a straw hat to shade his eyes, on the back: 'Perth. Hope Sydney is cooler!!!' The letter itself had been written in stages, different inks used, some more faded than others.

Two days out. Bay of Biscay.
Dearest Rabbit,
I don't know what to write. I love you!!!
But then, that's hardly news. How did we end up in this mess? But, we've been over that. Why? Why Shaunny did you not take the chance and come with me? I LOVE you. I LOVE you. My heart is breaking. I can't write any more just now. WHY wouldn't you come? I think I hate you for that.
Three days out. Somewhere off Portugal. (I think)
Of course I don't hate you. I LOVE you. I KNOW

why you couldn't come. GOD but I hope she does lose it. I'll expect you on the next day in Sydney. I'll expect you there anyway, no matter what happens. I'm so sick Shaunny. Seasick and Heartsick. Mostly Heartsick. This could be so much fun, indeed I know it would be, if only you were here with me. I cry myself to sleep everynight. I MISS you. I miss you more than I ever thought it possible to miss anyone or anything.

Six days out. Don't know where. Don't care. SHAUNNY. RABBIT. LOVER. Heart of my heart.

Where are you Shaunny? What are you doing? What did Little Mum say when you got back? She wanted you to go, you know that! OH GOD! Why didn't I knock you over the head and drag you on board? She's married now, got your name, it will be legitimate no matter what. God forgive me, but I hope she looses it, or it kills her. HOW COULD I have fucked HER! I'm sick everytime I think about it, and you know, I think about it all the time. I'm only glad that I can't remember any of it. Shaunny, I'm SORRY, SO SORRY, you KNOW that. Jesus I'm going mad, I can't stop thinking about it and what it has done to us. I see her face that morning, smug little BITCH! Then, when she knew she was PREGNANT! SHIT, SHIT, SHIT, Shaunny, what did I do. I don't think I can live with this. I stood on the deck last night (it's getting pretty warm now) just watching the water slide by below. So smooth, so dark, it would be so easy. But you know, I'm frightened by the thought of sharks, wouldn't want to be eaten. GOD, Shaunny you have GOT to come. That's the only thing I cling to. Love my RABBIT. Love you Shaunny. PLEASE come to me. I can't live without you.

LOST COUNT OF THE DAYS.
Arriving Cape Town.

This gets worse by the day. I get worse. Burst into tears with no warning. Taken to spending most of my time in the cabin. Thank God it's only two berth and the other is empty.

YOURS! That doesn't help you know Shaunny. I'm cracking up I think. I try to tell myself that she has lost it already, or she's dead, and you are going to be on the quayside in Sydney or maybe even Perth when we arrive. I warn you, I shall probably expire in your arms right there, but at least I'd die happy. Only hunger drives me out. I'm sure I'm loosing weight. Back to being all elbows and angles again. I feel your hands holding my ears, taste you in my mouth. I miss you. I miss you. I miss you. Wanking myself silly staring at your photograph. Do you feel me thinking about you? Or are the miles between us too much? How I wish now that we had fucked that last night in Southampton, instead of shedding all those tears, I've shed another ocean since we sailed. Think maybe I'll get drunk. Only thing is, who would I fuck this time? I swear it again, I'll never touch another drop as long as I live. TALK to me Shaunny. I talk to YOU all the time. Point out the dolphins and the Whales to you. Undress you at night. Wash your back in the shower. Kiss you and KISS you. And you're NOT FUCKING THERE!!! Can't take this Rabbit. You MUST COME!

Two days to Perth.
Rolling, heaving, slamming around and that's my belly. Can't begin to describe what the ship is doing, been like this for days, suits my mood. Please be in Perth. Then I can give you this. We'll read it together, have a laugh and, tear it up. Shaunny the thought of being with you again is keeping me hard every minute.

Two days to Sydney.
Promise me you are there. You have GOT to be there. I sat on the quay in Fremantle all day, waiting, hoping. Nearly jumped in the harbour when you didn't show. Of course I knew you wouldn't, Sydney is easier. I'm feeling better, now that it's nearly over, I'll be seeing you soon. God Shaunny, you'd better be ready for me, the first one is going to be the most fantastic fuck ever. I only hope we can wait till we are somewhere private. Behind the nearest tree trunk will do. Do they have trees in Sydney? Don't care.
Love you Rabbit. Say only that you love me.

Sydney Hostel.
Been here nearly a month now. Been working for two

weeks. Soft furnishings in a department store. Moving into a rooming house tomorrow. HATE this place Shaunny. It would have been great, if only you were here to share it. My little ploy on the boat did at least keep me alive, so far. Shaunny, I came so close, sharks or no sharks. I wont post this but keep it safe for you. Keep my heart safe for me, I know I don't have one here. Will you let me borrow it back when you come?

ALL, ALL, ALL MY LOVE AND SEX AND EVERYTHING.

YOUR WHITE GHOST.

I'd managed not to cry, but Harry hadn't, tears streamed down his face as he re-folded the sheets around the photos and slipped them back in the envelope.

"What a *bitch!* Sorry, Shaun."

"No, don't be, you're absolutely right."

I poured coffee before picking up number two, looked at him wiping his eyes.

"Okay, love?"

"Yeah, yeah. Go on. I want to find out what he did."

At Woolongong 1976.

("Jesus Christ.......Six YEARS Shaun.")

Shaunny-Rabbit-Keeper of my Heart-My Only Ever True Love.

Why don't I feel a fool writing that? Because my love, it remains as true today as it ever was. Oh, it's alright, I know you wont come now. Maybe when the child (boy or girl?) is grown, maybe not even then. It will have been SO long. I don't think you will ever forget though, anymore than I can. How are you my love? How do you look? How do you feel? I know you think of me constantly as I do off you. I had a copy taken of a picture of you and I have it on the car dash. All the 'queens' think it is great. And anyone that asks, I tell them I am in deep, deep mourning. That seems to please them somehow. You wouldn't believe the number of gay guys here Shaunny. But, don't worry, I'm only ever thine.

I'm Chief Clerk at the steel mill at Port Kembla now and, what's more exciting after all these years, I've managed to develop a TAN! Not very dark it's true but still a tan.

Remember (of course you do) how we dreamt of Bondi Beach, the surfing and all that? Well, I'll have you know I'm quite good at it. It's like having a wank (which

I do often with you in mind). Something you can do on your own. In fact it's best when it's just you and the waves, I haven't been eaten yet, though some girl was savaged last week according to the press. Lost most of a leg I think. Not that it would really matter. Anything, anything at all just to help pass the days, the months, the

YEARS! I'm truly only half alive Shaunny. The other half went into hibernation sometime during the first year here. Sometimes it tries to wake up, but I soothe it back to sleep with the promise that you will soon be here. It's getting harder now to make it/me believe that. I think, we both knew that night back in Southampton, we'd never be together in this world again. I hope I'm wrong, but I know your sense of duty once you give your word, and I know you wont break the promise made to my unborn child. What a thing to keep us apart!

Shaunny, my only true love, if I were to let myself go I could die tomorrow and gladly. To wait for you there, wherever 'there' is. So, I wont post this, I couldn't bear to read your reply. You know I can never come back. You knew then. I know now you will not come. I just wonder how long I can continue when there is no reason to do so? Only the knowledge of the hurt it will cause you holds me back. How long that remains true?... I don't know any more. Whatever happens my love. Blame me and my weakness.

Steadfast in my love for you, as always.
Your (slightly brown) Ghost.

There were no photos with that one. We were both dry-eyed, but my heart ached for him, and for Dad.

"I wonder why he wouldn't come back?"

"By then I think he was probably a little crazy, Harry. Couldn't think straight."

"It does read a wee bit odd."

"Make another coffee, love. I think we've got to see this through now. Don't you?"

"Mmm, I'm thinking the last one is probably going to be the hardest."

"Promise to hold me specially close tonight?"

"Only if you promise too, little goat."

"Promise."

"Me too."

The writing was very spidery, almost impossible to decipher in places, but we puzzled it out in the end. It also had a photograph. We were looking at a man old before his time. He was balding, grossly overweight and looked sadly tired.

Woolongong Feb. 1983

My lovely little Rabbit,

Do you exist at all? I've often thought I must be mad. You know! I saw you yesterday. Isn't that a surprise? You didn't see me. Well, you wouldn't would you, you were with me. I never realised how white I was until I saw my self with you. You haven't changed Rabbit. Still as young and as fuckable as ever. I had my first wank in, oh I don't know how long, sitting there in the car watching us as we crossed the sands. Where did you learn to surf like that? Although I must say I was at least your equal. Well, we always were equal, weren't we? I'm still at Kembla, still Chief Clerk, but it doesn't mean anything other than the fact that I'm pretty well off, or so the bank says. I had to go in before Christmas, they wanted me to select investments, cant think why. Oh yes, I made a will at the same time. It's all yours love. I cant wait to get home from work and make dinner for us. It's the only place I feel real now. I've had your photos blown up larger than life and I have them on all the walls so that I never loose sight of you. Until I saw those boys yesterday , I was beginning to think I was in a dream, if not the actual dream itself. Oh, I know it wasn't you and me. After all you are there and I am here. WHY is that Shaunny? Why are we NOT together? Will I REALLY have to wait until we DIE? If so, I'd rather it was soon. My mind plays little tricks on me at times. Not at work yet, or at least, I don't think so. Though even there it's getting difficult to stay quiet when you talk to me. I'm going to slip one of these days, I know it. How is our child Shaunny? If it was a boy, he'll be wanking by now. It's a pity we had to use her to have one, but no matter, you'll keep him right for me I know. I know you always keep your promises. Tell him how love ALWAYS hurts, promise me that Shaunny. I would love to wait till he grows up and you both come to me, but you know, I'm getting worse. Even I know that. There is STILL a LITTLE bit of me the same as when we were together. Oh, we had the best of times, didn't we? We talk it over every night at dinner. I just wish you didn't have to leave so early in the morning. You know how much I loved our early morning sessions. But there you are love, things change. If it was a girl, I hope you strangled it, and her too. Though if you had you would be here, I wouldn't be so disgustingly fat and half, more than half mad. Rabbit, I'm sorry. I don't think I can carry this guilt, this pain, much longer. I'm just not ME any more. I cant go on fooling people much longer. I sometimes wonder if I am fooling anybody, or is everybody laughing at this fat old fairy continually talking to herself? No. Not YET. They would surely have fired me by now. I think I must be fairly lucid most of the time, but really, I just want to get home and talk to you. I HATE going to work. I love the week-ends when I don't have to leave you. We go for long, long drives every Sunday with a picnic. Remember picnics at the shore in the tent? Of course you do, how could you not. Remember our first fuck in the tent? I do! Yes, I know you do too. I've got to see the lawyers tomorrow, I want them to put some letters and other things with the will. Nobody else will read them then, only you. After all they are yours, they're mine, so they must be yours as well. What's happening to me Shaunny? Why is it ending this way? I think we'll go for a run to Canberra this Sunday. Wont that be nice? I'll pack your favourite sandwiches and lots of cokes. They still do the glass bottles here. Remember floating them off the shore and throwing stones to see who could break them? I think I'm still the record holder. Do you still do that Shaunny? Will you teach HIM to skim the flat stones for me?

SHAUNNY, SHAUNNY, SHAUNNY, I don't want HIM! I don't care about HIM! I don't care about anybody, only YOU! I MISS YOU, I MISS YOU, I MISS YOU! I HAVE MISSED YOU FROM THE VERY FIRST DAY AT SEA. I MISS YOU, I MISS YOU, I MISS YOU. I wish I wasn't such a coward. I SHOULD have jumped that very first night and be damned to all the sharks. I bet it would have been some great blow job. What do you think?

Send me some roses Shaunny. The yellow scented ones from Little Mum's garden, I can smell them now. I really don't think we'll bother coming back on Sunday. Just keep driving. What do you think? Yes? Good!!

Bye, my FIRST, my LAST, my ONLY, LOVE.
GHOST.

We were both in tears, I could not see to put it back in the envelope, just picked everything up and piled it on the table. We fell into bed, holding each other blindly. How could the world hold such misery, so much pain? I *hated* the bitch. Hated her for what she'd done to Dad, to Seamus. I admired Dad more than ever for staying for what he had thought was Seamus's child's sake, then for me and Eileen. The fates seemed to have conspired to keep them apart, or as Harry said, perhaps conspired to bring us together. There was no other explanation.

Over a cup of coffee next morning, whilst waiting for him to wake up, I looked through the legal papers. The will was very short. Everything went to Dad, to do with as he liked. There was a hand-written note under the signature: 'For you Rabbit, all my love as always, Ghost'.

From what we could make out it seemed that Harry and I were now the joint owners of a small house somewhere in Woolongong. Dad apparently could not bring himself to sell and had got the lawyers to appoint an agent to let it out and manage it on a renewable yearly lease. There didn't seem to be a fantastic amount of money, and we couldn't understand all the legal terminology. Later, during the correspondence necessary to assume ownership, we learned of some one hundred and fifty thousand dollars in realisable investments. Harry was reluctant to accept any of it, but Dad insisted and in the end we decided to leave things as they stood until we went out to Australia the following year, that now being our plan.

Knowing my reluctance to fly Harry earned himself a big hug, and more, by suggesting that we follow Seamus's trip and sail out, taking the first half of one of the many round-the-world cruises on offer.

At home in Streatham, the anniversary of our first meeting dawned, with the quiet notes of 'The Sigh' waking me. He was naked at the piano, his back to me. I drank in the interplay of the muscles in his back as he caressed the keys, and the thickening line of silky black hair down his spine, like a smudged pencil stroke. I lay silent and totally content as he came to the end.

"You're awake!"

"Mmm."

With a smiling glance over his shoulder he gently stroked the keys. The 'Anniversary Waltz' was followed by Cliff's 'Congratulations', sung sotto voce. Finally, closing the lid he looked over his shoulder again, a wide and wicked grin spreading over his face. Turning on the stool, he revealed himself to be hugely erect, a blue bow tied round his cock and balls.

"Happy Anniversary, Shaun."

"Happy Anniversary, Harry," throwing the duvet back to show him that I was just as ready for the celebrations.

David and Nu bunked off work that day after conning Dessie and George into running the store. They admired the small bronze of a crouching boy that I'd given Harry and the scale model of the motorbike that he gave me. Then they presented us with a glass paperweight containing two of the most beautiful butterflies I've ever seen, one all green and the other white and grey, before whisking us off to reveal their latest passion. A broken-down old house, two miles from the nearest paved road, on the edge of the Salisbury plain.

Harry listened with visible disbelief as they raved about sun rooms, conservatories, en suite bathrooms and a 'playroom' in the cellar, which turned out to be a black hole in the floor.

"Oh, about three years. With a little help from 'friends'."

"Oh God,." I moaned. "Just so long as I don't have to do anything more complicated than waving a paintbrush around."

"He'll be a worse slave driver than Dad," Harry warned.

"Rubbish! Bet we can live in it by the end of summer." Nu was itching to get started.

During dinner that night with them and Dessie and George, we all agreed to christen it 'The Folly'. It certainly looked like one to me.

The 'friend' that Dad had mentioned in his letter turned out to be Graham. They arrived for a visit towards the end of July – Kath and her fiancee, James Perry, were off to Majorca taking Eileen along – staying with Dave and Nu but spending most of their time with us. Neither of them seemingly able to get over how much the two of us had changed. We couldn't quite work out what, if anything, was going on between Dad and Graham, but finally agreed that, as they were both adults, they should know what they were about.

When we saw them off at Heathrow we had three months and one little week left.

Part Four: Pain and Partings

18

Big, soft loveable George and small, waspish Dessie. Each one's heart as soft as the other, though Dessie strived mightily to hide it. The first night we really saw them together, the night we celebrated the completion of the conservatory at 'The Folly', changed our perceptions of Des completely. Dave and Nu had both said that we were misjudging him totally, basing our belief on his vinegar wit and talent for malicious gossip, without even trying to see the little vulnerable Gorbals boy hiding behind it. If only we had known at the time what lay behind the prickly exterior, what really caused him to appear to be downright rude at times; but his shield, up till that night, was pretty well perfect.

We'd all been treated to dinner at an Indian restaurant in Andover by David and Nu, a sort of thank you for all the work we'd put in, and to celebrate the completion. Des had really hit the scotch before, during and after the meal, and after returning to 'The Folly' we laid low the two wine boxes purchased earlier. Dave and Nu had retired to the one as yet habitable bedroom. The four of us were ensconced in sleeping bags on the conservatory floor admiring the sweep of the heavens and the multitude of stars when he began to cry. At first Harry and I put it down to too much booze, and tried as best we could to ignore it.

George was the first black boy either of us had known personally, in fact a beautiful silky coffee colour. His humorous outlook on life, his raw sexuality, his cuddliness, his sheer intelligence and maturity, so far in advance of our own, had all been a beacon of attraction from the very first introduction. Dessie had been harder to take to and we hadn't been able to understand the obvious attraction George felt.

Had the two of us been sober I expect we would have worked out exactly what was going on, what Dessie's problem really was; on reflection there were certainly more than enough clues dropped that night. We had no option but to listen as George comforted him and over the following hour or so, before he fell asleep, Des expressed his love, his complete devotion and his sorrow.

That was what Harry and I were too slow to get. We were too new, too self-centred to realise what the drunken conversation was really about. Des apologised very handsomely in the morning for being such a wet blanket and for the first time ever, hugged us both. From then on he was much more relaxed around us, less inclined to use cutting remarks and altogether younger in a way.

But this does me no good. And anyway the memories are private, mine! I don't know whether I can do this.

Continuing to relate the major and minor events of the next few months is only to delay recounting the detail of the tragedy that was to be Harry's and mine. Is mine still.

In a way Dad was right! Time does heal, but never completely, and I WILL NEVER FORGET!!

I have literally dreaded putting what follows on paper. Despite Dr Singh's assurances that it will help, and his continual nagging. I think that had chance not provided me with the opportunity to balance the scales somewhat, it would have remained unwritten. In that case my end would probably have been an inglorious descent into madness or suicide, perhaps both. As things now stand, after years of depression, disbelief, even madness at times, I have reached a point where a flame I thought long dead has begun to flicker faintly. A point where I can begin to see the future at a further remove than just one day at a time.

* * *

On an evening in early November we were sitting at the kitchen table comparing brochures detailing world cruises, consulting itineraries, accommodation and rates when the phone rang. Harry was nearest.

"Eighteen sixty-one," he chirped, always saying it in words, never figures. "Oh, hi Kath. How does it feel to almost be an old married lady?"

"Yeah, yeah, yeah. I only hope he's as good looking and sexy as me."

"Oh ho, don't you worry. He's safe on that score. *No one* is as good looking and sexy as your little brother."

"Okay, here he is," handing me the phone.

"Hi Kath, hope you weren't teasing my other half? How's things?"

"Shaun, hi. Look, it may be nothing much, but Eileen's not

well."

"How not well?"

"She's been taken to Daisy Hill, the..."

"When?"

"About an hour ago. The ambulance was just arriving as I got home from work."

"What's the matter Kath, appendicitis or something?"

Harry's face registered concern and he came round the table, draping an arm over my shoulders, leaning close to listen.

"No. Nothing like that. Dad went with her. I only had a minute or two with him. He said that one of the teachers brought her home about two o'clock."

"And?"

"Well, it seems she took ill after lunch, vomiting, severe headache and feeling very dizzy."

"Food poisoning, you think?"

"I honestly don't know, Shaun. Dad called the doctor straight away, I think at first he thought it might be because she's recently started her periods. You know what I mean?"

"Now Kath, just because we're gay doesn't mean we're idiots you know."

"Sorry, guys."

"Go on."

"Well, the doctor came back about five and she was worse, not vomiting, but the headache was worse. She didn't want to move her head at all, he sent for the ambulance."

"Did you speak to her at all?"

"Yes Shaun, that's what worries me, it took an age for her to recognise me. Shaun... you know the ould bitch has hardening of the arteries, it couldn't be that, could it?"

"Don't be silly, Kath, she's only a kid, it'll be all those hormones racing around. You wait and see."

"Yes. You're probably right. Pray God that you are."

"Is Dad going to call you or what?"

"I don't know, he's pretty beat up, only got in from a trip this morning. I've rung James, he should be here any minute, we'll go up. I just thought I'd better ring you first."

"Good girl, Kath. Try not to worry, and give us a call from the hospital, you can always reverse the charges."

"Okay, Rockefeller. Talk to you guys soon."

We hadn't seen Eileen since leaving Northern Ireland, though we did speak to her nearly every week. I hoped that there was nothing much wrong, despite the fact that on many occasions I could cheerfully have strangled her (well, maybe not). But little sisters can be, and usually are, the bane of a teenage boy's life.

We put the brochures aside and made coffee. Harry rang his mum and she urged us both not to worry, talking in easy terms about 'women's problems' and puberty. By ten that evening, when we hadn't heard from anyone, I rang the hospital. Following the usual shunting around, strange background noises and silences.

"Are you family?"

"Yes. This is Eileen's brother calling from London."

"I see."

"How is she? Can you tell me what the matter is?"

"All I can say at the moment is that your sister is holding her own. You should call back in a couple of hours when we should have a better idea of how she is."

At that point I began to be more than a little worried and concerned.

"Please nurse, what *is* the matter with her? What do you mean, holding her own? Where is she?"

"Ah, Mr McKenna, I really cannot discuss these matters over the ph... "

"Too bloody right you'll discuss it! This is my sister we are talking about! I get a call from my other sister to say that she has been taken ill, with no one seems to know what, and is in hospital. Now you talk about her holding her own, as if she was at death's door. Then you refuse to *discuss* the matter! What am I supposed to do here in London, sign a pledge of secrecy? Talk to me, damn you, or put me on to someone who will right now."

Harry's eyes had assumed saucer proportions as I fairly yelled down the phone. Again he came close to listen, I wrapped my free arm round him, just for the comfort of his touch.

"Just a moment please, Mr McKenna."

There was some blurred conversation in the background, then: "Mr. McKenna?" A different female voice, quiet and tired.

"Yes?"

"I'm Dr McVeigh."

"Yes doctor, what *is* the matter with Eileen?"

"Well, you must understand that at this stage we are not one hundred per cent certain. We're still awaiting the results of some tests."

"And?" I prompted.

"We think, that is I think, your sister may have meningococcal septicaemia."

I looked at Harry and raised my eyebrows; he shrugged and shook his head.

"Mr McKenna, are you there?"

"Yes, I'm here. What does that mean, doctor, and what did the nurse mean when she said that Eileen was holding her own?"

"Yes, that is a good sign. She's managing to retain her grip on consciousness, and believe me, we are doing everything we know how."

I was taken aback and Harry paled, put both arms round me and hugged.

"But doctor, you sound as if she was... I mean, is it *that* serious? " Faintly incredulous at what I was hearing.

"I would be doing you a grave disservice, Mr McKenna if I was to pretend that your sister's condition was other than critical. I can give you no guarantees, and should your sister slip into a coma, well then, I'm afraid the situation would be very serious indeed."

"Should we come?"

"I would suggest that you call back around midnight, we will know for certain then what we are dealing with here. But Mr. McKenna, I won't mislead you or raise false hopes, Eileen's condition is very grave."

"Is Dad there, can I talk to him?"

"Not now, your father and sister are with Eileen, helping to keep her going. I'll tell them you called."

"Thank you, doctor."

Harry immediately rang Jean. "Ask her to tell Gran, would you love, I don't suppose any one has had time to think of it yet."

Jean had a brief word with both of us, declaring that she would go out to Ballymartin and take Gran to the hospital, if she wanted to go, and in any event would go up herself.

"Thanks, Aunt Jean."

"You two stay right there until I call. Do you hear me?"

"Yes Mum."

"No dashing off to airports now. Do you understand?"

"Yes Mum," we both chorused.

"That's my boys. Talk to you soon."

Dave and Nu came round, more for the company than anything else. Dave looked and acted decidedly uncomfortable, fidgeting like mental as he knocked back a couple of quick whiskies, unable to meet my gaze. Nu muttered at him in Chinese when he got up to refill his glass again.

"Yes, Dave," Harry grumbled. "What *is* the matter with you?"

He sat down heavily. "Look Shaun," he cleared his throat. "Aw shit! I can only suppose the doctor didn't want to say it over the phone."

"Say what?" I ventured.

"I don't see why I have to be the one to tell you, but with the way the doctor spoke to you, she did say Eileen's condition was very grave?"

I nodded.

"Shaun." He drew a breath. "Meningitis is a killer. I'm sorry."

"Come *on*, David." Harry was angry. "She's not fourteen yet."

"I know, I know that. Believe me, I'm not out to scare you, but you have to be prepared. I'm truly sorry."

"I don't believe any of this, guys. Surely they can do something? I mean, she is in hospital, they have everything there. And what the hell is meningitis anyway?"

The phone rang.

"Hi, Mum."

"You both there, boys?"

"Yes." Sharing the receiver.

She sighed. "Not good news I'm afraid, they have confirmed the meningitis."

"Is she awake?"

"Just barely, boys."

"Did she know you?" Momentary silence.

"Mum?"

"I'm sorry boys, no. Her dad is the only one she's responding to now."

"Is she going to... die, Aunt Jean?" I felt ridiculous asking, she was only a kid. Kids didn't die that easily or quickly. Did they?

"God help me, Shaun. I'd give anything to be able to tell you that she'll be alright... and I'm afraid... I can't do that."

"She *is* going to die?"

"We should all pray for a miracle, son. But I'm sorry, it seems that, yes she will."

"Jean... NO!" My heart stuttered and I turned my head into Harry's shoulder.

"We'll be there in the morning."

... ...

"Yes. Both of us."

... ...

"No. We'll hire a car."

....

"Yes, we'll be careful."

....

"You'll call us if there is any change?"

"Okay, Mum. See you in the morning." Harry put the phone down to hold me tightly, caressing my hair.

* * *

We got seats on the early flight to Belfast.

David and Nu stayed until about one thirty, Nu giving me a long hug as they left, tears in both our eyes. They insisted that they would drive us to Heathrow in the morning. We rang the hospital again at three, there was little change, but the tone of the nurse we spoke to seemed very sombre. Dad knew we had called but didn't want to leave her side. Kath was asleep in James's arms and Jean had left to take Gran home. We said we'd call again around six, just before leaving for the airport, had a shower and shave and lay down on top of the bed. Lights out, cuddling in the dark. Harry strong and reliable stroking my hair, being my rock, my love, my life. He insisted that we have something to eat before leaving, encouraging me to have two boiled eggs and toast. He rang the hospital to be told that there was no change and lessening hope.

Nu arrived alone at six-ten. Dave had gone on a bender when they got home, passing out about five.

"You know him," shrugging as we went out to the car. "Don't be silly," he said, followed by grumbles in Chinese, when we protested that we could take a cab. "You are *my* brothers. Did you not know that?" He glared at us in the mirror. "My Davy didn't want either of you going back there. So, you be very careful, okay?"

"Okay, brother mine," being rewarded with a smile. At the airport we hugged and kissed him.

"Remember to be careful and don't worry about the flat or plants or anything. If you have to stay a few days I'll look after everything."

We waved, and turning away, boarded the plane.

By ten we were having tea with Gran, having decided to stay with her, as it would be less likely to draw comments. She'd shrunk, even on what she'd been when we last saw her, a cigarette dangling from her lips, ash dropping where it would.

"Aye, boys." She surveyed us over her specs. "Aye, boys. Tis men ye are. Aye. And two fine ones at that. Let me look at ye."

Taking my face between her hands and turning it to the light. "Och aye, laddie. Ould Shaunny'll nivir die." She turned to Harry. "And yer mother hit the jackpot wi' ye. Ye must be breaking hearts by the dozen. Not that I suppose ye'd notice."

He grinned at her and planted a smacker on her withered cheek. "It's great to see you again, Grannie McKenna."

"Wheesht! But would ye listen to the grand English voice on him. No childer." she continued when we asked if she wanted to come to the hospital. "I'm too ould, too slow, and I can't bear to look on the child. I'll say a wee prayer for her. Aye. I'll away down the chapel. Take a key, and if I'm in my bed when ye get back, just come in and tell me how the wee creatur is." She shook her old head. "I'm afeared it'll not be good news, boys. Aye, I am that." She sighed as we stood to leave. "God in his wisdom sends burdens no man should have to bear. Hasn't my wee Shaun put up with enough, that he should have to bear this too?"

"Gran, I'm sorry, we must go. Are you sure you won't come?"

"Away wi' ye boys and drive careful now. I'll talk to ye when ye get back. Aye. God speed."

Driving into Kilkeel, the fields of childhood, so vast and strange then, were like postage stamps now. Harry commented on how narrow and twisting the roads were, compared to the dual carriage-ways and motorways of England.

"Can't believe I used to do seventy along here," as we passed my old school at Maghereagh.

* * *

'If looks could kill' was the thought that blazed in my mind as we entered Jean's kitchen. The venomous disbelief in the glare from the toad-like figure slumped at the table should have been enough to puddle the pair of us there and then.

"Morning, Charles," Harry said after hugging his mother. Whilst Jean embraced me the words "Fucking slimy, perverted, *popish bastards!*" rang out explosively. Chair rasping on the stone floor. Back door bouncing off the wall, he'd slammed it so hard on leaving.

"Oh dear," Jean sighed. "Shaun, Harry, I'm sorry." Ruffling my hair.

"I take it he didn't know we were coming?"

"No. Though he knew something was going on. I think you may just have spoiled his day."

"I hope Uncle John's warnings still hold good. Sorry, Aunt Jean."

"I wouldn't worry on that score, boys. Now, you go on, I'll be there in a wee while. Take these for your Dad and Kathleen." She gave me a shopping bag with toothbrushes and paste, razor and other toiletries. "Go on now, I'll see you soon."

* * *

"Dad! Kath!"

Eileen looked *so* small, about ten years old. Lost in the bed and the machinery attached to her. Tubes in her nose, arm, the back of her hand and snaking out from under the bedding. The incessant clicking and beeping. An oxygen mask covered most of her face. She looked dead. You had to watch very carefully to see the rise and fall of her chest.

Dad was red-eyed and aged, two or more days' stubble on his face, misery in his every movement.

"Shaun, Harry." He rose stiffly to envelope us both. "My poor wee girl." He sagged between us, his tiredness and grief palpable in the very air. "You two are taking a chance coming here."

"We'll be alright, Daddy. Don't worry."

Kath was crying openly, relief on her face that she was not going to be left on her own to cope when the inevitable came.

We eventually got Dad to go and have a wash and shave. The nurses coaxed him to lie down for an hour or so, backed up by Jean, who arrived as he was cleaning up. "Just an hour or two, Shaun," she urged. "We'll call you if there is the slightest change. You know you're going to collapse else."

Eileen! My Eileen. My poor wee frog. Harry and I talked to her. Called her Frogface and Goblin, talked maths, reminded her I needed someone to cover for me when I stole the talc. Asked about Majorca. All to no avail. By three in the afternoon it was evident she was well along the way on her final journey.

Dad shook his head, mute, tears streaming down his face in a river that would not stop.

Jean looked after us all as late afternoon and early evening rapidly descended into darkness. She held Kath when emotion and tiredness at last broke her strength. Harry never let go my hand. Dad just sat with a hand on Eileen's arm, his eyes fixed on her face. His own face wet and tortured as her breathing became the merest sigh.

Doctor McVeigh and the consultant assured us she was not

suffering. They increased the flow of liquids into her body, gave her a series of injections during the day. Then, as evening became night, they advised that very little time was left. A young priest, summoned from somewhere in the building, gave her the last rites at eight o'clock.

Against all expectations, it was not until 3.50 am that a slight change manifested itself. Her face, already pale, whitened to bone colour. Her pitifully shallow breathing grew ragged and stopped, started again, and then – undramatically – ceased altogether.

Doctor McVeigh checked her heart and reflexes, then turned the machines off.

The silence was complete, incredible.

I looked at death with utter disbelief.

"Aye, God." Dad's voice was low and venomous. "Why a *child*, God?" He didn't see any of us as he shuffled out of the room to rest his head against a window, staring unseeing into the dark. Kath was folded in Jean's arms, both in tears, my hand was numb from the pressure of Harry's grip.

James Perry arrived a few minutes later. Taking in the scene at a glance, he went to Dad and drew him away down the corridor. It should have been me, but I was incapable of movement. Jean took Kath out. Harry and I remained at the bedside a few minutes longer, until Dr McVeigh gently urged us to leave – the nurses, one in tears, needed to prepare her.

We all sat silent in the waiting area at the top of the stairs; for maybe twenty minutes nobody spoke. The machinery was removed, the nurses washed her, brushed out her hair and laid her out.

I couldn't stay in there, I felt faint, ill. I kissed her forehead, as did Harry, then he took me back to the waiting area. Kath and James knelt down with Dad and said a rosary. Jean had disappeared a little while earlier. Eventually Kath and James joined us. My composure had at least partially returned.

I looked at James. "Dad?"

"He won't leave her."

Then Jean came back – with Graham! He must have broken every law in the Highway Code to have reached the hospital so quickly. She walked him down to the side ward, returning alone a moment later.

"Graham will look after him." She looked at us. "You two should go to bed. You're staying with Gran?"

Harry nodded.

"Go on then. Be back at your Dad's by three tomorrow. Go

on now." She turned to James. "Can you take Kathleen with you? If not, she can stay with me, plenty of room."

"Kath's coming home with me," he confirmed.

"Off with you then."

Harry and I went along to see Dad before we left. He and Graham were sitting side by side at the bed. Dad's face was ravaged, eyes burnt into his head, hand resting on Eileen's crossed fingers.

"Aye, boys. Away out to your Gran's. I'll be alright. Has Kath gone?"

I nodded, not trusting myself to speak, I couldn't look at Eileen, bright sparks skittered before my eyes.

"Catch him Ha... "

I came to in the waiting area, a nurse holding a compress to my head.

"Sorry Aunt Jean, Harry."

Jean followed us to Kilkeel, flashing her lights as she turned into the Harbour Road. Ten minutes later, as we let ourselves in, Gran's door opened.

"Thought I heard the car." She looked at our faces and drew an unsteady breath. "Och, childer, childer." Tears beginning to leak down the wrinkles. "God ha' mercy on the poor wee soul." She shuffled into the kitchen. "Come away in boys, sit yerselves down." She lit a cigarette with trembling fingers. "Why should I have lived so long?" She looked all of a hundred years old.

Grief and exhaustion poleaxed me, though I had thought sleep would be impossible. I was swallowed up by the feather mattress, under a welter of blankets, secure in Harry's arms. I had time to kiss him, thank him for his strength and love, then sleep claimed me.

19

Eileen's body was released to us at four o'clock the next afternoon and Dad had her taken direct to Massforth chapel. He said he wasn't having any of the Scrogg Road scum trailing through the house with their false sympathy.

"We'll 'wake' her at my mother's this evening. Just the family" – including John, Jean, Graham and James in a tired smile. Well, they are all family.

The funeral was set for the following day, and Father Sheridan met us at the church door. From the scowl which spread on his face, I gathered that he would have loved to refuse entry to all the Hannahs as well as me. However, as all Eileen's classmates were there, along with most of their parents and teachers, he seemed to think better of making a scene.

There was an audible murmur from some quarters when Harry and I took the rear of her coffin on our shoulders and followed Dad and John, supporting the front, into the church. Father Sheridan was livid particularly as John, Jean, Harry and Graham joined us, the immediate family in the front pew. He no longer bothered to try hiding his feelings, standing glaring so long that even the altar boys started to fidget.

Dad stared back calmly.

"Lost your tongue, Eamon?" Murmuring from the congregation was beginning to grow, accompanied by an increasing amount of foot shuffling and throat clearing.

"This is an innocent child," the voice still quiet, without inflection. "Do your God-given duty by her soul,"

By this time the priest was literally shaking with rage at the altar. Clenching his fists by his sides he took the two steps to the altar rail.

"I want to see you, in the vestry, now!"

"No, Eamon," Dad answered. "Anything you have to say, you say here. In front of your God and your people."

Eamon Sheridan bore a close resemblance to Ian Paisley, both in his manner and volume of speech and in his bullying self-righteousness. He didn't hesitate.

"God has delivered a judgement on you, Shaun McKenna, you and your perverted family. You have been judged and found wanting. You and yours have indulged in incest, sodomy and collusion with the enemies of the One True Church. Your daughter has been taken from your care before she could be tainted, and rightly so. I tell you, all you people, there is no place in this House of God for perverts and Orangemen! There will be no prayers offered for this child until the pollution present in our midst is expelled." His face was red and beaded with perspiration as he stood shaking a clenched fist in our direction.

There were muted cries of 'shame' and 'bigot' but, also words of encouragement. "You tell the proddy bastards," and "Right, Father".

Dad stood up and faced the body of the church holding up a hand for quiet.

"We come here today, my family and friends – along with

Eileen's friends – to pray for her and to see her properly laid to rest. Anyone here for any other reason should leave. There will be no confrontation, no argument. Me, and mine, we remain until right is done by my daughter Eileen." He faced the front and sat down. I could tell he was furious by the narrowing of his eyes.

"You may wait till hell itself freezes over, Shaun McKenna, I will not do it."

"Then the bishop will be so informed, Eamon," Dad replied. "I shall also inform him that you used the occasion of an innocent child's funeral to display your bigotry, prejudices and lack of Christianity before half your congregation." Dad looked round the Church. "It's a grand display you are putting on for young kids, *father!*"

Veins were throbbing in the priest's forehead.

"There will be no service in the presence of *perverts and Orangemen!*"

"Is that your last word, Eamon?"

"Aye! It is that."

"In that case, if you will excuse me," turning back to the body of the church and raising his voice, "I'm sorry everyone, due to the bigotry and lack of Christianity on display here today in this house of Christ, my daughter's remains will now be transferred to the Church of Ireland on Newry Street. All are welcome to attend her burial at eleven tomorrow."

There was a united gasp of disbelief all round and the priest left the altar to grab Dad by the arm. "You cannot bury the child in unhallowed ground." He was practically foaming at the mouth.

Dad shook him off. "It is you who are denying her a Catholic burial."

"You are condemning her soul to eternal hellfire!"

"Rubbish, Eamon, her bodily resting place has no bearing on her soul."

"I will *not* do it," and he literally stamped his foot.

"I will!" came a quavering voice.

Dad smiled. "Thank you, Father," taking the arm of a very old priest approaching from the vestry.

"You are retired," Father Sheridan snapped.

"Once a priest, always a priest." The man raised a palsied hand. "And if you attempt to stop me, *my* voice will be heard in Armagh and it *will* be listened to."

Father Sheridan seemed about ready to explode. Suddenly I remembered who the old priest was, Father Sweeney! Dad and

Seamus had been altar boys for him years ago.

Eamon Sheridan's voice was full of loathing. "God will see that you rue the day you were born, Shaun McKenna, for you will be cast out and cast down. Your sins are many and great and this is but the first, and the least, of the punishments the Lord has in store for you."

"Prophesying now, Eamon?"

"I speak only as I know," and he turned to Harry and me. He was cold, dismissive, yet brimming with pure hatred. "*You!* You and your kind are an anathema in the sight of God and man. You are lower than the serpent and like the serpent, you will be ground into the dust of the earth. The torments you will suffer in this life are as nothing to those you face in the eternity to come." Jean, John and Graham he did not even look at. "I wash my hands of this whole affair."

"Better for you in the eyes of God that you should pray to Him for forgiveness, pray to Him to send you His Grace to see your way through the hatred in your heart and to the light of His true love." The old man's voice, like his hands may have trembled, but there was no doubting his compassion as we watched Father Sheridan shoulder his way through the now silent people and out of the church.

"My good people." Father Sweeney had ascended the altar and turned to face us. "You are *all* welcome in this house of God. God makes *no* distinction between man and man. Only man himself does that." He raised his hand and made the sign of the cross. "We will now pray for the child laid here before us, and tomorrow, you are *all* welcome to the Requiem Mass for the repose of her soul."

He smiled at our thanks after the short service, refusing to accompany us from the church.

"I will say a prayer here to cleanse this house and ease the child's soul. Do not worry on her behalf, she is with the Blessed Virgin now." He took Jean's hand and blessed her. "You are all welcome in the sight of God. When you truly believe in Him, it matters not where or how you express that belief, so long as you do so with love and forgiveness in your heart. God does not check a true offering to see the sender's address," he went on, his old eyes resting on Harry and me, flicking to Dad standing with Graham. "Love has many expressions. True love, whatever it's form, is no bar to the love of God. Times are changing and though I may not live to see it, I believe that the true heartfelt love of a man for a man, or that of a woman for a woman, will yet be accepted by this Mother of Churches for what it is. *Love!* That being so, and sure in the love of Christ for all mankind, I tell you there is no sin in love. Go in peace, children, and pray for me."

The boiling anger engendered by Father Sheridan drained away with the words of this frail old man. The conviction in his voice, the compassion in his eyes and the logic of his words remain with me always. And though my belief in any God was due for rapid extinction, I cannot help wishing that more of his ilk were in positions where they could be heard.

* * *

The following morning, Massforth was packed, people standing at the back and down both sides. I didn't think they had all come to honour Eileen, and wondered whether it was a show of Christianity, or had some come in the hope of witnessing another row with Father Sheridan? Afterwards, Dad said it was probably a bit of both. Eamon Sheridan had been vindictive enough not to have allocated altar boys for the Mass and – reverting nervously to being ten years old again – I assisted the old man when he made the lack known from the vestry door. Which was the biggest scandal of the two days? Oh, definitely the sight of a well-known, self-confessed pervert at the altar.

The merest trickle of people came up for communion despite the crowd in the chapel. I could see parents preventing friends of Eileen's from doing so. Harry was white-faced and suffering on my behalf and I shocked half of Kilkeel by flashing him a big smile as I held the patten for Dad. It was just as well so few did partake, I was having serious doubts as to Father Sweeney's ability to carry through with the service. I thanked God at that point for the warm gentle day, despite the lateness of the season, at least he wouldn't catch pneumonia at the graveside.

I need not have worried. Following prayers after communion his voice steadied remarkably, he seemed to gain strength, as he made a short speech from the pulpit on Christian love and forgiveness. It really wasn't preaching, more a reiteration of what he'd said the previous day. I had to smile though when he omitted the part on man to man and woman to woman. Old he might have been, ninety-three to be precise, and shaky he certainly was, but no fool.

He took my arm to steady himself as the coffin followed us to the newly-dug grave. Two of Eileen's teachers and two of the crew from the 'Mary Jean' carried her to her last resting-place. Dad with

Kath and James stood alongside Harry and his family as the final blessing was given, the final rosary said. Dad, John, Graham, Harry, James, her teachers and the boys from the 'Mary Jean', they all helped cover her with the dark rich soil. Floral tributes, including a single white rosebud from David and Nu, covered the little mound of bare earth.

Eileen! Eileen my wee frog. Oh God!

* * *

Harry and I helped Father Sweeney disrobe in the vestry. He turned down an invitation to come to the house. His holiday in the parish he had served so many years came to an end that day.

"God was good to me here, boys. I spent fifty-four years tending His flock here." His voice quivered with emotion. "Aye, all is as He wills, but I would that He had seen fit to let me see my time out here. Not that I dispute His will you understand." He laughed. "It's just, sometimes His decisions take a lot of prayer, even then they can be hard to understand and accept. Forgive me Jesus," fixing his eyes on the cross, "and bless my two young friends here. Give them ease in their grief and strengthen the love in their hearts." Again he traced the sign of the cross over us and obediently we crossed ourselves.

"Thank you, Father."

"Now, if you'll just walk me up to the house, you can rejoin your families."

Only the two families remained at the graveside when we returned. Kath in tears, as she rearranged the flowers, assisted by James. Dad, John and Graham stood watching whilst, a little way off, Jean was pretending to read the gravestones and crying at the same time.

"I think we should go to Gran's now."

"Aye, son," his eyes filling with tears again as he looked on the flower-covered mound. "There's nothing more we can do for her now."

John and Graham left together, Graham to be dropped off at home as his dad returned to the hotel. Dad went with Jean and of course Kath went with James. Harry and I followed on after a final farewell to Eileen.

Gran had sandwiches ready to go with the bannock and cakes that Jean had sent out earlier. The three women disappeared into the bedroom, presumably to have a little weep in private. That left us four men to twiddle our thumbs, until Harry took charge and started making tea. James Perry was never at ease with us and I suspect he was having serious doubts about Dad, he couldn't have failed to notice how close Graham and Dad were. I think he was still of that school of thought which says 'married men cannot be queer', but he was evidently having a great deal of difficulty reconciling what he saw with what he thought he knew. He would flinch in the most obvious way if Harry or I bumped into him, and given the lack of space in Gran's kitchen, that was inevitable. Recognising his acute discomfort, Dad took him into the front room.

"Phew, what a relief." Harry grinned. "Do you really think he's *that* scared of us?"

"Don't know, love. Don't really care."

"Sorry Shaun, said the wrong thing."

"No, you didn't, Harry," putting my arms round him. "I can't wait to get you home tonight." Kissing the back of his neck, cock nudging his arse.

"Ah! That's it. Is it?" leaning his head back on my shoulder. "Why wait that long?"

"Where?"

"Do you not think we could find that little dell in Kilbroney again?"

"Sure of it, Harry. When, now?"

"No. We'd better have a sandwich first. Then just say we're going out for a couple of hours. Back say at six? That'll give us plenty of time to get to the airport."

I released him as we heard the bedroom door open. "Yeah, our flight's not till nine."

"What is not until nine?" Jean taking over laying up the tray.

"Our flight, Mum."

"Oh that! Come on, you bring the cups, and you can bring the milk and sugar."

We were all struggling to reach acceptance of Eileen's death and I felt sure that over the next few days the burden of grief would only increase. Worry about Dad and how he would cope over the coming weeks warred with the desire to be away, back at home in our flat, with Harry. I needed time with him to make my own adjustments. I knew it would be bad. I also knew he would be my rock and willing helper as I came to terms with death.

"Shaun! You okay?"

Tears were rolling down my face without my realising it.

"Yes, sorry love. It's just... I can't bring myself to believe it."

"I know, son." Dad's voice was calm, far too calm. "Belief is the very hardest part. You *know* it is true... Believing takes a great deal longer, and, I'll tell you something else. Acceptance? It *never* comes. *Never!*

"I think Shaun and I will go out for a wee while."

"Go, where?"

"We'll take a walk in Kilbroney, Mum, don't worry, we'll be back by six."

"Shaun, Harry, don't go. Can't you just have a walk on the shore?"

"Don't worry, Kath," I followed Harry to the door. "We'll be alright."

"Drive careful, childer."

"See you later, Gran."

Accustomed as we had become to the constant traffic flows, we found the roads very quiet, even Kilkeel seemed more than half dead as we turned up Newry Street.

"If this was the Continent, I'd say that everyone was having a siesta." Harry mirrored my thoughts exactly.

"I shall be very glad to get on that plane tonight."

"Me too," he agreed. "This just isn't home any longer."

* * *

Oh God. Oh God. Oh God Oh God... ... ... I CANNOT DO THIS.

* * *

Damn you, Singh. Damn you, Singh. Double damn you. I don't believe you!

* * *

A few minutes later we swung into the park entrance followed by an old white Transit. As we took the fork for the Forest Drive it turned into the bottom car park.

"Didn't recognise that one Shaun, he was behind us most of the way."

"Maybe gypsies," I shrugged. "Who cares?"

The top car park was completely deserted as he pulled up beside the toilet block at the bottom.

"Too much tea, love," he said apologetically, hastily unzipping his flies as he scampered into the loo. I locked the car and rested against the bonnet, lighting two cigarettes, giving him one when he rejoined me and inhaling deeply through my nose.

"Mmm. Isn't the pine fantastic?" We walked up the slope towards the path. "You know, it's just about the only thing I miss in London, the fresh air."

"Never mind, love, in three months time we'll be getting plenty of fresh air."

"We'd better make a definite booking when we get back."

"First thing tomorrow, love," crushing the cigarette butt underfoot as we ducked beneath the branches and on to the path.

"You sure you remember where we turn off?"

I punched his shoulder lightly. "Oh, we'll find it, and of course I remember. Don't you?"

"Oh, just the occasional flash," grinning like the proverbial Cheshire cat and almost succeeding in tripping me up.

"Not fair, Harry," regaining my balance and giving him a push from behind. "Go on, slowcoach."

"Okay, okay. But it's steeper than I remember." He began to pant.

"Rubbish, Harry Hannah, you're older and not as fit as you were, too much good living."

By the time we reached the relatively flat stretch before the last steep climb, I was ready to admit that I wasn't as fit as I had been either.

"Nah," he said when we stopped to regain our breath, looking with distinctly jaundiced eye at the steeply curving way before us. "It's these damned fags. Mum did say we were idiots to have started."

"I know. Did you hear Gran yesterday? Oh no, that's right, you went to the loo," as he shook his head. "Anyway, she said that only people over eighty should be allowed to smoke."

"You ready to go on?"

I nodded.

"Did she give any reason?"

"Oh yeah. She said that at her age it hardly mattered. And if it did kill you, it would at least save the NHS from having to look after you when you got too old to cope."

"She has aged, hasn't she?"

"Mmm, she's gotten very slow."

"Shaun?" he hesitated.

"Go on, love."

We broke out of the trees, and at a nod from Harry, made our way to the old bench set amongst the heather. I sat down gratefully, sweat beading my brow. He stood, shoulders heaving, looking down on me. Then, with a small smile, he lay down full length on the seat, his head resting on my lap. Taking my right hand, he slid it inside his jacket over his heart, covered it with both of his. My eyes stung a little as I stroked his hair back, revealing the broad, white forehead.

"Do you remember...?" we started together, then had a fit of the giggles. He almost rolled off the seat. Grabbing him by the shoulders I leant over and kissed his brow.

"What was it you were going to say just now?"

"Oh that!" suppressing the giggles sternly. "Now, don't be mad at me, Shaun," gazing up into my eyes.

"You'd better say whatever it is you've got to say, otherwise I just might."

"Might what?"

"Get mad." I pinched a nipple through his shirt.

"Owww, beast." Clutching my fingers. "Mind you, that kind of mad I could get used to."

"Have got used to you mean." I went back to stroking his hair. "Well? Come on, out with it."

"What! *Here?*" mock alarm, raising his head to peer around.

"Harry!!!!"

"Okay, okay." He adopted his best martyred expression. "I don't ever want to come back here." He looked at me expectantly, but I said nothing. "To Northern Ireland, I mean. Not for Christmas, not for funerals and I don't care whose. I never want to see this country again."

I looked over the lough far below, to the grey mountains on the other side, and smelt the heather mingled with the pine. I listened to the cawing of the rooks and the rustle of the wind in the branches.

"Well?"

I looked down and met his gaze, green and deep.

"Good!"

Leaping to his feet he pulled me into a crushingly hungry embrace.

"Love you," I gasped when my ribs had resumed their normal position.

"And so you should, McKenna," reinforcing that with a kiss, long, light and very satisfying.

272

"Do you want to go on?" As he released my lips at last, drawing back a little, so that we were nose to nose.

"Mmm," brushing the impertinent snub of a nose with the tip of my tongue. "I'd really like to find that little dell again. Maybe take a twig or something as a souvenir. You know?"

"Romantic soppy git." A pleased smile as he gave me a push. "Come on then, we'll have to start back pretty soon." Taking the lead. "How about a pine cone?"

"What about a pine cone?"

"Well, when we settle on a place, maybe we could grow our own pine tree to remind us."

"Now who's soppy?" managing to trip him up and into a big bank of heather.

"Hey! That's not fair." He took my extended hand and yanked me off my feet instead of getting up. "And from behind as well," caressing my arse.

"Come on, come on. No fooling around." I dragged us both upright.

"You started it."

"Okay, okay. Say, do you think we've passed it?"

"No. Isn't it just about here we passed the old boy?"

"Mmm, could be. I don't really know." I looked to the right, and sighed. "I don't suppose it really matters."

"No! Go on. Go on." I got a gentle nudge. "Look there, no. Just here, see?"

In truth, I didn't see at all. But he was off, bent double through the trees. Following, I was almost sure this wasn't the place. The branches were a great deal thicker and lower than I remembered and it seemed to be taking much longer.

I heard him laugh joyously from somewhere close in front, and we were there, just as we both remembered, but without the sun. His head was down scanning the floor of the dell.

"Look here." He bent down to pick up a cone. "This one has plenty of seeds, we could have our own forest."

"How long will they keep?" rolling it round in my hand.

"Oh, years I should think," as I put it in my pocket. "We'll have to take the seeds out when it opens and keep them somewhere safe."

I leant back with a sigh of contentment when his arms encircled me from behind. Warm breath brushed my neck and he nibbled on an ear, his hands sliding down my front to the crotch, and eagerly awaiting cock.

"Too cold to get undressed," I voiced as his fingers lowered my zipper, ferreted round inside, and released cock into the fresh air. Reaching behind me, I pulled him close, so that I could feel his hardness nudging me through the cloth.

He has never been a great one for words, my cock, shrugging aside any awareness of the cold. Plainly he was not going to be intimidated by a little coolness in the air. Leaning my head back to rest on Harry's shoulder, keeping him tight against me, I gazed on the racing clouds and gave myself up to the entreaty of his knowledgeable hands.

As was normal, on those rare occasions when he had been denied any outlet for more than thirty-six hours, cock was determined to make the most of every stroke, pinch and squeeze. His nerve endings were super-sensitive, just the touch of cool air on his head everytime it was uncovered sent a shiver all the way up my spine.

"Ahh, my lovely man. I love you. Truly I do." Kneading his buttocks harder as my leg gave a warning tremor. He gripped the side of my neck with his teeth, his left hand cradling and squeezing my balls, the right now flying on cock's shaft. Tight, short hard strokes then light and teasing, pulling the foreskin up, tickling cock's head through it and releasing him into the air again. Another tremor and the clouds seemed to stand still.

"*Now*, Harry! Hard and fast."

"*Oh, God yes!*" as he obliged.

I had to screw my eyes shut as I shot forth gob after gob, smearing his fist, his left arm now encircling my chest and supporting me as I trembled at the knees. Bringing a hand to the front, I stilled his without having him let me go. Cock and I groaned as the final twitches diminished, his hood slowly covering his head against the chill. Turning in his arms, I kissed Harry, slipping a hand between us to grasp his straining hardness.

"Not in your pants, again?" I laughed from the sheer joy and release.

"Not yet, but you'll have to be quick, little goat."

Even as he spoke I was dropping to my knees and undoing his zipper at the same time. In a second he was jauntily savouring freedom from the restriction. Pausing only to lick the bright bead of pre-cum from the eye, I engulfed him, his hands coming to grip each side of my head.

"Easy, Shaun. Easy." Groaning as I caressed the underside with my tongue, pushing him against the roof of my mouth, swallowing

274

rapidly to mimic contractions on its head.

"Jesus, Shaun! Go easy." But we'd been together too long and too often for me not to know what his real preferences were. Fumbling just above my head I managed to undo his trousers and lower them to his knees. I ran my hand up the back of his thigh and inside the boxers. "Oh God! Shaun. Love." Panting as I parted his cheeks and my questing finger found his hole. Cock in my mouth, he would have screamed in ecstasy had he had a voice. Failing that, he attempted to burrow past my tonsils, and again as my finger slid in. Again as I tickled the inside of his arse just where cock's root curved under the pelvis.

"Ooh yes, yes. YES!" hands frantic about my head. "Jesus. Don't stop *now*!" as I paused momentarily to draw breath. Nothing loath, I rammed my nose into his pubic hair, nipped him lightly with my teeth and slid the finger all the way in. At the same time I endeavoured to increase the suction and speed up the tongue flicking. Reward came swiftly, heralded by the first contraction beginning under my finger.

"Ahh, God! Shit! Coming, Shaun. Coming."

By then he didn't need to tell me, I was busy trying not to drown in the first flood of salty sweet liquid filling my mouth. Only by the most rapid swallowing did I make way for a second, then a third spasm. Reaching behind himself he urged my hand away from his arse, which snapped shut with an almost audible 'pop', propelling the last gout onto my tonsils. Gingerly and with a series of little moans he moved backwards, holding me still with a hand on each shoulder when I tried to follow.

"Aww, spoilsport, you know how I like to hold you."

"I do know. How would I not?" His face wet with perspiration, eyes glowing. "Too sensitive today, love," in a tremulous voice. "You know the old saying 'absence makes the cock grow fonder'. " A pleased smile when I whooped at his sally.

As I stood up, we both realised that that indefatigable cock of mine, whom I had neglected to tuck away in the urgency of the moment, was bouncing up and down, drooling, begging for second helpings.

"Put it away, you randy little sod!" – both of us dissolving into the giggles, effectively putting cock into a sulk. "Honestly Shaun, you're sex mad."

"I know," grinning happily as I tucked the offended member away. "And isn't it lucky for me that you're even worse?"

"Perfectly normal boyish behaviour, McKenna."

"Aye! Well, we'll discuss boyish behaviour later. We'd better get a move on." We checked each other to ensure no tell-tale gobs of spunk had added an extra decoration.

"What *is* the time, Shaun?"

"You tell me."

"Where's your watch?" looking round in surprise. "And where's your ring?"

"Both in Gran's bathroom," I admitted. "Forgot to put them back on. Sorry."

"Honestly, McKenna, if I wasn't around to check up on you, you'd leave your head behind."

As he led the way back under the branches he took a quick glance at his wrist. "Hey! It's only a quarter past five. How about an ice cream with raspberry sauce before we go back?"

"Sounds good to me. Got any money on you?"

"Now don't tell me," hands on hips, head tilted to one side, as I straightened up from under the branches. "You forgot to pick up your wallet as well?"

I nodded sheepishly.

"Come here, cotton head," arms extending, long easy comfortable hug, ending with fleeting lip contact.

It was the last!

19

They took us as we entered the carpark.

We paid no attention to the old white Transit parked at the end of the path. Someone was behind the wheel trying to read a paper in the rapidly dying light. Harry raised an eyebrow at me and I shrugged.

Memory is hazy as to the exact sequence of events that followed. The months and years spent re-living every nuance may have distorted some things, but the end result remains inevitably the same.

As we passed along the side of the van, to go round the rear and down to the car some fifty yards away, the sound of the driver's door opening caused us both to look round.

From the corner of my eye, I saw a figure rushing round the back of the van towards us, arms raised to shoulder level and swinging something in our direction.

"RUN HARRY. RUN!" Screaming, pushing him out of the way, simultaneously trying to protect my face. I took the full force of the blow on my left cheekbone and the bridge of my nose.

The crunching thud of wood on bone.

The incredible pain. Accentuated when the back of my head bounced on the side panelling of the van.

Harry roaring: "BASTARDS! FUCKING BASTARDS!" as I slid to the ground.

I was awash with pain tinged with incredulous disbelief. I had the blurred impression of figures struggling practically on top of me. I could not get off the ground.

"SHAUN! SHAUN!"

His anguished scream was followed by another meaty crunching thud.

I passed out.

Came to in a complete daze. Head bouncing on cold metal, every bounce heightening the facial agony. Every time I bounced I tried to scream, only to realise I was almost choking on my own blood. Couldn't push myself up. Hands tied behind my back, lying on my right side, continual bouncing. I was in the back of the van, going up a very rough track.

Where was Harry? With only one eye that would open and in almost total darkness, I could not see a thing. A particularly violent lurch lifted me completely off the floor. Nearly blacked out again as I slammed back down.

"Fuckin' shite!" from above and in the direction of my feet.

"Shut yer sodding hole." Harsh, older voice.

I thought there had been a soft thud beside me. Then came a low tortured moan. Harry?

"Harry," whispering through the pain. "Harry?" I couldn't see him. Everything was so dark, my eyes didn't seem to be working.

Another low moan, filled with pain. Tried moving my leg. Tied together! Slowly bent my knees, touched something both soft and firm.

"Harry."

"Harry!"

Blinded by sudden light. Savagely kicked right between the cheeks of my arse. Cried out, head banging on the cab partition.

"Shut the fuck up!"

Another equally savage kick rendering my lower body completely numb.

"Sodding pervert."

Light on long enough to see Harry stretched out on his stom-

277

ach beside me. Back of his head towards me. Hair looking matted and shiny. BLOOD! Time enough to see three indistinct figures bracing themselves at the rear door. That meant at least four, if there was only the driver in the front. Light snapped off, darkness, blacker than ever, little shivers of sheer panic making me tremble.

Seconds later the van lurched to a halt. Short pause, engine still running, door slamming and we were off again. Dead slow, dipping to the right, dipping. Rolled me over, slammed my face into the panelling, passed out gratefully.

Half came to. Someone fumbling with my wrists, then my feet. I was sitting upright, tried to lift my head, only made myself cry out.

Head pulled up by the hair. Smashed across the face open-handed.

Scream after scream ripping from my throat as the pain increased a thousandfold.

"Leave the wee shit-licker." Voice helping to focus my vision. Harry?

Directly in front of me. Tied to a chair, which was tied to what? Bare two-tiered wooden bunks. Light, yellow and hissing. Tilley lamps? Where *were* we?

"LEAVE HIM, I said," as my head was yanked by the hair and bounced off wood behind me.

"Wake his boyfriend up."

Three of them. All in new blue overalls, wearing balaclavas. Hands looking very odd – my eyes? No, surgical gloves, against fingerprints!

Harry wasn't moving. Was he DEAD? OH GOD NO! PLEASE NO! We'd get over this somehow. My heart shrivelled at the sure knowledge of what was to come. My testicles crawled into my abdomen.

This was going to be a 'punishment beating'.

"Harry?" I could barely form the word. Sounded more like a grunt than speech, even to me.

The smallest of the three had left the room. Where was the fourth? Smallest returned carrying a tin bucket of water. He poured it over Harry's head, soaking him thoroughly but bringing him round. Enough so that he slowly raised his head. Slowly, so very slowly.

Apart from a 'mouse' under one eye, his face was unmarked, but his eyes! His EYES, rolling in his head, the whites bright scarlet with burst blood vessels.

"Harry! Jesus Harry." Answered by a low listless moan, a moan that went on and on. He can't see, I thought. HE CAN'T SEE!

At some signal I'd missed, the one who'd slapped me around left the room, returning moments later carrying a stool and a couple of long pieces of wood. Hurley sticks? Hockey sticks? Same thing.

He set the stool in front of Harry, whose head by then had sunk back down onto his chest.

The one who had spoken (I realised the others hadn't yet) lifted Harry's left foot and placed it on the stool. Gripping it by the ankle, he leant all his weight on it and nodded to the other two.

Harry's head came off his chest at the second blow to his knee. The other two – 'Smallest' and 'Slapper' were raining blows on his knee with all their strength. 'Slapper's stick had a couple of six-inch nails hammered all the way through it.

The low moan changed to a thin high-pitched continuous scream. His face wet and white. He vomited a little. Head flailing, eyes starting from their sockets.

The seventh blow, a soft scrunching sound and an incredible animal-like wail announcing the shattering of bone.

Releasing his grip, 'Speaker' pushed the leg to one side. Another tortured wail as the foot hit the ground. The leg bent the wrong way! He picked up the other foot. Why didn't Harry struggle? Must have been the blow to the back of his head in the car park. I vomited as his other leg was pulped. Ten, maybe eleven blows this time and all the while that thin never-ending scream. JESUS, let him pass out, but no. Just how aware he was, I really don't know, I only know what the doctors said afterwards. I *do* know that he felt *every* blow.

My mind crouched shivering in some hole as they turned their attention to his hands. The stick with the nails! OH GOD!!!!

The room permeated with the smell of shit, His, mine? I don't know.

As a finale, 'Speaker' held Harry's head steady by the hair, and 'Slapper' measured up with his stick. Screaming "NONONONO" didn't do me or Harry any good. He smashed Harry full in the mouth with the edge of the hockey stick. The wail cut off. Harry's head jerked out of 'Speaker's' hand, leaving him holding a hank of black hair.

Head slowly tilting forward again. Face shedding blood and teeth. Jaws broken, dislocated? My brain spun.

"Well, boyfriend no beauty now, eh?" 'Speaker' standing beside me.

Surely Harry was dead.

"Aye, it'll be a day or two till he looks human again." Patting my broken cheek, laughing as I screamed.

"Take a break, lads," and he left the room followed by 'Slapper'.

'Smallest' looked round to ensure I was watching. He flipped his dick out and pissed on Harry. In his mouth and eyes, down to his crotch and back up again. Laughing low, he tucked himself away, and left. Something tried to surface in my mind but I was too terrified to grasp it. I was under no illusion about not receiving similar treatment and vomited at the thought. My face felt like several pneumatic drills were working on it at the same time.

"Harry, Harry. PLEASE Harry." I knew it was hopeless, but what else was there?

"Harry. Harry my love. HARRY!" No response. Dead? God, NO! ANYTHING! Anything but that. As if in answer to a prayer, his right arm twitched, a low moan reached me.

"Harry, Harry, I LOVE YOU. Oh GOD HELP US. Harry?"

How long did they stay away? Long enough for a smoke, a tea break? Do punishment squads have tea breaks?

They came back.

My mind was scurrying around in my head, like a rat in a cage looking for a way out, trapped. I prayed that I'd pass out.

A different strategy for me – arms and feet, arms first. I struggled, I really tried, but I was weakened and in no condition to offer much resistance. GOD! Bone is hard to break. I felt it snap above the left elbow. Came round when dashed in the face with cold water. Went through the same with the right, the elbow joint itself giving way eventually. More cold water.

Right foot beaten to a pulp, nails slammed all the way through. Wrenched out, slammed in again, out. SWEET JESUS, let me die, let me die NOW! HarryHarryHarryHarry Help ME! Alongside the agony, the sheer disbelief that this could be happening to US. Surely this was all some terrible nightmare.

Subconsciously aware of strange sounds emanating from Harry, audible even over my screams. Loud gurgling noises, half speech, bordering on comprehensible. Through my blurred vision, the tears, the pain, I could see that his head was upright. Poor smashed limbs hanging useless like some discarded doll. Head tilted, almost a listening attitude, useless bloody jaw agape. I knew then, really knew, that he was blind. Spittles of blood shooting from the cavity in his face as he tried for words. Louder now but no more distinct.

"HARRY!" I screamed as they removed my other shoe. "OH HARRY LOVE!" I never knew that the human voice-box was capable of producing sounds like those coming from the bloody ruin opposite.

Then, as the first blow dug the nails into my flesh, "HARRY" in a falsetto I'd never before reached, even as a boy soprano. His body strained and he roared, a sound that raised the hairs on the back of my neck, frustration and terrible anger combined in one wordless bellow.

"Fuck this!" 'Speaker' released his grip on my lower leg. I could see perspiration dripping from his balaclava. Crossing the few feet to Harry, he backhanded him across the ruin of his face, once each side.

"SHUT THE FUCK UP."

Silence for a second. Then, I will swear it, those amazing green eyes seemed to focus.

The doctors said this wasn't possible, but I KNOW what I saw.

"'aun, 'aun, 'aun." Jaw still gaping uselessly, blood flowing. Was it 'Shaun, Shaun, Shaun?' I believe it in my heart.

"FUCK YOU." 'Speaker' pulled a small gun from his pocket and put the barrel against the left side of Harry's head. He pulled the fucking trigger!

THERE IS NO GOD! THERE ARE NO FUCKING GODS!

Don't believe it when you read reports of death having been 'instantaneous'. It is not true. There is no such thing. I KNOW. I SAW IT.

He knew what was coming the instant the metal touched his head. He knew!

Those eyes! They smiled at me. One last sound: "Lau'." 'Love?' Yes, I KNOW it was. The force of the bullet knocked his head onto his shoulder. I saw the right side of his head bulge. Bulge as in slow motion. Bulge, and burst, shooting blood, bone and brains across the room.

His eyes were still alive. Looking at me. A slow tear from the right. For as long as a second, maybe two, they retained life. Harry was still looking at me. Then they went out, they stopped shining. Just like that.

He died.

STUNNED!

My good eye locked on Harry's.

My heart, falling, falling, falling down an endless drop.

All pain cancelled. STUNNED!

I was barely aware of 'Smallest'. "You said no killing." Something stirred in my brain but I barely registered anything.

"Shut the FUCK up."

Although my gaze was locked on Harry's corpse, I knew when 'Speaker' raised his arm, knew he was pointing the gun at me.

I neither heard the shot nor felt the bullet strike. Time enough to realise we would be together again, thank you God.

WAIT FOR ME HARRY.

* * *

I lay near death for twelve days and took another three weeks to regain consciousness. One thing I knew, from the moment I opened my eyes. Harry was DEAD and I wasn't. At that point my heart broke. I lost all interest in living, only the fact that the body was young and possessed of a strong survival trait kept me going.

Both my eyes had been saved, that, despite my other cheekbone having been smashed when I was chucked over a ditch on the Head Road, Harry's body thrown on top of me.

"Extensive bone and plastic surgery will be necessary." The surgeon was falsely cheerful. "When we've finished you'll be breaking even more hearts."

"Fuck off."

The bullet had passed through the chest, missing all vital organs, and lodged itself under the shoulderblade. "You are a very lucky lad." Broken bones would mend eventually, though likely I'd always have trouble with the left foot. For a few days, as my memory started to return, everyone thought I was on the way back to a full life, even if I'd never be completely okay.

The first memory? Sucking his cock in the dell, I could taste him on my tongue.

The second memory? Holding each other in that first sexual embrace in the darkness by the Mourne Cinema. Harry coming in his pants, wanking behind the pillar at the Royal Hotel.

Like doors, in a long corridor full of doors opening at random, it all came back. As it did I sank deeper and deeper into a never-never land. I may have been alive to look at, but on the inside I was dying by inches.

Always there was someone there and in the beginning I would

respond, even talk quite rationally. I had a long talk, several in fact, with the police. The beatings and murder had taken place in a mountain refuge above Dennywater, high on the slopes of Slieve Donard. The van had been found burnt out near Spelga dam and, either by quirk of fate or design, proved to have been stolen earlier that day from Hannah Building Supplies.

I couldn't tell them much about the beating or the 'punishment' squad, what was there to tell? Of course I knew why we had been taken! We were from opposite sides, we were perverts, why bother asking when they already knew? Why didn't they just fuck off and leave me alone? They weren't likely to catch them. And even if they did, they would only get a smack on the wrist from from Number 10, accompanied by an invitation to tea.

As the days passed, more doors opened in my mind, the enormity of my loss grew. I spoke less and less, saw people less and less. I knew they were there, I mean, I could see them perfectly well and hear them. I even imagined I saw Nu a couple of times, but it was all less real than my memories. They were all living illusions, even the doctors and nurses.

Four months after we had been found by two boys bunking off school, I wasn't even bothering to open my eyes; memories are more real played out on the inside of the eyelids, like a wide-screen movie. I hadn't managed sound effects as yet, though the colours were brilliant, especially his eyes. I would lose myself for hours, for days in their regard. I feel sure I wore a permanent grin, all the memories were so happy.

I didn't want the last door at the end of the corridor to open. Yes, I knew he was dead. Yes, I knew how. But no, I wasn't about to relive that anytime soon, probably never.

Time moved on as I continued my retreat into my own world. In March I was transferred to a hospital in London, triggering memories of our first flight together. How terrified I'd been, how tightly I'd held his hand. Other associated memories, making love on the Gatwick Express, piano in Portree, the blue bow round his cock, the feel of him inside me, his head on my shoulder when I woke!

Let me die.

GOD I WANT TO DIE.

WHY WONT THIS FUCKING BODY DIE?

The voices, always voices in the background. Murmur, murmur. I'd long since stopped listening. It's funny, the last one I responded to, Kath's boyfriend James Perry! Now, though I heard them, I didn't even try to comprehend.

* * *

"Love you, Little Goat... "
??
"Love you Shaun..."
"...Harry?..."
"...HARRY!!!..." What had happened to my voice? I could barely croak. My eyes snapped open, well more likely levered themselves open a fraction.

"Promise you'll never leave me... PROMISE!"

I knew his voice... could never mistake it.

"... Harry?..."

My eyes were almost fully open, but I was so weak, I couldn't turn my head.

"... Harry... Where?" Tears washed my face.

"Oh God... Harry... Stay... Don't go..." I couldn't see anyone. Darkness swooped.

20

It was a very dangerous game Dr Singh played with my mind in the weeks it took to bring me back. He told me it was a last resort – I might have died sooner, rather than later. At the time I couldn't understand why they bothered, did they not know that was what I wanted above all else?

I was reduced to a living skeleton, despite their best efforts. The internal organs would have broken down eventually as the body consumed them in the fight for survival. He couldn't say what the long-term effects were likely to be.

Nu had found the entry into my closed mind in the dozens of tapes we had made at the flat. Sometimes one of us would put the recorder on without the other's knowledge, then try and seduce him. Sometimes it was recordings of parties or piano music, even bouts of love-making, nothing had been sacred.

They'd lifted phrases and single words from the tapes, and remixed them to make a programme which it was felt might reach me. This was allied with a drip-fed drug regime, all timed to coincide with Harry's voice, to knock me out after each session. Apart from Singh and the nurses, I had no visitors for a period of over ten weeks, again part of the program whilst Singh rebuilt my mind.

And with Harry's help, he dragged me out of the fugue state.

The date of Harry's twentieth birthday, followed by that of my nineteenth, then what should have been our second anniversary, all passed unheralded. June was well into its last week before I really began to relate to the world outside the confines of my own skull. Dad turned up two days after I'd cursed out the nurses who were washing me – my first interaction with anything other than Harry's voice for months.

I awoke, yet that's not quite true, maybe it was the drugs. But instead of waking, there came a very gradual encroachment of awareness. Really akin to dawn breaking. At first, all is dark, then you're surprised when you realise that you can make out the shape of the chair on the other side of the room. A little later, and you're struck by the ability to see the differences in colour of objects. Then their varying textures, such as the differential between cloth and wood or metal. Finally, the ability to focus on edges brings distance into perspective.

He was sitting in a chair a little way from the bed, in my direct line of vision, not moving. Even though his face was not yet clear, I knew him by his outline.

I lay, watching him watching me, until I was far enough along to register his features and his white hair. His WHITE hair!

"Your hair." My voice as yet barely above a whisper.

He didn't answer, didn't move, but slowly, tears began to track down his face.

"You REALLY here?"

"Yes, son."

"Not Harry though?"

"Harry is with you always, Shaun."

"Harry is DEAD!"

"Yes, son."

"Go away." Darkness dropped softly over me.

Next conscious period, Harry was back, telling me of his love, telling jokes, playing the piano.

Next time, Dad was back, just as before. As though he had never left. Same place. Same clothes. Same questions. Same answers. And so it went on. The strain on him was enormous, his every word scripted by Singh. His every movement, or rather, the distinct lack of the same. They were reducing the level of the medication over the weeks, both to wean me off it and at the same time to test the viability of what Singh was rebuilding, almost reprogramming in my mind. Progress was painfully slow and on looking back, I don't think I'd have had the patience to do what Dad, what Singh and the nurses did for me.

The rages I indulged in as I regained a little strength. The terrible depressions, which saw me lash out at the slightest provocation, or more often than not without any provocation at all. I didn't want to move, and the first time Singh had the nurses lift me out of the bed and into a low pillow-filled chair induced a rage so great that had I had the strength, I'd have killed the lot of them.

From that point, however, things began to get easier, for them if not for me.

Harry is DEAD. Always at the forefront of my mind. Harry IS dead.

I longed for death too, but realised that as long as I remained in my present condition, I'd never get my wish. Too many people were dedicated to preventing that very thing. That realisation came not in a flash, but over a period of days and weeks, as Singh's rebuilding of my mind began to lock into place. I *had* to do what they wanted, if I was ever going to be able to do what I wanted. Above all else, I wanted to *die*!

Singh, clever man, knew all this of course, he was prepared for all eventualities. (I've wondered since, are people really so predictable? It certainly seems so.) He pushed his campaign forward by having a blown-up picture of Harry and me attached to the wall at the foot of the bed. Arms round each other's shoulders, eyes focused on the lens, so that they never released you. I knew immediately where and when it had been taken, by Nu at 'The Folly' ,, the night we had celebrated the completion of the conservatory.

I wanted it taken away, but Singh ignored me, as did Dad and the nurses.

"Why? It's a great photograph." I gave up.

Within days however, I'd asked about David and Nu, Dessie and George, and John of course. That was just the signal Singh had been waiting for.

Nu came first, and alone. I could see he was scared. I also realised from the way he flinched when he first set eyes on me, that quite apart from the constant pain, my face must have changed a great deal, and not for the better either.

"Shaun... Shaun." He choked the tears back. "You're awake."

"Scared you... didn't I?"

"Don't you joke!" Looking *so* young, thoroughly miserable and scared half to death. He'd been coached by Singh as well. Reaching out I took his hand, whereupon he immediately departed from the script by bursting into tears.

"Nu...don't cry... enough tears already."

He shook his head as he fumbled for one of the paper tissues he always carried. (Handkerchiefs were *so* unhygienic.)

"Nu...please." Trying to squeeze his hand in mine. It was a pretty weak squeeze "Where is David, is he alright?" when he had managed to stop the tears.

"At home. Shop. He's fine. Sends his love. He's fine."

Once started, he did ramble on, I'm sure he wasn't supposed to. But Singh could have stopped him at any time, I found out later that he monitored all visits during the early stages of my recovery. Nu, however, frothy gossip and camp as he is, was no fool. He filled me in on George and Des (but not everything there), on happenings in the store, the latest orgy at the flat. Who was sleeping with who, and who wasn't. Managed to drop the fact that Uncle John and Jean were coming to London for a break the following month.

"What can I say to them, Nu?"

"No need to say much. Just be getting better."

"But, Harry's DEAD!"

"Well don't you be going and breaking their hearts completely, and it's about time you lightened up on your Dad as well. He's cracking up on the inside about you. Oh God...Sorry, Shaun. Shouldn't say things like that. Your Dr Singh will probably ban me from seeing you again." He muttered on for a minute in vehement Chinese, just as he used to when Dave failed to respond to his blandishments.

I giggled.

I know, I embarrassed him. But he was so incongruous. There he sat, looking for all the world like a schoolboy, when in actual fact he is ten years older then me. He blushed and added a couple of epithets in my direction.

I giggled again.

"I'd better go." He was a little hurt as well as being embarrassed.

"No. Please don't go." Trying to retain the grip on his hand. "It was just, I mean, it's just so good to see you. I hadn't realised how much you mean to me, meant to Harry and me. Please Nu. Don't go."

Hurt and embarrassment melted. "Really?" blushing again.

"Really. Don't go yet. I'm not tired."

"That... doctor, he said I could only stay ten minutes," looking at his watch. "I've been here nearly an hour. Are you sure you are alright?"

"I'm okay. Really."

"I..." he hesitated, "brought you something." He reached into his inside pocket and brought out a small yellow rose. "Is it alright? Maybe I shouldn't have."

I stared at it. Memories came surging in a flood, threatening to drown me.

Skye. Sligo. Letters. Seamus. Piano. Dad. Harry. HARRYHARRYHARRYHARRY! Jesus CHRIST, HARRY! GODGODGODGOD HARRY! OH GOD, HOW LONG MUST THIS GO ON? Take ME. LET ME DIE!

"Shaun? Oh *shit*... What have I done. Shaun?"

"Okay... Nu...okay."

"..................." In tears again.

"Really Nu...it's okay...Let me smell it...Please."

That broke the ice. John, David, Dessie and George came next day. Didn't stay long, just long enough to assure themselves that I was indeed back and sane.

It was Dad, Dad who was always there for me. Dad, whose heart had survived one blow after another, and whose first concern was still for me. Gran had died at Christmas, of a broken heart I know. My mother's deterioration was speeding up, by then she was reduced to a bed-bound vegetable, she would die before the end of the year. Aunt Jean had had a heart attack two days after we'd been taken, and when she visited the following month I would almost fail to recognise the tall thin old woman she had become. It was Dad, aided and abetted by Singh, who encouraged me to face the future. It was Dad who showed me I was not alone. And it was Dad, with Singh's help, who got me to relive those last dreadful hours, finally enabling Singh to get me to face the huge weight of guilt which was mine because I'd survived.

It was Dad who first brought me a mirror and showed me the horror picture travesty that was my face. I could not understand how anyone could bear to look on my skewed features. The 1930s – or was it 40s – version of the Hunchback of Notre Dame was the first thing that sprung to mind.

Singh snorted. "Couldn't operate while you were so weak, and besides, you need to say what you want to look like. A film star maybe?"

I stared.

"You have no idea just how good the surgeons are today.

Within reason, you can have anything you want."

"A snub nose," I paused, "like Harry's."

Dad grimaced, but Singh was quite straightforward.

"Why not! I will tell you, it's not going to be fun for you. We need you to start building yourself up before we can begin. Not only that, you have other problems as well, you know."

"I do?" Mustering all the sarcasm I was capable of. "You do surprise me."

"Good. *Very* good. A bit of spirit." He laughed, eyes disappearing in the little rolls of fat. "You need a joint replacement for the right elbow. Your left foot is a mess, and until they can look inside, they won't know what is best. You know you may lose it at some stage? Your right foot is pretty well okay, only minor correction needed there, that bullet really needs to come out from under your shoulder-blade. Finally, there is the question of your heart."

"Even *you* can't mend a broken heart."

"Ah, but there my dear young Shaun, is where you are wrong."

"Oh, don't talk shit. And, what about my arse?"

"Shaun! That's not being very nice to the doctor."

"Well, he shouldn't spout rubbish, and frankly, I don't feel like being nice today."

"Ah, but *dear* young man, it is not rubbish. You have a congenital heart defect, and now at your age, this is the perfect time to repair it. Thus ensuring a long and happy life."

"What heart defect?" Dad and I simultaneously.

"Let me first ask. You have experienced blackouts, faintings, blurred or double vision at times?"

"Don't be silly."

"Think, please, young man."

I blushed for the first time in I don't know how long. My little stars. Sex!

"Ah, I see you have. Describe for me what happens please."

Still crimson, I told him (and Dad) about my stars and the very occasional greying of vision during sex.

"You see, young man, you were born with a little door between the two sides of your heart. Normally it does not affect you, but when the heart has to work very hard, the little door opens too wide. That reduces the flow of blood to the brain which is what brings on your little stars and the faintness."

"Harry knew." I marvelled. "He said there was something wrong."

"Yes, if anyone would notice, it would be your lover."

"More than my lover, my life."

"Yes. Believe me, I know that." There was a moment's silence. "Now, what is this about your arse? Or do you make jokes today."

"No joke! Amongst other things, I was kicked very hard, several times. It hurts every... every time I crap."

"Ahh. Forgive me young man, I may be at fault there. Surgeons have examined you, we have X-rayed you and made plans for your operations, whilst you... slept. But truly, I don't think we ever X-rayed or examined that particular area, we shall rectify that in the morning. Now, enough for today, your father may stay a little longer, then you must eat and rest. Tomorrow, thank God, you start the rest of your life."

Two days before John and Jean were due, Dad sat chatting aimlessly for over an hour, constantly fidgeting and unable to hold my gaze.

"For God's sake Dad, sit still, you're making me dizzy."

"Sorry, son."

"Come on, out with it, what's eating you?"

The door opened and Singh's vast bulk rolled in.

"Sorry to be late. Another patient you understand." He looked at Dad. "Have you told him? No! Ah, that is good." He settled himself into a chair.

Told me what?"

Dad looked at Singh, despair writ large on his face.

"What is it. Is it Aunt Jean?"

"Young man. Listen to me please. Harry's mother will be here in a few days. She is going to ask you something which will require you to be sensible, and to give her a gentle and honest answer." He held up one fat hand as I went to interrupt. "She is a very sick lady now. Her heart cannot stand a great deal. In fact, she should not be making this journey at all, but she will not rest until she does."

"What *is it*?"

You need to decide, Shaun, my brave young man, what you want to do with Harry!"

Totally at a loss, I looked from one to the other, a cruel joke? But no, not these two. My mind was busy trying to deny the implications of what he'd said.

"Harry is *dead*!"

"Yes, your Harry *is* dead. None of us can change that. But, you see, his mother says that he is yours still. She has had his body embalmed and will not permit a burial until you decide."

Blackness swooped very close, my breath failed me.

HARRY, HARRY. OH GOD, WHAT NEXT? HARRY. I could hear my heart quite clearly, squish-thump, squish-thump, my breathing would not restart. I was falling, falling, falling.

"Shaun?" I felt a sharp pain in my earlobe. Singh was bending over me.

"I told you." Dad's voice, panicking. "This was too soon."

Vision firmed, blackness receded and the breathing came back.

"Okay... I'm... okay," feeling very far from it.

Would she let me?

My God, if I thought at all, I thought he had been buried months ago. How long was it now, eight, nine months? All on his own, in a cold dark box. No one to talk to him. No one to hold him. If I'd died it wouldn't have mattered, we should have kept each other company. But he was waiting, waiting all alone, waiting all this time. Waiting for me. HarryHarryHarryHarry, I'm sorry love. I didn't know. I'm sorrysorrysorrysorry.

Dad sat grimly shaking his head as Singh hovered over me. Watching, gauging, as I struggled with my emotions. I was not ready for this, but if I didn't do it for him, who would take care of him?

"Where... Where is he?"

"Downpatrick mortuary."

"I will *not* go back to Northern Ireland."

"No need. He can be brought here if you so decide."

"Will she... Will she let me keep him. Won't she want an interment?"

"You will need to ask her that. But I don't for one minute think she will object. She is adamant that the decision on what to do is yours and yours alone."

"So, I *can* keep him?"

"That decision is yours," Dad repeated.

Oh yes. OH YES! GOD YES!!

How long would it be before I could get out of here? How long before I could get around again? HOW LONG?

* * *

Two and a half months was how long.

Jean had come. She shocked me by her appearance. She agreed to whatever I suggested, and never by word or deed gave any indication that she blamed me in any way for having been the one to survive. For having put Harry in the position that led to his death.

But, OH GOD I could FEEL it. I could FEEL her agony, HEAR her screaming inside, almost FEEL her hands on my throat. "WHY MY HARRY? WHY NOT YOU?"

The *guilt*! The sheer weight of it on me.

John was different, swearing that one day, one day he would find out who was responsible and then, ah, *then*! He kissed me hard on the cheek. "For your Harry, Shaun." He urged me to hurry up and get better, and joked about how my new face should look. Wept and wept and wept when Dad took Jean out for a coffee.

"If ever you remember anything, son, *anything* at all, tell *me*. Not the police, I wouldn't trust those bastards not to know already, not to have had a hand in it. You tell *me*, and I'll see to it that they pay in the same coin, you tell *me*!"

His grim fury both terrified and exhilarated me and I hugged him long with my good arm. At the last, he took an envelope from his pocket and spilt the contents on my knees. There, blinking on the blanket, an emerald ring along with the two watches and a gold wrist chain. I picked up the ring and squinted to read the inscription. Mine.

"Good. Harry still has his ring then." Pleased to think he was still wearing it.

"Isn't that Harry's?"

"No, this is mine from him."

"Your Gran, God rest her soul, said it was Harry's."

"No, he was wearing his when we... when it..."

"He had no ring when he was brought to the hospital."

"Are you sure?"

"Are you sure he was wearing it?"

"Of course, he was joshing me about mine, just before... just before. God. Who would steal his ring. Who would rob the dead?"

"Maybe someone took it before he died."

* * *

By the end of September my elbow joint and foot had been rebuilt, my tail bone or coccyx had had to be removed. (Harry would have at the very least, have had a fit of the giggles at the unfortunate name.) I returned to our flat at the end of the month, I'd had a very hard time convincing everyone that I could cope with the memories and emotions by myself. Twice-weekly sessions with Singh were my prop. When things got particularly rough he was always available on the phone. Without his help, and Dad's unwavering support, I would not have made it.

Nights were the worst, lying alone, listening to the muted sounds of the traffic. No one to hold. No one to talk to. No HARRY!

That first month on my own, with all our things, all the happy memories associated with them, that was very nearly the worst period. With my face such a mess I went out very little, always being the target for stares. I needed then – and still use today – a cane to walk any distance. My foot was never to recover more than 60 per cent mobility and I will always have to wear specially made shoes to compensate for the distortion.

I still had to regain a lot of strength before the heart op, and starting the long series of operations necessary to rebuild my face. The heart job was provisionally scheduled for the end of November and I decided to have Harry cremated on the anniversary of his murder. I don't know about being morbid, it just seemed right somehow.

His body was flown in two days before the cremation, and as he was in a sealed casket, that removed the dilemma as to whether I should or shouldn't look. John had been due to accompany him but by then Jean was very ill indeed and he couldn't leave her. Graham came alone.

Dad, Nu, David, John, George, Dessie, Graham, myself and good old Singh followed him from Stanstead to the crematorium at Roehampton, the casket laid in the Chapel of Rest until the actual cremation took place.

I wouldn't have any religious mumbo-jumbo, nor so-called sacred music. I'd had a rosewood box with a brass insert made for him and handed it to the funeral director when we reached the chapel. The morning of his cremation we sent him to his rest to the sound of his own music, a tape of various pieces made in the flat, including of course 'The Sigh' by Liszt. I didn't feel like crying as the casket moved through the curtains, I felt oddly at peace, almost as if he was truly coming home to me and not just his ashes. I was calm all the way through, even when the director placed him in my hands – how very light he was! No apparent increase in the weight of the little casket at all. We drove in silence back to the flat. Harry on my knee. My hands holding him again.

Of them all, only Nu had *not* argued with my decision not to inter Harry, but to keep him with me in the flat. I don't think anyone knew quite how to react when I placed him on top of the piano between the two silver candlesticks. Little retaining battens had been affixed to the piano, though as the box was locked there could be little damage in the event of an accident.

Singh had a good look round as David and Nu made tea and coffee and took the sandwiches from the fridge.

"My dear young man, if it wasn't for the fact that you will be spending considerable time in hospital, I would not recommend that you stay here alone. It has taken me, and many others, months of very hard and difficult work to bring you back to where you are today. I would not have all that destroyed just because you turn your home into a shrine or mausoleum to Harry."

"I promise I won't. Really."

"Easy to say, Shaun, but I would be happier if you were to make that promise to Harry. So much more difficult to break. Yes?"

Seeing my hesitation, he took me by the arm and turned me towards the casket.

"I do not ask that you ignore him. I ask only that you do not turn him into a god and allow him to control your life. You know he would not want that from you. Am I not right in this?" – giving me a gentle shake.

"Sorry, Singh." I reached out and laid my hand on the casket. "I promise not to be silly, Harry." I turned back to Singh. "That doesn't mean that I can't talk to him, does it?"

"When you have pain, young man, whether it be of the mind or body, by all means let him be your father confessor, but do not let him rule you. Your mindset is such that you will want to let him take control to appease the guilt you feel. I tell you now, I will be watching you closely over the next year. And if I think it necessary, with the help of your father and friends here" – including them all in an expansive wave of an arm – "I will bring you back under my control and into full-time care. Yes?"

The hardest time of all came just a few days later when Uncle John rang to say that Aunt Jean had passed away in her sleep.

"She just could not go on, son. I think she only held on this long through sheer will power."

"I'm truly sorry, Uncle John. She was more of a mother to me than my own ever was."

"She just wanted to know that Harry was at rest before she went. I think she just wanted to be with him."

"What will you do now?"

"Och, son. What is there to do? I'll just carry on. But you'll know what I mean when I tell you that the main reason for carrying on is no longer here."

"Yes. I know exactly what you mean."

"I only wish that you and Harry had had our thirty-odd years, Shaun. You know, Lass was so pleased when you two got together, we were both relieved. Lass was just saying the other day, she was sure he would have attempted suicide around that time if it hadn't been for you. She loved you very much you know. So my lad, no feelings of guilt. You hear me?.. "You listening, Shaun?"

"I'm here, Uncle John."

"Aye well, you gave him what, eighteen months full of love, which he wouldn't have had otherwise. I *do* realise how you still feel, Shaun, but you must learn to accept in your heart, nothing that has happened is any reason for guilt. Remember the happy times son, remember how happy he was with you. Make your life happy again. Harry would not have wanted it any other way. You know that."

"I am trying... truly, Uncle John...God knows I do try... It's just so hard without him... you know?"

"I know son, I know. But we'll both get over this in time. Shaun, son, I'm only at the other end of the phone and if things get too much for you, I can be there in a couple of hours. Don't be eating yourself up, or locking yourself away, I'd be very angry and so would Harry."

"Please don't be angry with me Uncle John. I do, I get very very depressed, really down at times. But somehow, I'm managing, so far. Will you call me a couple of times each week? Just for the chat. You know?"

"You know I will, son."

* * *

Dad went to her funeral, as did David and John, against everyone's advice and wishes. (Nu spoke nothing but Chinese all day). They flew into Belfast in the morning and back the same evening. I sent a dozen yellow roses with them from Harry and me.

Dad cleared up his things in Northern Ireland. James and Kath (who'd gotten married as I lay in hospital) took over the tenancy and he moved to Leeds. Why Leeds? I don't think he knew himself, at least, when I asked he just shrugged.

"Time to start over, why not Leeds?"

Part Five: Revenge and Renewal

21

Following on my recovery from the heart operation and removal of the bullet, the next two years consisted of regular hospital visits as slowly my face was rebuilt. I can honestly say that I do not remember one day of that period when I was completely free from pain. On the first visit to Singh after the heart op, I told him that taking into consideration how sore I was, I'd just as soon have stuck with my little stars.

He laughed and launched into an inquiry about my sex life. Solitary and infrequent.

"My dear young man, that will not do. No, no. Not do at all."

I had to point out that with my face in its then condition, I'd probably have to wear a bag over my head before I'd even get near a man. "When I look human again, I promise you, I'll fuck from one end of the country to the other."

"Mmm. Promise me, young man. Safe sex only. Yes?"

Which brings me to my unwitting anchors during that period.

After the heart job, David and Nu took me down to 'The Folly' for a couple of weeks' rest and to help me regain a little fitness. I wasn't up to much other than to lie around and be waited on. Or to watch as they put the finishing touches to the kitchen. A 'folly' no longer, a number of very minor jobs remained to be completed but it was all coming together very nicely, no more sleeping in bags on the floor and no more chemical loos.

Dessie and George were running the store whilst we were away and although I wondered how they could do that, knowing their dance schedule as I did, I really didn't give it more than a passing thought. Essentially, I was at least 95 percent self-centred still, brooding endlessly on my loss. On my Harry. Still not sure, promise or no promise, that it really was worth carrying on. I kept asking myself 'what for?'.

Anyway, three or four days before we were due to return to London, David got a call during the night from George, and when I woke he had gone, leaving Nu with a promise to return for us on the Sunday.

"You need the rest and the country air. Besides, there's nothing you could do," he replied when I taxed him with it over breakfast.

As Nu never was very good at keeping secrets, within a couple of hours I had learned that both Dessie and George had been diagnosed as HIV-positive some years earlier, with Dessie recently developing full-blown AIDS. He had been admitted to hospital during the night with viral pneumonia and Dave had gone back to cover the store.

Although George showed no signs of AIDS, when it became apparent that Des was too sick to continue dancing, they'd both given it up to be there for each other. With Harry and I out of the picture Dave had taken them on full time at the store.

Talking to George some months later I found out that they had both been pretty promiscuous as teenagers and not overly careful every time. "I mean, you just didn't think about it. It wasn't something that was going to happen to you. Know what I mean?"

I said I did.

"Once we'd been together a few times and realised that we wanted to be with each other, it was too late to start taking precautions anyway. We went for the test together, as a sort of commitment to each other and well, when we both tested positive there was nothing to do but carry on. Know what I mean? Enjoy life as much as possible and try not to worry too much about the future. After all, there was always the possibility that they'd find something in time for us." He shrugged. "Que sera sera."

When Des was released from hospital after the pneumonia, David insisted that they give up their tiny place and move in with him and Nu. When I wasn't in hospital myself, I spent most of my time round at the store helping to look after Dessie, and trying to ensure that George got his proper rest as Des deteriorated.

During what was to prove his last hospitalisation, when he became blind, he announced that he didn't want to die in hospital and asked if we'd take him home. Around that time George started developing lesions on his body and neck, but despite some weight loss, he seemed physically well enough. Des was down to five stone and dropping fast when we brought him home. The hospital ensured that we had the drugs and body linen necessary for what proved to be a very short period. Despite his physical frailty, his sense of humour and biting cattiness never left him, right up until he slipped into the final coma. He stopped breathing in the early hours of the third day, cradled in George's arms. Nu had woken David and rung me when it was obvious that he was dying. We all sat touching him as he breathed his last. George was devastated, just saying through the tears "Thank you for all the years, and all the love."

The funeral was very quiet, no outpourings of grief. No family members either, both Des and George had been ostracised by their respective families. Looking at those present, it was obvious that more than one of them were going to follow him soon.

Within six months of the funeral, George began the unstoppable slide. He grew obsessed with not wanting to die in the same room where Dessie had passed away, and refused to go to hospital, terrified that he'd die amongst total strangers.

I moved him to the flat.

For the first time since Harry's murder I shared our bed with someone! Over the months and years George had built up a huge collection of all sorts of drugs, and one night as I was changing the soaked sheets, he took my hand and made me sit on the bed beside him. "You know Shaun, I'm not like Des. I don't want to fight for every breath. Know what I mean? I don't want to become helpless, not able to get to the crapper, that sort of thing. Know what I mean?"

I nodded, I'd seen this coming for some time.

"When I decide I've had enough. When I don't want to fight it any more. Know what I mean? Will you help me, if I need it?"

I nodded again. "Yes George, I'll help. You know I will, love."

He cried then for Dessie, which he hadn't done since we buried him, and a little for himself too I suppose.

We went back to bed and fucked. The first for me since Harry. We played it safe, George insisted. I wished Harry had been alive to see (I told him next morning anyway) just how easy it was to take George's ten-inch dick. It felt *so* good! My own poor old cock, who'd practically become celibate during the three years since Harry, woke up with truly indecent haste. Overnight he seemed to revert to being seventeen again. Once more anything and everything made him hard at the most inconvenient times.

I was still seeing Singh a couple of times a month and that crafty old lecher knew straight away.

"*Aha!* My young man has got himself a lover. Am I not right, yes?" and that was before I'd even sat down. So I told him about George and Des and George and me. It could never take the place of our respective partners, it wasn't love as either of us had known it, more a mutual bolstering of each other. Good for me as I finally began to re-surface from my long night. Good for George, in that it helped to fend off the loneliness after Dessie. Following that first night, we never went the distance again. Cuddling, mutual masturbation and a little protected cock-sucking sufficed for both of us.

Towards the end of a subsequent visit with Singh he wrote out a prescription and handed it to me. "You may find, young man, that you will have difficulty in sleeping." He held up a fat hand. "After George. You understand? Good! Now, you will find that one of these ground up in a hot whisky is very effective. More than fourteen would be fatal. Very peaceful, but fatal. You are understanding me? Good! I would not recommend that anyone use old drugs. No knowing what they may do, possibly nothing. You do understand?" I nodded. "Good. Very good. I also think now that you are far enough along for me to be able to trust you not to be doing anything silly. I also think that maybe we can begin to reduce the frequency of these visits. I will still be here if you have need of me, but I think now after your last operation, how many more scheduled?"

"Only two more, thank God."

"Thank God indeed, Shaun. My very brave young man. I am so very, very proud of you. So, we make your last visit for the week after your final operation. Yes?"

I just had to plant a kiss on his forehead.

"Thank you, Singh. Thank you for everything and I mean *everything.*"

He beamed, well content with the miracle he had wrought. "Go, live your life to the full, Shaun, and try not to forget this lonely fat old man."

"I could never forget you and what you have done for me. Thank you again from the very bottom of my heart." That was when I really began to feel human again. No more compulsory visits to the head-shrinker.

Over two months passed before we resorted to Singh's pills. George had perked up remarkably, going so far as returning to the store and manning the till whilst I had my penultimate op. We were down to the fine detail now, tightening sagging flesh under the right eye and realigning the errant left eyebrow. That left the droop to the left side of my mouth and some unsightly loose flesh under the right jaw for the last job.

George looked strained and very tired as we drove back to the flat on what was to be our last evening.

"Shaun, let's go out to dinner?"

Glancing across, I met his steady gaze, and knew immediately what he really meant.

"You sure you want to go out tonight?"

"If you wouldn't mind. I feel that this will be my last good night and I want to enjoy it. Know what I mean?"

"Okay."

We dressed for the first time in ages. George looked a million dollars. His dinner jacket tended to hang a little and I suppose if you knew what to look for, the signs were there. The bones shining through the flesh of the cheeks, the undeniable yellowish tinge underlying the coffee colour and the over-bright glitter in the soft black eyes.

"Just you and me, Shaun. Know what I mean? I can't relax with other people around, always having to pretend to what I don't really feel."

We taxied to Topo Gigio's, a long-time favourite of Harry's and mine. I knew several of the staff, but with my new face I went unrecognised, despite claiming the table in my own name. I was happy enough with that, this was George's night, what would I have not done for Harry in similar circumstances? I wanted to do as much for George, if I could.

We gossiped through dinner, George relating stories of sexual escapades whilst on tour, which I was more than half inclined to disbelieve. I told him of Harry's reaction at 'The Folly' when it was still mostly rubble, and we all slept in bags in the same room, his utter astonishment at how easily Dessie coped with his – George's – huge cock.

"I told him about us the next morning, you know."

"Oh." He blinked, then smiled. "And what did he say?"

"Not much. But I swear he had a hard-on. I'm sure the top of the casket bent up. Just as well it was locked."

He nearly choked on his fish. "Oh you! Just you wait till I see him, I'll tell him you haven't changed one bit."

"Oh, I've changed alright, but tell him I love him."

"I will Shaun. I promise, though I'm sure I don't have to tell him anything."

He hung on gamely through dessert and the coffee and liqueurs but he was perspiring heavily by the time we took a taxi home. I had to help him undress, then hold him when he lost his dinner, hold him up under the shower and dry him as he sat on the loo, fighting for both breath and composure.

"That was a waste of good money."

"Never mind love, it doesn't matter."

"Will you make a drink for me?" as I ran the razor over his face.

"Of course, George. Now, a little Brut and what about some talc for the balls and bum?"

"Mmm, got to smell sweet for Des. Know what I mean?"

I propped him up in the bed with pillows, switched the kettle on, and ground up the pills in the blender. Cloves, sugar, honey, lemon juice and whisky in the glass, then the powder followed by the water. I placed it on the bedside table and told him to wait a minute whilst I made myself one.

"Yours, it's not going to be the same, is it?"

"No, love. But had this been twelve months ago, it probably would be."

"Shaun... you won't forget me... forget us, will you?"

"Now, how could I forget a beautiful big butch number like you?" I slipped on to the bed beside him, and took him in my arms for a kiss. He hugged hard and we both cried a little.

"I'm ready now. Will you put Harry's tape on for me. You know which one."

"Are you really sure?"

"Yes... I'm sure Shaun. Will you hold me like this?"

"All the way, George. All the way."

"Oh God. I miss Des... you know what I mean... I just, I want to be with him."

"I know love... I know."

I stirred his drink and helped hold his hands steady as he drank. A little sediment remained in the bottom of the glass, I poured some of mine into it, swirled it around and helped him drink again. The gentle notes of 'The Sigh' filled the room.

"Thank you, thank you for everything Shaun. Kiss me."

I kissed him and helped him settle back into the pillows, my arm round his broad shoulders and my other hand gently stroking his face. One of his arms round my waist, his other hand on his chest. Watched with him, stroking his face, wiping away the occasional tear as the drug began to take effect.

"Love you, Shaun." Voice indistinct, eyelids beginning to droop, pupils expanding enormously.

"Love you, George." I kissed his slackening lips. "Rest easy, Georgie."

His eyes flared slightly, a contented semi-smile tugging at the corners of his mouth as he succumbed to the power of the drug.

For the first time in three and a half years, I cried. Really, really cried. For George, for Dessie, Jean, Gran, Eileen, so many, so very many. But my tears? Mainly for Harry, and for me.

He went very easy, in less than an hour. His breathing grew ever more faint and just before the end the arm round my waist slid slowly onto the mattress. I continued to stroke his face as long as he breathed, unsure as to whether he could sense my touch, unwilling to deprive him of it. I wasn't aware just when it was all over, only the slow relaxation of his body told me. I took him in both my arms, pressed his head into my shoulder, indulged in a paroxysm of grief which both shamed yet lightened me.

"Jesus, Harry, if only I could have held you, helped you, like this. I love you, *love* you."

The piano tinkled on, as for the first time I came to terms with all the pain and grief. My mind finally gelling, finally realising that there would be no suicide for me. I was sentenced to life, without Harry!

"But I shall always love you. *Always*."

I kissed George's shoulder, rubbed a hand over the tight curls on his head, as with his usual half-embarrassed giggle, Harry on tape announced the end of the recording.

"Always love you, Harry." I laid George down, kissing his still warmly moist lips. "Loved you too, you big black queen." I folded his arms across his chest, then washed my face and made coffee. I stood by the piano and stroked Harry's casket. "Show them the ropes and take care of them, love. Take care of me too. Love you." I kissed his casket, then phoned David and Nu.

I had thought there might be a problem with the death certificate, but his doctor didn't bat an eyelid when I called him in just after eight o'clock.

"It would have been perfectly alright to call me earlier, you know," he said after giving George a very cursory examination and handing me a paper. "Are you sure you are alright?"

"Fine, thank you doctor. Well, not fine. But, you know."

"Keep your chin up, son. He had it easier than most."

* * *

Following George's funeral, I had my last operation (not a complete success) and my last scheduled session with Singh. He confirmed then what I already had guessed. George had provided the final therapy that he had been unable to. Promising to stay in touch,

I walked out into the bright, bright sunshine; healed in mind, if not exactly 100 per cent in body.

Back at the flat, cock bounced impatiently as I surveyed myself in the mirror, I was almost twenty-three years old. Looking at a picture for comparison, I could find no trace of the eighteen-year old-boy depicted therein. Gone was the elfin face and slight sharp nose, even the hair was different. With so many regular operations I'd found a short crew-cut easier to manage. Looking in the mirror at the strange face I would be spending the rest of my life with, I could see that the hairstyle suited the broader, flatter features I now possessed and, oh yes, I'd gotten my snub nose. The cheek bones were much more prominent, as were the ridges of the eye orbits. The left had been rebuilt using bone from my hip and the right altered to match. The now sunken eyes aged the face somewhat beyond my years, and my eyebrows somewhere along the line had lost their natural curve, now being bar straight. It gave me a slightly oriental slant. With the final operation not having been a complete success, my lips still drooped a bit at the left side of my mouth (damage to a nerve), however I thought it gave me a quirky, half sardonic appeal when I smiled.

Looking down my body I could see scars aplenty. The facial ones tended to look like laughter lines or crease marks and it wasn't immediately evident that they were scars at all. But there could be no doubting my 'zipper' being anything other than what it was, with its dead blue-white line from collar bone to belly button. Likewise my right arm with its nightmare of lines and scar tissue around the elbow. There was a mini 'zip' on my right pelvic area where they had removed the bone to rebuild my face, and then – my foot! That would never be right, held together by a plethora of tiny plates and screws, I'd been very lucky not to lose it. That concluded my inspection, as without the aid of a mirror I could not see the last of my zips, concealed as it is in the cleft of my arse. I had regained almost all the weight that I'd lost and from under six stone was back at a more respectable ten stone four.

"I suppose you'll do," I told my reflection. "You're fucking well gonna have to."

I had never given serious consideration as to what I would do once all the physical and mental problems had been solved, and for the time being was quite happy to be led by cock. *He* at least knew *exactly* what he wanted.

For the following fifteen months I fucked my way through London, with occasional asides to Leeds, Weymouth, Andover, and quite often, places I couldn't remember afterwards. Remembering only the guy I'd picked up in a bar or maybe hitchhiking somewhere. I always took precautions, though deep down I believed that having survived being beaten and shot (if only just), a mere teaspoon or less of cum was unlikely to kill me.

I'd long since traded the Mini for an automatic Sierra, easier on the foot, though I shed quite a few tears when I drove out of the showroom leaving it sitting on the forecourt. I suppose I could have gone for something more flashy, just as I could have moved house at any time; after all I had plenty of money. On top of our joint savings and the money in Oz, the Criminal Injuries Board were due to cough up at any time and Harry had insisted at the very beginning that we both took out life assurance. But for that period I just didn't bother, in many ways I seemed to be marking time as cock surged to make up for the lost three and a half years.

I read voraciously or practised the piano for hours, that is if cock didn't drag me out hunting for something, anything to get into. With a good three-quarters of pick-ups being rent in one way or another, I quickly became adept at picking those likely to give value for money. Of those, before learning that I had to be precise as to my requirements, a good nine out of ten shed their butch street image once we got to bed – rolling over with their arse stuck in the air or remaining an almost totally unresponsive piece of warm meat.

Many nights, as I handed them their money and showed them out the door, I'd reflect that a good wank would have been just as satisfying and free besides. Cock would have none of that (or as little as possible), he wanted a hot living breathing presence and, if they did not appreciate his virtuosity, he shrugged and implied that there was always tomorrow.

I would complain bitterly to Harry as to the various disappointments and I'm sure he laughed his head off at my fulminations when I closed the door on some poor side of beef with the assurance that he had indeed been wonderful and that, yes we would certainly do it again soon.

"Pigs will fly, Harry Hannah."

I made quite a few trips to Leeds to see Dad. He was driving a bus and had an eighteenth-floor council flat. I never stayed very long, disappointed and hurt with the growing gap between us. If I was promiscuous, he was positively swamped with sex. Asking him about it only the once, he said that he had thirty years to catch up on and anyway, it was none of my business. He remained totally adamant in refusing all financial help, getting very angry when I unwisely tried to insist. I could never forget, have never forgotten, his love and care for me and Harry. I can only suppose that having fulfilled – more then fulfilled – his obligations as he saw them, he no longer wanted responsibility for anyone other than himself. I couldn't blame him really. Life had been undeniably cruel to him, but it did hurt that he now seemed to view me as a project completed. To be checked on now and again, but not for long, and preferably from a distance. When I asked about Graham, his sarcasm revealed another hurt to add to the list.

"Oh, him. A 'happily' married man, protecting his inheritance."

"But what about Charlie and Allan?"

"How should I know? I only know that at Jean's funeral he told me, John that is, that neither of them would be getting a penny."

"Oh."

"Aye, well." then: "I presume you are taking precautions?"

"Sure."

"Good. Well then, next time you want to come up, make sure and phone first. It isn't always convenient. You understand?"

"Sure, Dad. I know how it is."

"Right then, drive carefully on that motorway. See you."

"Be seeing you, Dad."

22

Back home some weeks later I'd had a couple of bad days sexwise. David and Nu were in Mauritius and I didn't know the guys running the store. Truth to tell, I was beginning to get very bored with the sexual chase. I had a key to 'The Folly' in my pocket and was on the look-out for something worth spiriting away for the weekend. The Brief Encounter had been packed beyond comfort and the Salisbury full of old queens. I had resigned myself to paying for it, again, and was in a window seat at McDonalds in Piccadilly. The same old tired faces drifted past, including my 'conquest' of the night before. He smiled hopefully when he spotted me, then moved on when I smiled back and shook my head.

Sitting there nursing a plastic cup of semi-cold liquid posing as coffee, I almost missed him in the hordes of lost tourists, druggies, rent boys, plainclothes cops and the very occasional person with a legitimate reason for being there. Just caught a glimpse of the back view as he sauntered towards Shaftesbury Avenue. Looking at my watch as I got to my feet, I reckoned that if this didn't work out, I still would have time to drive to Chaplins in Andover. More than once I'd found a local lad or a squaddie there at just the right level of intoxication to be interested in a little sexual experimentation. If not, well I had my hands and some pretty weird sex toys in Dave and Nu's 'playroom' to amuse, even abuse myself with.

I'd lost sight of him in the crowds, but felt confident that he wasn't going anywhere in particular, or in a hurry. Sure enough, as I sidled through a flock of chattering Chinese I spotted him again, only a few feet in front. My heart dropped and cock wilted. I was oddly sure that I knew him, even though I had yet to see his face. If I did, that meant that I'd already had him and I wasn't in the mood for any repeat performances that night. I very nearly turned away, then shrugged – what the hell, I could be wrong. Best to make sure.

As I expected, he wasn't going anywhere, hitching himself to the railings at the bus stop, accentuating the tightness of the blue jeans over a quite delicious-looking dish. I still couldn't see his face, but was growing more and more certain that I did know him, from where? Oh well, might as well have a proper cup of coffee since I was here, I looked again at the watch and decided I could give it twenty minutes. Got a capuccino and came out to one of the pavement tables. He was directly in front of me facing towards the road. As I lit a cigarette he straightened up, and turned to survey the jostling masses.

I almost burnt my new nose as I stared at him through the smoke and passing people. My reaction, as I singed my fingers on the forgotten match, drew his attention. As I was busy cursing and ridding myself of the match, he came over, I looked up to find him standing beside me. "Got a spare fag, mate?"

I indicated the pack on the table and was just about to call him by name when he reached over and picked it up. He made a production of lighting it, ensuring that his crotch which was level with my nose was well thrust forward. Absentmindedly I noted the apparent lack of underwear, but my entire being had become focused on his strong brown hands.

On the emerald ring flashing on the pinkie of the right.

* * *

Ten days later, despite all the oaths that I had sworn, I was sitting shivering and crying on the old bench in Kilbroney Park.

Was it really possible that five and a half years had passed so quickly? I almost lost it completely there on that bench. The memories surged and tumbled through my mind. The smell of the heather, the aroma of pine woods, the wind rustling in the trees! I squeezed my eyes tight shut, trying to believe and willing it to be that none of it had happened. That when I opened my eyes again, he would be there with his hands on his hips, smiling down at me.

But I opened them to... nothing! Just the wind soughing through the branches, rooks cawing hoarsely and cloud shadows spinning over the purple heather.

I hauled myself upright and limped up the hill towards our dell. Found that I had no trouble finding the path, someone else had found our outdoor refuge. It was quiet and empty when I straightened up from under the trees and I hoped that it might be two boys who had found it. I stayed long enough to pick up a cone to replace the one I'd had from Harry.

"I will, I swear it, I'll plant our forest for you."

I stood looking at the tarmac of the parking area before getting into the car. How could a place that had been the scene of such a vicious attack look so beautiful, so unspoilt? Wiped my eyes and left.

Theresa gave me a professional smile as she poured the Baileys. She hadn't a clue who I was and I had no intention of enlightening her.

"Is Mr Hannah in?" – knowing he was. He hadn't been at the house and I knew from our weekly chats that he spent most of his days, nights too, at the hotel.

"Who shall I say is asking?"

"Shaun Hannah."

I took my drink and turned away from the bar before she could make further inquiries. I crossed the empty room to the far corner. It was just on ten am.

He didn't see me till Theresa pointed out where I was sitting, in 'our' window seat, nor did he recognise me as he approached. How could he? He'd never seen my new face. Threading his way through the low tables he came over, a polite smile on his face and extending his hand as he neared.

"Well, Mr Hannah is it? And what can I do for you?"

His eyes narrowed slightly as I used the cane to stand, I was shivering more than ever, yet my face and hands were slick with perspiration. Propping the cane against the table, I took his extended hand in my left, turned it palm upwards. And as he made to withdraw it, I deposited the two gold rings, set with an emerald each, into his palm.

I thought he would faint. He swayed. The puzzled look, when I'd turned his palm up, changed to one of grief. Tears trembled on the brink and his eyes glinted.

"From Harry and, from me, Uncle John." I kept my voice low. He knew me then.

He was speechless, his bowed shoulders straightened and the tears fled. His left hand clasped my shoulder painfully, wonderfully tightly. He closed his fist so hard on the rings that I feared they would cut right through his hand. His face hardened like stone and several seconds passed before he could speak.

"Och, son. Och, son. God is good. God is good." He crushed me into a massive hug.

Over his shoulder I watched Theresa's face change. I could almost see the little cogs tumbling over, click, click, clicking into place. She put her hands to her mouth and her shoulders started to shake.

"Not one word, young lady," as he turned to lead me into the sitting room and saw her face pale, eyes wide and wet.

"He was never here, you understand. You never saw him. Say nothing to any one."

She couldn't speak either. I suppose after five and a half years – no, for her it would be seven years since she had last seen either of us – it must have been a bit like seeing the living dead. Once she'd worked out who I must be.

"No interruptions, no calls. I'm not here until further notice. You understand?"

She nodded, her tears flowing freely.

"Dry your eyes, child. Customers will say that I beat you." But his heart wasn't in it and he practically dragged me through to the sitting-room.

Closing and locking the door, he leant against it, his eyes never leaving mine.

"Shaun Hannah, is it now?"

"It is now, courtesy of deed poll. Hope you don't mind?"

"You couldn't care less whether I mind or not, is that not what you mean?"

"Not really." I shrugged. "I'd been thinking about it for some time. Now seemed ideal" – gesturing towards his clenched fist.

He controlled himself with a visible effort, crossing to the table and placing the rings in the centre of it, before going over to the bar cabinet. Handed me a large Baileys on ice.

"Let me see what kind of a job they did on you." Taking my chin in his hand and turning my head from side to side. "If I didn't know to the difference, I wouldn't give it a second thought. No one will recognise you as long as Theresa keeps quiet."

"Will she?"

"Oh aye." Releasing me and sitting down.

"The foot?" as I propped the cane and sat down in the same seat as I had used on the last occasion I'd been in the room. Seven long years previously.

"Awkward, uncomfortable, and it tells me when it's going to rain."

"Aye! Aye!" his gaze focused on the rings. "Who?"

And so it began. Not that it had ever ended for either of us.

* * *

"Oh sorry mate, thought you meant... ?" waving the cigarette.

Belatedly, taking the forgotten finger from my mouth, I managed a weak smile.

"No. No, go ahead. Sorry. I was just thinking how lucky I am running into you like this."

"Why? You looking for business?" Hooking a chair over and sitting down uninvited. Legs apart, easing forward on the seat, accentuating the crotch.

I was having the greatest difficulty in maintaining the smile and almost equal difficulty in not just sitting staring at the emerald winking on his finger. I concentrated instead on his crotch, even though I knew well enough what it was outlining. A riot of questions tumbled through my mind.

How?

Where?

Who?

Please, God! Don't make it that *he* had been one of the punishment gang. I didn't think that I could take that. Not for one minute, not for one second, did I doubt that the ring he wore was Harry's. And not for one second did I doubt that I'd see him dead, if it turned out that he *was* involved. In my mind it was only a question of when, not if, but I first had to find out what he knew? He had to know something, even if it was only where he had got the ring. That would be a start. How to proceed?

My momentary silence and non-answer slightly disconcerted

him. Then I could see the pall of boredom descend across his face, he was obviously well practised at this game.

"Well, if you're not interested... ?" looking at me as he stubbed out the cigarette.

I raised my eyes to meet his. "Oh, I'm interested alright," grinning genuinely as a plan struck me. Risky maybe but then again maybe not. "I'm always interested in a rematch with good-looking guys."

The smile which had been switched on again faded into puzzlement. "I don't think... I mean, I've never... I don't know you. Do I?"

"You know, when someone your age starts to forget things, it's a real bad sign."

"But I never saw you before," he protested, brow furrowed as he studied me. "You're having me on."

That very nearly did it for me. My grin left me and I stared at him intensely. I would have him arrested! There were always plenty of cops, both uniform and plainclothes, around the Dilly. I'd have him arrested, tried, convicted – and then? In four or eight years, when he was released, I'd kill him. I could wait. I'd been doing little else these last five and a half years.

"Tell me then. Tell me that you do not have a brown birth mark on the shaft of your dick. Or has it worn off by now with all the wanking, Padraig?"

"Patrick, it's Patrick. Nobody calls me... how did you know my name?"

He wasn't running. I took that as a good sign.

"Mmm. Why not come back to my place, see if I can't jog your memory a little?"

"Was I drunk, I mean, the last time?"

"No Padraig, you weren't drunk."

"But I could swear... I've never seen you before, I'm sure of it."

"Ah, I've changed a great deal since we last met. I doubt my own mother would know me. Or want to, come to that."

"It's seventy quid, mate... in advance."

"Now, now. You'll get paid after, as you usually do, I'm too old a hand at this to be caught by that one."

He grinned, puzzle temporarily shelved. "Can't blame me for trying. And if as you say we've met before, you'll know it'll be worth every penny."

"You've changed too, you know. We'll have to see just how

much."

"It was Birmingham! Must have been. God, that could be as much as four, five years ago. Used to drink a lot then, don't always remember who I went home with, you know how it is."

"Yes, I know how it is and no, it wasn't Birmingham. Never been there. You coming?"

"Yeah sure. You really got me intrigued." He frowned as I picked my cane up from the floor. "Now I *know* that I've never met you." as we walked round to the NCP.

"Happened since I last saw you."

"Oh, you had an accident?"

"Mmm, you could say that."

He whistled when he saw the low slung Sierra Cosworth.

"Some car. Are they really fast?"

"Fast enough. Fasten your seatbelt."

Going along Piccadilly he pushed his crotch well forward and ostentatiously rearranged himself. Swinging round Hyde Park Corner he reached over and groped me.

"Leave it till we get home," I advised and replaced his hand on his own crotch. "I should hate to have another 'accident'. "

"Is that what happened? Did you crash?"

"Something like that. But tell me, what are you doing these days? How come I haven't seen you round the Dilly before?"

"Go there a lot, do you? Not got a steady boyfriend then?"

"Mmmm."

He had, according to him, gone to Birmingham from Northern Ireland. Been working as a bricklayer. He'd quite recently gotten bored with the same old faces and routine and had come to London about six weeks previously. He was presently working days in a City pub and supplementing his income by renting in the evening. So far, he didn't think much of London, everybody was too snobbish and in too much of a hurry. He thought that after all, he might just go back to Birmingham and the bricklaying, though that wasn't much cop in the winter. And he still couldn't remember where or when we had met.

"Wait till we get in," as we crawled through Brixton. "I'm sure I'll be able to jog your memory."

"Just my memory?" Rubbing himself, half hard down the leg of the jeans.

"We'll see about that too."

I let him into the hall and closed and locked the door behind us, pocketing the key.

"Hey, this looks really... " Voice and enthusiasm dying as he entered the main room of the flat.

Above the piano I'd fixed to the wall the enlargement of Harry and me that Singh had used in the hospital.

"Who the fuck are you?" He swung round. No fear, but a mixture of anger and bewilderment on his face.

"Why don't you sit down."

"Who are you?" he insisted, eyes widening as he realised that the flat was full of pictures of Harry and Shaun. Harry and Shaun on their own, or with George and Dessie, or David and Nu, John and Jean, Dad and Graham, John and the girlfriend of the moment. Following his gaze around, I realised for the first time that maybe, just maybe, it was all a little over the top. Almost a shrine.

"I'm going to have a coffee. You want one?" going to the kitchen.

"I want to know what the fuck's going on here, and who you fucking are." His voice sounded hard, but was underlain with uncertainty and something else.

"And I want to know who else, other than yourself, has a brown birthmark on their dick. I also want to know where you got that ring?"

"What the fuck's it got to do with you? Whoever you are." Bristling, clenching his fists.

I picked up the meat cleaver, weighed it in my hand, my eyes on his.

"Where did you get the ring, Padraig?"

"You're mad." Eyeing the cleaver. "Let me out of here." Backing up to the door as I came forward. "I'm warning you."

Keeping my eyes on him, I moved to the bedside locker and opened the little box that I kept my jewellery in. I didn't need to look, I knew it by touch, and picked it up and lobbed it to him.

He caught it by reflex, never taking his eyes of the cleaver in my hand.

"Look at it, Padraig. Look at it, then tell me where you got the one you are wearing."

It was meant to be the merest glance, but he did a double take when he saw what he had caught. "Shit!" He threw it on the bed as though it had burnt him. "Where did you get that?" – looking from the bed to his pinkie. "Who are you?"

"Och Padraig, Padraig. I was your first. Remember dropping the books in the store room? Remember when I brought you off in Science class, and Miss McCoy asked if you'd said something? You must remember getting me back on the bus?" His face was a picture of disbelief and dismay, yet his eyes started to shine with unshed tears. "Earlier this evening you said 'You're having me on', remember? Remember the last time you said that to me 'You're having me on, nobody asks their Da things like that'. I see you do."

"I said he'd beat the shit out of me if I even mentioned it." His voice quavered a little "And he did too. That's one reason I left home." He sagged against the door. "But you... you're not Shaun. You're nothing like him. How do you know... I mean, what is all this?" Looking round the flat, looking at all the photographs. "Was he a friend, was he your lover, what *is* all this?"

I limped back to the kitchen. "Sit down, I'll make coffee." I was pretty well convinced now that he hadn't been involved – at least, not directly. He never had been much good as an actor.

"Please? Tell me who you really are."

"Your wanking buddy from schooldays, Shaun McKenna." I filled the kettle in the silence that followed.

"Don't you fucking do this to me, you bastard. I know he never recovered from what they did to him. I know he's in hospital somewhere. Don't you fucking dare do this... why... why are you doing this to me?"

I turned. He was crying, hands over his face.

"Sit down, Pat."

He stilled.

"What, what did you say?"

"I said, sit down, have a cup of coffee."

"*No!* What did you..."

"I said, sit down Pat." Puzzled.

"Oh shit! You wouldn't know." He wiped his nose with the back of his hand. He crossed to the table and slumped into a chair, pulling off the ring and dropping it onto the wooden surface. "What in God's name has happened to you? I mean, I know what happened. But, you've changed so much. It's not just the way you look... you're so... you're so hard! I thought you were going to split me with that axe thing... What have I done?... What did I ever do?"

"Just like that, you believe I'm Shaun, what changed your mind?"

"You called me Pat... He... I mean, you... Christ! I don't know what I mean. Shaun, the Shaun McKenna I knew, he was the only one who always called me Pat. And it was the way you said it. Just like... just like at school." His face was still wet, his eyes disbelieving, at variance with his voice.

"I've changed my name recently. It's now Shaun Hannah. But I am the same Shaun McKenna that used to fool around with you at school. As for changes, I have been through rather a lot. Seeing you tonight, seeing that ring. Well..."

"What about the bloody ring, and where did the other one come from?"

I picked the ring off the bed where he'd thrown it and put it beside its mate on the table.

"Do you see any difference, Pat?"

Silence as he blearily looked at them.

"Do you?"

"No. They look the same. Where...?"

"They are the same. Exactly the same. And the one you were wearing was on Harry's hand when he was murdered. Where did you get it?"

Silence. Prolonged silence.

"Well?"

"Oh shit!"

"Well Pat, where *did* you get it?"

"Maybe it's different. Maybe they just look the same?"

"HH. L. SMK. And the year. You must have looked at the inscription. Mine says SMK. L. HH."

"Shit, shit, shit." He looked at me. "Would you have hit me with thon thing?"

"Yes."

"Jesus. How did I get into this thing?"

"Tell me. Tell me now, Pat."

"You know, it wasn't until we left school, it wasn't really till then... "

"The ring, Pat."

"My Da... he beat me. Jarleth told him I was crying over you, and" – looking at the picture – "him."

"His name is Harry."

"You and Harry. I left home the next day. Couldn't stand to listen to them. To all of them crowing about what had happened... You know, I was in the chapel that day... saw him, Harry I mean...saw you on the altar. I hated you, or thought I did, because you were with him. Saw you smile at him...Saw him smiling at you. I wanted to be him. I should have been him. Jesus Shaun, I loved you. I loved you, and I didn't know it, really didn't know it till then... That night, that night you were both on the news, reported as missing... Oh God!...And Jarleth, he didn't come in all night." Tears trembled on the brink.

"Then, the next day, he, I mean Harry was dead. You ...You were in a critical condition, not expected to survive. I cried... I prayed...I cried all day. Jarleth asked me what was wrong? When I told him, he laughed, called me 'another wee poof' and told Da. *He* took his belt to me, told me he'd give me something to cry about... I left home next day, walked out, got a plane to Birmingham. Been there ever since." He snuffled. "The ring, Pat! Where did it come from?"

"Jarleth! He said he was sorry he'd told Da. He gave me some money, came with me to the bus, gave me the ring as I was getting on. He said it was as a keepsake." He buried his head in his arms on the table and sobbed.

* * *

John sat staring at the rings.

"What a tangled web we weave, oh Lord," he sighed.

"Sorry, Uncle John?"

"Nothing, son. It's nothing." Getting up to refill the glasses. "He didn't know who the others were?"

"No."

"You believe him?"

"Yes. Yes I did. I do."

"Where is he now, London?"

"No. He's in the States. I paid his fare. Wouldn't want anything to happen to him."

"Why?"

"Because he's innocent. Too many innocents have been hurt already."

"I see! Where's this brother, what did you call him, Jarleth?"

"Yes, Jarleth. I don't know, but surely, it should be easy enough for you to find out. Or should I forget what you said four and a half years ago, and go to the police?"

"Ach, Shaun. You've gotten hard. No, no police. I'll deal with this, I keep my word, you know that. I'll call you, let you know when... "

"*No!* I'm going to be there. I have as much right to be there as you do."

"Shaun, son, you shouldn't be involved. You should not even have come here. You should have called me, I'd have come to you. Things can go wrong."

"I'm going to be there. Either I go along, or I go to the police, now!"

"And if I arrange that what was done to Harry... If I arrange that, can you take it?"

"I'll take it. I'll take anything. I want to know, I want to hear it from him, from them. I want to look into their eyes as they die, just as I looked into Harry's."

* * *

As it turned out, I could not take it. I hadn't been as confident that I could as I had made out to Uncle John.

A few nights later Jarleth Cunningham was run off the road on his way home from a celeidh at the Ancient Order of Hibernians hall in Attical. Trussed up and taken to a semi-ruined farmhouse on Greencastle shore, he didn't prove to be as brave when he was on the receiving end.

Punishment squads do have tea breaks, by the way. They bring their own flasks. I was never to know who Uncle John's heavy gang were but when I first saw them in their overalls and balaclavas, my balls shot into my abdomen and I burst into a cold sweat.

I was similarly clad, to prevent identification, John being the only one uncovered. He let me into the room alone with Jarleth before they began, cautioning me not to reveal my identity. He was naked, and for a moment I thought John had found a medieval rack somewhere, then realised that he was spreadeagled on an old riddling table. The sight of it brought back memories of October school breaks when we would go potato picking. Worked by a manual lever, the double bed of the table vibrated acting like a sieve, separating wee stones and soil from the potatoes. I don't think they are used anymore, they were pretty ancient technology even in my schooldays.

He was scared, skin slick with sweat, cock shrivelled up like a snail. Like me, in a similar situation, he just did not believe he was going to be killed. Fuelled by the beer he'd drunk at the celeidh, he sneered through the fear, damned each and every one of us. Promised that the 'boyos' would get us, and generally fucked us all and our mothers off right up until the first blow landed on his knee,.

Even though he must have known exactly what was about to happen to him, I explained it all in detail. I showed him the hockey sticks, one studded with nails. Ran my hand up his inner thigh to his balls, encouraged his dick partially out of its shell. He obviously hadn't had a bath recently, under the foreskin he was cheesy, smelling strongly. He was a couple of years older than Padraig and me and just a few months older than Harry would have been. More heavily built than Harry but with less body hair, the birthmark on his dick standing out in stark contrast to the whiteness of his skin.

I agreed with him that yes I was 'a fucking shirt-lifter', as I manipulated him to semi-rigidity. Disagreed strongly that I 'would burn forever' and leaving him half hard, I pissed on his face. I left, and walked out to where the others stood in the hissing glow of a hurricane lamp. Nodded to John and continued on, out of the building, as he and his three heavies entered the room.

He cracked well before the bone in his leg did, naming an old classmate of mine, Brian Feeney, as the one I had known as 'Slapper'. It took several buckets of water to bring him round, and a bullet through the left knee, before he named 'Speaker' as – Dermot Swallow! – the wood and metalwork teacher who had inadvertently first put Padraig and me together. Despite having his hands pulped, and being held by the hair with a hockey stick resting against his teeth, he screamed that he never knew who the driver had been.

John shot him through the head. They left his face unmarked. All the while I stood outside, listening to the muffled screams, just audible over the pounding of the surf.

I re-lived every blow inflicted on Harry at Dennywater, and I cried.

"Sorry, Harry. Can't do this. Can't stay here. Can't do this again. Sorry love, but I was never as strong as you thought I was, love you."

I stripped off the overalls and balaclava, wedged them under the wiper of John's car, got into my hired car and drove away. I didn't stop until I reached Dublin airport. I returned the car, and sat in the terminal until daybreak until the first London flight was called.

* * *

"Sorry, Uncle John," when I called him later that day. "Sorry, couldn't stand it."

"Och son, I should never have let you. Are you going to be alright?"

"I'll be fine. Really."

"What do you want me to do with the other two?"

"I thought... I was sure I wanted to be there. You know? Wanted to see it. Have the satisfaction of knowing. You know?"

"Aye."

"I, I couldn't. All I could see... all I could hear... was Harry."

"Aye." Voice grim and old. "You realise that now that I know, I cannot let them continue to walk the face of this earth. I need to know who the other bastard was, and I need to face them. You do understand me?"

"I do, Uncle John, and I wanted to stand beside you. For Harry, if for no other reason, and I'm sorry I can't do it."

We were both silent for long moments.

"I want them gone, Uncle John. I'm not washing my hands of this, I didn't want to leave it all to you, but I want them dead!"

"Son! I told you. Remember? I told you that if ever I found out, I'd pay them back in their own coin. You remember?"

"Yes."

"Well, God will undoubtedly judge me, but I keep my word. You understand?"

"I do."

"Aye well, leave it to me then, I will avenge you both."

"Call me when it's all over."

"If that's what you want."

"I do."

"God bless you, son."

I put the phone down.

23

Three months later it was all over.

Brian Feeney was dead, his body dumped in a ditch on the Head Road.

Dermot Swallow – valued teacher, town councillor and recently promoted Head of St. Columbans – had disappeared. To date his body has never been found.

Uncle John was dead! Suicide. His letter was short.

My Dear Son,

     I have accomplished almost all that I set out to do.

     My only regret, we never learned who the driver was, so one at least has escaped. I am too old to start again and it was only the hope of revenge, for my Lass, and your Harry that kept me going up till now. Now it is done. Try not to grieve too much, I am where I want to be. I charge you, in

Harry's memory, to live. You are still very young and he would want you to enjoy this life. You know he would not want to deprive you of one minute. After all, in eternity, if there is an eternity, you will be together for all time. I'm sure that will be long enough, even for you two. Harry, Lass and I will look out for you, if we may (Lass and I promise not to peek when you get to the 'naughty' bits, honestly).

Be a good boy, go talk to your Dr. Singh, he will know how to help.

And lastly son, give Harry a permanent resting place. He is not in your little casket, he never was, he is in your heart. Lay his ashes to rest, for me, for Lass, for him, for yourself.

Love, (Uncle) John.

I inherited what would have been Harry's portion of his estate. I also cracked up completely. Nu saved my life, and for months afterwards, I didn't know whether to thank or curse him. Just last night, our second last night in the UK, Ray asleep on the settee with his head on my lap, Nu told me that he very nearly let me die. He said he'd had a premonition all that day that something was wrong. Dave had pooh-poohed his worries, joshing him about the spirits of his ancestors, the old gods. But Nu is stubborn, he'd called me to talk about his feelings and couldn't get a reply. I'd left the phone off the hook and disconnected the answer-phone. His worry had crystallised at that point. He'd rushed from the store, jumped in the car and raced to Streatham.

Ever since Harry's death and my slow recovery he had possessed a key to the flat. He had looked after the plants, dealt with bills, and coped with small emergencies during my frequent hospital visits. I had never asked him to return it, indeed, had forgotten he had it.

He let himself in when he could not raise me. Found the shower door closed and the shower running inside. When he failed to get an answer to his calling and thumping of the door, he'd kicked it in. I was sitting on the floor of the cubicle, under the hot water, the blood from my wrists swirling down the drain. I was pretty far gone by that stage, and he knew it.

This was when he had debated with himself, should he let me go, or should he try to save me? Nu had none of the Western squeamishness about death. If I really wanted to die, that was my affair.

Both he and David had noticed my increasingly erratic behaviour since their return from Mauritius and, though knowing nothing of my visit to Ireland or its results, had surmised that Harry once again was the uppermost thought in my mind. He did a quick sweep for a note of some kind, and came up with John's letter. He dragged me out of the shower, bandaged my wrists and called David. He then called an ambulance and Dr Singh.

Singh was furious with me. Within thirty-six hours I had been transferred to his care and he had instituted a suicide watch on me. For the next four weeks I was never alone for an instant, not even on the loo, and for those four weeks I was a complete zombie.

I don't remember doing it. I'd drunk quite a lot, swallowed whatever pills were in the flat (luckily none of Singh's were left) and I do remember having a long quiet argument with Harry. I can't remember how that turned out. I'd opened his casket and put the rings in on top of his ashes. Some of the ash had adhered to my fingers, and as I licked it off, the decision was made. I don't remember stripping, turning the shower on or, slitting my wrists. I can only remember seeing, really seeing, the warm, welcoming, velvety darkness wrapping itself round me.

I was going home! I was going to Harry.

My reaction, when I realised that I was breathing – I was in a bed. I was *not dead!* – was despair. Total and absolute despair. I tried to will a cessation to the rise and fall of my chest and couldn't. My mind switched off at that point. Singh didn't really need the suicide watch. I didn't even have the will to try again.

For four weeks I allowed myself to be led around by the hand. Allowed them to put me on the toilet at regular intervals, otherwise I just shat or pissed where I lay. Obediently opened my mouth when someone offered food, the body's demands automatically ensuring that it got a cursory chewing before swallowing whatever it was. I was mindless, I heard nothing and can remember none of it. Cannot remember anyone actually being there, I was oblivious to the passage of time.

Singh used a combination of drugs, hypnosis and electric shock therapy to bring me back this time. Though, he later admitted, he had not been sure that he could do it again. Under the drugs and the hypnosis he had apparently learned exactly what had transpired. What had brought about my collapse.

As I slowly started to connect with reality again there remained an enormous dead area in my head, in my heart. I felt myself to be just a very thin, very brittle shell, containing an ocean of utter blackness. Should that shell crack, I'd disappear like a pile of windblown sand.

I didn't rant and rave, as I had previously when he'd forced me back to life, I was too weary. I accepted that he'd won, again, and that he probably would continue to win. I went along with his programme without a fight, eventually to return to some semblance of normality, though I was just a black emptiness inside.

Four months after Nu had found me, I was back at the flat, twice-weekly visits with Singh reinstituted. I wasn't really in control, just running on automatic pilot. There was this thin shell applied by Singh which made me walk, talk a very little, eat and carry out the so-called normal day-to-day business of living. Inside I was in a coma, there were two of me – the false exterior shell and the death-like black reality contained within it.

As the subsequent months passed, the shell hardened and grew less brittle. It thickened and began to develop a personality of its own. A bleak and morbid personality, but one that began to take an interest, of sorts, in happenings outside the confines of the four walls of the flat.

Singh had long been nagging – no, not nagging, suggesting – as persuasively as only he can, that I wrote everything down. I had ignored him. Did he know what he was asking, that I go through it all again?

"My dear young man. Just what do you think it is that you are doing every day? Believe me Shaun, unless you come to terms with it all, all will have been for nothing." His concern was growing rather than diminishing, as the new bleak, morbid me stumbled aimlessly through the days and months.

Violence of any kind, films, theatre, the awful cacophony of most modern music, drew me. I wouldn't say that I revelled in it. I did not, but it seemed to provide some kind of weird solace.

On a cold wet evening, nine months after the abortive suicide attempt, I was limping past the Strand Palace Hotel, coming from some show or other. It may even have been Matthew Bourne's all-male 'Swan Lake'.

"Any spare change, guv?"

What passed for my emotions had been touched by whatever it was I'd been to see, otherwise I'd have ignored him. I resent the beggars who seem to be infesting this city more and more. But my emotions had been touched and that, coupled with the soft York-shire burr, made me stop.

He looked both pathetic and embarrassed as I fished for change, hand only half held out as though frightened of being slapped down. I pressed a handful of coins into his hand and his head came up. The other hand emerged from his pocket to flick back a swatch of very wet red hair.

I was utterly transfixed. In that instant the shell around me crumbled and disappeared. Disappeared as if it had never been. I was *me* again. I was utterly lost again.

"Hey, thanks." The smile was genuine, if wistful. He was shivering, wet through, looking half starved and all of sixteen years old; he was actually just seventeen then.

"Are you... are you looking for business?"

"Could be, but right now, I'd rather have a bath and something to eat." Direct and honest from the very start. That's my Ray.

"Come on, then."

Epilogue

That was almost fifteen months ago. Today I love Harry no less and I'm happy again. I know too that he is happy for me, it is just something I can sense. I'm sitting here at the bedside table in the spare bedroom at David and Nu's. We were late going up after my talk with Nu and Ray sleeps on as yet. He is just a formless lump in the bed, surmounted by a shock of carrot-coloured hair, one slender arm hugging a pillow in my absence.

The flat has gone, the car has gone, tomorrow we will be gone. We are joining the *Arcadia* for the first half of her round-the-world voyage. We are going to Australia. Of course Harry is coming with us, though he will be staying in Australia, even if we do not. I'm going to give him into Seamus's care. I know that *he* will help him settle into however long the wait turns out to be. Who knows, they may even get round to comparing notes. Everything we are not taking with us is in storage. Nu, dearest of friends, will forward it all when, or if we settle.

Ray is mumbling in his sleep, a sure sign that he will soon be up, bouncing around like the unruly cuddly pup that he is. My mind returns constantly to the taxi ride from the Strand Palace on the night that we met. Warming one of his grubby little hands in mine, I could not help but smile.

Fulfilled again. Beginning again.

Love you Harry.
Love you Ray.
He does have the most amazing green eyes!